Loretta Re and her sister Carolyn have been writing together since they were children, cranking out magazines and ripping yarns on an old home roneo machine.

Loretta's middle-grade novel, *Stand Up and Cheer* about the 1934 rescue of the Uiver plane over Albury during the Centenary Air Race, was published in 2015.

Carolyn has written numerous medical articles for newspapers and magazines and had a regular humorous column in Medical Observer based on her experiences in general practice. Her website can be found at https://outsidethesquare101.com

Secrets of the IN-group

Carolyn Re and Loretta Re

'The web of our life is of a mingled yarn,
good and ill together.'

All's Well That Ends Well

First published by Resisters in 2019
This edition published in 2019 by Resisters

Secrets of the IN-group

EPUB: 9780648481904
POD: 9780648481911

Cover design by Christa Moffitt

Publishing services provided by Critical Mass
www.critmassconsulting.com

PROLOGUE

It was time to act. If there was a vendetta against her, Andrea had to know who was behind it. She reached for the phone. Martin was the only one who might provide an answer.

This is all my fault, she thought, as she waited for him to respond. *Who'd have predicted that one tiny decision could ruin so many lives?*

If the vote had been different, Denise would never have risked all her savings. Sarah would be living the dream, exploring the canals of Europe with Rob as she'd always planned, instead of being—who knew where? And Libby's past would have remained a secret, instead of being exposed in such humiliating detail.

Andrea herself hadn't been spared either. If they'd stayed with book club, she'd still have her best friend and her self-esteem, and her home would be safe.

Stupid, stupid, stupid.

Chapter 1

Several months earlier ...

The Albury library was the last place Andrea expected to be hit with the shock of the new. But as she walked into the architect-designed, bright orange 'LibraryMuseum'—as it was called since its mega-dollar revamp—she looked around for Sarah with the same stranded feeling she always experienced in foreign airport terminals.

The space seemed vast now there was no central catalogue. Along one wall a computer class was being conducted loudly by a skinny young man with flat earrings the size of saucers. With their smattering of grey hair, his students looked about Andrea's age and vaguely fearful of computers. They were staring at their screens, heads forward, frowning while they hunted on the keyboards, using two fingers. Over in the corner half a dozen toddlers, with mothers and prams, were absorbed in a wriggle and jiggle session, while a sari-clad Indian woman wearing a council lanyard roamed around their circle taking photos and encouraging them as they belted out 'The Wheels on the Bus'.

As if this wasn't in-your-face enough, there was a metal stand on the library counter sprouting branches adorned with mini-posters advertising forthcoming events, like *Pom-pom Workshop* and *Spinning and Weaving Demonstration*, for heaven's sake, and one boasting *Discover Secrets Only Celebrities Know—Make-up class held here Friday mornings*.

She glimpsed a copy of *The Life to Come*—a book that had won some high-profile award—on the New Titles shelf. At least she could borrow it while she was waiting for Sarah. Yet even that mundane decision turned into a mild trauma.

'We don't do manual loans anymore,' the young librarian behind the counter explained, after staring at the old library card Andrea was offering. She reached for it and turned the cardboard relic over with care, as though it were some archaeological find. 'Gosh, these were way before my time. How long since you've been here?'

'I always planned to call in and update it when I retired, but … ' Andrea gave a small shrug. It wasn't the place or the time to explain why she wasn't engaging much with the outside world.

After issuing her with a new digital card, the librarian pointed to a screen at the end of a set of bookshelves. A scanner arched above it. 'You can check out the book by scanning it over there,' she said.

Damn, yet another thing Andrea had to work out for herself. To be fair, the staff member looked as if she was about to demonstrate the process, but at that moment her phone rang so, not wanting to be a nuisance, Andrea went over and warily poked the back of the book under the scanner. A warning blip sounded, then the screen flashed: 'Code not Recognised. Consult an Information Technician.'

Consult who? She looked around, hoping someone wearing a badge reading 'Information Technician' might be standing close, but could only spot other library visitors browsing through books. She returned to the librarian.

'Excuse me, where's the information technician?'

The young woman held the phone away from her face.

'That would be me. Did you present the bar to the scanner?'

'Yes, but it said to see the information technician.'

'This code?' She tapped a lustrous black fingernail on the back of the book.

'Yes.' Andrea beamed.

'That's not the right barcode.' The librarian/born-again information technician flipped the book over and pointed to a label with a row of squiggles and bars that obliterated the author's name. 'You'll need to go back and scan the one on the front.'

Was life always like this? Everything was so complicated these days, even borrowing a book from the library. She'd need to get to grips with modern technology. Not today, but one day.

She caught sight of Sarah, a little breathless, hurrying through the LibraryMuseum's sliding glass doors. A couple of heads turned towards her. Sarah had that effect on people. Wearing a simple pencil dress with a Hermes scarf draped at a perfect angle over her shoulders, she waved as she walked towards Andrea, on heels that would have had other women tottering.

'Never mind. I'll do it later,' Andrea said to the woman at the desk.

'Hope you haven't been waiting,' said Sarah. 'Isn't this place fabulous? Such a buzz.'

Andrea started laughing as they embraced—at her own disquiet at this new library and at Sarah's immediate enthusiasm for the whole rowdy shebang. It was so like Sarah to grab life with both hands. In their student days, Sarah was the one who took on glamorous-sounding jobs, working as an extra in movies or waitressing on the overnight train between Sydney and Melbourne. And although she was always busy with her committees and Rob's hectic schedule, somehow she found time to catch up every week.

'So, let's talk to the librarian about getting this book club started.' Sarah looked around as she spoke. 'Sorry to hurry you, but I have to dash off much earlier than I'd planned—the art gallery has brought its meeting forward. I was hoping we'd have time for a coffee.' She gestured towards the Help desk. 'There'll be a booklist we can use. I'm dying to catch up with some great novels. I missed *Satanic Verses* and *The Unbearable Lightness of Being*—too busy with the children. I want to enjoy a plain, good read again too.'

'And I need to meet new people,' added Andrea.

'Good heavens, I'm boring you after all these years.' Sarah pulled a face in tragi-comic dismay.

'You know what I mean,' Andrea replied. 'We see the same people at investment club that we've known forever. Not that I go often anymore. But let's find some new faces and invite them to explore our world of books.'

'Your world of books? Now that sounds most interesting.'

A little startled she'd been overheard, Andrea turned to see who was speaking. It was the Indian woman who'd been photographing the children a few minutes earlier.

'Would you allow me to take your photograph for the council newsletter?' the woman continued with a generous smile. 'We are wanting to showcase all of the activities that the LibraryMuseum has on offer. Your plan for a world of books would be one very good example of this.'

She looked to be in her early forties, with ebony eyes and hair like polished black onyx. Andrea knew she'd seen her somewhere before today. Yes, that was it. She'd been at the mayoral launch a few years earlier for an historical novel written about a daring air rescue over Albury during the Depression. Gliding around with a camera, she'd been taking shots of the party-goers as they nibbled on their canapés.

'Oh, no thanks,' Andrea said at the exact moment she heard Sarah's, 'Of course!' Sarah, still beautiful in her sixties, would never fret that her hair wasn't looking perfect or her make-up might need adjusting before she'd contemplate having her photo taken.

'Photos would be ideal. We're looking for new members,' Sarah said, 'so some advertising wouldn't go astray.'

'You are truly wanting new members?' the photographer replied. 'I am only now cutting back on my working hours, and have thought I should like very much to do something for myself. Would this club be open to someone like me?'

'Absolutely.' Sarah jumped at the possibility of their first member. 'I'm Sarah and this is my friend Andrea. Welcome to our Albury Book Club.'

Even though inviting strangers had been her own idea, Andrea hesitated. This was so quick. Wasn't there going to be a vetting process? Well, perhaps not *vetting*, but she'd thought she and Sarah would have a good chat about possible new members. Confer like a selection committee.

'Marvellous. I am Neelam.' The younger woman extended a slim hand. Her slender long fingers were at odds with her comfortable figure. 'You are very welcome to have the first session in my home. Vinod will make less fuss about me going out if he has met you all.' She gave a small smile. 'My husband thinks it is a bit naughty of me to spoil myself with outside interests.'

'I was going to suggest we meet at my place initially, but if that suits you better, then thank you,' said Sarah. 'I'll post a message at the Help desk for more members. People can RSVP me for the first meeting.'

Neelam took their photo, swapped contact details and, with another smile, floated over to the computer class. Andrea turned to her old friend.

'I love how you're so good at organising, but we *are* doing this together. I need you to consult me more before rushing to accept members in future.'

'But Neelam seems lovely ...'

'I know, and I'm sure she is,' said Andrea, *even though she did interrupt our conversation,* 'but I didn't get any say at all. And now you want to tell people to RSVP for our first meeting, when we don't know how big we want the group, who'll be in it, or when we'll hold our gatherings.'

'I hear you, but I'll be late for my meeting—I have to dash. Sorry, would you mind sorting out the reading list? We'll chat about it later. Rob's office manager can type up a notice for us and I'll pin it on the stand next week. Okay?' And with a flurry of movement that included an air kiss, she disappeared through the automatic doors onto the street.

Typical Sarah. So enthusiastic. So exasperating.

After picking up a book club guide, Andrea left. Goodness knows how this was going to work out.

BEEP BEEP BEEP.

A loud alarm ricocheted around her. Was there no end to the noise and cacophony of this new improved LibraryMuseum?

A moment later she felt a tap on her shoulder and saw, out of the corner of her eye, black fingernails.

'Excuse me, but you can't leave yet.'

8

'Pardon?' Andrea could sense the eyes of every passer-by on her. What a mortifying moment!

'You haven't scanned your book. You can't take an item out of the LibraryMuseum without clearance.'

Oh, how embarrassing. *The Life to Come*. She'd forgotten all about it.

Andrea stood without a word. Torn between thrusting the book back into the staff member's hands and fleeing the scene of her crime or owning her mistake, she followed the information technician back to the desk like a chastened puppy.

Chapter 2

Libby held her fingers up to the light, admiring the shimmering blue nails. Her hands were one of her best features, everyone said, and for a while a few years ago she'd even been able to supplement her income by working as a hand model. She placed her fingertips under the Thermal Spa nail dryer, one of the few little luxury items she still owned. Professional-looking toes and fingernails were important, every bit as much as make-up. Especially now, in a new town, with a new life. Good make-up—and she had plenty of skills in that area—could help you face anything, help you to be both seductive and defended against the world.

This morning's job interview for the TAFE position had to go well. Heaven knows she was well qualified for it. She figured that not many applicants for a part-time, temporary job as an office manager in Albury would have prior experience as the PA to the chief of a big engineering company in Melbourne. Not that she could mention that, of course.

She drove through town, an Albury that had changed over the years. There were still the gracious old buildings along

Dean Street, especially the cream-coloured Post Office and Conservatorium, with their similar brown-tipped arches that made her think of matching siblings, separated by size. But there was now also a modern-looking extension to the art gallery, a shiny glass façade in front of the grand old building, right in the centre of town. Next to it a generous town square, all wide green lawns and well-established trees was a welcome refuge, allowing visitors and shoppers to take a deep breath in the middle of their business.

School holidays spent with her grandparents, twenty minutes' drive away in the small town of Yackandandah, had been Libby's introduction to this regional city. First, there were the occasional shopping visits, then, in her later teens, those two magical summer holidays when she'd take the bus for work shifts in Albury. Crossing the flood plains of the Lincoln Causeway to pass over the Murray River into New South Wales was like entering a new world. She'd pass under a canopy of massive elms that formed an arch between the Botanical Gardens and the beautiful old buildings, thinking that Albury was the prettiest, greenest city she'd ever seen.

Her move here now would make the cost of living more manageable. If she could find a job in Albury that paid well—the one she'd left in Melbourne had a fabulous salary—then she'd be almost optimistic. Steve, her boss in Albury all those years ago, was one of the few people she could ask for a reference now. Thank goodness he was happy to help and didn't ask too many questions, but, realistically, her options were going to be limited at first. She needed to be patient. *Act like a success,* she told herself, *and good things will surely follow.*

*

Half an hour later Libby floated out of the TAFE interview. Both the women on the panel had been relaxed and friendly, so unlike the interviewers for her last position.

'Your referee, Steve … he's an old friend of mine,' Amy, the office manager, had said. 'But you've been working in Melbourne. How do you know Steve?'

'Years ago, when I was at school, I worked holidays at his cinema. He'll tell you there's not a thing I don't know about upselling popcorn and coating ice cream for choc-tops.'

Amy smiled. 'He has lots of youngsters passing through. If he's still willing to be your referee, he must have been impressed.' She was a maternal woman with salt-and-pepper hair. Highlights in the right toning would make her quite chic, Libby decided.

After that, the interviewers seemed to be going through the motions, and she sensed she already had the job. There was no need to mention how Steve had given her more and more responsibility, trusted her to order supplies, balance the books, reconcile cheques, and deposit the business takings back in the days when that was a physical activity. She used to be so proud as she carried a cloth bag full of notes and coins into the bank. Thanks to Steve, she'd mustered the confidence to go on to secretarial college, the first in her family to have further training, despite her father pooh-poohing the idea.

After she creamed the typing test, she was offered the position then and there—no short list and no second interview—to commence next Monday.

'Thank you, thank you so much. I won't let you down. It'll be wonderful to work in Albury again.'

She steered her old Toyota back to the centre of town and turned on the radio. 'Purple Rain', her favourite Prince track, was playing. With the window down, the wisp of a breeze was refreshing. She wasn't sure why she was heading to a make-up class, or what she would learn there, because she already knew the tricks of the trade. She'd come across a flyer listing activities in town run by council, and the class had sounded inviting. It would be fun and, now that she'd snared a job so quickly, it could become a celebration of sorts. The best thing about the lesson—being run at the local library, of all places—was that it would cost next to nothing. It could be a way of meeting local people too, and another step in starting over. If there was one thing she needed, it was a new start.

*

At the LibraryMuseum, Libby looked around in surprise. She strained to remember what it had been like when she'd visited it once before, as a school student, but that was over thirty years ago. She could recall nothing more than a vague image of a rabbit warren of a place with books crammed in every corner and the floor space taken up with several wooden chests of miniature drawers that she hadn't been confident enough to open. But this new library was huge and spacious and humming with people. All the tiny drawers had disappeared, replaced by the streamlined look of flat-screened computers.

She followed the signs for the makeover session and headed up the sweeping central staircase towards a group of about twenty women outside one of the meeting rooms. She spotted only one older woman among them—and she stood out because she resembled a small, bright-eyed rainbow lorikeet, flitting around in a loose cerise jacket over cobalt-blue trousers and wearing eye-catching, bell-shaped earrings. Unusual for someone that age—she must be around sixty—but worn with real panache. All the others looked like twelve-year-olds—young, anyway. Libby began to wonder why she'd signed on to learn the 'Secrets Only Celebrities Know'. She should have guessed it would appeal more to the Millennials.

'I need you all to buddy up,' announced a blonde woman with a ponytail who emerged from the room. Her exquisite, made-up mask—was it really due to cosmetics alone or had there been more extensive work?—relaxed in a brief smile. 'You'll be working in pairs for this session, helping each other with a make-over to look *AbFab*!'

Libby looked around the chattering women, hoping to pair with the lorikeet.

'Hi, I'm Kate. Have you buddied up yet?'

Libby turned to find the very partner she'd been seeking standing right at her shoulder.

'When I first saw you,' Kate said, 'I thought, *Oh, she must be the teacher—her make-up is fantastic!* You don't need to be here! I was expecting more wrinkly nannas like me. I don't think there's much Miss Ponytail can teach you. I love the way you use kohl around your eyes. Such a sultry look. Can you show me how it's done? My granddaughter would love it.'

Libby exhaled a slow breath. Maybe this wasn't such a bad idea. She prided herself on looking sultry, but she hadn't had so many compliments delivered at such a pace since—well, since the charming Gerald had picked her up in that bar, and her life had gone pear-shaped.

'Libby.' She smiled, extending her hand. 'You're much too flattering, but it's lovely to hear. And forget the "wrinkly" tag. I wish I'd had a nanna who looked as terrific as you. I'm a nanna, and you're an inspiration.'

'Surely you don't have grandchildren, already?' Kate said, placing her hand on Libby's elbow, as though they'd been friends for years.

'Just the one,' Libby said with a little laugh. 'Thanks to having my son at nineteen.'

'I came to sign up for the IT sessions, you know,' Kate confided, 'but they're so popular that there's a six-month waiting list. Can you believe it? Six months! My daughter'll only be in New York for a year—she's been there three months already. By the time I've mastered Skype, she'll be back. So, they talked me into this session and I thought, why not? Might be fun. I need to look more glamorous now my wedding planner venture is up and running.'

Miss Ponytail broke up their conversation, shepherding them into the spacious meeting room where small wooden tables, each with a magnifying mirror, were set around the edge to garner the light from the huge windows.

'How about the end, away from any foot traffic?' Libby pointed out a table in the sunlight towards the back.

There was a familiar, comforting array of tissues and cotton buds ready on the table, alongside a jumble of other make-up they'd need: foundation, concealer, lip stain, powder, eyeliner, mascara and blush.

'First things first,' announced Miss Ponytail, who'd introduced herself as Ebony, but whose nickname was now established in Libby's mind. 'Eyebrows shape your face. Like, totally.'

Libby caught Kate's eye and could see she was stifling a laugh too.

'Bad eyebrows will spoil a beautiful face. I know full eyebrows are all the rage, but full doesn't mean "bushy" or "wild".'

The next couple of hours passed in a glorious blur. Kate had been right. Libby had nothing to learn from Miss Ponytail.

'What? You've never heard of twenty-four-hour super-stay lipstick?' she asked Kate. 'I swear nothing can budge it. You can kiss, you can eat. You could deep-sea dive and still look glamorous when you resurface.'

'You're an artist,' Kate said. 'Can you show me how to give definition to my cheekbones? When I put on blush I end up looking like Andy Pandy.'

Miss Ponytail was having oodles of fun with the younger group, only flitting down to Libby and Kate once or twice to say, 'Oooh, fabulous' or 'You're both naturals', so by the end of the session Libby felt like she'd known Kate for years. Her first new connection since moving to Albury.

'That was brilliant!' Kate looked at her reflection and beamed, while Libby stepped back, mascara wand in hand, to admire the effect. She'd chosen muted colours to complement Kate's vibrant outfit and the new look gave her a moment of genuine pride. She *was* good at this.

'Neil—my husband—won't recognise me. He'll love it. *I love it*. You're so clever. Are you a professional make-up artist? Do you work with brides? You could, you know.'

Libby gave a modest shake of the head. When she'd modelled part-time for department store catalogues she'd learned all the trade secrets, but that was well over twenty years ago. She was as tall as the leading professional models—once she'd even been likened to Megan Gale—with the allure of glossy dark hair and almond-shaped eyes. But she'd been passed over for the better paying gigs. 'Sorry, darl, we're looking for perfect facial symmetry.' Ouch. It was then she'd turned to hand modelling.

As they were packing up their table, Libby thought about how she could meet Kate again, other than at one of Miss Ponytail's workshops. Kate was warm and bubbly and such fun to be with, there must be some way of getting to know her better.

Before she could speak, Kate swivelled towards her and gave an excited tap on her elbow. 'Did you notice downstairs—there's a new book club looking for members? I saw a flyer about it on the front desk. What do you think?' Her face was alight, not solely due to Libby's work. 'We could join together. My business is only getting started and I have more time on my hands since Louise flew the coop for the Big Apple and the twins moved out. Do you have time to discuss it over coffee? I'm parched.'

Libby hesitated. She'd love nothing more than to have a coffee with Kate, but …

'I'm not much of a reader,' she said wryly. If only she'd read what she was signing two years ago, she mightn't have landed herself in so much trouble.

'Gosh, no one in book clubs worries about reading.' Kate's mirth was infectious. 'I belonged to one when the kids were young and I was desperate for adult company. That's what book clubs are about—chatting together with friends. The book's only an excuse. Anyway, you can always cheat—read lots of reviews so you sound clever. Or better still, watch the movie and not bother with the book.'

Libby would never have joined a book club on her own, would never have considered anything so lofty, but Kate's enthusiasm was filling her with bravado.

'How can I say no to that?'

They headed down the LibraryMuseum's staircase, trailing the young women who sparkled after their makeovers, passing a young staff member, lanyard swinging, who looked enviously at the light-hearted group. They did all look quite stunning, their skin glowing with their freshly minted make-up.

After stopping at the Help desk to take down the details of the book club, they wandered outside, blinking in the sudden burst of sunshine. There was an inviting whiff from a cafe attached to MAMA, the new Albury art museum behind the library. The little eatery spilled over onto QE2 Square, the lush green gardens bordering the main street.

'Once you wouldn't expect a good cup of coffee outside a capital city, but that's not true anymore. It's everywhere,' Libby said.

'So you're new to town? That's why I haven't seen you before. I don't know *everyone* in Albury, but once you've put five children through school, plus been to endless cricket and footy matches, not to mention fundraisers and trivia nights, you get a pretty good radar for people, and I'd have remembered you for sure. Albury's a great place. Big enough to be a real city but small enough to be friendly—and convenient. You can always find a parking space! Why did you move here?'

Libby hesitated a moment before waving her hand, hoping the gesture seemed nonchalant. 'I used to visit as a teenager, and I guess I was looking for a tree change but instead chose a … river change.' She wondered if any such thing existed, but if it did, the Murray River was a worthy contender.

Libby looked around for somewhere to sit while Kate went in to order. Like all the rustic furniture on the sunny verandah, the table she chose was made from river red gum, making it seem as if it had been there for years, almost a natural part of the landscape, though she could see the cafe was new. The council had gone to a lot of trouble with the landscaping—paths bordered by purple agapanthus and climbing clematis were painted with eye-catching indigenous motifs in ochre and black and white. From the adjoining square, the squeals of excited children rang out as they tried to clamber over two giant, slippery, pink snails made of fibreglass, resting in the middle of the lawns.

'Righto, let's call straight away.' Kate plonked the table number down and pulled out her mobile. 'We need to sign up in case they restrict numbers. Our old club became too big—we had twelve members by the end, and honestly, it was like two warring camps. There was the "I only watch the ABC and read the classics" battalion versus the "What's wrong with *Who Wants to Be a Millionaire?* And for heaven's sake, it's summer, why can't we read a Jackie Collins?" squadron.'

'You're not making this sound all that promising,' Libby said with a laugh.

Kate made the call and spoke briefly, before holding her hand over her mobile. 'A "Sarah" and "Andrea" request the pleasure of our company at Coffee Mecca on Dean Street, Saturday week,' she said to Libby. 'Can you make it at ten?'

Libby raised her eyebrows. This sounded ominous, like another job interview. What was she letting herself in for?

She nodded before whispering, 'Dress code?'

Kate laughed soundlessly, her shoulders shaking. 'Fine, 10 am,' she said into the phone. 'We'll look forward to it.'

She slipped the phone into her bag and turned to Libby. 'This Sarah person said they already have three in the group and want six max, but she couldn't say a definite yes until we've met her friend Andrea—and she'll be away for a week.' Kate dropped her voice and leaned in a little. 'Reading between the lines, I think there may have been a slight "iss-ew" over the choice so far and Sarah has to placate Andrea. As long as we're our fabulous selves, we'll be fine.'

Kate grinned before adding, 'It looks like I'd better practise these new make-up skills so I'll appear irresistible.'

Of course Kate would be irresistible to this unknown Sarah and Andrea. Who wouldn't love a rainbow lorikeet? The big question, Libby knew, was what would they think of *her*, especially if they knew about her past?

Chapter 3

'Here's your coffee. That's three dollars, please.' The waist-coated cashier had a cascade of stars tattooed on her neck. She paused, waiting while Denise unzipped her wallet. Around them was the cheerful clang of the pokies, and the enticing bright lights of the Albury RSL Club, but in that moment they seemed to fade away as Denise gazed into her red leather wallet. Empty. Every compartment.

The twenty-dollar note she'd tucked into the side pocket to cover the lunchtime sandwich and drink? Gone. The money she'd set aside for the afternoon's entertainment? Gone. And she hadn't even noticed she'd spent it.

She felt her face go red-hot as she apologised, all the while scrabbling for coins at the bottom of her handbag. There was nothing to find there, of course, even as she stood in a shockwave of perspiration staring into the black chasm of her bag. She knew her credit card was maxed out, so that wouldn't help. But there was no harm in pretending to search, acting as though the coins had slipped out of her purse. The young cashier yawned, waiting for her payment.

She looked familiar—was she a pupil from years ago? There seemed to be no flicker of recognition on the girl's bored face. Small mercies.

The reprieve was short lived. As Denise fossicked around, her coffee was forfeited, and she was passed over for the next customer in the queue. She'd become another invisible older woman. The cashier wasn't the least bit interested in her or her pretence. Probably saw it every day, had picked Denise as yet another customer who'd come to the counter flat broke.

As she moved away without her coffee, Denise heard the cashier call after her. 'You've left your glasses on the counter, Mrs Robertson.'

Mortified, she turned and grabbed her reading glasses. She wanted her clothes to swallow her and to be as far as possible from anyone else who might recognise her, who once knew her in her other life as a confident woman who wielded authority and respect. She hurried out, past the rows of brightly lit gaming machines, past the transfixed patrons as they hunched over, looking neither right nor left, absorbed with the clanging and the garish lights. *That was me, only fifteen minutes ago.* The idea hit her like a slap. She was like them. She *was* them, hypnotised, caught in a vortex and focused only on the next push of the button. Near the hole-in the-wall proffering instant cash, she caught sight of the sign she'd managed to screen out of her mind so far, a sign that was now shouting at her: 'Is Gambling becoming a Problem for you? Are you spending more than you can afford? Confidential help is available. Call 1800 858 858.'

She knew it was becoming a Problem. She pulled out her phone and keyed in the number.

*

Nothing was familiar to Denise as she drove down the main street of a town two hours' drive from Albury, across the state border in Victoria. She rarely came down this way, always referring to the southern inhabitants as 'Mexicans,' a local in-joke that, when you thought about it, possibly wasn't acceptable these days. Anonymity, that was the key. It'd be safe here, nobody would recognise her because she knew no one who lived in this town, she'd never even visited the place. She glanced out the car window at the alien shops, the large community notice board announcing a dance in an unknown venue. The downside was she didn't have her bearings: she had no idea where anything was, and no clue how to find the office she was after.

With no cars on her tail, she slowed down and took the crumpled piece of paper tossed on the passenger seat, an address written in her scrawling handwriting. *87 Railway Crescent. Use rear entrance.* That shouldn't be too hard to find—she'd crossed the train tracks not a minute ago. Making a U-turn, she retraced her route and, sure enough, the sign to Railway Crescent jumped out at her, curling alongside the train tracks where you'd expect it to be.

The office of Gamblers Anonymous was tucked away at the back of a commercial building, its entrance via a dog-leg lane lined with wheelie-bins, hidden in a quiet area with a discreet sign outside that wouldn't alert passers-by to her reason for being there. A prickly itch crept up her neck, as the shame she'd been trying to hold back returned with a vengeance. Damn. That nervous rash hadn't surfaced for years. She'd have made a hopeless spy.

The building's door opened into a poky waiting room where several vinyl chairs sat along one wall below a sign reading: 'PLEASE BE SEATED. THE COUNSELLOR WILL BE WITH

YOU SHORTLY.' No one else was waiting, thank goodness. Imagine making small talk with a stranger in a place like this. A cork board on the opposite wall was plastered with posters bearing motivational messages: 'YOUR ONLY LIMIT IS YOU' and 'THE SAFEST WAY TO DOUBLE YOUR MONEY IS TO FOLD IT IN HALF AND PUT IT IN YOUR POCKET'.

A few minutes later, the door to an inner room opened and half a head poked out. 'Mrs Robertson?' Denise nodded. The rest of the body appeared, a scrap of a girl who didn't seem old enough to be paying off her student loan yet. She gave a quick smile as she gestured towards her room. 'Do come in.'

Denise pulled herself out of the chair with some difficulty. She suspected they were making seats low-slung these days; she'd rather not think that her struggle to get out of this one might be linked to her slowly increasing girth and decreasing fitness. Or her reluctance to be there in the first place.

She followed the girl into the consulting room, past a poorly aligned sliding sign on the door that read 'Claire Pulman. Psychologist'. It was one of those temporary nameplates that could be flicked out at the end of the session. Perhaps Claire shared this office with other counsellors, perhaps they could only bear to work here in small bursts and had other, better jobs elsewhere. Jobs with paying clients who had more acceptable problems, such as relationship issues or battles with their teenagers. No, on second thoughts, Claire didn't look old enough for that. This was probably her first placement. Ever. She was here to practise on Denise.

The counsellor gave her a level gaze as Denise sat down in the claustrophobic office. A room without windows; one wall had a blotchy stain, most likely rising damp. *Oh great. Get me out of here.* Claire's hair, a mousy colour, was pulled back behind her ears and held low with an elastic band. That, combined with a homeopathic dose of make-up gave her an earnest appearance, which was another worry. Fancy driving all this way to find that Claire was taking 'Counselling 101: Prac Classes' at Denise's expense.

'Thank you for coming, Mrs Robertson,' Claire said. 'Acknowledging you've got a problem is a big step to take. It's the first one on the road to recovery.' She paused and read from a laptop on the desk in front of her. 'I see you're self-referred.'

It must be the checklist of questions Denise had answered when she'd telephoned for the appointment.

'Oh yes, of course I'm self-referred. I haven't spoken to anyone else about this. I don't want my GP to know.'

'We'd never contact your GP without your permission. I meant that you've not been sent here under a Court Order.'

A court order! Does this girl think I'm some light-fingered criminal needing to feed an addiction? Denise's rash accelerated from itchy to hot-and-itchy as it spread from her neck to her face. She would not scratch it, would not draw attention to it. If only there was a window to open.

'No, no. Nothing like that. It's just … I've been playing the pokies a wee bit more than I want to, so I thought I'd better nip it in the bud. Before it becomes a problem. Not that it's likely to become a problem …' She noticed Claire's eyebrows lift a couple of millimetres for a split second before they resumed a neutral position, as though she'd remembered she needed to look professional and non-judgemental. Claire tapped a few notes into her laptop.

'Uh-huh, okay. So you've never found yourself short of money for essentials due to your gambling?'

'Oh, money's not a problem. I'm quite comfortable,' Denise said. That was a true enough statement. She was almost thankful Stan had left her when she was young enough to build a nest egg, and she was lucky with her job as a teacher with its generous super. Better not mention the Visa debit-card moment at the petrol station on her way home from the Club last month. Awkward to fill up the tank only to discover you're over your card limit and have no spare cash on you. It hadn't been a problem at all because Keith at the pay counter knew her, knew she'd be back with the money. Which she had been, of course, she'd just not had it with her at that moment.

Claire glanced at her list again. 'Or have you ever been in an embarrassing situation due to your gambling?' She gave an encouraging smile.

Denise hesitated. She didn't like these questions. Too personal. 'I wouldn't say embarrassing, no,' she said. If another teacher had spotted her at the Club last week unable to pay for coffee, *that* would've been humiliating, but it was only the young girl with the star tattoos. She'd barely noticed Denise's momentary financial lapse and Denise hadn't needed the coffee anyway. In retrospect, an uncomfortable situation, yes, but not an embarrassing one.

Claire cleared her throat and glanced at the computer screen again.

'Do you ever lie about your gambling, or minimise it?'

Goodness. This must be some checklist Claire had to follow. Nobody could set out to be this blunt.

'Lie is a strong word, isn't it?' Denise leaned forward, shifting her weight. The chair was becoming quite uncomfortable.

'I've made this appointment and travelled quite a way to see you, so I'm very committed to getting help before it becomes an embarrassment or I start lying about it.'

Claire nodded. She leaned forward mirroring Denise's posture.

'So giving you some strategies to overcome the triggers to your gambling before it becomes an ... embarrassment ... might be the best approach?' she asked.

Here comes the jargon used by most newly hatched professionals. No one had spoken to Denise about 'strategies' since the last Department of Education meeting when she was still the principal of East Albury Primary School. If Claire mentioned Key Performance Indicators or Strategic Outcomes, Denise wasn't sure if she'd roll on the floor laughing or get up and leave this suffocating little room.

'It helps if we can identify your gambling triggers,' Claire said. 'I see you're retired. Has the gambling increased since you stopped work?'

This one was easier to answer, and now she was here, Denise thought, she may as well go along with the whole exercise. 'Yes, it has,' she said. 'In fact, it started then. I have a lot of time on my hands now.'

'Husband? Children?'

Denise shook her head. 'Neither. I've been divorced for years.'

'Having too little to do is a common trigger. Being on your own is another.'

'That sounds right. I do drift down to the Club to fill in time, not because I get a huge buzz out of it. I mean, you don't make friends there. We're all regulars, but there's no friendly hello or the chance to have a coffee together.'

'So if you don't really get a buzz out of gambling, what is it that you like about it?'

Denise considered the question before answering. 'The structure it gives my life, I guess. Knowing when I get up in the morning that I have somewhere to go, something to do. Maybe it's also the thought that I have a fifty-fifty chance of winning something ...' Denise marvelled at Claire's ability to type notes into the laptop while she could maintain eye contact with her.

'If you had something better to do, would that make you think twice about going to the Club every day?'

'It probably would. Maybe I didn't plan my retirement well enough, work out what I'd like to do. It was such a relief to be free of all the responsibilities that I somehow imagined I'd be happy every day for the rest of my life.' Denise smiled. How naive she'd been. 'Sounds silly, doesn't it? Of course it hasn't quite worked out like that. There are parts of work I really miss.'

'What parts?' Claire was more probing than Denise had expected. She took a long, uneasy breath. This office was too small, too confining.

'The company for one. Having great people around me every day to bounce ideas off.'

'If you're missing company, perhaps you could join a club? A bowling club, maybe? That would be good exercise too, and help lift your mood.'

Good Lord, she hadn't exercised since she'd played school netball—or basketball as it was called in those days—at Our Lady of Perpetual Succour. 'I'm not one for exercise—though my doctor keeps nagging me to take it up. Slow torture as far as I'm concerned.'

'What do you enjoy doing?' Claire turned her full attention on Denise, joining her fingers into a steeple. 'You'd need to find a leisure activity you truly enjoy, if you're to keep going with it.'

'Enjoy'? The word sounded like an indulgence. There'd been little time to enjoy leisure over the years. 'I used to love classroom teaching, though the chance to do it faded over time. It's odd, but the higher you rise in your profession, the further you move from doing what you enjoy. You get caught up with planning and administration, as though they're the most important part. I miss being with the littlies.'

'What about volunteering at a school, then?'

The thought had crossed Denise's mind. Schools were always looking for people to take reading sessions, and it could be enjoyable to give it a go for a few hours a week. Especially when someone else has all the responsibility for running the show.

'I love books, I could do something along literacy lines. Mind you, I'm pretty strong at maths, too.'

Claire sat upright, like a meerkat. Denise couldn't believe she could manage to look even more earnest. 'If you're a reader, what about joining a book group? Or do you know anyone who'd start one with you? Local libraries can often help with that. Having an interest—and setting goals—is a great way to take you out of yourself.'

'I had close friends who'd have been interested but they both moved to Melbourne. To be closer to their grand-children. Not something I'll ever have to worry about.'

Claire glanced back at the notes she'd taken.

'You mentioned earlier that having a fifty-fifty chance of winning on the pokies was appealing to you. But you can't ever win playing pokies.'

'Oh, I understand all about the maths. Just because you've thrown, say, ten heads in a row doesn't mean the odds favour tails for the next throw. It's still fifty-fifty.'

'But you're talking about odds where all things are equal. Did you know the machines are programmed—fixed, you could call it—to always return less than you put in? You can only win over the short term if you leave the machine the second you've made more money than you've spent. You can't ever win over the long term.'

Denise looked up, surprised. 'But that wouldn't be fair. I assumed it was random. Are you sure?'

Claire sat silently, her hands resting on the desk. Denise gave a disbelieving shake of her head. Tricked by spinning wheels and unfair tactics.

'Are you saying I've been suckered into believing players have an even chance?'

'Don't blame yourself. I'm embarrassed to say it's psychologists—experts who understand human behaviour—who've designed these machines. It's the same with the venues—the bright lights, no windows, the enticing graphics, even the lairy colours. Nothing about the industry is random, I promise you. It's all orchestrated, smoke and mirrors and trickery, designed to make you lose track of time, and find it hard to leave. I think for you, once you really get that, you're well on the road to recovery.'

'That's diabolical. So that's why I just kept pressing and pressing that stupid button, believing in something that doesn't exist.' Denise paused in her outrage. 'Those machines should be treated like cigarettes and covered in plain khaki wrapping with graphic wealth warnings on them.'

Claire laughed, a relaxed, easy sound that made Denise more comfortable. Perhaps she wasn't so earnest after all. 'And the casinos target people with free chips or special offers,' Claire said.

So that explained the email in her inbox. She'd been browsing gaming websites when, out of the blue, this offer had popped up describing in detail a lucky chap in Queensland who'd won the jackpot after his first attempt on their roulette site, and showing him smiling in front of a red sports car. And they were giving her—yes, actually giving her—a free voucher worth fifty dollars as a gift. The phone had rung then and somehow the offer had slipped her mind, and she'd never used it. Well, that was one win to her.

*

The trip home in the twilight was different, almost enjoyable. The countryside spooled behind her in black and white. The road was straighter, the trees on the horizon sharper, the distance between towns shorter. Amazing. It had been worth the journey. Denise even felt lighter, slimmer. Claire may be young, she may be inexperienced, but she knew what she was doing and there was nothing like talking a problem over to gain a new perspective. She—and all the others—had been targeted, that's what had happened. Now she knew that all these mug players had been hoodwinked by the poker-machine heavyweights, she would not set foot in the RSL Club again. Not even for lunch. She'd show them she wasn't to be taken for a fool. It had really only been a time filler until she found something better. How stupid to hand over your hard-earned cash to grasping strangers. And Claire had given her some ideas to play with. Set new goals: that would be her strategy. She could change her life, be more frivolous now, with no planning meetings, no staff training, no angry, estranged parents. And she could let other people in more, no need to keep up that distance that went with being a principal.

She glimpsed the setting sun in her rear-view mirror, a slash of gold and pink and red, glowing against the darkening blue. Red sky at night, sailor's delight, as her father used to say. No doubt about it. Tomorrow was going to be a very good day.

Chapter 4

The telephone was ringing as Sarah stood on the front steps of her house, high on Monument Hill, and punched in the home security code. 5 pm. Lovely. That would most likely be Andrea calling. Andrea had always been quiet, but she was turning into a recluse since Brian's death, her once warm and lived-in home seemed like a mausoleum whenever Sarah visited. Dark and gloomy, curtains remaining drawn in all the rooms that weren't in use, piles of newspapers or books-to-read that didn't change position for weeks at a time.

'Hi, Sas, it's only me ...'

Why, Sarah wondered, did your closest friends use phrases like 'It's *only* me?' That should be reserved for annoying strangers calling at dinnertime, wanting you to change your electricity provider.

'Never "only me",' Sarah said. 'Only one of the most important people in my life.'

'Oh, thank you. That's very kind. Any progress on the book club? Any callers?'

'Yes, and I've been giving it some thought. What say we limit it to six members at the beginning? We could meet on the first and third Tuesdays of the month. Fortnightly at first to get to know each other, with the hostess providing a light supper. Looking at the list you picked up, what do you think of *The Hare with Amber Eyes* for our first book?'

'Wow, you've really thought this through.' Andrea sounded nonplussed, so Sarah changed tack.

'A couple of women phoned, but I want you to meet them first. I've teed up coffee with them the Saturday after you're back from Canberra,' she said. 'Here's hoping this book club doesn't implode like our last one. Mind you, it *was* fun to watch Fiona and Bernadette bicker over whether the Pope was to blame for all the misery in *Angela's Ashes*. And I swear, I might have a lot of catching up to do if serious readers join. I'm so out of touch. I was mortified last month—I twisted Rob's arm to take me to one of his medical dinners and I was the only woman on our table who hadn't read any Richard Flanagan. It's as if I haven't turned a page since I read Chaucer for my master's.'

'Chaucer?' Andrea laughed. 'From memory, most of your time that year was spent treading the boards with the drama society. You'll soon catch up. You were always a great crammer. I'll see you after I'm back from Canberra doing my share of grandchild-minding.'

With their conversation over, Sarah made a quick calculation of the time zones. Ringing New York and waking Lucy at two thirty in the morning wasn't on, and it was seven thirty in the UK, so Anna would be getting ready for work. Her gaze fell on the silver-framed photograph resting next to the telephone, the three of them laughing together at the river, the week before the girls left for overseas. Andrea had taken the shot, capturing them in a moment of unselfconscious fun and abandonment, arms around each other, heads back laughing. Sarah found herself looking at it a lot now. She had no idea if they would ever come back home and settle down. No idea how they felt about men and marriage and children.

She envied Rob's sister, who lived a few streets away from her grandchildren. Her home seemed welcoming and busy, filled with photos of toddlers on swings, bright finger-paintings on the fridge door and toys scattered around the room. For a moment Sarah allowed herself to wonder if she'd get the same someday, whether there'd ever be photos of happy grandchildren in silver frames to display on *her* living room sideboard. *I have two children I love*, she thought, *and I don't live near either of them.*

* * *

As she stood at the front counter of the LibraryMuseum the day after her session with the gambling counsellor, Denise's eye caught a small sign. It seemed to be winking at her, as if conjured by magical thinking:

DO YOU LIKE READING?
ARE YOU INTERESTED IN FORMING A COSY BOOK
CLUB WITH NEW FRIENDS?
CALL SARAH FOR MORE DETAILS.

Wasn't this exactly what Claire, the counsellor, had suggested? That she needed to explore new interests, new friends, now that she'd retired? A distraction from playing the pokies, with its rock-solid guarantee of losing money. A book club might be the perfect antidote, the first step back from the abyss. No harm in giving 'Sarah' a call in the next few days and exploring what was out there.

***

'I can't believe you did it again, Sas!' Andrea had called in for news about their book club plans the day after her return from Canberra, and she wasn't about to let the issue pass. Honestly, Sarah had to be pulled up every now and then. 'You jumped at inviting Neelam into the book club without any discussion and I said then I wanted to be consulted about new members. Now you're telling me you've said yes to a Berenice without running it past me. Or either of us even meeting her, for that matter.'

'I think it was Bernice, not Berenice.' Sarah poured them both a glass of wine. 'She's a retired teacher, so she'll fit into a reading group well. I didn't want us to lose momentum while you were away. And she had a very pleasant telephone voice ...'

Andrea accepted the wine but remained firm. 'Letting me meet with her first would've been nice, that's all I'm saying. And don't forget that it's not going to be *your* book club when we settle into the final numbers. Everyone gets a say—about the books we choose, about the times of the meetings, about everything!'

'I'm sorry. You're right. And I need you to remind me if I begin to treat everyone like a committee.' One of Sarah's more endearing traits was her ability to take criticism without offence. Whether she was able to change as a result of it was another matter. 'But don't forget Coffee Mecca this Saturday at ten—we can both meet the other women who were interested.'

Chapter 5

Andrea reversed her Mazda into the narrow space left between Sarah's imposing Mercedes and a cute little BMW parked outside a house in West Albury. Neelam's home, which looked no more than five years old, was in an upmarket area of the city, where the houses were so huge that they all shone with the reflected pride of their owners and dominated even their substantial gardens. The sort of places that had large swimming pools and spacious barbeque areas out the back. The front gardens were landscaped with native trees and Grevillia shrubs to cope with the scorching summer heat, and without fences, the whole suburb had an open plan look, as though the neighbours here would be friends, waving to each other as they mulched and tidied and pruned on a Saturday afternoon. Quite a change from her own Californian bunga-low, tucked behind its high picket fence and screened from the neighbours by bushy hedges.

She could hear the burble of voices through the screen door as she stood at the entrance, the scent of exotic spices wafting her way. She made out figures at the end of a long hallway lined with vibrant Indian wall hangings. Before she could press the buzzer, Neelam was gliding down the hall towards her with a warm smile. Despite being a little overweight, she had a walk so graceful you wished you could capture it and hang it on the wall.

'Welcome,' she said. 'Andrea, isn't it? We met in the library. This is so very exciting for me to be in a new club. Most have arrived already. You will know them all, I am thinking?'

'Not all,' Andrea said. 'I haven't met Bernice yet.'

'Bernice?' Neelam tilted her head slightly, her forehead puckered. 'I do not think we are expecting a Bernice, though I may have misheard. Let us come in and introduce ourselves.'

Andrea followed her into an open living and dining area, her eye first catching a silk-covered table laden end to end in scrumptious-looking samosas and other Indian delicacies. A plate of pink and white coconut ice was at one side. The message about 'light supper, nothing too elaborate' mustn't have filtered through—no doubt thrilling for the passionate foodies among them like Sarah, but daunting for mediocre cooks like herself. She could never hope to match this marvellous spread. Two bottles of Prosecco were sitting on the table. Sarah must have decided the first meeting was a good reason to bring along her favourite bubbly from a local vineyard.

Andrea kissed Sarah and turned to greet Kate and Libby who were both holding a glass of the Prosecco. Kate gave her an exuberant hug. It was the first time Andrea had seen them both since their meeting at Coffee Mecca to get to know each other, and she was struck by how Libby, standing so tall next to the diminutive Kate, wouldn't have been out of place on a catwalk.

A moment later, Neelam ushered in the last of her expected guests. It was fortunate the others were all too busy chatting to notice her arrival because Andrea couldn't suppress a sharp intake of breath. *Oh my God.* Neelam had been telling the truth. There was no Bernice at all. Andrea was in a book club with, of all people, Denise Robertson. *Mrs Robertson. Nooo.*

As they shook hands, there was no sign of recognition on Denise's plump face. Fair enough. It had been years ago and Andrea didn't doubt that she herself no longer looked like she had in her mid-thirties. What was slim and fit then now passed on a good day as wiry. Denise had certainly rounded out even further in the intervening period, but Andrea would know her anywhere. Her heart plummeted. Of all the people she might have liked to join their book club, Denise Robertson would have been so low on her list she'd have fallen off the bottom.

Andrea picked up a long-stemmed wineglass and reached for the Prosecco. She filled her glass to the very top. Kate was standing at the table, eyeing off the spread, so Andrea made a beeline over to speak with her.

'I'm afraid we won't be having anything like this when it's my turn to host,' Kate said, reaching for a samosa. 'How does reheated pizza sound?' She gave a wicked smile. 'It worked a treat with my boys.'

'I was thinking along the same lines.' Andrea swept a wedge of naan into a dip. 'Yum.' The exotic spices hit her senses the moment she bit into it and she swallowed it in one gulp. 'The height of my culinary expertise is adding basil to a tomato sandwich.' She took a second, larger wedge of the home-baked bread and dip. 'This is divine! Forget book club. I could eat it all night. Stop me now, please, before I turn into Monty Python's Mr Creosote and burst.'

Kate held out the last sliver of her samosa and feigned a French accent.

'A waf-fer thin mouthful of samosa, madame? Only a tiny little thin one?'

They both burst out laughing as a puzzled Neelam came to shepherd them across to the living room, where the others were taking up their places on sofas adorned with silk throws and bright red and gold triangular cushions.

They made themselves comfortable—Andrea sitting as far as possible from Denise Robertson. She scrabbled for her copy of *The Hare with Amber Eyes* while balancing the wine and her dip-loaded naan. A prehensile tail would come in so handy at times like this.

'Welcome everyone to our inaugural book club meeting.' Sarah spoke first, of course. 'I hope you've all had a chance to read our book and have your copy with you?' Everyone nodded. 'On reflection, maybe I should've chosen a novel rather than a memoir for the first session, but I'm sure everyone's given it the best go they can.'

'And I'm so pleased you chose it, Sarah.'

Andrea was taken aback at the interruption. *Heavens. A generous comment from Denise Robertson.*

'It's not a book I'd ever have read without this club, but I loved it,' the older woman went on. 'And now I'm besotted with Japanese netsuke.'

'And *that* was going to be my first question.' Kate leaned forward. 'How did you pronounce the name again?'

'Okay, confession time. I had no idea either, but in an episode of *Downton Abbey*, the Dowager Duchess thought the young gardener had stolen her precious ivory carving—it was a tiny fisherman—and she called it *net-ski*. I figured she wouldn't make a mistake.'

'I've heard it called that too, so I agree with you.' Sarah gave Denise a radiant smile. 'And wouldn't it be marvellous to have a collection? They sound exquisite.'

'Was anyone else uncomfortable with the affluence of the family?' Andrea interrupted, emboldened by the Prosecco. She didn't like Sarah and Denise Robertson cosying up to each other quite so quickly. 'Not that there's anything wrong with money, of course,' she said, by way of concession to her friend, 'but I always fail to see how one person's labour can be worth massively more than another's. I got bogged down a little with all the tales of acquisition in the early pages of the family's history.'

'But there's something wonderful about having beautiful objects.' Sarah smiled again at Denise. 'And collecting them is such a pleasure.'

'Somehow, I felt the expansion of the family's collection of *objets d'art* bordered on greed,' Andrea said, surprised at her own insistence.

'You may be accused of harbouring socialist tendencies if that view gets out!' Kate said. 'But you have a point. At the end of the day, it's all just stuff, isn't it? And when trouble comes to visit, you can't take it with you. Well, unless it's the size of a tiny netsuke that can be tucked into a mattress.'

'I would've liked more photos. Especially colour pictures so I'd have a better idea of what they look like. Unless I missed something …' Libby's voice faltered. 'I haven't quite finished the book,' she added, with a half-smile, as though admitting to a fault. Perhaps she wasn't an avid reader.

Neelam was topping up everyone's food and drinks, but stopped for a moment, samosa plate in hand.

'You are right,' she said to Libby. 'I too would like to see all the beautiful treasures of this family. Photographs are so important.'

Denise turned to her, taking a proffered pastry. 'That's why there are shows like *Downton*, so we can ogle an opulent life we'll never know. Imagine living in such grandeur.'

'I think you'd cease to notice it after a while.' Andrea paused for a moment, thinking it over. 'I mean, if art is in a public space, like a gallery or a church, it allows everyone to share the experience, so in that way, the beauty is constantly renewed because it's being seen by fresh eyes. If I had the talent to create something original, something exquisite, I'd hate to think it was purchased by some billionaire for his own personal viewing, or worse, kept in his vault.'

'Or hers,' Kate added.

There was spontaneous laughter and suppressed spluttering.

'Sure, or hers!' Andrea wondered how many women amassed great art collections, especially using money they'd earned themselves.

'It's not unheard of,' said Sarah, making eye contact with Andrea. 'Think of Catherine the Great. Or Peggy Guggenheim. And there's our Gina. But jewellery collections are more our thing, and at least we wear them out and about for others to admire … or envy.'

'If this memoir proves anything,' Denise said, shielding her mouth with her hand as she ate, 'it's that it's much cleverer to have small items like netsuke—or precious stones, I guess—that can be smuggled out of harm's way, as opposed to something the size of Michelangelo's *David.*'

The others laughed again, and they continued their discussion until a slight man padded into the room and stood at the rim of their circle. Obviously 'Mr' Neelam.

He cast his handsome dark eyes around. 'Good evening, ladies, welcome to my home. I am Vinod.' He turned to Neelam. 'It must be time for coffee, isn't it? It is getting quite late.'

Andrea glanced at her watch, surprised she hadn't noticed that their two hours had almost passed.

'We haven't even been aware of the time,' she said, and turned to their hostess. 'You've looked after us so well, Neelam. Such luck that we bumped into you in the LibraryMuseum that day.'

'I would have to agree. I, too, am lucky that I was there. It has been a most entertaining evening.' Neelam headed for the kitchen, and Vinod, after a little nod to the women, followed her.

'Before we finish business, why don't we choose next meeting's book? I've printed out the library's reading list.' Sarah handed copies to everyone as Andrea suppressed a giggle. Sas could never resist a chance to forward plan. 'If we pick one tonight, we can discuss an ongoing schedule at a future meeting.'

*

As Andrea slid between the sheets that night, she realised her arthritis hadn't given her a twinge of pain all evening. There was no better cure for an ailment, she decided, than pleasant distraction. *Mrs Robertson* notwithstanding.

Chapter 6

'What would you think about us buying a small pad in Sydney?' Sarah pulled off her gardening gloves, wiped her forehead and paused for a moment. The work had been harder than she'd expected.

It was Saturday, and she was able to snare Rob's attention as they hefted the limb of an old eucalypt that was blocking the path to their front door. With the gardener away, she'd had to leave it until Rob came back from Sydney. They'd worked together in companionable silence to clear the debris until she threw the last of the branches that he'd dismembered into the back of the trailer. The gardener could take it for mulching and recycling next week.

Rob was in an easy mood, so now seemed as good a time as any to float her idea. 'Think about it, Rob. It would be fun for me to stay there some weeks, now the girls are living overseas.'

'It's unnecessary.' He took off his gloves and handed them back to her for safekeeping. He was a stickler for protecting his hands. 'Could end up being a white elephant. I'd never be there. The room I have at the hospital on weeknights is all I need because I'm operating until late. And this place is so good to come home to at the end of the week, why have the hassle of another property there?'

Sarah slapped the gloves together. 'But I'm seeing you less and less.'

'It's the Sydney work that provides our comfortable lifestyle—and the best house in Albury. You love that. Plus your friends are all here. If you ever want to come to town, you can always book into the InterContinental and I'll join you, if you give me notice.'

Come to town, he'd said, as though Sydney was his home base. Not *visit Sydney.* His InterContinental suggestion might sound fine in theory, but any visit she made would have to be planned weeks in advance so he could rearrange his operating lists.

Rob was already wandering back towards the house, keen to dictate follow-up letters to his referring doctors. If she let him go now, she mightn't see him till dinnertime. She followed him along the landscaped path.

'But the "Best House in Albury" seems a bit empty now the girls have left. I'm so far from them, and from Sydney. The farthest reaches of the state.'

'You were keen to come to "the farthest reaches of the state" when I first suggested it.'

'Of course I was. You said it would be quicker to build up a reputation here. You said I'd see you more.'

'And you were extra keen when you knew Andrea and Brian were moving here.'

'Sure, and it was great—but that's all changed now. You're away all the time. What started as a day a week in Sydney is most of the week now.'

'Can't help it if so many women there need me to make them look twenty years younger,' Rob said in a lighter tone. His smile disarmed her as it always did.

Back in their university days, Sarah had dreams of becoming a professional actress. She'd poured every ounce of energy into the theatre, spending hours rehearsing her lines with Andrea's help, underlining key passages and scrawling accents on the page. The script for *All's Well That End's Well* had been even more dog-eared than the rest after she snared the role of Helena over other aspiring young hopefuls. And there'd been plenty of those once word got around that Rob Carpenter had been cast as Bertram. 'He's the one for me,' she'd whispered to Andrea in the wings, and so it had been ever since. He *was* the only one for her.

'You haven't forgotten the MAMA fundraising ball, have you? I've arranged a table with your medical friends.' She twiddled with his gardening gloves.

'Well, make sure my office manager knows so she can schedule it. But I've got referral letters to answer now.' And with that, he headed back to his office inside, where he'd no doubt stay working until dinner was ready.

* * *

The camaraderie of the book group had set Andrea thinking. She was spending too much time alone now that Brian had gone. Maybe it was time to face the future, time to clear out the past, and let go. She could start with all the stuff out the back. She slid open the doors to the large workshop crammed with Brian's collections and stared at the mementoes of his life. The musty space was chock-a-block with all his treasures.

She opened an old biscuit tin and carefully picked up the small, solid silver DC-2 model inside, holding it with both hands under the smooth fuselage, as Brian had done. It had been his favourite. He'd found it at an auction of aircraft memorabilia when they were on holiday in Queensland. The expression on his face when he spotted the treasure and held it aloft from the other side of the crowded room was all she needed to give him a thumbs-up. She didn't even consider the price. If she totted it up, they must have spent a small fortune on all these banners, old flight manuals and other assorted aviation paraphernalia that filled the shed.

As Andrea picked her way past more assorted storage boxes, a wall of mounted model aeroplanes confronted her. Little dust motes fluttered around. She placed the DC-2 back in its resting place. *No, not today.*

Other couples often seemed to drift apart once the children left home, discovering they had no interests in common and nothing to talk about, but she and Brian hadn't been like that. They'd always had the same sense of humour and, for her sake, he'd even feigned interest in the local choral concerts. She wasn't ready to clear his stuff out yet, and didn't even know how to go about it.

It was already late afternoon, a hot summer day of bright light and set-square shadows. She turned to go back to the house and paused to pick up the secateurs near the back step, then she slipped on her gardening gloves and confronted the rosebush. The ivory and red-tipped Double Delight roses were too fragrant to be left to shrivel in the overgrown garden. She cut half a dozen flowers, keeping the stems long, and snapped off the thorns. Maybe these would cheer up the house.

She walked down to the living room to get a vase from the sideboard, the click-clack of her steps on the polished floors echoing in her ears. Strange, she'd never noticed it when Brian was there, filling the space with his laugh and his constant queries about where he'd put things—his keys, his wallet, his mobile phone. At first, after he died, she'd been too numb with grief to understand the full weight of her loss. She'd felt as if she were living behind a pane of glass while she'd kept busy following her routine at work. But since she retired, his absence was enormous and ever-present.

Nicole and Jason were grown up and gone—the very thing she'd looked forward to in a guilty way, even though of course she wouldn't be without them—but that secret desire of middle age to be child-free and fancy-free must have been a crazy phase she had gone through. She'd have them back in a heartbeat now.

After filling the vase with water from the kitchen tap, she dumped the roses in it. Her hands felt too stiff after cutting the blooms to fiddle with an arrangement. This wretched lack of energy since the rheumatoid arthritis hit her. She looked at her painful, swollen fingers, wondering if she'd need to enlarge her rings at some stage. Stress, the specialist said, was often a trigger for an autoimmune disease. Most likely all the worry with Brian's illness. The frequent trips to chemo with him had left her vulnerable, he'd told her.

By this time of day, she and Brian would have been collaborating on the cryptic crossword. She missed sharing these myriad little moments with him. Even doing the dishes. For some reason, they'd reverted to washing and drying them by hand once the children had left, as if it were a way to recapture the early years of marriage. How good it would be to still have someone to care for. Being needed was central to Andrea; it was who she was, her sense of self. Now that her family no longer needed her and there was no niche for her in the nine-to-five world, she wondered who she was—what was her purpose?

She tried to focus on the crossword. One across: 'Partner revamps team (4)'. Too easy! She pencilled M-A-T-E into the grid. Ah, the eternal search for a soulmate.

Before she'd left work, some of her younger colleagues had spent their lunch hours logged onto RSVP and Yvonne Allen websites in the tearoom, working through the mysterious abbreviations and sharing war stories about disastrous dates with unsuitable men. It sounded like a battle-zone out there, and yet they kept on trying, even assuring her in a lighthearted way that they'd look for her perfect match, too.

'Here's one, Andrea,' Tracy said one lunchtime, between gulps of coffee. '"Sixty-four-year-old retiree, GSOH, loves walks in the bush and romantic dinners. Looking for mature lady to share his retirement years."' The women put down their salads and hooted with laughter at the prospect.

'I expect he's looking for mature lady to cook said romantic dinners and prevent him falling without his walker!' said Andrea.

Years as a social worker had opened her eyes to the realities of life, but unbeknown to her younger workmates, who were treating it as a joke—as if anyone so *old* could still be interested—she did harbour a desire to at least investigate what was out there. Maybe Mr GOSH, as she took to calling him, was sincere in his loneliness. Just like she was.

The abbreviations in those lonely-hearts ads were a cryptic language of their own, and it was time to explore them. She put down her pencil. She was a bit rusty on the computer, having abandoned it during the dreadful time when Brian was ill, and before that she'd always relied on him to upgrade the various applications and unjam the printer. Those tasks would all have to be learned now ...

When she was settled in her study, her Google search threw up Internet Slang.

GSOH cropped up in every ad Tracy found at work. Who wouldn't want someone with a Good Sense of Humour? Did anyone ever write BSOH on these sites? Or ASOH if it were absent? Maybe not. People might think these meant something else altogether.

AL: What sort of animal lover? And was the emphasis on 'animal' or on 'lover'? Now that would be a worry.

GEM: Gemini? *Oh, please.*

NM: Never Married = Never-Been-House-Trained.

DF: Drug Free. Was that cryptic-speak for 'drug free nowadays'? Why would you even mention that unless you wanted to convince someone? But come to think of it, now that she was taking so much medication herself, would she have to admit to being DA (Drug Addled)?

Most confusing were the dual meaning abbreviations like 'P'. It would be quite a challenge walking into a cafe not knowing if you were meeting a Professional person or a Petite one.

Engrossed in the search, Andrea reached for her guilty pleasure—a chocolate Flake, enjoying the slow melt in her mouth. What qualities would be essential in any new partner she might consider, and how would she abbreviate them?

SE: Smiling Eyes. Yes, a man with smile lines at the corners of his eyes—and lips for that matter—was always appealing. Think Detective Chief Superintendent Christopher Foyle from the TV show *Foyle's War*.

GC: Good Company. Nothing too spectacular, but an intelligent and interesting man was not too much to want.

HATH: Helpful Around The House. The ability to bring her a cup of tea in bed in the mornings would be priceless.

UMAG: Uncomplaining Mower and Gardener. Yes, please.

Hmm. She could be describing Brian. That might be a problem. If she found somebody like Brian, she'd spend her time noting all the little not-Brian things about him. The ways he failed to measure up.

And what would Nicole or Jason think of her looking for an ersatz Brian, or *any* type of companion, for that matter? Nicole—always a dependable soul, even as a child—had been Dad's little helper, his shadow, remembering where he'd left his hammer, handing him his nails and screws and making herself indispensable around the workshop. And Jason relied on Brian to help him out whenever he found himself in some far-flung country, short of funds. No, the children mightn't take to another man in her life.

Maybe she should stick to small steps, like the new book club. Not that she'd come across men there, of course—she'd have to go to Bunnings for that—but at least she was meeting new people again, getting out a bit, having more interesting events in her life.

Did men ever have book clubs? Brian had enjoyed being busy with his hands. He liked to do repairs, to hammer and chisel and do whatever men do in their man caves. His choice of reading topics had been restricted to politicians' memoirs, cycling magazines and anything to do with airplanes. Plane crashes, plane rescues, air investigations. Lucky that she'd grown up in a family of plane tragics and could share this interest. All those aviation-related events she'd attended over the years meant she could hold her own with any man on that topic.

She swallowed the last of her Flake.

This new club with new people was a good start and even Denise Robertson's presence couldn't spoil that. She headed towards the kitchen; her chocolate appetiser had made her hungry. Time to arrange the roses before making a stir-fry. And she'd throw in some cashews for a change.

Chapter 7

When Sarah later tried to figure out where things went wrong, she blamed *Moby Dick*. The weighty nineteenth-century novel was so dense that none of them could conquer it, despite all remaining conscientious about reading. Even with a master's in English literature, Sarah hadn't been persuaded to complete the arduous tome, deciding it needed a good edit. They should have stayed with more titles like, say, *The Guernsey Literary and Potato Peel Society*. That was so endearing with its themes of loyalty and courage, and its small-town sense of community. Or *The Hare with Amber Eyes,* the one that had been such a hit with Denise. Instead, after a few meetings, Sarah had suggested the group try an old classic as a challenge. Big mistake!

The LibraryMuseum only had a few copies of *Moby Dick* available, so Denise said she'd be happy to download an ebook instead, because she'd bought an iPad that week. Sarah wondered if she'd heard correctly. Denise, who looked to be the oldest in the group, and was coming across as quite staid, even old-fashioned, didn't seem like someone who'd embrace ebooks. Well, chalk that up to Andrea for suggesting they open their book club to people they didn't know. Denise must have hidden depths. The only problem was that Andrea still seemed a little piqued that Denise had been invited into the group without any discussion, and remained cool towards her. That was a bit unfair. It wasn't Denise's fault—she was reading and contributing so well to the group.

But when Denise sank into her chair for the *Moby Dick* meeting you could see her mood was dark. The women were gathered in Kate's comfortable family room. The casual throws over the chairs, the boxes full of dolls and trains and draught sets, and the side tables crammed with photos of laughing children and smiling parents all reflected Kate's welcoming personality. Even the golden retriever lying beside a couch seemed to wear a perpetual smile, as if to confirm how good it was to be a part of the family.

'Hideous iPad.' Denise looked far from happy. 'I had to buy *iPad for Seniors* to try and work out how to use it.' She pulled a magazine out of her bag. 'May I read the first line from their "Out of the Box Set-Up Guide"?'

May I? Sarah could hear the former school principal in Denise's choice of words.

'*The PC Free option removes the need for a PC and iTunes when it comes to activating and syncing your iDevice.*' She laid down the guide and snorted. 'What the hell does that mean? My neighbour's teenage boy finally came over to download *Moby Dick* for me, but his explanation was as clear as the *iPad for Seniors*. And delivered at umpteen times the pace. I had to get an Apple account—and password—so I could download some sort of Kindle gizmo that can read books, then I had to go into Amazon to buy the book. That meant yet another account—and password—before I could even open the so-called "book" on screen.

'I ask you, what's wrong with using an old-fashioned paper book from an old-fashioned bricks-and-mortar shop? Or borrowing one from a library?'

Kate moved to take another bottle of wine from the sideboard. *Hardly surprising,* Sarah thought, *that nobody's rushing to fill the silence.* It had been Denise's idea to download an ebook to her iPad in the first place, and it was called *book* club after all, not Kindle club.

'And what's wrong with turning pages with your hands, and knowing how far you're into the book?' Denise was warming to her outrage. 'Or enjoying the scent and the touch of a real book? And knowing how many pages you've got to go?'

Sarah almost felt embarrassed for her. This about-face was as total as it was shameless. It now seemed the idea of replacing paper with an ebook was close to treachery.

'Take bookmarks. I love them,' Denise continued. 'I've discovered those clever little ones that fold over the page and grip together with magnetic strips. That sort never falls out. You know the ones I mean?'

Sarah relaxed, sinking back into the cushions. This was more familiar territory, as everyone took a comforting detour into a topic unrelated to *Moby Dick,* and for the next ten minutes meandered around the pros and cons of bookmarks.

'I love a good bookmark, I used to collect them,' Andrea said.

'It's hard to find good ones now. They're so often paper ones that come with the book—you know, those shameless props for advertising,' Denise said.

'I like the mini-versions of Old Masters,' Kate said. 'I have one of Van Gogh's sunflowers.' That triggered a discussion of visits to galleries in Europe and memories of their favourite paintings before Denise returned to her grievances.

'*Moby Dick* is so dreary!' she said, flicking her hand towards her iPad. 'I *know* it's a classic, I *know* we should persevere, but I gave up after twenty-five pages.'

'Twenty-five?' Kate asked, pausing as she poured more wine. 'Clever you! That's five more than I managed. I was beginning to think this club is too brainy for me. I said to Neil maybe I should leave gracefully.'

Sarah sat up quickly and turned towards her. She was still getting to know Kate, yet already felt very fond of her. 'Don't you dare leave! You know that rule of mine about giving a book my undivided attention for at least fifty pages before passing judgement? Broken this time. And quite early.'

The competition quickly became intense to find who'd lasted the longest in the quest for the great white whale. Or rather, the shortest.

Kate shifted in her seat before slapping one hand on her knee. 'I've had an idea. How many of us have iPads?' She looked around at everybody.

Only Denise raised a hand, her wineglass sloshing close to spilling.

Andrea's forehead crinkled. 'I'd been thinking about it, but from what I'm hearing today, I might reconsider that!'

'What about smartphones?' Kate added. 'Do we all use them?'

Sarah pulled a little face. She knew a bit about smartphones, having inherited Rob's iPhone when he'd done one of his regular upgrades, but she'd resisted any of his further offers. Too much hassle relearning each new phone, and Rob's latest discards were too big. Who'd want one like that? When mobile phones first came on the market he and his friends all competed to own the smallest model. Now they all wanted to show off how big the screens were, provided they were cigarette-paper-thin, of course.

'Yes, I have a smart phone,' Sarah said, wondering where Kate was going with her questions. 'That's why I can't be bothered with an iPad. Don't need it.'

Libby pulled a clunky little Nokia out of her pocket. 'This is smart enough for me. Only use it for emergencies.'

Neelam giggled when she saw it. 'Do they still exist? I believed they had been retired due to old age.'

Sarah hadn't seen a little mobile like that for years either, but if Libby didn't need a slick smartphone, why would she bother? It was fine for Neelam with her council job: PR or publicity, or something. A smartphone was part of her package. *And* she had an IT department on tap. Anyway, Sarah had heard her admitting that she had a mere basic-level smartphone because only team leaders in council's strict hierarchy rated an iPhone. Neelam's wasn't a state-of-the-art device by any means.

Sarah turned to Kate. 'Why are you asking about smart-phones? We're veering off course, nothing to do with book club. We need to get back to the ...' She was about to say *agenda* but caught Andrea's eye '... book, don't we? Make sure our next one is better?'

'Bear with me, Sarah,' Kate said. 'This *is* going somewhere, I promise. Who has a blog or a vlog?'

Denise looked puzzled. 'What's a vlog?'

Her question wasn't answered as Kate continued to quiz them. 'Okay, how about a Twitter account?'

They all looked from one to the other, shaking heads.

'Instagram? WhatsApp?'

More shakes, a couple of blank looks.

'Anyone joined Facebook?'

As they all began to speak at once, Kate lifted her palms in mock surrender.

'Of course people have Facebook accounts,' Sarah said, relieved she could contribute something positive. 'It's almost impossible to get through life without one these days, even if you're worried about your data being used. My daughter Anna set it up for me before she moved to London.'

'And I've got one,' said Denise. 'We had a teacher's college reunion a few years back—that's how we all communicated. Mind you, I haven't used it since.'

'I sometimes look at what little Emily and Jesse are up to at school,' Andrea said. 'My son-in-law Tim organised it for me last Christmas. And Jason might post photos on it someday,' she added.

Sarah heard a wistful note in her voice. Ever since he was a little boy playing with her Anna and Lucy all those years ago, Andrea's whirlwind son had been a challenge. He was in Thailand now, being entrepreneurial and living the life of Riley. He was a clever one, if unpredictable.

'Don't you see?' Kate returned to her idea, eyes shining. 'We all love books. We'll read with or without a book club, but we're being left behind by modern technology. We don't need *Moby Dick* and book club as much as we need an IT club. Otherwise, we're going to be irrelevant to these smart Gen Xers and Millennials coming after us. It's time we pulled ourselves into the zeitgeist. Maybe we need a Social Media club!'

Sarah glanced over at Andrea, but she was intent on pouring a glass of water and didn't notice. Sarah knew how much Andrea loved reading, and setting up this club had been their shared adventure. What would she think of their grand plan being railroaded like this?

Sarah had no need to be on top of technology. When Rob was home, he sorted out the rare IT problems she might have, and his office people were so competent at upgrading her home software remotely that they could teach most computer geeks a thing or two. Anyway, there was no need to be part of 'the zeitgeist' and Andrea would think the same. A social life with real people was more important to them than a social media life.

Neelam leaned forward and cut herself a small slice of cheese. 'Hmm. I *am* a Gen Xer. But if I can say to you, being born in the early 1970s is not making me a smart woman with all this modern technology. I am often to be heard lamenting the disappearance of old-fashioned film!'

'I work with IT at TAFE, but I could always learn more,' Libby added. 'And I don't want something like this again.' She lifted her copy of *Moby Dick* as though it was a block of cement.

Kate turned to Andrea. 'What do you think?' She smiled. 'Would you be interested in learning more about social media?'

Poor Andrea. She'd be too polite to say 'no'.

'I mean, our local car dealer rang the other day,' Kate continued, 'saying my car had emailed him that it needed its service. When your car can email the dealer, but you can barely boot up a computer, maybe it's time to take action. The car will be sending twits next.'

Sarah stifled a smile. She wasn't Mrs IT Expert, but even she knew they were called tweets. But better not say anything in case someone asked her how to actually send a tweet.

It was time to come to Andrea's aid and defend their baby. 'We're a book club,' she said firmly. 'This would be quite a change of direction. A case of the ignorant leading the uneducated.'

Denise murmured agreement. Her iPad was sitting next to her, abandoned.

'And if you ask me,' Sarah continued, 'self-directed learning, despite being all the go in education, is seriously overrated.'

Denise beamed, nodding vigorously. Sarah was pleased she'd hit a chord with the ex-teacher.

'I agree,' Denise said. 'I might've known how to look up Facebook for the reunion last year, but that means nothing now. And judging by my success with the iPad, it's not like I could help you, if anyone else gets one.'

'Sorry.' Kate looked apologetic. 'It's me being too enthusiastic again. Neil says my mouth moves faster than my brain sometimes. I think he means that in a nice way.'

'It's an interesting idea.' Sarah began to back-pedal, contrite that maybe she and Denise were coming across too forcefully. 'But I tend to agree with Denise.'

There was another awkward silence for a few seconds until Neelam spoke. 'A friend has a blog about painting, and I have considered, also, writing a blog about Indian cuisine in Australia. I have very many photographs of my dishes. But I would not know how to create a blog.'

Sarah didn't doubt that Neelam's food could garner quite a lot of interest. On the visits the women had made to her home so far, her platters of samosa and pakoras, dips and curries had been superb, enough to have Sarah experimenting with Indian cuisine at home. Not that she would dream of serving Indian food—or any Asian dishes—to the group now. She'd only come off second best to Neelam. No, she'd been delighting everyone with her European pastries and tortes, all lavish icing and piping and gold leaf. A feast for the eyes as well as the tastebuds.

'I know what you mean about wanting to do something but not quite knowing where to begin.' It was Libby who spoke, now alert with interest. She gave her crooked little smile. 'When I see those Twitter messages at the bottom of the TV screen, I do wonder if I should know how to send tweets. Not that I'm desperate to "join the conversation".' She gestured air quotes. 'They're often dumb and distracting, but I should understand the process ...'

'I imagine there are things we don't even know that we don't know,' added Andrea. 'I saw something called Grindr the other day, but it was spelled without an "e". Is that something we should be using?'

'No idea,' Kate replied. 'That's what I mean, though. I need to know more. Maybe Grinder-without-an-e is like Tumblr—that doesn't have an "e" either.'

No one spoke. They seemed to have reached an impasse.

Chapter 8

Sarah began a mental calculation. She'd chaired enough art gallery meetings to understand the importance of counting the numbers. Now was the time to work out their views before putting anything to a vote. Libby and Kate would plump for the IT idea, of course. They came as a package, supporting each other on everything. Neelam seemed interested in changing direction, too. But Denise, with her unshakeable views, was not for turning, and Andrea would be sure to support their original book club.

'We could vote on it,' Sarah suggested. She managed to sound tentative, as if she hadn't thought it through fully. 'If it's a three-all tie, we stay as is. Otherwise we go with the majority. How does that sound, Kate?'

'I don't want to cause a rift or anything,' she replied, a little subdued. 'And in the interests of full disclosure, as they say, I went to the LibraryMuseum in the beginning to enrol in an IT course, but couldn't get in. But I do love this group and I want to stay—though I might get a mystery lurgy and be unavailable if we do another book like *Moby Dick.*'

'Don't worry,' said Sarah, 'we'll all do that! So ... shall we vote on it? Kate, you'd like to switch to an IT group. I'll vote to stay with a book club.' Sarah looked directly at Denise. 'And how are you leaning?' she asked.

'Definitely book club,' Denise said, her arms folded across her chest.

'Your turn, Neelam,' said Sarah. 'Book club or an IT group?'

'I am tempted to give an IT club a go, if that is forgivable? And if my blog should ever eventuate, I will *promise* to mention you all, as I may be testing new and strange recipes on each of you,' she said.

Sarah turned to Libby and raised her eyebrows.

'IT club.'

Libby's choice was not unexpected. She and Kate were so tight they even hosted together at Kate's home when it was Libby's turn.

'That's three votes for IT group, two votes to stay with book club,' Sarah summarised, ticking off the numbers on her fingers. 'Andrea, you have the final say.'

Andrea took a deep breath and paused for a few seconds. 'I'd like to move to an IT group. A change might be stimulating.'

It took all of Sarah's strength to remain silent. Blindsided by Andrea, of all people! She felt winded, as though the one ally she knew as well as Rob was, in fact, a stranger. *Keep calm, look unperturbed*, she urged herself.

'Wow. The I-Ts have the numbers.' Kate gave an apologetic smile, looking stunned and pleased and embarrassed all at the same time. 'Now what do we do?'

Sarah struggled to control herself, wondering if this was how political leaders felt when they were felled by a party room coup, even though they'd been sure of their support. She leaned back against the couch, with nothing to say.

The silence grew noticeable, starting to weigh on the group. Andrea gazed into her wine.

'I could approach the LibraryMuseum and see if they'd run more IT sessions, now that there'll be six more people.' Kate answered her own question, sounding quite tentative. 'They might be prepared to schedule another class.'

'But then we couldn't meet at our homes anymore,' said Denise, picking up the last piece of chocolate, 'and it's been so nice getting to know you all. We won't have our delicious suppers if it's at the library.' She sounded as though she was already missing Neelam and Sarah's culinary delights. 'That's if it even opens at night.'

Sarah didn't want to seem put out in any way. Gracious— that's what she had to be. It had been a fair vote after all, even though she'd miscalculated badly. And perhaps it would be fun to learn about IT.

'What if we look for a computer wiz to come and give us social media sessions in our homes, so we can meet like we do now?' she said, relieved to have inspiration at last. 'Someone trustworthy. I'd be happy to investigate. We'd need to pay an expert, though. And if it doesn't work out, we can always return to book club.'

'Would you do that for us?' said Kate. 'That'd be great.'

'It would be an Information Networking Group, isn't it?' said Neelam. 'So we call ourselves "The IN-group". And who does not wish to be part of the IN-group?'

The tension eased as they laughed and nodded, reaching for their wine glasses again.

'Why not?' Andrea lifted hers in a toast. 'Nothing to lose. To the IN-group.'

Denise pulled a face, though she didn't look seriously upset. 'I'll go along with it if everyone else is keen,' she said. 'But I hope we don't regret it.'

*

As Sarah locked the house before bed that evening, she recalled a conversation she'd had—*When was it?*—a couple of months ago. It was at the hairdresser's, while Chelsea was applying foils to highlight Sarah's natural blonde locks and camouflage the ever-encroaching silver.

'I've been busy helping my father-in-law settle into Albury,' Chelsea had confided. 'Martin moved to town three, no four, weeks ago now. So he can be closer to the family.'

'Has he been divorced?' Sarah asked. You heard about this sort of thing so often nowadays—women tiring of being the ministering angel, and then upping and leaving their husbands.

'Oh, heavens, no,' Chelsea's voice dropped. She carefully stroked the colour onto Sarah's hair strands with her flat paintbrush before flipping and folding the foil like origami.

'My poor mother-in-law died in *awful* circumstances. Let's see, it must be over six months ago now. He and Christine— that was my husband's mum—had moved up to the far north coast. Martin took early retirement—he was in the army so he got one of those rivers-of-gold service pensions.

'They were going to do the whole grey nomad thing, tripping around Australia looking for platypuses in the rivers.

'But before they set off, Christine went for an early morning ocean swim—alone. She was such a strong swimmer, but she got caught in a rip and drowned.'

'How awful.' Sarah couldn't imagine losing Rob in that way: the person who was the centre of your life gone, forever, in a moment. 'That poor, poor man.'

Chelsea told Sarah that Martin blamed himself for not being there to rescue her. 'He still hasn't gotten over it because he's known in the family as the Trouble Shooter. He was the army's go-to man in IT security for years, protecting their computers from hackers—but now he's quite lost.'

'Is he working?' Sarah asked.

'No, and you're right. He needs to work. There must be part-time jobs around. Or maybe he could volunteer at a men's shed. I talked him into updating the salon's computer system and improving our Facebook page. It's working so much better. But he needs more contacts. Moping around the house all day is doing him no good at all.'

Pausing at the front door, Sarah smiled. Martin deGraff could be the ideal man to give lessons to the brand new IN-group. She'd ring Chelsea in the morning and find out if he was likely to be interested.

Chapter 9

Libby's route home from her new job at TAFE took her close to Kate's place, so she'd taken to dropping into the welcoming California bungalow after work, and arriving early on book club nights. The gracious old homes in the street were nestled among towering pin oaks that formed a canopy across the central Albury street.

She couldn't help but compare the area with her own suburb. Gateview was a puzzling name, since she could find neither a gate nor a view anywhere near her unit. Despite the struggling saplings, it was still a flat, featureless area that, in her bleaker moments, she'd renamed Ghettoview.

What a long way she'd fallen from the chic Prahran cottage she and Gerald shared only eighteen months ago. The memory of him felt like the twist of a knife. Their life had been a lie. She remembered the nausea that had risen from the pit of her stomach when the police had seized her computer and files after Gerald came under suspicion. And now she was wearing the burden of endless debt.

This evening she was meeting up with Kate before travelling together to the IN-group meeting in Kate's car. Libby pulled over to the kerb and picked up her basket from the floor under the dashboard. She often arrived with a treat, like decorated cupcakes or shortbread biscuits. With both marshmallows and Turkish delight on special today at the supermarket, she'd brought some homemade Rocky Road for Kate's grandchildren.

She went up the wide steps, knocked on the door, and was welcomed by an excited Kate who gave her a big hug.

'Quick,' she said, without preliminaries, 'come and meet Esmerelda and Estella, the latest additions to the family. Before they go to bed.'

'New grandchildren?' Libby asked in surprise. 'You haven't mentioned them.'

Kate laughed. 'No, no, they're my newest chickens.' She led the way to the part of her backyard she'd converted into a coop and chicken run for a small flock. 'Aren't they gorgeous?'

'They're beautiful,' Libby agreed. Their black and brown feathers shone in the golden twilight as they pecked at insects in the dust. 'So different to white chooks. I've never seen ones like these before.'

'Barnevelders. And wait till you see their eggs. All speckled and dark brown.'

'I wish I had the space for some chickens. Or for anything. I don't even have enough room—or chairs—to host the group in that poky little flat,' she confided.

Despite the time that had passed since she'd lost her home, her well-paid job as a PA on St Kilda Road, and her favourite blue Honda Jazz—now that was a wrench—Libby didn't have a sense of herself as poor and in debt. And if she couldn't get her head around her impoverished state, how could she expect the others to accept her? They all seemed so comfortable.

Kate didn't hesitate in her support. 'Heavens, didn't I tell you Neil and I used to sit on milk crates in the early days? You know you can keep holding meetings here for as long as you need. It's fun preparing together.'

She led Libby back inside and opened one of the doors that ran off the hallway. 'And have a look at this bombsite,' she said. 'I've finally decided to resurrect the twins' old bedroom.'

Libby peeped in at the jumble of teenage boys' needs and wants. Bunk beds topped with duvets sporting Star Wars motifs were pushed up against one wall, while posters of footballers and former tennis stars obliterated the opposite one. Their bookshelves were crammed with comics and sporting trophies—most looking tarnished and in need of love. Hockey sticks, basketballs and tennis racquets were scattered higgledy-piggledy, jostling for space in any spare corner.

"What are you going to do with the room?' she asked.

'You'll find out in good time,' Kate responded with an enigmatic smile. 'Come on, we'd better go before we're late.'

They walked out to Kate's BMW in the front driveway. Libby took a deep, satisfying breath as she was cradled in the luxury of its cream leather seats. New money and new cars, she'd always been a sucker for them. There was something special about the scent of leather in a brand new car. What a pity that the chances of experiencing it again in one of her own were so remote. It was a relief to leave her old Corolla at Kate's tonight. She'd bought it in Melbourne, before leaving, for a pittance, and it showed. The car caused her grief at regular intervals—the battery had died only last week—and it probably wouldn't pass its next roadworthy test. Leaving the car behind meant the other book club members still didn't know she drove such an embarrassing old clunker—that was a reprieve too.

They were taking the scenic drive to Sarah's elevated home on Monument Hill, through streets lined with massive elms. Houses in this part of Albury commanded the best views of the town and the river, with the peaks of the Great Dividing Range visible in the distance.

'Did you notice Sarah's face when Andrea voted to switch from book club to the IN-group?' Libby said.

'What did I miss?' Kate glanced at Libby, her eyes widening. 'I was a bit guilty that I'd suggested such a frightening change—everyone was so hesitant.'

'It was a fleeting look, but she seemed … shocked, I think. Blindsided even.'

'All credit to her then,' Kate mused, her eyes back on the road. 'She recovered before I noticed.'

'Mmm. Sarah's got control down to a tee.'

Kate grinned. 'Her organising skills are something else, aren't they? I'm looking forward to tonight. I bet she's found someone clever to take the IN-group sessions.'

Chapter 10

Sure enough, Sarah had managed to source someone who was up to date with technology and social media. What a pity Libby had sworn off men since her last disastrous relationship, because Martin deGraff was attractive. Very attractive. Perhaps mid-fifties, dark eyed with flecks of grey through his hair and the lean, energetic frame of someone who kept himself in shape. His direct gaze was both warm and reassuring.

'Now you're all connected, where would you like to begin?' he asked, looking around at the unusually subdued group.

They were sitting around a large oak dining table in Sarah's downstairs living area, a room that was part glamorous Hamptons, part French provincial comfort—a perfect match for her persona. Libby always felt as if she'd walked into the pages of *Vogue Living* when she came here. Behind them like a stage set was a backdrop of white flowers—an artful arrangement of tulips, orchids and gardenias. When she'd asked for the bathroom on her first visit hoping to sneak a peek upstairs, she was instead directed to the guest bathroom built into a cavernous space, hidden under the stairs, that was all clever curves and gleaming silver and marble.

Sarah had relayed a flurry of instructions via phone and email so they could prepare for their inaugural IN-group meeting. Now that they'd abandoned the comfort of the book club for the unknown, all the members seemed serious about embracing 21st-century technology. Neelam and Sarah had laptops open in front of them, while Denise, Kate and Andrea arrived with iPads. Thank heavens for TAFE, Libby thought. Amy had given her the nod to borrow an old laptop after being persuaded that these classes would be useful for work.

'So ... where would you like to begin?' Martin repeated.

They all eyed each other, hoping someone else would speak. Libby remained silent. She knew more about technology than she'd let on to the group. It had seemed inappropriate to admit to more knowledge than the others. Somehow boastful.

'Let me rephrase it—what are your interests? How could more IT skills help you? Anyone?'

'I'd like to know more about these chat rooms where you can meet people and share things—like, say, craft tips,' Andrea ventured at last.

Libby looked at her, astonished. *Craft tips?* That didn't sound like the Andrea she was getting to know. She'd only visited her home a couple of times, and couldn't recall seeing anything crafty there. No patchwork quilts, no hand-sewn cushion covers, no knitted cosies. If anything, it had been a gloomy house, rather untidy, as though Andrea didn't care for it very much. When Libby offered help with the trays, the older woman had mentioned that her rheumatoid arthritis was flaring up again. Libby knew how limiting that could be—her mother had suffered with it. Why would anyone look to do craft work with stiff, painful hands?

'Right-o,' Martin said. 'Let's show you how to find these sites and get you signed up. But don't forget, not all chat rooms are safe. *Never* release any personal information. *Don't* give your surname, and *never* give any clues that identify you. And of course, *only* use safe services like PayPal if you're buying online. I can't emphasise enough how important security is with the internet. Even Mark Zuckerberg, Facebook's founder, covers the camera lens on his computer when it's not in use so he can't be spied on. And for security, it's best if we set you all up with new anonymous email addresses.'

'*Nooo.*' The wail came from Denise who was frowning. 'It's bad enough keeping track of one email address, who wants a second one?'

'It's not as difficult as you might think, Denise,' Martin said.

It was impressive how he'd learned their names already. Perhaps Sarah had given him a heads-up somehow. Probably provided him with mugshots of them all to memorise! Libby had a mental image of Martin arranging their faces on his computer.

'We'll set up a Gmail account for each of you. Easy as.'

He turned to the keyboard, signing them up to their own anonymous email account with an ease that impressed Libby. She took mental notes of his methods, deciding to try them at work when Paul, the head of department at TAFE, came to her fretting that he couldn't get his computer to work. Martin was diplomatic and calm, helped by a ready smile and a direct gaze that made you think you were the most important person he was talking to at that moment.

'I've found a chicken-keepers' forum I'd like to join,' Kate suggested. 'Esmeralda and Estella seem to have different habits from the rest of the brood.'

Denise gave a suppressed snort. 'Your chickens have names?' She shook her head, incredulous. 'Mine would be called Maryland and Kiev.'

Libby flinched. She liked hearing about the little brood, and the idea that Kate would eat one of her beloved pets was ridiculous, as Denise well knew. Some meetings Kate would be concerned about one or the other bird—if it seemed off its food, was losing feathers or wasn't laying as often as she expected. The others were fine with these updates, but Denise would make a joke of it. She was a hard one to fathom.

Kate looked unperturbed as she clicked on a website, and a picture of three chickens with black and copper feathers flashed on screen. Libby recognised them as Barnevelders, the new chickens she'd seen at Kate's. To think that a few months ago, she'd assumed all chickens were white, like the ones her granddad had kept.

'I've been browsing through these posts for a while, but I want to be able to ask questions and contribute to the chats,' Kate told Martin.

'Simple,' he said, holding two fingers over the keys. 'Type your new Gmail address here,'—he indicated the login area—'then choose another password.'

'Another password? Oh, they are so impossible,' interrupted Neelam, a look of dismay crossing her smooth features. 'I am always forgetting mine. So now I use the same one. PASS-WORD. Or, if they insist on numbers, PASSWORD123.'

'Exactly what I do,' Denise said.

Her comment was like a teacher's stamp of approval. The others looked up from their devices, agreeing.

Martin turned from his screen, alarm on his face. '"PASSWORD" is the commonest password, you know. A bit like handing over your credit card details and PIN to a stranger.'

Denise looked put out. 'But it's much simpler, and I've had no problems so far. As if you can remember a different password for every website you sign up to.'

'Here's a tip I use.' Martin's tone was light and coaxing. 'Choose numbers or letters that you know well, like an important birthdate or your middle name, then put a letter from the website you're on, at the beginning and the end. This way all your passwords will be different, but easy to remember. So, Kate, if you want to join the Backyard Fowls website, surround your birthdate, say, with a 'B' for Backyard and 'f' for fowls.'

Kate typed B090957f as they all watched.

'So … does that mean if Kate wanted a password for her Visa Account, say, it would be …' Libby glanced at the numbers, pleased to have Kate's birthday for future reference, 'V090957a?'

'Spot on, Libby,' said Martin, turning to her for a moment. She felt a flutter of pleasure. 'It's not a perfect password, of course, but so much harder to guess than PASSWORD.'

A murmur of appreciation rippled around the table.

'Where were you when I was doing my business course? If my lecturers had been so clear, I'd have made CEO instead of remaining a PA. Are you a teacher?'

Martin flexed his knuckles. 'No, but I like taking problems and breaking them down into smaller steps. Making them solvable, that's all. Comes from thirty years in the army. You can't mess around there and assume everything will be hunky-dory. Planning and foresight. That's the way to go.'

Hunky-dory. Libby smiled at him. She hadn't heard that term in ages, but it had been a favourite of one of her devil-may-care boyfriends.

'So, you can show me please an easy way to set up an Indian cooking blog?' Neelam said. 'I have written my first entry, and the photographs to go with it are on my laptop. But I do not know where to go from here.'

The next hour was spent learning the ins and outs of blogging, and before long, Neelam had published her first post—'Simply Samosas', complete with mouth-watering pictures of golden platters piled high with Indian snacks, against the backdrop of her living room, furnished in the rich colours of India. The others all crowded around the laptop, *ooh-ing* and *aah-ing* over her artistic eye.

By the time Martin had shown Kate how to post a question on the poultry site about Esmeralda's lost feathers, and introduced Andrea to the finer points of chat rooms, the room was buzzing.

'We'll have plenty to ask you if you're available to continue the classes,' Sarah said, picking up her pen to make a list. 'I'd like a session on upgrading my phone. I've resisted so far—it all seemed too difficult—but with your help it'd be a different story.'

'And I'm keen to learn all about eBay,' Denise said. 'I used to scour the Trading Post with my dad when I was growing up—he liked to buy old farm machinery to fix—but buying and selling seems to be done online nowadays. I'd love to try it from home.'

'This might take a few months, but if you're all happy to keep our sessions going, we can cover everything you want,' said Martin.

'Can we learn about Twitter?' Libby asked, bouncing forward in her seat.

Despite her earlier view that tweets flashing like ticker-tape during TV shows were distracting, she'd decided it was better to keep up with the times and learn more. Martin had the ability to make the unfamiliar appear non-threatening, and based on the session so far, she was sure he could help her learn to enjoy the medium.

'Of course,' he said. 'Twitter's a great tool for communication.' After explaining how it could be used to suit each person's purpose, Martin paused. 'But Twitter has its own language and rules, so to speak. Easy to learn but they'll take time to teach. We could tackle that at another session.'

*

'Wasn't that amazing?' Kate was shaking her head as she squinted through the frenetic movement of the windscreen wipers on the drive home. A torrential downpour had hit them out of the blue.

'What part?' Libby asked. 'Coming away with new email accounts? Our easy to remember passwords? Or the glory that is Sarah's flower arranging?'

She didn't add the word 'Martin' to her list. No need to sound like an excited teenager.

'All of the above. I'm so empowered now, it's scary. I'm dying to move onto Facebook and get a web presence for the wedding planning business. I'm getting heaps of bookings. At the start, it was through people I know, but that's changing now, and I need an online presence. And all the info Martin gave us about tweets was great. So having a Twitter account doesn't mean you MUST follow the latest attention-seeking starlet. Who knew? Maybe I'll tweet about Neelam's fabulous blog.'

'How do you reckon Sarah found Martin?' Libby was on a fishing expedition now, keen to know more about him. 'He said he was in the army, but Sarah doesn't seem like the service people I've known.'

'He's related to a friend of hers … I think.' Kate slowed a little, trying to see past the rain hammering the windscreen. 'Sarah has lots more money than an army family. Even when I heard her surname, I didn't twig at first. But then the penny dropped. Her husband's Rob Carpenter. *Doctor* Rob Carpenter. He's a big shot, a cosmetic surgeon. I might need him when simple make-up isn't enough to hide the crevices. In the meantime, I have a favour to ask you. And a proposition.'

'Sounds fascinating.' Libby sat upright. 'I'd love to return a favour—or favours.'

'I have a wedding Saturday week, and when I rang to arrange my make-up for it the salon couldn't fit me in. I forgot it was the Platinum Cup at the races. Fake tan salons booked out from here to Sydney! I'm not good enough to trust myself to do my own face yet, and this bride's mother is very exacting.'

'You'd like me to do your make-up? I'd love to.'

'I'll pay you of course …'

'You'll do nothing of the sort.'

'I guessed you'd say that, so here's a proposition for you. How about I recommend you as a make-up artist for my brides—and their bridesmaids—when they book me? Most of them grab onto any guidance, and I won't pass on any bridezillas, I promise. In fact, I'm developing a nose for them, and I'm "already busy" on the Saturdays they want to book their wedding. The two I've had were quite monstrous!'

'I'm not sure that I'm expert enough …' Once upon a time Libby'd had Kate's confidence and self-belief, but Gerald had managed to take that away.

'Of course you're expert enough! I heard Miss Ponytail telling one of the girls at our make-up session she had three wedding parties that weekend. Three! You were miles better than she was. There's good money to be had, although as far as planners go, I'm not pricey. I think this idea of bumping up the charge because the event has the word "wedding" in front of it is a bit off. If you want, you could start charging at the low end too, until you're more confident. So what do you think? Shall we go into business together?'

Libby imagined the boost to her meagre income. It could mean paying off her debt in a few years instead of in the never-never. She could move out of Ghettoview, maybe buy a better car. It would mean she'd be free again. But she shouldn't get ahead of herself.

'Let me think about ...'

A massive lightning flash, followed a millisecond later by a shuddering thunderbolt, startled them both.

'Come on, Libby! The cosmos is speaking to us. I wasn't sure if I could be a successful wedding planner until I did it. Let's give it a go.'

An exciting future whirled in Libby's brain as the rain pounded on the car roof. A future of brides and their parties having fun, of earning good money doing something she loved. No more scrimping and penny-pinching. A chance like this could change her life.

'If you have this much faith in me, it would be a bad look not to have faith in myself. And I'd hate to ignore the universe. So ... why not? Yes, let's give it a go.'

Chapter 11

Denise stood at the entrance of the Albury art gallery, willing herself to walk through the automatic glass doors at the front of the imposing building. She never felt she belonged in galleries; they were reserved for people with a true appreciation of fine art. Denise and Art—she saw it in her mind's eye with a capital letter, illuminated by a mediaeval monk—had no more than a fleeting acquaintance, and for that she blamed her third-grade teacher.

In the first few years at Our Lady of Perpetual Succour she'd enjoyed her colourful experiments with finger painting and lop-sided potato prints. But that all changed when she hit Grade 3. Sister Pius, her class teacher, took pleasure in announcing at every art lesson that Denise had no talent whatsoever. Denise could still recall the mortification she felt when, in front of a cowed group of eight-year-olds, the nun mocked her drawing of a girl in a two-toned dress.

'Now, look at this!' said Sister Pius, her puffy red face screwed up in disgust. She held the offending picture above her head while the other girls gave compliant, nervous giggles.

'Lord, grant me strength! This morning in composition class you were writing that caves "dotted" the shore, as if caves were polka dots. Now you're upsetting the laws of nature and giving a red skirt a green outline. Are you colour blind? A red skirt has a *red* outline. Not green, not blue. Red. Now, here.' She thrust the picture into Denise's trembling fingers. 'Tear it up and start again. And this time, use your eyes.'

Denise spent that year of her life in a state of misery—and puzzlement. Why was she praying so hard to become pious herself, when a nun with the very same name could be so cruel? The subtleties of spelling escaped her at that age. Art became something to dislike and dread. Once she was permitted to change to a language instead of art classes, they were banished forever. Latin declensions, with their black and white rules, now made more sense and held less fear than a visit to an art gallery.

But as she entered this one for the first time, she had a revelation: this was no sombre grey building built to intimidate, but a bright exhibition space with soaring ceilings and a clever use of light. She looked around her, upbeat and interested. She'd heard the building had been extended and revamped—its name had even been changed from plain old Art Gallery to MAMA—but she wasn't expecting it to have such a wow factor.

The one drawback was when her quest to find a netsuke began to prove unrealistic. As she wandered around, the pieces on display all seemed contemporary and many of the artworks looked as though they reflected the indigenous history of the Murray region. The pressed-metal ceilings and scraps of wire unearthed in the recent renovations had been recycled into arresting animal images by Wiradjuri artists: a wire wombat, a spindly echidna, a pressed-metal turtle with a Victorian-era shell. The bits and pieces of scavenged material had been reworked to reflect a hybrid culture and now dominated an entire wall over the staircase. What would Sister Pius think of such creative fusion?

Looking around for help, she spotted Andrea, of all people, entering from behind a heavy steel door. 'Hello, this is a surprise,' Denise said.

Andrea was clad in black, her t-shirt sporting a prominent MAMA logo. She indicated a bright pink lanyard around her neck with the label 'MAMA Volunteer', and said, 'My first day on the job.'

She was the only IN-group member who always seemed reserved with Denise; perhaps she was shy until she knew somebody well. Or was it more than that? There was an ongoing hint of coolness, a wariness that wasn't shown towards the other women. There was something familiar about her, but Denise couldn't pin down the memory.

'I think I'm on a wild goose chase,' she said, 'but would you know if there are any netsuke in the gallery? You remember—those Japanese ivory carvings we read about in *The Hare with Amber Eyes*.'

Andrea gave a small shrug. 'Sorry, I do remember them, but I'm not front-of-house. I've been learning how to 'nest' down in the basement. It's a way to safely store exhibits that aren't on display. And I haven't had time to acquaint myself with all the pieces in the gallery yet, because they've been in storage during the renovations.'

She looked around as if hoping a sign saying 'Netsuke Room' would appear in front of her. 'I know the names of the smaller galleries, and I can direct you to the restrooms, but … netsuke?' She gave a self-deprecating smile. 'A bit out of my league, at this stage. To be honest, even if we have them,

I doubt they'd be on show. But give me a few minutes and I'll find out. In the meantime,' she gestured to a room behind them, 'there are some displays in there that might be a good place to start looking.'

The first gallery Denise went into disappointed her with its modern pieces that were as ugly as they were incomprehensible. The text that accompanied them on the wall didn't help either. One exhibit declared *'The meeting of the artist's experiences with that of the viewer's is joined by an understanding of the texture and tenor of the thing suggested, even if the language is replaced with something else'*, whatever that meant. And the rest of the comments were equally opaque. Denise itched to take a red pen to the rambling and obscure explanations.

She wandered off into a spacious room whose walls were adorned with black and white photographs and political sketches and cartoons that reached back to Daumier, including one that showed a mid 19th-century woman who indulged herself by writing while her poor neglected infant tripped into the bathwater. Now this was interesting. Much more accessible than modern paintings with their jarring stripes and distorted shapes.

She spotted a set of display cases against the far back wall and walked over to inspect their contents. She glanced into one of them and felt a sudden thrill of discovery. Surely this couldn't be? Yet there they were. Not one, but three beautiful ivory netsuke, each small enough to fit in the palm of her hand—a laughing pig, a large-eared rabbit and a cowering rat—staring back at her as though they'd been waiting to be discovered. Housed in one large rectangular glass box and illuminated from above, each was standing on its own small mahogany plinth to best display the artistry that had gone into its making. They were gorgeous. Denise wanted to hold and turn the tiny carvings around in her hands, to be able to delight in them from every angle. That settled it. She'd do more research and one day perhaps she'd have her very own netsuke, like the Dowager Duchess of Downton.

Keen to share her discovery with someone she knew, Denise walked back to the main entrance where she and Andrea had last spoken, but she had left, so Denise began the slow climb up the wide staircase to the second level. She was out of breath by the time she reached the top, and leaned against the railing to recover, pretending her purpose was to look more closely at the impressive wire and pressed metal indigenous displays that were now at eye level on the wall beside her.

'Ah, there you are.' It was Andrea, exiting a room with the exclusive title 'Staff Only'. 'Good news. Apparently, we do have netsuke displayed downstairs after all. I'll show you.'

'I know! That's why I came to find you. Come and see them, they're terrific.'

Andrea was as impressed as Denise when she saw the exquisite treasures.

'They're beautiful. Isn't it interesting how the memoir introduced us to a world we didn't know about?' Andrea said.

'And what a story that family had,' Denise replied. 'I do enjoy our meetings. They're keeping me young. I was wondering, would it be possible …?' Denise hesitated. Perhaps what she was about to ask might be a step too far for Andrea.

'Yes?'

'If I came back one day when you've been here a bit longer, would you be able to give me a tour, and explain some of the works? My knowledge of art is woeful. I'm such a dolt beside people like you.'

'I could do that,' Andrea said. 'But I'll bet you know more than you think. You've been a school principal. Brian used to say, "Always have a teacher on your table at Trivia Night."'

'I don't know who Brian is, but I like him already,' Denise said.

'He's my husband. My ... late husband, he passed away two years ago. Cancer.'

'I'm sorry. I didn't know. That must be very hard for you. Stan, my ex, is about to have cancer treatment, so I've been taking him to his doctor's visits. It's such a stressful time for everyone. And now he's heard about some expensive new operation only available in Sydney, so we're driving there soon.'

It was important to have someone looking out for you, Denise thought, as she made her way home. Andrea must be lonely since Brian died. Maybe she should make an effort with her, extend a hand of friendship. Perhaps that was something Andrea would appreciate.

Chapter 12

Andrea turned on her computer that night convinced it was time for action. Talking to Denise had given her a jolt. The IN-group activities were invigorating, but she needed to go further. If a faint heart never won a fair maiden, then it wouldn't win you an older man either. Thinking about joining a dating website was pointless without action.

A few weeks ago, she'd spoken to Nicole during one of their regular phone chats about joining RSVP, but her daughter, usually so affable, had been ... less than encouraging, she'd have to say.

'A dating website? You? At your age?'

Ah, the comfortable arrogance of youth. Nicole had no idea that every sixty-year-old exterior with its lines and wrinkles and reliance on reading glasses hid a thirty-something soul. Without any intention to be hurtful, Nicole really knew how to make Andrea feel desirable! And sexy. It was probably a good thing that her daughter couldn't see how peeved she was with the comment.

'Yes. *At my age.* I'm not totally past it, you know.' She detected a faint giggle. 'And I've been on my own now for over two years. Some days, I think company would be lovely.'

'We'll get you a dog, then,' was Nicole's helpful response.

Martin may possibly have guessed what she was up to. She'd read about people using fake photos on their profile page, so asked him if there was any way to check the bona fides of photographs on the net. It turned out to be as easy as pasting the picture into Google Images. Wonderful Martin. No hint of a laugh or snort, or a suggestion that she might prefer a website about rehoming furry animals.

Deciding how to write her bio to create a good impression was more of a challenge. She supposed there were etiquette rules, and tips on finding a good match. How awful to be stuck with someone totally unsuitable on a date. A *Wake in Fright* miner, say, or an astrologer.

She returned to ever-reliable Google and trawled through an article called 'The Things You MUST Do Well On Your Profile'. Not surprisingly, lame comments like 'I enjoy long walks on the beach' were an absolute no-no. Not that she, living in an inland city like Albury, would be writing that old cliché.

Women do best, she read, if they describe themselves as easygoing or sweet. Did she want a man whose first pick was easygoing and sweet? Someone who was a pushover? Brian wouldn't have wanted—there she went again.

Scrolling past the cartoon couples enclosed in a heart, she decided that the best piece of advice she'd read was for women to cast a narrow net; there was no point trying to appeal to everyone. She could mention that she was genuinely interested in aviation history. Nobody in her right mind would say that simply to snare a man, would she? Perhaps she could include her interest in planes in the catchy name the sites urged her to adopt. Highflyer might be a good screen name, but was hardly easygoing or sweet. Any prospect would expect a woman with a leather briefcase and a power suit.

Then there was the added challenge of how to describe herself. She'd had so many compliments over the years about her shapely legs that it seemed like a disservice to leave them out, but perhaps it wasn't the done thing to talk up your best feature. She could try a bland note: 'Pleasant-looking widow, early sixties, in good shape, with wide range of interests.' That, while far from headline-grabbing, was at least truthful. Would she have to include a photograph? She could use an old one from twenty years ago when she still had coppery lights in her hair rather than a current snap showing it had faded to a sandy colour, but how awful to see disappointment in a potential suitor's eyes when they met in person.

Show them the real you, that's what she needed to do. She could showcase her interest in cryptic crosswords. What about a cryptic clue in her post? Brownie points to any man who picked that up!

So many of the profiles she was examining sounded like they'd been workshopped at an ad agency. 'Down to earth, raw and homegrown,' boasted one man, smiling as he laid a trowel on a stack of mud bricks. 'Artistically reconstructed' was attached to the photo of a blonde-tipped woman whose taut face had been lifted so high she was at risk of altitude sickness.

It was important to sound like a real person, yet interesting enough to pique the attention of someone with personality. *Prefer indoor activities?* Better not say that, lest it be misinterpreted. At last she was able to settle on: *I'm in my early sixties and alone since my husband died. I'm loyal and companionable, an introvert but worth getting to know if you'll take the time. Interests include deconstructing pralines and early long distance transport modes (9). Do contact me.*

Maybe the cryptic clue was too much, but what the heck. This was a bit of fun, and anonymous, so if no one answered, it wouldn't matter. The worst that could happen was that an eager but literal-minded suitor might turn up with almond toffee for her to crunch on, or book tickets on an antiquated steam train.

She looked at all her photos, focussing on the more recent ones, but they all seemed much the same, her expression polite and contained rather than come hither. According to Google she needed to be smiling, so she was relieved to at last find one taken in good light, shortly after a visit to the hairdresser. Flattering without being dishonest. No one, having only seen the photo, would look shocked on meeting her. It may be her best self, but still herself.

Using her new, anonymous Gmail address, Ant62 pressed the *POST* button. Her future was now in the lap of the internet.

*

The next morning when she logged on Andrea was stunned. She had no idea there were so many lonely men out there. There were several responses to her RSVP posting, all from middle-aged or older men declaring their single status and their readiness for commitment.

One wrote back: *Also age 62. For the right woman, I'd be willing to find employment.*

For the first time? Andrea wondered.

Another, who must have been sending out replies ran-domly, declared he was *Age 62, want marriage to start a family.*

As they kept trickling in the next day, she became sceptical of some of the senders. When she copied a photograph of one of the better-looking men, a chap who lived in Perth, Western Australia, and then pasted the picture into Google Images, what should spring up but the identical photo—except that it belonged to a fellow hailing from Nebraska.

But several days later came the warmest, funniest email she could hope for.

Hello Ant62. Your posting intrigued me because I enjoy solving cryptic crosswords too (such a clever clue!) and have a passion for airplanes/aeroplanes—though intact ones rather than the deconstructed type!

I'm lucky enough to pilot light aircraft every day for work. My base is in Queenstown. If you haven't visited there, it's a beautiful place, not too far away from you, across the water.

Queenstown? Beautiful? That wasn't her memory. She'd been to the town on a school holiday back when, as a naive teenager, Tasmania was an 'exotic' location. It was her first flight, her first trip 'overseas', as she and her friends giggled, her first holiday without the halter of parents. She'd been delighted with Launceston and seduced by Hobart's hills and bay, but when the busload of tired schoolgirls pulled into Queenstown at the end of the holiday it was like a trip to the Wild West circa 1850. She'd stared at the desolation of discarded pink and grey soil, lying in mounds around a town that had been denuded, by years of mining, of any trace of life and knew she'd reached the end of the world.

I lost my wife twelve months ago, the email went on, *after nursing her through a long illness, and miss her terribly, so understand where you're coming from. It isn't an easy time of life. As we didn't have children, I'm on my own now, and although flying's my reason to live, I'd love to share my life again with a special person. I'm wondering if you fly yourself. It's exciting to find a woman who's interested in planes. How did that come about? I'd love to find out more about you, so I'm hoping you'll reply soon.*

She decided to verify his photo, and a New Zealand website appeared with the same image of a strong-jawed, middle-aged man with a receding hairline and a welcoming smile, under the banner *Ken Ashton Aviation Services, Queenstown*. Exactly as he'd told her.

But wait … New Zealand? What an idiot she'd been. Since that school trip, she'd shuddered and dismissed the name Queenstown out of hand, in an Aussie-centric way, wondering why anyone would choose to holiday in such a wasteland. But with the touch of a computer she could check out this Queenstown where Ken lived, and take a virtual tour, in lieu of the real thing.

As her mouse clicks took her deeper and deeper into images of the South Island town and its surrounds, she shook her head in amazement at the awesome crystalline lakes and rolling snowfields. Why had she never known about this truly breathtaking Queenstown? Poor Queenstown NZ, unfairly maligned by its plainer namesake. Did Queen Victoria ever know she'd given birth to two such disparate children?

How long to leave it before she replied? She was itching to contact him, but that might look too keen so she checked out 'The Etiquette of Online Dating'—was there anything you couldn't learn from the internet? Two to three days was considered optimal. But that was for younger people: life was too short and she was on a roll. So twenty-four hours later she wrote to him.

Clever you for solving my cryptic. And how amazing to find someone with the same interests.

My father and older brother were flying fanatics so I absorbed it from a young age. When we were in primary school in Victoria, one of the local soft drink manufacturers ran a competition where you'd win a model aeroplane if you collected the letters A-E-R-O-P-L-A-N-E *from under their bottle tops. So Eric and I, aided and abetted by our uncle who had a corner store and could find us the elusive 'P's, both won a kit. I've been hooked ever since.*

The next morning, when she took her coffee to the computer, there it was, another email from Ken. This was more fun than receiving letters from her penpal as a girl. In this post-modern digital world there was no such thing as delayed gratification, no 'wait and see', no 'in a minute', none of the admonitions to take it slowly that had punctuated her own youth.

Loved your story about saving bottle tops to win such a wonderful prize. It took me back to my childhood, too, only my brother and I made a billycart from bits and pieces we found lying around. Nothing as exotic in this little neck of the woods as an aeroplane kit in the seventies!

How old were you then? she wrote back.

About three. No, seriously, I'm 55 now, if that's what you want to know.

So, a younger man. But a difference of seven years at this stage of life was like seven months to a teenager, and she enjoyed hearing about his life. The ins and outs of his business gave a glimpse into another world, too.

My light aircraft trips involve showing tourists around— they love to see the sights on the South Island. You should see the views flying over Milford Sound, his email continued. *We have sights you Aussies can only dream of—genuine, lofty mountains, and glaciers with winding fjords below. And our cascading waterfalls deserve to be world famous. They're as good as any on Earth.*

To prove his point he had attached a picture of a breathtaking fjord whose sheer face soared upwards towards a blue sky.

She gazed at his message thinking how Brian would have loved such an adventurous life—and felt a small pang of longing. Gorgeous views were well and good, but what was the point to them if they were discovered alone, if there was nobody to reminisce with about them? But better not mention Brian—it would surely be a turn-off to prattle about a lost husband.

Deciding to take Martin's advice and be cautious, Andrea slipped in a 'wrong' snippet about aviation history in her next message to test him, mentioning the '1937' MacRobertson International Air Race, but he seamlessly corrected her straightaway—*it was in 1934, five years before the outbreak of war*—he pointed out, without mansplaining or sounding a know-it-all. She felt a little frisson of excitement. This was a man who knew what he was talking about.

She turned off the computer. It was a pity he lived so far away, but maybe that would work in her favour. Take it slowly, get to know each other; perhaps she could fly over there in a few months if she was up to it and they kept enjoying each other's emails.

Then she might think about telling Nicole of her success. *At her age.*

Chapter 13

How, Denise asked herself, could she help Stan earn money to pay for the expensive state-of-the-art surgery he might need in Sydney? It struck her how good it was rekindling their friendship since his prostate cancer diagnosis. She'd never have dreamed that would happen, but she'd long forgiven him for leaving her for a younger woman. Their marriage had spluttered out some years before they separated, partly because she'd had no luck producing an heir and partly, she could admit it now, because she'd been keen for promotion in the teaching hierarchy. After he left, she'd adjusted so quickly to her independence that she wondered why she'd bothered getting married in the first place. There were no children in Stan's second marriage either, so it seemed infertility hadn't been solely her problem. And young wives might be fun for older men in the early days, but you didn't see them for dust when things went wrong.

Denise was a little shocked at first that Stan now seemed to expect her to be there for him, his 'real' first wife driving him to various doctors' appointments and hospital visits, as if they'd been together all along, as if there'd been no lengthy interruption, no Christmases without a word. Not that she minded taking him to see the specialists. She was very fond of him in a sisterly sort of way and they'd settled now into an easy companionship ... and yet ... if the positions were reversed, would Stan be there for her?

An idea came to her in a creative flash talking with Andrea. They'd spent a couple of hours together at MAMA while Andrea gave her a brief introduction to art as she led her around the various exhibits, pointing out their merits—or otherwise.

'I'm beginning to realise my primary school art teacher had no knowledge of art at all,' Denise told her as they shared a ploughman's lunch in the museum's cafe afterwards. 'Thanks to you, art's starting to make sense. I hope MAMA knows what a great volunteer you are.'

'I find it so comforting being among works of art,' Andrea said. 'Like when you mentioned how you loved watching shows about opulent lifestyles so you could imagine yourself a part of it. A gallery gives me that opportunity too, especially when the treasures are displayed so beautifully. I wonder whether we'd give a small netsuke a second look if we found it lying unloved at a trash and treasure market, and hadn't read the book and understood they were collectibles? Once it's showcased in its own cabinet, with spotlights and an elegant backdrop, we can appreciate its artisanship and its worth.'

Of course! Denise had already begun researching netsuke on the internet with the long-term aim of finding the perfect one to buy, but now Andrea had given her an idea.

'Some of them are quite inexpensive. People probably don't know how valuable they can be. You've given me a brainwave. I could buy one and sell it for a profit, then put the money towards Stan's operation.'

'You'd need to learn how to clean and polish them in the right way—you know how on those antique shows the experts are always saying 'What a pity it's been restored, it's worth tuppence ha'penny, but in good condition it would have been worth twenty thousand dollars.'

Denise laughed. 'Oh, don't worry, I'll read up all about them. And Stan's an electrician and a dab hand at carpentry, so he'd help me display them to look as good as the ones in the gallery. I could post pictures online.'

'Neelam would give you photographic tips, she's a very generous soul,' Andrea said. 'I'm sure you could make the netsuke look quite valuable.'

What a wonderful thing. Denise felt uplifted, as if she'd joined a choir, one where all the voices were in unison. She'd be helping Stan and enjoying herself at the same time. If they approached this project seriously, they could actually raise some money.

*

'I refuse to drive in Sydney traffic,' Denise said, as Stan lifted her overnight bag into the boot of his car, in preparation for their trip up to the Sydney specialist. 'So if you want to take advantage of a second driver, now's the time. Otherwise you'll be doing the six-hour drive yourself, I'm afraid!'

Stan gripped the keys of his Ford Mondeo with what Denise interpreted as a deep reluctance to trust his baby to anyone else.

'I'm a good driver, Stan,' she said. 'I haven't had a car accident in … oh … years and years.'

'It's not an accident that worries me. I don't like anyone else driving me on long trips, that's all,' he said.

'What say I do the first couple of hours. It's dead straight freeway at the start. Then we can have a break and I'll shout you morning tea. My IN-group were all raving about a cafe at Jugiong. Then you can drive for the rest of the trip and take us into Sydney. It'll give you a chance to relax and enjoy the scenery for a bit.'

Stan snorted. 'Like you said, it's dead straight freeway. Not a lot to see, unless barren paddocks, dying gums and fading towns are your thing.'

Stan wasn't normally this irritable, but he released his grip and handed the keys over before walking around to the passenger side of the car.

Denise settled into the driver's seat, adjusted the mirrors and dragged the seat towards the steering wheel. Stan grimaced.

'Oh, relax! I'll put them back when we swap over again. I know you're a bit worried, but think of this trip as a holiday. You're only seeing the specialist for an opinion. You don't have to commit to anything he says if you don't like the sound of this new surgery.'

'I know, but I don't like the sound of any surgery that's on offer.' He clicked his seatbelt into place and sighed. 'It might help if you'd come into the consulting room with me tomorrow. You know me—I always end up forgetting details.'

'Of course, I'll come if you want me to. And after the appointment, if you're up to it, we might take a quick detour to the Art Gallery of New South Wales. I've had an idea about how to raise funds for the procedure, if need be. I'll explain as we drive.'

*

The next day as they left the surgeon's rooms in Macquarie Street, Denise noticed Stan's fretful look, present for weeks, seemed to have vanished.

'Well, that was encouraging,' he said. 'He's so confident that I'm right for this type of surgery. Who knew smokers don't heal well? Your nagging to give up the fags back in the day wasn't such a bad thing after all. But we'll need to raise some serious cash now. Better find out more about those ... what were they called ... netsuke things?'

Denise opened her eyes wide and looked at him. So Stan had been listening to her fundraising ideas on the trip. Even remembered the name. He'd seemed rather quiet and non-committal.

'Yes, netsuke. I especially want to see how they display them. I've already done a bit of searching and know I can buy small bone ones online at a good price, but if we want to sell at a profit, we'll need to value-add. Present them as irresistible to collectors who don't have the time or skills to do that themselves.'

It would be good to see more netsuke and then get out of this nerve-jangling city. Sydney's weather was fine with a crisp hint of autumn, and the travelogue-quality views of the Harbour Bridge and Opera House were spectacular, but that didn't quite make up for the downsides of the city: the crowds at Central Station, the confused maze that was the underground. Denise had been astounded to see on the last leg of their journey that the woman in front of her was actually putting on her deodorant. *On the bus.* But at least it was possible to look away. Worst of all was the unrelenting roar of the city. Massive buses everywhere, moaning and hissing as they pulled to a stop, bumper-to-bumper delivery trucks stopping and starting and changing gears. And the ubiquitous jackhammers! It seemed every street in Sydney had its own hard-hatted team competing to make the most racket. George Street was under construction and closed to traffic—had been for ages, according to her sister Kay, who'd made her spare room available for them.

They headed towards the art gallery, strolling first through the heart of the Domain and the Botanical Gardens. Peace at last. What a relief to breathe in the fragrance of the gardens and leave the city behind. By the time they reached the gallery, Denise had mellowed—and the building itself, with its fine columns echoing a classical Greek temple—was glorious. To think it housed a collection of beautiful netsuke that they were about to see. There was no greater pleasure than having a purpose.

She and Stan spent the next thirty minutes wandering from one room to another, amazed at the diversity in the vast gallery. One giant sculpture—a bowl of dancing female figures, wild and abandoned—would look wonderful in her front garden if she ever won Lotto. She was sure it was inspired by some famous painting, probably French, but she couldn't recall its name. Something to ask Andrea when she got back home.

'I think we need the Asian Collection to find our netsuke,' Denise said finally. 'Otherwise we'll be here for hours.'

Eventually they found a gallery with a glass cabinet displaying tiny exquisite carvings along one of the walls. Denise marvelled at the milky luminescence of the carved pieces, minute objects reflecting the philosophy of an ancient culture. She paused with Stan in front of an artist's brush-rest made from a pale, greenish-grey nephrite stone that was decorated with a scene of a peacock among rocks, then examined a tiny carved carp swimming near lotus flowers that captured the quick flash of movement within stillness.

She loved these delicate green jade pieces, so finely wrought, and timeless in their beauty. Jade held a special place in Chinese culture, she read, and was often made into weapons because of its strength. Believed to make a person immortal, jade powder had been used for consumption to prevent the body from decay.

She shivered a little. We were not so far removed from ancient times. All these centuries later, and Stan was here in Sydney in search of a way to stop the inevitable decay.

They kept looking, but couldn't find a netsuke anywhere. Almost defeated by the fruitless search, Denise left Stan to keep looking, and approached the information desk manned by a gaunt young attendant—probably an art student, he looked all of twenty-two or three—who turned to his computer after hearing her request.

'Yes, the gallery has netsuke. Several, in fact.' He sounded pleased with his find.

'That's good news. Where are they? We've looked everywhere.'

'Oh, you won't find them on display. They're all in storage.'

'None on display?' Denise asked in shock. MAMA down in Albury had three, but not one to be found in the state's major gallery? Had no one else read *The Hare with Amber Eyes*? She couldn't be the only person in New South Wales who wanted to see them.

'Do you know if they'll ever be displayed?'

'Not sure,' the young man responded. 'Our exhibits are rotated, so they'll be back some time, I guess. But I can't tell you when. Do you have a computer at home? You could check on our website. You might see some online.'

Denise took a deep breath. Was there any point in a bricks and mortar gallery if she had to view its treasures in a virtual space?

She returned to the Asian gallery to find Stan sitting on a bench looking tired. He'd done well to stay so focused. 'They have a few netsuke, but they're not on display,' she explained. 'I was told to look them up on their website.'

'So you came almost six hundred kilometres to see some antique thingos and then got told to go back home and look 'em up on your computer?' And for the first time since his diagnosis, Denise heard Stan's deep, familiar chuckle. 'Still, it's not a total lost cause, old girl. Seeing we're in Sydney, why don't we take a squiz at some of the jewellery stores on the way back to Kay's?'

That was sweet. 'Are you sure you're not too exhausted?'

'Nah, while we're here … might give us ideas on how they make their stuff look a million dollars. And I can check on how they do the lighting. My guess is LED strips. They're all the go now for display lighting.'

Denise smiled. If Stan was already planning the lighting, he must have liked her idea. 'Then what are we waiting for?'

*

Small parcels from Hong Kong and the United States began to arrive in the post on a regular basis. The netsuke were in Albury at last. This was better than Christmas, because the presents never stopped coming, and they were always what Denise wanted. And because she was never certain what particular netsuke would be delivered on any given day, she felt like a child plunging her hand into a lucky dip.

She never tired of the pleasure of unwrapping the little objects from their bubble wrap, of holding the exquisite items in her hands. They felt weighty and substantial and were so cool to the touch. She was in awe of the artists' ability to capture expressions and emotions in the miniature carvings, loved running her fingers along the grooves and curves of their workmanship.

With every delivery, she fell in love with a new netsuke. A corner of her living room was turning into a shrine to the miniature ornaments. Thanks to Martin's guidance, she was becoming a wiz on Google, finding out all the information she needed about the small sculptures.

That's not to say she hadn't fallen into a trap or two with a few early purchases, though. Like assuming the term 'ivory' meant a netsuke made of animal tusks or bone. When one of her first purchases turned out to be an ugly, mass-produced plastic netsuke, the penny dropped that some sellers used the word as a description of colour.

But she quickly became better at identifying the material used for the netsuke's creation—well, as best she could from a photograph and its brief description—and more accurate in estimating its age and, the most important part, in understanding its probable value.

Stan's enthusiasm for making money had gained momentum since their Sydney explorations.

'People won't pay for something they can get themselves,' he told her, as though she didn't know that. 'We've got to value-add.' His zeal was unstoppable.

'I know. That's why I picked up this backing material. I've done my research on the impact of colour in marketing, and sapphire-blue is considered mysterious and exotic.' She held up the rich blue velvet she was working on.

'Looks good,' he said. 'I'd pay more for that.'

Denise stroked the soft velvet. 'Then let's hope the punters do.'

Chapter 14

Sarah felt a buzz of pleasure at her latest coup. Martin brought an extra spark to the IN-group, a little charge that hadn't been there before. There was a vibe in the room, and she could see the others all respond to his easy manner, almost competing for his attention, wanting to learn more. What a stroke of luck that Chelsea was so chatty at the salon, and that he was her father-in-law. No, it was more than luck. Sarah's own organisational skills had come in handy. Born to network.

Kate, in particular, seemed to have taken to the new technology and was using it with instant expertise. She'd even been clever enough to tweet about Neelam's blog and post photos on Instagram of her *malai kofta* dish. *Food that's grown, not born, #vegan* she'd promised.

Thanks to all these glowing reviews, Neelam's blog was becoming noticed. What had begun with the few followers who knew her had now jumped to hundreds, with plenty of 'likes'. Her luscious photographs made the recipes irresistible and Sarah was trying them all out herself, and freezing them for later meals. Not when Rob was home, of course. He wasn't a fan of even mild Indian flavours—or Thai or Vietnamese, now she thought about it.

Not wanting to lag behind, Sarah arrived at the meeting at Kate's home with a plan to upgrade her iPhone. Here she was hanging onto it, when Rob—who wasn't any more computer literate than she was—changed his all the time. His very efficient staff did all the upgrading for him, but now that Sarah had Martin's help, she could become as switched on as Rob.

'I found this old iPhone in a drawer in Rob's study,' she told Martin as she took her usual seat on the sofa. She held up a large-screen mobile. The phone didn't have so much as a scratch on it, but had been tossed aside in Rob's desire to find a newer, sharper model. 'Rob offers me his old ones when he upgrades but I haven't been keen to learn how to use them. Until now.'

Martin took the mobile from her with a slight shake of his head. 'This isn't an iPhone. It's a Galaxy Smartphone. A superseded model, though a good one. But if you've always used an Apple, do you want to switch?'

Was there any real difference between a Galaxy Smartphone and an Apple iPhone? Sarah hadn't a clue. But how strange that Rob was changing brands. He was an Apple man from way back. Maybe he'd got a great deal from this not-an-Apple mob, or perhaps it had been a freebie from a drug company. They were always giving him amazing stuff like watches and executive toys and overseas holidays.

'I'm keen to learn about mobile phones, so if you say it's a good one, I'll give it a try. If I don't like it, I can always switch back. But I couldn't get it to turn on. Is this the right button?'

'The battery's flat,' Martin said, fiddling with the on-switch. 'It'll need recharging.'

Sarah reached into the mezzaluna-shaped carry bag that stored everything she might need for the classes. After scrambling through her lip gloss, wallet, leather diary and keys, she located her iPhone charger.

Martin held up his hand apologetically. 'That's for Apple. Annoying, I know, but every gadget has its own charger—more or less. I have one that'll work for this phone. It will take thirty minutes to get going though.' He scrabbled around in his box of tricks until he found the right charger and plugged it in. 'While we're waiting, what else would people like to cover?'

Sarah turned to Neelam, who was sitting at her elbow. 'Your blog recipes are terrific. I've been trying them all out. How about showing us your methods on a video? The edges of my curry puffs don't crimp anywhere near as well as yours. I'd love to know your secret.'

'Yes, videos are fabulous for cooking techniques,' Kate said, her face alight.

Neelam beamed. 'Well, this is a very amazing coincidence. Just last week, my sixteen-year-old son has asked if he could video me while I was cooking. He is to create a short film for his drama class and has decided to show aspects of life in a chaotic Indian household. For some reason, the family found my efforts at speaking to camera while I am cooking very amusing.' She turned to Martin. 'Can short videos be uploaded somewhere for others to see?'

'Sure,' he said. 'Do you have it with you?'

Neelam brushed back her dark hair with one hand and passed her laptop across. All it took was a few clicks and about five minutes for Martin to upload Neelam's cooking demonstration to YouTube.

Kate gasped. 'Ooh, look! How gorgeous.'

They all crowded around to watch the homemade show on the full screen of the laptop. Draped in a glorious royal blue and gold sari that followed her curves, and with her shining hair and vivacious smile, Neelam exuded photogenic beauty, but it was when she tilted her head, looked straight into the camera and began discussing the joys of Indian cooking that they realised what they were watching.

'You're going to be a star,' Libby said, as the real-life Neelam bowed her head in modesty.

The camera caressed Neelam. Sarah knew quality, and it was on show there in Neelam's sheer enjoyment of her role. They all chuckled as she declared in her musical voice with its rippling inflections that poppadums 'sun-dried in Madras' were nothing of the sort, and if you checked the small print, you'd find they were made in a factory.

'They come only from a town called Epping or Wapping. So why not make delicious poppadums yourself and dry them under the Aussie sun instead?' she asked directly to camera.

'You have the choice of posting this for public view,' Martin said, 'or you can keep it private, only for the people you choose.'

'Oh, public for sure,' Kate said. 'This video is gorgeous. People are going to love it. I want to see you rustle up every dish on the menu. Would your son film more demos?'

'He would *adore* it,' Neelam said. 'Not unlike thousands of other teenage boys, he dreams of being a famous movie producer—of Bollywood films, of course. I said to him, "We did not come here to give you a better life to see you disappear into this exciting new India you keep speaking of!" He will probably succeed in his Bollywood dream. He is most persuasive. Already he is trying to talk our extended family and friends into dancing Bollywood-style in the background of his movie!'

'Now that's something I'd love to see,' Libby said, smiling.

Martin turned towards Sarah's recharging phone. 'We should have lift-off,' he said, glancing down to check it was sufficiently powered. 'Do you know the password your husband might have used?'

Sarah hesitated. 'He uses Bradman, I think. Rob's a cricket tragic from way back.'

'This is asking for a nine-digit code,' Martin said. 'I'll try Bradman99.'

The Galaxy phone sprang to life once Martin had entered the code.

'What genius.' Libby clapped lightly. 'How on earth did you guess?'

'From one cricket tragic to the next,' he said, his eyes still on the device. 'Here we are. And it appears to have a screensaver of your family on it.'

Andrea, who was sitting next to Martin, glanced down to look at the screenshot shining up at them. 'Yes, there's Anna with Rob—and with a stethoscope around her neck! How funny.'

Sarah felt as if the air had been sucked from her lungs. She saw her own manicured hand reach out and take the phone from Martin's. It was as if she were watching from thousands of miles away, in another universe. She drew the screen closer to her eyes.

'That's not ...' she began, but her throat tensed, like a belt was tightening around it.

Rob was standing with his arm around a young woman who, dark-haired and with a roguish grin, was a carbon copy of their elder daughter. Except it wasn't Anna. Anna didn't part her hair that way, nor would she have been photographed with a stethoscope. Ever.

Sarah tried to smile, but her face felt stiff, as if she'd had Botox injected. 'Yes. Rob, with an intern from the hospital,' she managed to say, and then wished she'd said nothing. They must have seen it was a lie. Rob didn't take his interns to Bennelong Restaurant at the Opera House. With the view of the Harbour and ferries in the background, she could tell that was where the photo had been taken. It was his favourite Sydney restaurant—well, the whole family's. The one where they celebrated on rare special occasions when they were all in Sydney.

Her mind screamed: *Who is this girl who looks so like Anna? Why is she on Rob's home screen? And why is he enveloping her in some sort of ... horrible hug?* It wasn't the kind of hug you'd give a girlfriend, more like a father's proud embrace.

Andrea cleared her throat loudly in a distracting way, quite out of character.

'Sorry, but I have to go soon,' she said, gathering her things. She slid her iPad into its leather satchel. 'Such a nuisance. It's been fun tonight.' She looked at Martin. 'There's only ten minutes left, would you mind if we finished early? Pick up on this again next week?'

'That suits me, too,' Denise said. 'I have to drive to Sydney tomorrow with Stan for his operation.'

Thank you, Andrea. The ploy had given Sarah momentary breathing space. Her internal scream quietened a little. She had to get out of here, away from the goodbye chatter and the polite offers to take a slice of cake home. She needed to digest what she'd seen and work out what it meant. She had to have time to think.

She *dreaded* time to think. With the flick of a switch—what a cliché, but how true in this case—her life had changed.

It was all so confusing; her fragmented brain whirled with questions. But an answer, barely thought out, misshapen but insistent, was boring into her brain.

Rob has another daughter somewhere. A daughter who's the image of ours ...

Chapter 15

Sarah gripped the phone in her hand all the way home, even while driving, as if she didn't dare let go of the evidence. Once she let herself inside, she focused again on the mobile, letting the door swing shut with a bang. But the noise didn't register; she was turning on the phone again with nervous hands.

It turned out Rob's old Galaxy phone wasn't so different from her iPhone, and navigating it wasn't as difficult as she'd feared. She sat on the sofa scrolling through the sparse *Contacts* file, an unfamiliar list that was remarkable for its omissions. The Albury practice rooms, local hospitals, Rob's Sydney consulting suites—not one of them was entered there. Nor was their home number, or Anna or Lucy's international numbers, anywhere to be found. He was using the phone for his own limited purposes.

The blood seemed to drain from her, leaving her weak and numb and empty. She went to the fridge and poured a glass of pinot gris, her hands shaky, her mind jumbled. *Face up to it,* she told herself. This wasn't a phone Rob used every day. This was his 'Other Life' phone, the one hidden from the world, the one she was never meant to see. As she took several long swigs of wine, the shock of her discovery began to wear off. A cold, burning anger was replacing it.

She found a couple of telephone numbers for a Madeleine Stevenson—one a landline, the other a mobile. Sarah felt the name *Madeleine* was a perfect match for this doppelganger, this carbon copy of Anna, for no other reason than that she looked the right age to be called that. She typed the landline numbers into a website Martin had shown them during one of their earlier sessions—reverseaustralia.com, it was called—in the hope it would give her more information about this woman's whereabouts. Before the IN-group began a few weeks ago, she'd had no idea it was so easy to become a cyberstalker. Of course, a few weeks ago, in all her IT ignorance, she'd had no idea what Rob was up to either, no idea that he might have a secret life.

A stroke of luck. The name *P Stevenson* appeared on the website with an address in Balmain, an inner Sydney suburb. Balmain was familiar territory. She'd taken the short ferry ride from Circular Quay across to the Darling Street wharf for many years, to visit her late aunt who'd lived near the Dawn Fraser Swimming Pool. Perhaps she could stake out the Stevenson property, hide in the shadows and wait for the doppelganger to come home. Or knock on the front door and ask her outright: 'Are you Rob Carpenter's daughter?'

Sarah checked the address on Google Maps—another skill recently mastered—and zoomed in on Google Earth for a closer view. Up flashed a picture, not of a freestanding home, but of a block of apartments about three storeys high. The doppelganger could live in any one of these identical apartments. Imagine if she hadn't checked. Anyway, what was she thinking? The idea of hanging around for hours, like a half-baked PI, in the hope that a young woman who looked like her daughter would appear, was insane. Though *so* tempting.

She pored over Rob's screensaver again with as much care as a forensic pathologist. That wasn't a new jacket he was wearing; it didn't have the nipped-in waistline that men's fashion now favoured. She'd bought it for him four, maybe five, years ago, so perhaps the photo could be as old as that. And she hadn't noticed before, but there was a middle-aged woman standing in the shadows to one side of the photo. A petite, fair-haired woman in a shimmering dress and wearing a strand of pearls was watching Rob and the mystery woman with a look of pride, and ownership. *Look at my family*, she seemed to be saying.

It was no one Sarah knew and there was nothing otherwise special about her—she could be any blonde, no doubt attractive in her day. That gave no clues. But the younger woman who was flaunting the stethoscope did. No one would drape a stethoscope around their neck *at lunch* unless they were making a statement.

A wave of nausea flowed over Sarah as a possible reason came to mind. They were all celebrating the doppelganger's graduation from medical school, she was sure of it. The look of pride in Rob's eyes, and the confident gaze of the young woman in her look-at-me dress—I'm pretty *and* smart was the unspoken message—reeked of success and complacency. This young upstart might now be working at a hospital or in a clinic in Sydney. Sarah needed to know where, but there were scores, maybe hundreds, of medical establishments in the city. It was impossible to check them all, much as she'd like to knock on the door of every single one.

Google again. She typed *M Stevenson* into the Australian Health Practitioners register. *Bingo!* One name jumped out at her. Madeleine Stevenson was working as a general practitioner in a clinic in Rozelle, a stone's throw from Balmain.

If she wanted to know more about this young woman, and her relationship to Rob, Rozelle would be the place to start.

Rob had a secret life, one she was only discovering now, one he'd managed to conceal for years. If she confronted him without evidence, how could she trust him to tell her the truth? She would have to know everything before she could do that, and the only way to find out what was going on was to be on the ground herself, investigating.

* * *

Sleep eluded Andrea. As she twisted in bed to check the glowing numbers on her clock radio for the umpteenth time, she blamed herself yet again. Only ten past midnight. This was going to be a very long night.

How tactless she'd been to blurt out Anna's name and then draw attention to that odd photo of Anna's lookalike. But she'd been caught off guard. She knew that feisty Anna would never drape a stethoscope around her neck for anyone, least of all for Rob. The other women probably didn't know Sarah well enough yet to pick up on how devastated she was by seeing that screen. Perhaps bringing the session to an end had worked as a distraction, but it was also possible the others might have caught a whiff of Sarah's seismic moment and watched, silently eyeing each other off, as her world had shifted.

Andrea should have considered this might come out one day. It was like ignoring a lump and then finding out about its menace too late. The old memory she'd suppressed for years began to surface. It had all happened years ago. She hadn't even mentioned it to Brian.

It had been during a short-term placement at the Royal Charlotte Hospital in Sydney, where she'd been busy in the understaffed social work department. Her days were a crowded march of meetings and appointments, arranging for children's services to rescue 'battered babies'—as they were called then—or finding Vietnamese translators to help communicate with bewildered and traumatised mothers.

In the noisy hospital cafeteria one day, grabbing a quick lunch with a colleague, she'd noticed Rob Carpenter leaving with a woman through the back door. He probably had a short-term placement there, too.

When she saw him again in the cafeteria a week or so later, deep in conversation with one of the hospital's senior registrars—Tricia, her name was—it took a moment to click that it was the same woman he'd been with the last time. Something stopped Andrea from bowling up and saying 'hi' to the pair of them, though that would have been the natural thing to do. Once she'd missed that opportunity, it became impossible when she spotted him again, this time entering the laboratory where Tricia was doing research. The lab was deep in the bowels of the hospital, opposite where the social work department had been given a couple of basement rooms, almost as an afterthought. Andrea, who was involved in a limited way with Tricia's work, couldn't think why Rob would visit her there as part of his work. Cosmetic surgery wasn't related to Tricia's job.

Over the next eight weeks, Andrea glimpsed him stealing into the lab several more times. Her antennae quivered with suspicion. But it was way too late to seek him out on the wards and speak to him—he might think she'd been spying and anyway, she was soon to leave the hospital for her next placement at RPA.

This is nothing to do with me, she'd told herself. The reason she was privy to his comings and goings was by virtue of her position. It wasn't her role to speak to Rob about his personal life and she couldn't tell anyone else her misgivings, especially not Sarah. After all, she'd not known anything definite. It had been nothing more than a suspicion, and you didn't act on suspicions if it wasn't your business. And she'd discovered the information in a professional capacity—another reason to keep silent. Confidentiality was paramount in her profession. And Rob's. If she told Sarah, it would only cause her friend distress. And she would have to seek her out deliberately, as they'd slipped out of regular contact then. How mischievous that would look. No, there was nothing she could do.

But it was different now, all these years later. Now, she'd glimpsed that photo on Rob's screensaver—a photo of a woman instantly identifiable as Anna, and yet not Anna. The evidence that Rob might have another child, only a few years younger than Anna and Lucy, seemed credible. No, more than credible—very credible. Maybe even probable. Should she tell Sarah what she'd suspected all those years ago?

By the time the eastern light hit her windows, breaking the darkness, she'd given up on sleep. It was nudging five o'clock. That would make it almost 7 am in New Zealand. Ken might be up checking his emails before work. It would help to discuss her dilemma with him. No names, of course.

She sighed. Here she was blaming herself for keeping a secret from Sarah for more than twenty-five years, and yet she was doing it again about Ken. But her burgeoning internet friendship was too new to tell anyone about, even her best friend.

Good morning Ken, she wrote. *Sorry to bombard you with this email first thing in the morning, but I've had a sleepless night worrying about a problem with my best friend, and hoped you might be able to give me wise counsel.*

She paused, unsure where to go from there. Telling the whole story, beginning years ago and ending up at last night, might turn into a novella, and what chap would want that before heading out to work? She pressed DELETE. This wasn't the sort of chatty email Ken was used to, and it might be a complete turn-off for him. Besides, this was such a big issue, it was way too much to foist onto a new friend.

Andrea picked at her toast and vegemite, her appetite missing. She'd have to ring Sarah, apologise for her indiscretion last night, and arrange to meet later this morning. That gave her a few hours to work out if it was possible to reveal her long-hidden suspicions about Rob in a way that wouldn't devastate her friend.

* * *

Soon after sunrise Sarah forced herself to have an egg on toast. She would need the protein to sustain her, though she didn't care if she never ate again. The yolk tasted like clag in her mouth. She washed it down with a milky coffee that she hoped wouldn't leave her nerves any more brittle than they already felt. Once eight o'clock ticked over, she rang the Rozelle Clinic and made an appointment for 2 pm that day with a Dr Madeleine Stevenson.

'You're a new patient?' asked the receptionist. 'What name is it?'

'Mrs Emily Thorne,' Sarah replied.

When the telephone rang before ten, Sarah assumed it was the taxi driver, letting her know he was close. It wasn't the cabbie, of course. It had been years since they phoned on approach. She wasn't thinking straight, but that was hardly surprising.

'Sarah, it's me.' Andrea's voice was strained.

'Sorry, Andrea, I can't talk.'

The statement was true on one level, but the real truth was that Sarah couldn't bear talking right now. Not to her friend, not to Rob, not to anyone, until she'd worked out what was going on. She flinched at the memory of Rob with his arm draped around the doppelganger.

A taxi sounded its horn at that moment. She twitched back a drape and saw the silver cab idling by the front gates.

'My lift's here,' she told Andrea. 'I'm booked on the eleven o'clock flight to Sydney. You understand. I'll contact you when I'm back.'

'How long will—'

'Bye.'

She ended the call and took a deep, ragged breath.

Sorry, Andrea. I may not have a clear idea of what to do, but I'm not going to talk about this for hours, and then sit and wait for Rob like some pathetic version of a modern Madame Butterfly.

Chapter 16

When the front doorbell rang, Denise stood up from the kitchen table where she was draping sapphire-blue velvet as a backdrop for display. That would be Stan, ready for their drive to Sydney.

'I've brought around a few more perspex boxes for you. What do you think?' Stan showed her half a dozen clear boxes, some small, some large. They had no base to them so they could be placed over the netsuke, as she'd requested, and were made with Stan's usual precision and attention to detail.

'As good as the displays we saw in Sydney, if I do say so myself,' he said with pride. He looked as eager and excited as a youngster mastering a Lego tower. 'We can list these on eBay before we head off, so the fortune can begin to flow.'

It was good to hear Stan use the word 'we' now. It made her part of something bigger, something that had been missing in her life since she'd retired.

'They're terrific, Stan. Great job.' Denise turned the boxes over with genuine admiration, inspecting all sides. 'I can't even see how you've joined them.'

She'd sourced some miniature stands for the carvings at the local two-dollar shop and had painted them a glossy mahogany colour. The finished product would look so impressive in photos on the auction site. She'd already written a description that would speak to the customers.

'When do you have to start repaying your loan?' she asked.

'You know banks. Once you get the overdraft, you start paying interest.'

'So, fifteen thousand then?'

'That's only for the wiz bang surgery. A letter from the specialist arrived last week listing all the charges. Even my private insurance doesn't cover it all. Like the gap in anaesthetists' fees and extra tests. I went back to the bank and upped it to twenty-five grand.'

Denise let out a soft sigh. This was quite a bit more than she'd planned for and would take much longer to earn. She wasn't expecting a massive profit on her sales, but a slow and steady gain trickling in would be welcome. Maybe she'd been a bit too optimistic with Stan.

'And the bank agreed?'

'They bloody well ought to! I've paid them plenty of interest over my lifetime. And I own the house, so there's no risk to their money.'

Denise did a quick mental calculation. At the going interest rate, it meant Stan had to find at least another hundred and twenty-five dollars a month. That mightn't be easy for him now. He might not have much in super. It was important that they turn a profit so the loan could be paid off bit by bit.

'About the downlights to display them,' he said. 'I brought some LED strips. I'll rig that up for the photos. We can offer them with or without lights. Now, which one's going on sale first?'

'That's the million-dollar question. I'm becoming so attached to them, it'll be like selling my pets.'

Stan rolled his eyes. 'Emotion can't come into business decisions, Den. Gotta be hard-nosed. Let me put it this way: which pets are digging up the yard and chewing your shoes? We'll start with them.'

Denise looked at her darlings. Perhaps the fat fisherman could go, even though she rather liked his rakish look. And the bone dragon with the leering expression made her a little uncomfortable, so he was out. Neither had been too expensive, so she was interested to see if they could turn a profit once they'd been cleaned and displayed like the crown jewels.

'Only two up for sale?' Stan looked surprised. 'Why don't we list a few more? We can't lose if we put on a minimum price. When we get back, we'll know straightaway if we're on a winner by how many people are watching or bidding.'

He was right, of course. Denise hadn't got into buying netsuke to build up a collection. This was strictly business. Oh, but she did love the sweet little pair of mice, and she definitely wasn't ready to let go of the adorable plump sparrow made of antique bone. Maybe she'd keep one or two of the most exquisite ones …

Once the lighting had been set up and two netsuke displayed on the plinth in their perspex cages, Denise took photos and uploaded them to her iPad. She and Stan sat close together, inspecting the images, neither speaking.

Then Stan gave a low whistle.

'They're great, Den. I'd buy them in a heartbeat!'

Denise had a sudden urge to lean in and kiss him, but resisted. She wasn't sure if either of them really wanted to go where that might lead.

'Value-add is right. How expensive is it to make the perspex boxes?'

Stan grinned. 'The material's cost price and my time's my own. So selling the netsuke *in the boxes*, like framed works of art, would barely add to our costs.'

'And I can buy all the stands the two-dollar shop has. Painting them's easy-peasy. We could offer a choice—the complete package with the stand and box, or buying them cleaned and polished but without the extras. What do you think?'

'Yes. Looking at that,' Stan gestured to the photograph, 'I reckon people interested in buying one would pay a few hundred for it. That's a huge profit for us! We can upload photos of a couple of 'em as the complete package, and list a couple more as netsuke without the bells and whistles, and see what does better? As a trial?'

Great idea. Why not indeed?

Chapter 17

Sarah sat in a cramped waiting room full of restless, wriggling toddlers and tired mothers as the clinic's phones rang nonstop in the background. It was a rather unprepossessing practice, housed in a two-storey building crying out for a makeover with a plain shop frontage that sported frosted glass windows. The names of the doctors were printed on the glass. *Dr Madeleine Stevenson MBBS* was one of them. So different from the practice Sarah attended in Albury with its floor-to-ceiling glass windows and views of the distant hills.

'Mrs Thorne.'

She didn't respond the first time she heard the name called. Nor the second. But she started on hearing *Mrs Emily Thorne* spoken in a loud voice a third time and, remembering with a bolt that this was her new persona, she stood up rather flustered.

'Sorry, in a world of my own,' she said to the receptionist who directed her down a short corridor. She sat again in a narrow chair outside Dr Stevenson's door, her heart thumping as she waited for it to open. She wasn't even one hundred per cent sure she had the right person. Was she crazy to be here?

You can do it, Sarah, she told herself. *You once played Shakespeare. Bring out your acting skills now.*

The door swung open and the doctor was there, standing right in front of her. The wretched doppelganger. Despite Sarah's conviction that Madeleine was going to be the woman in the photograph, her flesh and blood presence came as a shock. She was smiling at Sarah as though the world was quite normal and this was the routine visit of a new patient for a standard consultation.

Madeleine was taller than Anna, her hair cut à la Audrey Hepburn's, and she was wearing an elegant cowl-necked shift dress with a colourful belt and matching earrings. More feminine and made-up than Anna, but the resemblance was striking.

After exchanging pleasantries and the details of her medical history—Sarah was glad she had such a healthy past and didn't have to lie too much as she denied a multitude of previous medical conditions—she went for the direct approach. The sooner she could get out of there, the better. Sitting opposite your daughter's double pretending to be someone else was—what was the word—discombobulating?

'I'm down from Coffs Harbour, visiting my sister in Rozelle for a few months,' she said, 'and I'm after a referral to a cosmetic surgeon in Sydney. I'd like some work done on my face. Possibly liposuction to my thighs too. Now's a good time because my sister can help me recuperate here. I've been given the names of a couple of Sydney specialists who people say are very good. A Dr Rob Carpenter and a Dr Barry Glover?'

Barry Glover was a contemporary of Rob's in Sydney, a friend for years. She was on safe ground using his name.

'I know them both well,' Madeleine said. 'They're excellent surgeons, so you can't go wrong. But in the interests of transparency, I should tell you that Dr Carpenter's my father.'

It was the information Sarah needed, the detail she was fishing for, but the answer came like a punching bag swinging from a great distance. Right into her solar plexus.

Dr Carpenter's my father.

Those four words were all it took for Madeleine Stevenson to confirm that the life Sarah was living was built on nothing firmer than a cloud.

She was spinning like a twirling marionette whose strings were being controlled by some malevolent force. All the background noise in the surgery receded, the air left her lungs. *Suffocating, suffocating.*

She reached with both hands for the solid reality of her chair, gripping the arms tightly until her palms throbbed. It seemed to be the only way she could regain some semblance of control, find her equilibrium and take back her life.

I knew this, she told herself. *I knew it! This is not a surprise.*

Sarah could hear her pulse thudding in her ears now, knew her breaths were coming faster than normal, but Madeleine had swivelled away for a few moments to concentrate on her computer screen, and seemed oblivious to Sarah's reaction.

What sort of doctor doesn't notice? Sarah wondered, while her inner voice was pleading, *Get me out of here.* But she needed to know more, she had to find out *every* fact she could, and this would be her only chance. Trusting Rob to fill in any details was fanciful now.

'Aren't doctors allowed to refer patients to a family member?' She tilted her head, trying to look politely interested—and innocent—about Madeleine's connection with Rob. 'I suppose there might be the temptation to discuss patients' details at home?' she added.

Would Madeleine notice that her voice was high and strained, that her queries sounded ridiculous?

Her mind was scrambling to stay one step ahead of her questions, but it wasn't easy. The insubstantial cloud she'd found herself on was bursting into a violent storm. Here she was in a consultation room with her daughter's spooky double, having given a false name and an imaginary medical history, and asking for an invented referral. She was so unused to lying that an old cliché flashed into her mind: *Liars have need of good memory.* Was her memory up to it? Rob had done this to her—turned her into someone she wasn't, a person she never wanted to be. *The bastard.* She was feeling sick to the core.

'Yes, doctors can refer to a family member,' Madeleine informed her. 'But it's best if we let our patient know that we're related. I do talk shop at home with Dad. We both love medicine, but we don't go into specifics.'

So there it was. Not only was Rob this wretched woman's father, but he lived with her—and presumably her mother—during the week, too. *In the same house.*

A flash of jealousy pierced her as she pictured their dinners together: Rob indulging in medical chatter with this young woman, bantering back and forth across the table. How dare he? For years he'd rarely made it home in time to eat with Anna and Lucy. What good luck Madeleine wasn't thorough enough to test her blood pressure. It would be sky high by now.

'Does your mother mind the shop talk?' Sarah's question was tiptoeing over the doctor-patient boundary, but she had to learn all the details about this murky, *shoddy*, other life Rob was leading. 'They must both be proud of you.' She could hardly bring herself to say it.

The young doctor gave a straight smile, and Sarah could tell that the last comment had probed a little too deeply and Madeleine was distancing herself.

'Yes,' she said, turning back to her computer. 'I'll give you the referral to Dr Glover, shall I?'

The printer spat out a letter based on Sarah's fake request and Madeleine scrawled her signature at the bottom before handing it over. 'If there's nothing else I can help you with today …'

She rolled her chair back and began to rise. Sarah realised the consultation was being put to bed, like a child who was showing a hint of over-excitement.

Nothing else you can help me with? Ha! What a joke. There were a thousand questions she had, but she could hardly grab Madeleine Stevenson by her chocolate-brown cowl, stare into her eyes and demand answers. Who was Madeleine's mother? Did this slip of a doctor know how Rob and her mother were cheating on another family?

And what year was she born, what month? Based on her appearance, Anna and Lucy might have been toddlers or in primary school. Had she, Sarah, been so absorbed in her mothering role that she'd missed the signs of Rob straying? And where did Madeleine—and her mother for that matter—think Rob went on weekends? They might know he'd had other children growing up in Albury. Not to mention a wife.

No wonder he'd resisted her suggestion of buying a place in Sydney. *The lying creep!* How could she have been so naive? She felt staggered that she'd been so trusting, so stupid.

She felt much sicker on leaving the consultation room than she had when she'd arrived.

'I'm sorry, I don't have my Medicare card,' Sarah told the receptionist. 'I'll pay in cash, if that's okay.' She wasn't going to leave a paper trail. Nobody need ever know she'd been to the surgery, and Rob could never find out.

Chapter 18

'It's gorgeous.'

Libby leaned on the doorframe of Kate's latest achievement—the redecorated room dedicated to brides, their wedding desires and their beauty needs. The higgledy-piggledy jumble of adolescent nostalgia was gone. 'This is so far from the old bedroom I can't believe it. Here was I thinking you were turning the room into a simple office! How did you manage to keep this glorious makeover a secret from me?' She hesitated. 'And what will the boys think of it?'

Libby knew how delicate it was reclaiming your adult children's bedrooms. A balance between accepting that they'd never live at home again so you could utilise the room for other pursuits, versus not wanting them to think you were pleased they were gone. She'd wrestled with that problem a few years ago, and Marcus was her only child. Imagine juggling five people's sensibilities.

'Don't worry, I told the twins that their room was going to be revamped. They were fine about it,' Kate said. 'Since they moved to Sydney, that space hasn't been used. To tell you the truth, I think they were embarrassed when their girlfriends saw it. Such a den of testosterone! Maturity's a great thing. I should have redecorated ages ago, but there's been no need. And it's not as though there's nowhere for them to bed down when they're here.'

It was true. Kate's rambling home had oodles of spare rooms, now all four boys and Louise had created new lives for themselves.

Kate had repainted it in Antique White USA, the colour *du jour*, she said, that gave a fresh, bright look to enhance the warmth of its furnishings. And now that the heavy masculine curtains had been replaced with delicate cream blinds patterned with sprigs of red and green flowers, light tumbled into the space. Outside a late-flowering jasmine was trailing its white blooms over a trellis. There was a wide dressing table with angled mirrors that took up most of one wall, large enough to house Libby's growing collection of make-up essentials.

'Are you sure it's okay to have me here as well? I don't want to crowd you out,' Libby said.

'I've got tons of room,' Kate declared, indicating a desk on the opposite wall with comfy chairs on either side. 'I'll be able to do all my paperwork there. And I can't *wait* for you to be working here, too. We're going to have a ball. It's the most exciting thing to happen since Louise got married. And wait till you see this ...' Kate slipped a latch at the side of a stand-alone cheval mirror, opening it like a door to display a hidden compartment for jewellery. '*Ta-da!* We can hit the op shops and stock it with costume jewellery for everyone to try while they're waiting their turn. Wouldn't that be fun?'

'That's inspired! It'll help me persuade them to choose their best make-up colours, too. They'll be able to see that silver

126

jewellery needs different blush and lipstick shades compared to gold accessories. You think of everything. How can I ever thank you? It's simply wonderful.'

Impossible to show enough gratitude to someone who'd pulled you to safety when you were about to drown, and then wrapped you in a blanket with the soft embrace of security.

Kate glanced at her watch. 'Time we went to Neelam's. She's expecting us at five thirty.'

Libby had agreed with her that an online presence for their new business was now essential, and Neelam was the ideal person to guide them in making their pictures look professional.

'I'm struggling a bit with our web page, though,' Kate said as they walked out to her car. 'Things like how to navigate around it and organise cyber security. Not to mention PayPal and credit cards. It's all very well for it to look good, but it's more important to be user-friendly. What do you think about asking Martin to give the two of us a private session on setting it up? I'll pay for it ...' Kate raised her hand to stop Libby interrupting '... and you can reimburse me when you get some clients. We'd best do this apart from the IN-group sessions. It's not fair to the others if we hog an entire lesson for our business needs.'

I would love, love, love us to have a private lesson with Martin, Libby thought. With no pressing requirements for Martin's skills—unlike most of the other women—she was hovering in the background at their sessions now and worried she might be coming across as the quiet mouse, with no personality. There were times when she felt like one of the contestants on *The Bachelor* having to make do with group dates, never being granted the thrill of a one-on-one. Silly, she knew. This wasn't a competition and Martin wasn't the prize.

'We *could* have a private session,' she said, as though Kate's idea needed more consideration. If she let slip how much she liked Martin, Kate, being Kate, would rush in and begin to matchmake. That's if he were in the market, which of course was unlikely for such an attractive man. But there was something about him, a slight vulnerability that didn't speak of a wife or partner. Libby used to think she was good at picking up cues about men, but since her major misjudgement of Gerald, her confidence had taken a battering.

'We do need a snappy website. I wonder if he'd mind?' she added. She opened the passenger-side door.

'If you don't ask, you don't get!' Kate said, as they set out for the drive to Neelam's place.

When they arrived, Kate parked the BMW to take advantage of a shady crepe myrtle on the street a few hundred metres from the house. They were early, so they took their time ambling towards it.

They passed the Sharmas' car in the driveway then walked up the steps. From deep within the household, they could hear raised voices. The front door was open, so the words wafted uninterrupted down the hallway and through the security screen door.

'I am getting tired of this!' It was Vinod's voice, exasperated.

Neelam's husband was often present when the group met there, and always quietly spoken and polite, but the way he hovered round the periphery of the meetings made Libby a little uncomfortable. She wasn't sure if he had an interest in what the women were discussing—unlikely—or liked to keep a close eye on Neelam.

Libby raised an eyebrow and tilted her head towards Kate. *What do we do?* Neither Neelam nor Vinod seemed to realise they might be arriving soon. The last thing Libby wanted was to witness a domestic argument moments before their meeting.

Kate gave a nonchalant shrug.

'You are out all the time, till all hours, at these stupid computer meetings.' His voice was irritable. 'As if you need to know such silly things as Twitter and Facebook. Then you go and put ridiculous ideas in our Raj's head telling him he could be a Bollywood producer! He ignores his studies to film you cooking every day. Cooking, of all things! Do you have any idea how foolish your video posts will make me look when our friends see them? And you have all these, these ... *followers*! Is that a respectable thing for a family of our standing?'

'For goodness' sake, it is one night a week, Vinod, and we are having some fun!' Neelam's voice was not as loud as her husband's but at least she was taking it up to him.

'You think it is *fun* for me to come home to an empty house on Tuesday nights? You think it is *fun* that our boy is so deluded he is forgetting the importance of his study? You think it is *fun* that women you never even knew a few months ago come here at all hours to talk about photography? To pick your brains?'

Libby winced at that comment.

'It is five thirty, Vinod. I would hardly call that *all hours*.'

'What about that dumpy old woman? She sat for hours one evening, going on about a stupid collection of trinkets she had not even purchased yet!'

'Netsuke are not *trinkets*.' Neelam's voice was annoyed now too. 'They are sculptures with centuries of history from a cultured civilisation. As an educated Indian, you, of all people, should have some appreciation of that. Do not insult what you do not understand!'

By this stage, Libby's heart was racing as a familiar but long-forgotten sensation flooded back, of needing to escape to her bedroom and put a pillow over her head when her father went on one of his tirades. She beckoned to Kate, pointing to her car further down the street. *Why not wait there?*

But Kate was having none of it. With an airy wave of the hand, she strode forward and jabbed the doorbell for several seconds.

The bickering stilled in an instant and twenty seconds later, Neelam came gliding up to the front door, all greetings and smiles. Perhaps she was used to arguments and they were a regular part of her life.

Libby shuddered. Gerald might have ruined her life and left her in debt, but at least he'd never had loud arguments with her—not like her father, or Vinod. Then she had to choke back nervous laughter—how ridiculous that sounded.

They heard the back door shut, and as Neelam ushered them into the ornate living room and they stepped onto the gorgeous silk rugs, Libby saw the car backing out of their driveway. Relief! Vinod wasn't planning to loiter during this visit. She wondered what they'd have heard about Kate and herself if they'd stayed listening for much longer. You never did know how people saw you, but calling Denise the 'dumpy old woman' was a bit of an injustice. Denise might be on the plump side, but she was kind and very well-meaning, and not *that* old.

Neelam said not a word about what they had overheard as she chatted with her usual charm and grace, but it was like an elephant in the room. As Libby glanced around, she had to stifle more nervous laughter. A large, ornamental bronze Indian elephant took pride of place on Neelam's mantelpiece. Make that *two* elephants in the room.

She pulled out her notebook in a businesslike manner and took a seat on the sofa, keen to get their business done so they could get away as soon as possible.

'We have a few questions about managing the lighting and close-ups when we take photographs,' she said. 'We're not professionals or anything. I mean, we don't even have real cameras. We'll be using Kate's iPhone to take them.'

'IPhones take excellent shots,' Neelam said. 'Too good, in fact. Sometimes I think I will be out of a job soon because everyone is a photographer now. But I have jotted down a few ideas. With these to assist, you can take flattering photos of your clients.'

Half an hour later, armed with a plethora of tips about when and why to use angled lighting, how to reduce camera shake, and the benefits of using burst mode to take several photos in quick succession, she and Kate thanked Neelam and left. The awkwardness had dissipated, but Libby was still keen to go, her ears pricked for the sounds of a returning car. Vinod mustn't find them there, filling up his living room with their presence and their questions.

She was envious of Kate, who had seemed oblivious to any underlying currents, chattering away to Neelam as though everything was normal, as of course, it was. Libby knew she was making far too much of a minor tiff between a married couple not meant for others' ears, but it would have been easier to dismiss the argument if the reason for Vinod's annoyance hadn't been quite so tied up with the very existence of the IN-group.

*

'Are you okay?' Kate briefly rested her hand briefly on Libby's shoulder as they drove off. 'Couples do have disagreements from time to time, you know. And Neelam handled it with her usual charm and serenity.'

'I know,' Libby said. 'I had flashes of memories from my childhood that I'd rather forget, that's all. My dad wasn't a very nice man.'

Libby had grown up thinking all fathers must be bad-tempered and irritable. Her best friend's father was the same, except he had a reason for it—he'd been to Vietnam during the war and had nightmares every night. Her own father had no reason for his nastiness, as far as Libby could tell. Finding herself pregnant at the end of her year at Stott's Secretarial College didn't improve his temper or his opinion of her, of course, especially when Marcus's father did a runner shortly after his birth.

'Life's a roll of the dice, isn't it?' Kate's voice was whisper quiet. 'If you're unlucky with the parents you get, there's not a thing you can do about it and it can set you up for a challenging life.'

'Oh, my mother was lovely. I adored her, but I couldn't wait to leave home to get away from *him*. And then she died a couple of years later without achieving any of her dreams. She always wanted to set up a gift shop serving afternoon teas, but Dad was having none of that. My problems with him seemed to carry over into my choices in men afterwards.'

'Sounds like you took after your mother. I'll bet she saw you as one of her great successes. I don't want to pry, but did you move to Albury to get out of a bad marriage?'

'Yes and no,' Libby said. 'It was more a case of a bad marriage got out of me.' She hesitated. She hadn't spoken to anyone about her experience, but knew she could trust Kate. 'His name was Gerald, and he wasn't angry or violent or anything. He was a charming white-collar crim. I fell for him completely. He left me with a mountain of debt and no reputation ... That's why I arrived here with less than nothing and have to start over again. I'm so wary of men now. I figured I'd found a great guy in Gerald because he was as far removed from my father's type as imaginable, but then I discovered sophistication and success can be a total veneer. It was a shock I didn't see coming.' She sighed. 'But you've got a great partner in Neil. How did you two meet?'

'I became close friends with his younger sister Maggie while we were nursing. Mags and I went to their parents' place one night for dinner and he was there too. I noticed he helped prepare the meal, and cleared up afterwards as though it was second nature to him. I thought at the time: *Neil will make a lovely husband for someone.* Then it hit me like a bolt. *He'll make a lovely husband for me!* And he has.'

'What a great story! I bet your kids enjoyed hearing it.'

'Are you kidding? They think it's the most boring courtship imaginable. They'd have preferred we met at a rave party backpacking around South America, or that our eyes locked across a glass of bubbly in a drunken bar one New Year's Eve and shooting stars danced around us.'

'Been there, done that. Remind me to set them straight when I see them. It looks like you might have discovered the secret to a perfect match, though. Watch someone on their home turf and if you love what you see, go for it.'

'Amen to that!' Kate said. 'Martin's a good example, too. I always think he's so patient when we're being a bit dense during classes.'

'I wonder what his wife's like. It would be interesting to meet her.'

'Martin's a widower. Neil mentioned it to me, but he didn't know any details.'

The news was not a complete shock to Libby, suggesting her antennae had not been too far off the mark. It confirmed her suspicions about Martin—that he, too, was alone.

Chapter 19

After she left the doctor's rooms, Sarah caught the bus back to Balmain to explore the block of apartments in Rowntree Street, the address matching the telephone number of one *P Stevenson*. Was that Madeleine's mother, living there with her daughter?

Another horrible thought blitzed her, one she hadn't contemplated before. Madeleine may not be an only child. Perhaps Rob had a son—the son he'd longed for—with Madeleine's mother.

Sarah gazed out the bus window as the terrace houses of the inner suburbs flashed by, barely noticing the wide umbrellas of the frangipani trees with their delicate yellow and white flowers.

Had she ignored the nagging little clues that had cropped up now and again during their thirty-five years together? The conferences he'd only mentioned at the last minute, too late for her to travel with him; the odd weekend he stayed in Sydney, to schedule more surgery sessions at the private hospital where he worked, or so he'd said.

Then there was the waning of intimacy and the often perfunctory lovemaking, with no romantic gestures anymore and foreplay a distant memory, but after so many years, wasn't that almost normal in a marriage? There was nothing so obvious as lipstick on his collar or the lingering scent of another woman. He was too meticulous for that.

Sarah had known his life in Sydney presented opportunities to stray, but his days there had expanded so insidiously it was hard for her to identify exactly when this second life might have begun. His time away from Albury had crept up on her and whenever it bothered her, she'd let it go—partly because her job was to care for the children and make his life easy, and partly because she'd filled any empty spaces with her meetings and committees.

Was it wilful on her part? A case of sleeping dogs and all that, better for her to ignore the red flags than stir up anything that might lead to the truth and the end of her supposedly perfect life?

She'd suspected Rob had had flings over the years, the odd affair that could be painfully ignored as part and parcel of marriage to a good-looking, successful man. But if he had had affairs, they'd never lasted very long as far as she could tell, and she'd convinced herself that being his wife, the one he came home to, was all that mattered in the end.

But now she couldn't imagine why she'd been satisfied with these crumbs. As if being the wife of a man who had no respect for you was worth anything, and it was clear he had no respect. Were there other signs that she'd completely missed? How he must have laughed to himself over her old-fashioned, stay-married-at-all-costs values and, she had to be honest, rank ignorance. *Worthless,* that's what she was to him. *Worth less.*

Sarah left the bus and walked around the corner into Rowntree Street, where she found the three-storey building she was looking for almost immediately. So striking were its Art Deco lines and pastel colours that she could hardly miss it. Located on the high side of the street, the billboard outside this recent renovation showed stunning views that the upper floor apartments would enjoy of the shimmering harbour, circling all the way from the north to the east, with the lights of the city skyline flooding in.

It was infuriating to think that the money Rob had earned—*their* money—might be going towards keeping this other family in such style. The rage inside her was growing by the minute, teeth-grinding fury making her muscles quiver. She took several deep breaths in an effort to stop the anger spilling out. An unfamiliar urge to smash something flooded her body.

She'd always made sure Rob's life ran so smoothly, always been the good wife. She'd sacrificed the ability to earn any money for herself. Who knows what she could have achieved if she'd given herself the chance? What kind of fool had she been?

Rob might argue he'd supported her very well financially for years, so why shouldn't some of his earnings go towards his time in Sydney? Well, let him try. He had no right—absolutely no right—to set up another, secret family while he neglected the first one. And Sarah determined in that instant that he wouldn't get away with it, whatever the cost.

There was a gleaming coffee shop on the ground floor of the apartment block. She'd skipped lunch after her discoveries, her appetite all but vanished, and now she needed sustenance and strength. A battle was looming, and as Napoleon once said, 'An army marches on its stomach.'

But first, she walked into the foyer of the building, with its own entrance to the cafe. Everything there was glistening, and elegant, and hateful—the vertical silver lights in keeping with the Art Deco appearance of the whole space; the twenty-odd mailboxes, all with silver trim and silver locks, lined along one wall. Her eyes slowly scanned the titles.

No, it wasn't possible.

'R Carpenter and P Stevenson' screamed letterbox 24. It might as well have added *And isn't Sarah Carpenter a fool?*

As she stared at those names, the world around her faded, she saw little bubbles of light, and in an instant she was underwater, trying to draw breath but paralysed, doubled over and sinking.

*

'Are you all right? Hello?'

Sarah opened her eyes to see a dark-haired woman, her kind face puckered with concern, kneeling beside her as she lay crumpled on the foyer floor. A twenty-something blonde woman in a bright, arty T-shirt was standing behind, holding a mobile phone to her ear. 'She looks shocking. I'll ring an ambulance.'

'No, no. No ambulance! I'll be fine.' Sarah raised an unsteady hand and flickered a smile. She wasn't quite ready to stand up, but at least the feeling of drowning had passed and she could breathe again.

'My fault,' she added. 'Shouldn't have missed lunch. It was nothing more than a faint. I do that sometimes,' she lied. 'Low blood pressure. I'll be better in a moment.'

'That's a relief.' The brunette, whose name badge identified her as Katrina, still looked concerned. 'You were out stone

137

cold. I'll help you up when you're ready. Can you make it into the cafe? How about a nice hot cup of tea with loads of sugar? And how does a cream cheese bagel sound?'

Sarah let herself be helped up and guided to a seat at a table near the counter. She focused her eyes on the large peppermill. So now, as well as being the cheated wife—and the cheated mother—she'd become a doddery old woman who keeled over in public and needed saving. How many more humiliations would she have to endure today?

Her embarrassment prickled her, but the women were being so caring, and the food and cup of tea so comforting, that she let it go. There was only so much she could deal with right now.

'I was looking for a friend of mine who lives here,' she told Katrina, once she was feeling stronger. 'I thought she said she lived at Apartment 24, but the mailbox out there says an R Carpenter and P Stevenson live there. Do you know them?'

'Penny and Rob? Yes, they're regulars. They come for coffee most mornings—with their daughter.' The pain of those words was intense.

'I must have it wrong,' Sarah said. 'My friend's name is … Helen, not Penny. I'll have to check the address again. It's not important. I dropped in on a whim while I was in Balmain.'

With another part of her mind she wondered if she should worry that making up a new life story every thirty minutes was coming to her so easily. Now that her real life seemed to have evaporated, she was able to say anything and it immediately became true.

'Is there anyone we can call for you?' Katrina asked. 'Can you make it back home on your own?'

She took another sip of her tea. 'No, I'm visiting Sydney. Staying at a hotel in town with my husband. I'll get a cab back there now. You've been so kind. What do I owe you for the food?'

Katrina gave a wave of her hand as though it was nothing. 'As long as you're sure you have someone to look after you,' she said.

The words hit Sarah hard. That was the problem. If someone had asked her twenty-four hours ago, she would have been confident in her answer. *Of course* she had someone to look after her. But the future was a different land now. Now, she wondered if anyone would ever be there to look after her again.

'What hotel are you staying at? I'll call the cab for you.'

Sarah was startled by Katrina's offer. There was, of course, no hotel booking. She wasn't used to this, to being so unprepared.

She hesitated a moment. 'No need for that. You've been so helpful, but I'm much better now. I still have one or two things to do in Balmain. I'm looking for the local library. From memory, it's somewhere close to here, isn't it?'

'Right round the corner. Walk back to Darling Street and it's almost directly opposite, past the police station. You can't miss it.'

Sarah gathered her belongings, but when she tried again to pay for her tea and bagel, the two women wouldn't hear of it. How kind they were. They may not have realised it, but their warmth towards her—a complete stranger—on this horrible day meant more than she could express. She walked out of the cafe ready to tackle whatever lay ahead, and she wouldn't give a backward glance at Rob's alternative home, the place where he lived his *seedy* other life.

The fog in her brain was clearing now. Balmain library had only been an excuse, but it would be the ideal place to organise accommodation in Sydney. She waited at the lights, jiggling the button over and over, as if it would have any impact at all on how soon they'd change.

Good, she hadn't locked in a trip back to Albury that evening. Her finger had hovered over the 'Return flight' button when she was booking the journey in the early hours of the morning, but something had made her hesitate.

Even though there'd been a chance that the Madeleine Stevenson in Rob's contacts list would turn out not to be his daughter after all, that her spontaneous trip to Sydney might have been the silliest of goose chases, an inner voice had cautioned her. If it *were* true, if Rob did indeed have secrets there, she'd need to stay. So instead, she'd clicked on 'One way' and packed a small overnight bag, just in case. Smart thinking.

It was well after three by then and the library was abuzz with the excitement of children released from confinement for the day. Sarah found the quietest corner and logged onto her iPad using the free wi-fi. She wouldn't bother with Wotif or any other money-saving site. Even though money had never been a barrier to anything she might want, she'd always been careful. After all, she wasn't the breadwinner, she hadn't wanted to be wasteful.

Well, that was about to change. Rob didn't know it, but he was about to pay for the most expensive suite she could hire on Level 29 at the InterContinental Hotel on Macquarie Street. Then he would shell out for an in-house massage, a three-course room service dinner—lobster perhaps?—plus every other luxury she could put her hands on. Come to think of it, she wouldn't mind purchasing a luxurious white bathrobe, either, to slip into after a bubble bath in the marble spa. So she'd be comfortable while she planned her future, and worked out what she'd say to Rob when she invited him to the hotel. *Surprise!* She'd flown up on a whim. He'd be surprised all right.

Seeing his name nestled next to P Stevenson's on the mailbox had cemented her decision and wiped out her past life as his wife. Her story was nothing more than a cliché—yet another naive, wronged woman married to a cheating, lying, two-timing bastard. And Sarah Carpenter, MA in English Literature from Sydney University, did not plan to live the rest of her life as, of all things, a cliché.

Chapter 20

As Andrea sat waiting at her GP's clinic, her thoughts turned to last night's shocking discovery. How would Sarah approach the mystery of the Anna lookalike on Rob's screensaver? No doubt he'd be busy all day in Sydney with surgery, forcing Sarah to wait until later that evening before she could confront him. Was there anything more frustrating than waiting?

Andrea looked around at the other patients, thinking that there must be a better way to manage the stream of people whose lives were also on hold as they waited, and waited. Most doctors never spent any time in their own waiting rooms, she decided, before realising that she'd never sat in her own, either. Oops.

A woman in a navy puffer jacket came in, looked around and then pinned a laminated notice onto the display board near Andrea:

ARE YOU LOOKING TO MEET NEW PEOPLE AND
HAVE FUN?
TWIN CITIES CROQUET CLUB WILL WELCOME YOU.

Andrea, whose eyes always chased the written word in much the same way as a collie dashed after a ball, was immediately absorbed in the sign. The newcomer came and sat next to her, offering the smile of an ally.

'We're trying to raise the profile of croquet,' she confided. She had smokers' lines around her mouth, although there was no trace of tobacco about her. She must have quit for a healthier lifestyle. 'Are you interested in giving the game a try? The first six lessons are free.'

'Sounds appealing, but I'm not at all sporty and not many of my friends are, either. I'm not sure my ageing joints would cope.'

'You won't know till you try! Croquet's a pretty gentle game, not like golf where you're forever twisting your back. They call croquet "snooker on grass". Quite strategic, moves have to be planned like chess because you're trying to outsmart your opponent. I've become quite a convert! I'm Debra, by the way.'

'Nice to meet you. I'm Andrea. My doctor's been encouraging me to get more active. He suggested I take up swimming but ...' She gave a slight shudder.

'Swimming? Oh yes, women our age love squeezing into a pair of tight-fitting Lycra swimmers and floundering around gulping chlorine.'

'So I'm not the only one?' Andrea said. 'Then he suggested I get a dog. My daughter recommended that, too. Not that I'd mind one, but I'm starting to think I must have '*Needs a dog*' tattooed on my forehead.'

'They do help get you out and about. I call Buddy my personal trainer, because I wouldn't go for a walk every day if he didn't pester me. But all the details for croquet are on the notice, or Facebook, if you use a computer.'

Debra's doctor called her then, almost as if they had been waiting in the post office and Debra had fluked the fast-moving queue, even though she'd arrived later. There was no chance to continue with the conversation, but Andrea had a spark of interest. Croquet wasn't such a bad idea, and meeting more people there would give her news to share with Ken. His life in Queenstown sounded so exciting compared to hers. Sarah might have been interested in joining too, but she had too much on her plate at the moment. Denise was a possibility, but Andrea wasn't sure if she was ready to socialise with her at that level.

Her appointment didn't take long as she only needed a script. Perhaps the whole way of delivering repeat prescriptions needed to be revamped with quickie Skype consultations for regular patients.

When she arrived home, she went into her study and logged onto Skype herself to speak with Nicole. Having Martin link them up was a great advance on phone calls.

Nicole carried her iPad into the family room so she could get comfortable for a long chat. Gazing up at the face of her daughter while she was walking made Andrea a little disoriented, as if she were a patient on a gurney being wheeled into surgery. Yet at the same time she couldn't help noticing how like Brian Nicole was—the same crinkly smile lines and reliable good humour.

'I was talking about you with a friend five minutes ago. Wondering how you're getting on with RSVP.'

'I haven't plunged into that yet, I'm still finding out how it all works.'

Nicole's mobile rang then and she ran off with apologies and a promise to catch up tomorrow.

For once Andrea didn't mind the interruption. It saved her from having to compound her small fib. It hadn't occurred to her that her foray into online dating was already being chatted about with persons unknown. It was too soon yet to be talking about Ken; she'd have to think of other gossip or tidbits of news for Nicole, and that was another good reason to consider joining the croquet club.

Andrea skyped Jason instead. He was often hard to catch, but his green contact light was on.

'Hi, Mum.' He wore his usual big grin. She gazed at the cheerful look in his eyes. How wonderful Skype was. 'Great to hear from you.'

There was something about the relationship with a son that was so clear and uncomplicated—there were no agendas, no expectation he'd see the world the same way she did, and no perceived criticism ever seemed to worry him.

Truth to tell, as a teenager it rolled off him, even when he needed to take it on board. At that age Nicole had been very sensitive to any reproach, not that she had received many. And Jason didn't judge his mother about RSVP, in fact he didn't even seem to remember she'd signed up, though she'd told him all about it the last time they'd talked.

'When do you think you might visit?' Andrea asked.

'I'm pretty flat out.'

'That means the business is going well?'

'Exactly, I've tapped into the Aussie tourist market and it's flourishing.' He leaned back in his chair, arms folded, his familiar look of confidence. 'Everyone, but everyone, wants to be rock climbing or bungee jumping. I think I told you, I've taken on a business partner now, another expat. I look after the surf and climbing side of things and he does the rest. At the rate we're going we'll need more staff soon.'

That was wonderful news, but Andrea could see the chance of him coming home for a trip, let alone returning forever, was receding as his success increased. How good life must have been when sons followed their father's career and lived a stone's throw away. But imagine Jason as an accountant—he would have been bored to sobs. He needed a job and a life where he could burn up his energy finding adventure and creating it for others.

No, he would never come home. It seemed to be the way now. Children scattered around the world.

Yet it was worse for Sarah and her daughters. They lived farther away from their mother and weren't even in the same time zone. Poor Sas was going to need a lot of support when she uncovered the truth about Rob. She'd be devastated if Andrea's suspicions turned out to be true. Was it her role to tell Sarah, or should she wait and see how the flying visit to Sydney unfolded?

Chapter 21

Sarah signed the registration card at the check-in counter in the expansive foyer of the InterContinental Hotel, with its arched pillars rising up to vaulted ceilings, its flooding light and air of old-world glamour. Beside her was a huge crystal bowl of the shiniest apples she'd ever seen.

'Would you like another swipe card for your husband, Mrs Carpenter?' It was the young desk clerk drawing Sarah back to reality.

'No, thank you. One's fine. My husband won't be staying with me tonight,' she replied. She didn't add what she'd decided: *and he won't be staying with me again. Ever.*

It dawned on her that life wouldn't be as different without Rob as she might have imagined. In a sad way, she'd been living alone for years. She wondered if he ever brought work home to his Balmain pad, or did he find discussing medicine over dinner with the doppelganger so absorbing, so pleasurable, that he chose it over paperwork? Did he save all the time-consuming letters for his boring country life on Saturdays and Sundays where his compliant wife would let him get away with it?

* `

The bubbly spa was warm and intoxicating, and as Sarah slipped into it, she felt free in an unexpected way. It was reminiscent of that memorable final day at school when she'd raced out of the imposing gates of her private girls' school on the North Shore, exulting in the knowledge that she could now be the master of her own destiny. Only it hadn't quite turned out like that. Was this the gateway to her second chance? Did sixty-something women get another bite at life?

Although she was tempted to open the bottle of Moët from the bar fridge to add to her sense of decadence, she decided against it. She needed a clear head for her call to Rob. Wrapping herself in a soft white robe, she sat down at the head of the mahogany dining table in the living room and regarded the Lobster à l'Américaine she'd ordered. She couldn't possibly eat it all, but what the heck? She wasn't paying!

But first things first. Better get the phone call to Rob out of the way and set things up for tomorrow's meeting. No, call that tomorrow's denouement. It was seven forty-five by now, a time she never contacted him after once interrupting an important meeting. 'This is a bad time,' he'd grumbled. 'What do you want? I can't possibly talk.' Or so he'd said. Sarah realised now that she couldn't believe a single word he'd ever uttered. She pictured Rob and Penny—and Madeleine—sitting down to dinner at this very moment, probably with Rob about to carve the roast beef, something he'd never done in all their years of marriage. Carving a joint of meat would be something he did to impress the doppelganger, to appear the perfect father. Well, let him.

'Hi Rob, are you busy? In a meeting?'

'What is it, Sarah? Yes, I'm busy. This is an odd time for you to call.'

'I know, but I'm coming up to Sydney tomorrow. I've decided to book accommodation at the InterContinental. We could meet for dinner there.'

There was a long pause. Sarah could hear the television on in the background. Penny and Madeleine must have been told to shush!

'Why on earth are you coming to Sydney? I mean, it's a busy workday for me. I can't spend any time with you.'

Sarah was enjoying having him on the back foot, hearing him struggle to comprehend the logistics of her being in the same city as his other family without him having organised it. Maybe family number two had plans for the next evening.

'I didn't expect you to be free. Anyway, I've got an appointment in the city later in the morning and then some shopping to do. I was thinking dinner tomorrow night at the hotel restaurant? Like a date night? It seems ages since we've talked to each other.'

'What do you mean? I saw you on Monday morning.'

Not unsurprising that Rob skipped over the fact that she had an appointment in Sydney. He knew nothing about her life, rarely asked about her activities. She could fly to Africa and go on an overnight safari as long as she was back by Thursday evening, ready to pour his gin and tonic when he returned from Sydney. He wouldn't notice her absence. Not that she wanted him to know that her appointment was with Collins Trent Forrest, the solicitors her side of the family had used for aeons. She was about to lock in Richard Arnold, the best divorce lawyer in the company, confident he would be one of the best in the state. Rob would have no idea of her plans.

'Anyway, I'm operating late tomorrow, and I have to do post-op rounds after that. Can you cancel the visit? Tee it up again when it suits me?'

Typical. *When it suits me!* Her whole life had been geared to suiting him. *Not anymore.*

'Not possible, I'm afraid,' Sarah struggled to keep the lid on her pleasure at hearing him squirm. 'Here's a better idea. Why don't I come out to your hospital digs? I've never seen where you stay when you're in Sydney. It'd be fun. I don't mind if it's late.'

There was a long pause. In normal circumstances, Sarah would rush to fill in the awkwardness, to placate Rob as though she'd caused his discomfort, but she let the silence play out. This was too delicious for words.

'The hospital's right up on the North Shore. It's not easy to get to without a car. Especially at night. You wouldn't like the accommodation anyway. All brown walls and uncomfortable furniture.'

Sarah gripped the mobile. *What a liar!*

'Even better,' she said. 'How remiss of me not to redecorate the space to make it more like home. I'm sure the hospital wouldn't mind if I gave it a makeover.' She had to stop herself from giggling.

'No, don't worry about it.' He was sounding panicky now. 'If you must come up to Sydney tomorrow, I'll rearrange my schedule and meet you at the hotel for dinner. Make it seven thirty. But give me more notice next time, please.'

'Sure, I understand how difficult it must be for you. See you at seven thirty,' Sarah said before hanging up. *And here's to it becoming much more difficult for you in the months to come.*

Her heart was thumping, but she was proud of herself, of the way she'd kept her cool and levelled her voice to remove any emotion. She'd annoyed him without giving an inkling of her true intent. Very satisfying. Tomorrow night was panning out exactly as she wanted, meeting in a place of her choosing under conditions that she'd control. A small victory at last.

She sank onto a long, padded couch under the window to catch her breath, closing her eyes for a few minutes. The tsunami of emotions that had flooded her this past twenty-four hours, and prevented her contemplating anything more than the next step, was waning, and a vacuum was replacing it. She was devoid of plans beyond tomorrow's meeting, her future unravelling ahead of her without the one person she'd always assumed would be by her side.

Except the truth was he hadn't been by her side, not for years and years. Her husband, her partner, was an illusion, a chimera. What would life be without the role she'd played so well for so long?

Her phone gave the familiar swoosh of a message arriving.

Are you okay? Call me anytime. A xx

Andrea. Always there for her, but Sarah couldn't face explanations right now. Couldn't even be coherent. Maybe tomorrow, after she'd seen her lawyer.

Talking it through with Anna or Lucy might help, but the time zones were all wrong to call either of the girls. Besides, what would she say? They had no idea their father was this sort of man—a cheater who'd had a child with another woman, who was blatantly living a second life with no concern for his first family. She imagined their hurt, especially when they discovered the child was now a woman, almost their age, and was practising as a doctor, the one profession he'd long steered them towards. What a shock for them.

A bombshell of this magnitude would have to be approached carefully, groundwork laid first. Maybe she should talk about a temporary separation at first, mention that she and their father needed some space. No. That sounded corny even to her. Why would she need space from someone who both the girls and she knew was so often MIA?

Sarah rubbed her eyes. These were conversations to be had later, when she was home again.

Home. Funny concept now. Her eyes wandered over the city skyline, taking in the beautiful but remote lights and harbour water that stretched out in front of her. Where was home? Was it still Albury now she'd be there alone? The rumour mill would be churning. Then there was their big house on the hill, the Best House in Albury. Empty, abandoned, maybe never to be filled with the sound of a happy family again. What would be the point of living there?

And with the exception of Andrea, who were her real friends? Not the couples she and Rob socialised with, the people she met at drug company dinners, nor the people she knew from her hospital committees or gallery boards. She had few real confidantes. A knot of nausea burned in her stomach as she realised her own emotional life had been sacrificed for so many years as she'd worshipped at the altar of Rob.

If the question had been asked of her before today, she'd have said, without hesitation, that she believed in women's equality. Of course she did. She believed in women's independence, in their right to become whatever they wanted, and yet … she'd hardly lived that life. She was nothing but a fraud who'd set a terrible example for her girls.

Then she pictured Anna and Lucy, and managed to smile despite her pain. No, they were the epitome of the modern, well-educated, independent woman. She must have done something right. And when this was all sorted, she could go and visit them. Take in the Tate with Anna, the Met with Lucy.

The prospect lightened her mood. How she missed them. Now she could fly off on a whim, no worrying about how Rob would manage without her. *Ha!* Let that Balmain woman become his doormat now. Sarah's days of sacrifice were over.

She'd spent her life in suspended animation keeping her man happy long enough. But Rob wasn't happy, that was clear. He was so bored or selfish or out of touch with his family that he'd made the choices he had.

She stood up and moved back to the table, lifted the silver cloche and picked over the lobster waiting to be eaten, the tomato-wine sauce now cold, congealed. She looked at it with disgust before turfing it into the bin.

What a waste.

Chapter 22

Libby was trying to persuade her workmates to provide headshots for Bridal Bliss, the new website she and Kate were planning for their wedding business. Surprising Kate with stylish photos would be a thrill for her, and perhaps a small way of saying thanks for all her support. Imagine if they could establish themselves as the go-to organisers for weddings in the area. But though Amy and Michaela were very keen to have a makeover and to learn professional hints, they baulked at the idea of being exposed to the public by appearing on a website.

'Oh no, I'm not good-looking enough to be used in an ad like that,' Amy protested. 'Michaela, you'd be fine—you have that lovely fair complexion. But look at me, I'm getting crow's feet. Who wants to see big dark circles on a website?'

'You'd be lovely,' Michaela said, 'but my cheeks are *sooo* fat, I'd come across like a moonface.'

'No, you wouldn't. Those photos of you on your Facebook page are terrific,' Libby said. 'Both of you,' she added, in case Amy worried she was only referring to Michaela.

'And you'll both think differently when you see how you look after I'm done with you,' Libby said.

'I wouldn't mind a few tips,' Amy said. 'Come on, Michaela, I'll do it if you will. And it will help Libby's new business.'

So instead of going to the tearoom for a drink, they went into the back office, surrounded by stationery, and well away from the teaching staff or any students dropping by to hand in assignments. Libby applied the lotions with deft confidence.

'See? A touch of concealer will do wonders for shadows under the eyes.'

She was careful to stay well away from words like bags, or crow's feet, or even dark circles. Shadows might come from nothing more worrying than an unflattering angle of the sun.

Amy beamed at her reflection in the vanity mirror Libby had set up, moving her head from side to side.

'Thank you, that makes such a difference. You're a wizard. I'll bet this Martin guy has his eye on you.'

'I'm not finished yet,' Libby said, ignoring the reference to Martin. She must've been talking about him around the office more than she realised. *Martin says to tailor-make your password. Martin says this is a helpful shortcut in Word.*

'The secret of good make-up is for it to look natural,' she continued. 'So men think, "You're looking well today", not "This beauty is way out of my league".'

But Amy was not to be thwarted.

'Has Martin asked you out yet?'

Libby focused on the beige foundation. 'And here's a great tip on how to be photogenic. *Squinching.*'

Her pirouette worked.

'What the heck is squinching?'

'It's a trick models and actors use. Make your eyes tight as if you're about to squint.'

Amy leaned forward to check in the mirror that the instructions were working.

'Now relax your top lids a little. Yes. See? The lower lids are doing the pinching. So we get squinching. No, no, you had it right before. You don't want a squint as if you forgot your contacts.'

Amy laughed. 'Without the squinch, I look like a deer trapped in headlights.'

'Everyone does,' Libby assured her. 'But you're both going to look like real pros once we get you up on our website. Let's take these photos, we need to get back to work.'

They returned to the front office where Paul, the head of department, was waiting with a coffee mug in his hand, looking adrift.

'Ah, I was wondering what happened to you,' he said. He paused a moment, then smiled. 'You're all looking very well today.'

* * *

Sarah opened the curtains of her hotel room and drank in the distant harbour view glinting in the sunlight. That she'd slept so well and woken so refreshed was nothing short of astonishing. Her forty-year marriage was a farce, her husband had betrayed her in an appalling way, and yet a new future was not only beckoning, it was opening its arms and singing out for her to join in.

She should be grieving, in floods of tears, rending her garments, calling on everyone she knew to come and soothe her and make it better. Oh, she was angry all right, she'd make Rob pay. What was that fabulous line from Ivana Trump in *The First Wives' Club*? 'Don't get mad. Get everything!'

156

But perhaps Sarah was too old to experience the depth of emotions she would have felt years earlier. Maybe deep down, she'd felt unloved for such a long time that she'd filled her days with busyness and meetings, trawling through the colour lift-outs of weekend newspapers in search of the perfect recipe, the ideal throw for the living room, and organising the masked balls and champagne suppers for charity. Maybe that's how she'd ended up blotting out her own needs.

Marking time, yes, that was it—ever since the girls left home, she'd been waiting for the next stage of her life to begin, denying the possibility that that may never happen. If only she'd known about Rob's secret life earlier, when the girls were young, she could have waited their schooldays out and then escaped the day after Lucy left home. No, the same day. The very next flight. Ten whole years wasted on that man since Anna and Lucy had moved away from Albury.

Now she could travel whenever, unimpeded by a grumpy companion who wouldn't take sufficient time off work for a proper holiday, and when he did travel, always linked it to a conference. Away at lectures all day, leaving her on her own to shop or be trundled around in a minibus with other wives she didn't know and who would be replaced before the next trip by their cosmetic surgeon husbands in need of a more up-to-date model. Perhaps he so often dissuaded her from accompanying him overseas because he took someone else. *His floozy.*

Not anymore. It was her time now. She'd be able to spend holidays with the girls as often as she wanted. How marvellous would that be? Maybe neither of them would be upset to hear that she'd left their father. They might even congratulate her on this flight to freedom, tell her that she's being *empowered* and *strong*, that her liberation hadn't come soon enough. They were clever enough to identify his self-absorption years ago, and vote with their feet.

Time for Sarah to do the same—and Sydney was the best place to begin the journey.

*

She sat in the soft leather chair at the black and white salon in Double Bay—*Le Bain de Jouvence*—hoping that Chelsea would forgive her for ducking into another hairdresser. It would only be this once.

'I'm after a stunning new look,' she told the young stylist, Ellen. 'A cut, colour and style that would turn a man's eye.' One that would make Rob realise that he'd made a terrible mistake, that he'd lost something important.

Ellen gave a wise nod. Perhaps it was the sort of request she got every day.

'At my age,' Sarah continued, 'I'm not expecting you to turn me into a supermodel, but I was born the same year as Christie Brinkley, if that's any help.'

Ellen looked confused. 'I don't think I know a Christie ... Brickley?' she started to say.

Sarah smiled. Of course not. No one born in the nineties would know someone that old.

'Don't worry. I know miracles are difficult, but do your best to make me look gorgeous.'

'Your colour's great,' said Ellen, lifting Sarah's hair and running her fingers through the blonde locks, 'and you have a very stylish cut. In fact ...' She stepped back to look at Sarah with a critical eye. 'Beautiful bone structure and great skin. I think you look fabulous already.'

'Wow. Thank you. That's what I needed to hear,' Sarah said. 'I'm from out of town, but Chelsea, my usual hairdresser, is on the mark with foils and cuts. But today I was thinking of something audacious and different.'

'Not a problem,' said Ellen. 'I'll get a couple of magazines and we can discuss the sort of look you're after.'

Two hours later, Sarah stepped out of the salon, exultant about the new sculpted cut that underlined her high cheek-bones. Foxy. Definitely looking foxy, and ready to start a new phase of her life.

This would make a statement at dinner tonight, one that'd destabilise Rob. She'd be a new woman. Not that he knew the old Sarah all that well, but with a revamped look and a chic new outfit—that was a Zara Lampelli boutique she'd passed on the way in—she'd be able to play her hand to win.

*

Judging by the greeting Richard Arnold gave her, she'd hit the mark. He was her longstanding solicitor, but more important than that were the personal ties that went back to when he was at school at Shore with her elder brother. He gave her a warm kiss on the cheek.

'Sarah, it's been ages—and you're looking so well.'

Richard was being more attentive than she remembered, but that may have been nothing more than good business practice, especially once he heard about her divorce plans and the business it might bring.

They sat in his large, sunlit office at an asymmetrical low table. Over a freshly brewed coffee, Sarah explained what had happened.

'I suspect Rob may have hidden assets to go with his hidden life,' she said. 'I've discovered he's living in a glossy Balmain apartment with a woman called Penny Stevenson.'

Richard asked for the address and jotted a note in his file. 'If he's bought a property with another woman, he may have put it in her name,' he said. 'That would make it hers.'

'Most of our assets are in my name, though,' Sarah said. 'For tax purposes, because I don't earn an income. I'm not sure if that will help?'

Richard inclined his head as he made another note, concentrating on the details. 'Don't worry—leave it with me. I'll make sure it's an advantage. Rob won't want to go to court. Judges don't like it if the joint earnings of the marriage have been spent on another woman. And it usually is a woman. If he's taken major steps to dodge tax, then the ATO can get involved. That's the last thing he'd want.

'We'll dig out every morsel of information about his assets—that includes his superannuation of course. You're entitled to half. Relax, Sarah, this type of law is our bread and butter.'

'Excellent,' she replied. She replaced her empty cup on the coffee table and stood to leave. It had been a satisfying meeting and she was comfortable she'd locked in the best representation she could. Her future and that of Rob's *legitimate* children were all that mattered now.

Chapter 23

In the foyer waiting for the lift to arrive, Sarah checked her iPhone for messages. Nothing from Rob. Good. He must have managed to rearrange his schedule so he could meet her for dinner by seven thirty. The possibility that she might arrive in a cab at his North Shore hospital and discover that he had no accommodation there, no brown-walled shoebox, must have given him the heebie-jeebies!

It was Andrea who'd left her a message—a short text sent an hour ago. *Are you ok? Pls text or call. I'm worried.*

Will call soon. Lots to discuss, she shot back.

It was three thirty, plenty of time before dinner, so Sarah walked the few blocks from Collins Trent Forrest's offices to the hotel. Stopping to speak with the concierge, she ordered ribbon sandwiches and a pot of Irish breakfast tea to be delivered to her suite.

She knew she'd been abrupt with Andrea yesterday morning, but her expertise would be a godsend now. She'd have plenty of tips on how to approach the discussion that was looming with Rob.

'Thanks for the text, Andrea,' Sarah said when they finally made contact. 'Sorry I couldn't talk yesterday morning. I knew you'd worry, but—'

'No apology needed. Are you back home?' Sarah could hear the relief in Andrea's voice. 'Do you want me to come around?'

'No, I'm still in Sydney. I don't know where to begin, but there's one thing I do know. My marriage is over.' Sarah ran her fingers through her hair, forgetting about her new style. The enormity of her own words made her head spin. *My marriage is over.* Once you said it aloud like that, it made it true. She sank onto the king-size bed. 'The woman who looks like Anna but isn't. The one we saw on the screensaver ... it turns out she's Rob's daughter after all.'

'Oh no. Sas, I'm sorry. That's awful, truly awful.'

'I've found out that low-lifer's got a secret life up here and she's a part of it. Not only that, she's a doctor, the very thing he always wanted our girls to be.' Hot tears welled in her eyes. 'And he's living in Balmain during the week. With her.' She took a sharp bite of her sandwich and swallowed the mouthful whole.

'With her? Living with her? How is that possible?'

'Oh, it gets worse. He lives with her mother, too. Some woman called Penny Stevenson, in a fabulous penthouse. Newly renovated apartments with a trendy cafe underneath.' It was the final straw, for some odd reason. 'They all have breakfast there in the mornings, playing happy families. God knows how long this little ménage à trois has been going on.'

'Are you sure? I can't believe he's living with them. What has Rob said?'

'We haven't spoken about this yet, that's not happening until tonight. He has no idea that I know.'

'How *do* you know then? Could you be wrong?'

Sarah paused. Could she be wrong? Perhaps she'd assumed too much, jumped to conclusions.

No, not possible, she decided. The evidence was overwhelming: Rob's secret phone burning a hole in his desk drawer, a phone that in normal circumstances she would never have accessed; the screenshot of her daughter's double with Rob's arm around her; Madeleine's admission of a father-daughter relationship between them; the letterbox in Balmain. And then there were the two lovely women in the cafe, who knew the three as a family, a family who drank cappuccinos together in the mornings.

'No, I'm not wrong. Believe it or not, I made an appointment with the daughter this afternoon—actually spoke to her. And you'll love this. Remember that series we were addicted to a few years back—*Revenge*? I chose Emily Thorne as my pseudonym!'

'No! You devil.' Andrea laughed. 'What if she'd guessed?'

'Too busy to have caught the series, I suspect. Anyway, she had no reason to be suspicious, I presented as a regular patient. My acting was quite good, if I do say so myself.'

'I've never doubted that you could have been our first Cate Blanchett, had you chosen that path. But what else did you discover? How many other children does he have then? Is he in touch with them too?'

'Good question. It did cross my mind that Madeleine—that's the girl's name—might have a brother or a sister.'

'Well, I expect there were quite a few more. Up to twelve others, I'd guess. They weren't so careful to limit numbers in those days.'

Sarah had taken a sip of her tea, but a sharp intake of breath sent it down the wrong way. She began coughing and thumped her chest. It was a good minute before she could speak again.

'Twelve children?' she spluttered, trying to catch her breath. 'Twelve? What are you talking about? Who's "they"?'

It was Andrea's turn to hesitate.

'Um ... the fertility specialists. Isn't that how this Madeleine was conceived? Using Rob's sperm donations?'

Sarah's mind deadened, her body went still as if it were no longer her own. Andrea may as well have been speaking Russian. Or Latin.

'You didn't know that? Did Rob not tell you about his time at the Royal Charlotte and the progress they were making helping infertile couples?'

Sarah opened her mouth but no words came.

'Sas, are you still there? I hate that you're in Sydney and I'm not with you. Say something.'

'I'm here.' Sarah managed to find her voice. 'And no, Rob didn't tell me. I recall years ago him mentioning the hospital needed sperm donors. I said I'd be uncomfortable with that, with the possibility of someone knocking at the door in twenty or thirty years' time claiming to be his child. He never mentioned it again.'

She racked her brains trying to remember their conversation, but it hadn't lingered in her memory. They'd decided no and that was the end of it. Or so she'd believed. But Andrea seemed to have a different view.

'It seems that you know more about my husband than I do.'

'I don't know for sure.'

Oh, yes. Try and backtrack now, Sarah thought.

'It was only because I was working there at the same time, counselling married couples who couldn't conceive. It was confidential information.'

'It was enough to make you think Rob was donating sperm,' Sarah said with difficulty. 'So why did you think that?'

She was aware that her voice had developed a sharp edge, that the space between them was stretching to a chasm, but she refused to make it easy. She had to know every last detail before she met up with Rob.

'I saw him visit the laboratory. Lots of times. And he had no reason to be there otherwise.' Andrea sounded reluctant. 'Plus, they identified the donors by initials, and I started to notice 'RC' was listed as the donor sperm on several patients' files after his visits. But I didn't know, not for sure. I still don't. Back then, the files were locked, the donors were guaranteed lifelong anonymity. Secrecy was paramount. How could any of them—how could this Madeleine—have found out?'

'You've suspected for years that *my* husband donated sperm to random couples and you never breathed a word to me? That there might be, what—twelve or more little Robs and Robyns running around the country with their stethoscopes in hand and you never warned me? Never bothered to tell his wife, the mother of his children? Never a quiet word in my ear. My best friend!'

'My work's confidential. I couldn't tell you. I didn't *know*.'

'So you looked the other way and decided to ignore the evidence that was dancing before your eyes.' Sarah could hear the bitterness in her own voice. 'History's littered with people like you. They're called cowards.'

'Sarah, I'm sorry, but what could I—'

'Don't bother contacting me again.'

'No, no ... Listen, we'll talk when you get back.'

'Not happening, Andrea. Just not happening.'

Chapter 24

Sarah struggled to get her head around the shock. Rob had chosen to donate to a dozen or more infertile strangers, without consulting her further *and he'd never breathed a word of their existence*. This was worse than if he'd had an affair with Madeleine's mother years ago, even worse than finding their names nestled on the Balmain letterbox. To think he'd kept this massive secret for over thirty years. And somehow, despite promises that donors would always remain anonymous, he and Madeleine had managed to find each other, maybe even sought each other out, and he'd gone on to play an important role in her life.

She leaned forward, head in her hands, and rocked back and forth. *And to find out that her best friend had known about it.* No sense of empowerment now. She was adrift—betrayal by Rob and now Andrea, her closest friend, was too much. And yet, in a few hours, she had to confront him, tell him she knew his secrets and that she was planning a new life where he would have no part. She'd need to pull herself together, not play the victim.

She stood up and went over to the corner window, wanting a glimpse of light. Across the road in an office block she could see all the workers at their desks and filing cabinets, looking as if everything was normal, as if this were a day like any other.

She turned away and began to pace the room. Maybe it was better that she was aware now, rather than later, that there might be more children. Maybe he had a whole menagerie of sons and daughters scattered around the country. What a shock if Rob had sprung that on her tonight. Madeleine's mother wasn't a mere notch in his belt, an affair from years ago that had unwittingly produced a daughter. He was actually living with Madeleine and that floozy.

She felt her throat constrict and a hint of nausea mingled with her fury. She had to find out more. There was no way she could trust Rob to tell her the truth.

His Galaxy smartphone, the one that had started all this trouble, was sitting on her bedside table. That's what she needed. There weren't many contacts in it, but Madeleine Stevenson hadn't been a lone listing. There'd been at least another four, maybe five, unknown names and numbers there. Sarah had concentrated on the one female contact because of the screensaver with the two women pictured, but perhaps the male names in the phone were also his children. Maybe this was the contact list for his offspring, his *donor* offspring—or at least the ones he juggled in his other life. She grabbed the phone and turned it on.

Scrolling down the names in his *Contacts* list, she reached for the complimentary biro from the bedside table and jotted them all down, trying to commit them to memory: Matthew Brown, Scott Jacobs, Ben Wilson, Nathan Pickering. It might be worthwhile checking them against the medical practitioner's register again—that had worked with Madeleine. His influence with these 'anonymous' children could have stretched back years for all Sarah knew. He may have championed them through medical school too, like he seemed to have done for the doppelganger.

She found a few Matthew Browns and Ben Wilsons practising in Sydney and around various Australian states. Generic names. There was nothing that pointed to them being connected to Rob. She could hardly zigzag over the country making false appointments everywhere to check them out.

She tried to channel Martin's tutorials—what would he do to chase up information about someone he didn't know? Checking out Facebook was a possibility. If only she'd paid more attention to the details. The day that Kate had challenged them all about their social media skills, she'd agreed that yes, of course she had a Facebook page, but the truth was she never used her account and had no idea how it operated.

All the young ones seemed devoted to theirs, recording the details of their lives. Every time some Australian backpacker got into trouble in an out-of-the-way corner of the world, it was a given that news programs would broadcast photographs and details lifted straight from the wayfarer's Facebook page.

She logged into her own sparsely chronicled account and typed *Nathan Pickering* into the *Find Friends* section, hoping there wouldn't be too many people with that name in Australia.

She was in luck—only three—so she scrolled through the photographs of events in the lives of these people she didn't even know—their mates, their rave parties, their sometimes drunken antics.

As she stared at them they laughed, they leered, they Liked. It didn't seem right to be looking them up, intruding on their space—much too voyeuristic. She'd have assumed that you had to be a 'Friend' to access all this personal information, but based on what she was seeing, it was splattered right before your eyes, no questions asked.

She pored over a group photo posted by one of the Nathan Pickerings, then sat bolt upright. This Nathan-person was standing in a cheerful group with four other men ... and Madeleine Stevenson. *Rob was at its centre.* As if to rub in more salt, the caption read 'Me and my "Family". LOL!'

Sarah's heart was racing, and with a sharp click, she logged out of her account and out of all the lives of all the Nathan Pickerings in the country.

Enough! I don't need to know any more. She sat still, blood pounding in her ears. This nightmare had to end as soon as possible. Bring on the meeting, bring on the confrontation: this sham life couldn't be over soon enough.

* * *

BEEP BEEP BEEP ...

The bedside machines in the postoperative recovery unit sounded with hypnotic regularity as Denise sat waiting for Stan to wake from his anaesthetic.

He looked so relaxed when he was asleep. Age lines smoothed out, and as she watched him, she was reminded of the slight, young electrician who'd come into her classroom late one afternoon, forty years ago. He needed to fix the dodgy light switch, he told her. As he worked, he chatted at length about his favourite school teacher, and had her laughing about the scrapes he'd got into. They shared a similar sense of humour and she'd liked him straightaway. So before she knew it she had a boyfriend.

Two years later they were married. That was how it worked in those days. No living together, no serial boyfriends—you met, you liked one another, you married and then you had children.

Except the last bit hadn't happened for them, and so they'd sort of floated apart. No fights, no animosity, nothing more than a fading away—to another partner in Stan's case—before a very civil divorce.

Denise turned around as she heard someone walk into the room behind her. It was Stan's surgeon, an imposing man, mid-fifties with a spotted red bow tie.

'Mrs Robertson,' he acknowledged, looking somewhere over Denise's head.

'Yes.'

She and Stan had discussed what her role would be around his surgery, and come to an agreement that as far as the health professionals were concerned, she was his 'wife' and entitled to sit by the bedside and be included in all the medical discussions about his health. After all, they still had a marriage certificate somewhere, and nobody was going to ask if they also had a *decree absolute*.

'It went very well,' the surgeon announced, his voice a little louder than necessary. 'It's a complex procedure—new techniques needing a high level of surgical skill—but superbly done, so there shouldn't be any of the usual side effects of prostate surgery.'

Denise hid a smile, trying to look impassive. Better to have a surgeon with oodles of self-confidence than a diffident one who addressed his shoes when he spoke to his patients. He left as quickly as he'd arrived, without waiting to speak to Stan, perhaps eager to tell his other patients how well their surgeries had been performed.

Stan stirred in his bed, turned his head and saw Denise sitting by his bedside. 'You're still here,' he said in a hoarse voice.

'Of course.'

'Good. I need to ask you something. Something important ...'

He wasn't fully awake; his lips were parched and his words slurred, but there was an urgency in his tone that made her lean forward.

'Yes? What is it, Stan?'

He waved an arm in the air as though grasping for words, licked his lips, then gripped her forearm and looked at her with a serious expression as he pulled her towards him and their eyes met.

'Have we had any bids yet?'

It took all of Denise's strength to keep a straight face. 'We're in the hospital recovery unit, Stan. Not supposed to use my mobile phone. And to be honest, it wasn't my main worry today. I could slip outside and check if you'd like?'

He nodded, screwing up his face in an effort at concentration. 'That would be most helpful,' he said, dropping back onto his pillow.

Denise had to stifle another smile. He sounded nothing like his usual knockabout self. *Most helpful*? He never used pompous phrases like that.

She took the opportunity to grab a coffee from the hospital's vending machine on her way out to the car park, but regretted it on the first sip. As appealing as sump oil. The nearest nandina bush, ubiquitous around city buildings and looking scraggly and unloved, took the brunt of the hot beverage, but it was a hardy variety. It'd cope better than her stomach.

She logged into their sale site on her phone, guessing it would be too early for much activity, but already there were up to a dozen watchers.

'Good news,' she told Stan when he finally opened his eyes again, twenty minutes after she returned to the recovery unit. 'There's quite a bit of interest already.'

'I should think so,' he said groggily. 'It was state-of-the-art surgery after all. And superbly done.'

'No, not your operation,' she began.

'What was that about a … high level of surgical kill?'

'Not kill …'

But Stan was asleep already, his chin tucked into the white linen sheet. And that was the reason, Denise realised, why his surgeon had advised him against making any important decisions too soon after surgery.

Chapter 25

At seven thirty, Sarah waited in the hotel's dining room for Rob to appear. Normally, she would have revelled in the calm beauty of such an elegant room, in the massive flower arrangements like works of art on the sideboards, their mirrored reflections enhancing the display, in the dessert trolleys the colours of the rainbow. But not tonight. Tonight, she wanted to escape her marriage as quickly as possible.

He'd be late, he always was. It was the story of her life. Always waiting for him—so busy with his practice, with his patients—always the second or third priority. She'd waited at home, in empty hotel lobbies during conferences, in theatre foyers as the bells shrilled, hopeful he'd make it on time, this once. And no doubt he'd arrive even later than usual tonight, to make the point that she should never have sprung a surprise like this.

After the day's revelations, she'd taken less time with her appearance than originally planned, because she didn't care enough now to want to make him jealous. She was no longer bothered if he regretted his choices either. This stranger she'd been living with had become a nasty little irrelevance, one that she was itching to discard.

Now seven fifty, with the waiter hovering, she figured she might as well order. If she'd already chosen and eaten something before he arrived, it would save her time. It wasn't as if she wanted to linger over dinner with the bastard. She'd tell him her decision, then up and leave.

'A dozen oysters, please.'

'And did you want to order for your companion?' The waiter gestured to the still empty seat. His hands were slim and expressive and his smile inviting.

She waved away the suggestion. 'He may be a while. But bring a bottle of champagne. A good one.'

Rob hated champagne.

'Ah, a celebration. Certainly, madam. I'll find you something special.'

Half an hour later, when she'd almost finished her oyster platter and was onto her second glass of bubbly, Rob appeared opposite her, pulling out the chair and sitting down heavily.

'Well, this is unusual. What was so important that it couldn't wait til the weekend?' he said.

No greeting, no kiss, no comment about her new look. There was no apology for keeping her waiting almost an hour, either. But that was normal.

'Champagne?' She held up her glass.

He grimaced and gestured to the waiter. 'The wine list, please.'

'I may as well come to the point,' she said, looking directly at him. 'Our marriage isn't working for me anymore.'

He withdrew a little, the unexpectedness of her comment seeming to unsettle him. He looked around the table, as if he wished the wine list were there to hide behind. His eyes then scanned the dining room, but there was no escape. *Good.*

'What do you mean? You were fine when I left on Monday morning. Nothing's changed.'

Maybe nothing's changed for you.

'I'm not happy that you're never home. First it was a day a week in Sydney, then it slowly increased. For ages now, it's been four—'

'I have to earn, you know,' he interrupted. 'There's more work in Sydney, a much better income.'

'But how much money do we need? You don't have to support the girls anymore. We've paid off the house. We never travel for pleasure. Why, exactly do you need to make so much money?'

'For you to drink expensive champagne,' he shot back. 'And for my retirement, of course.'

He didn't say 'our' retirement, the louse.

'And when will that be? I'm marking time, waiting for a future that's moving out of my grasp. And the present's no fun. The girls have gone. I don't have grandchildren, and if I did they'd be on the other side of the world. You have no interests you share with me—'

'What about all your own interests?'

'Such as?'

'I don't know. All those committees you're on.' He shrugged. 'How would I know?'

Sarah wanted to slap his smug face. *Control,* she told herself. *Keep control.*

'That's what I'm beginning to see. You know nothing about me, and I'm realising I know nothing about you. Would you consider cutting Sydney back to two days a week, so we can do more together in Albury, or go travelling, maybe tour the French canals? I was looking forward to that when we retired.'

'I can't do that,' Rob said. 'I've given the hospital a commitment to work for at least another five years.'

He focused on the red wine that had been brought for tasting and tapped his glass for it to be filled. Sarah put her hand over her own glass and shook her head at the waiter.

'And you didn't discuss it with me. Interesting.' She leaned forward across the table. 'Okay, here's a better proposal. Why don't we sell up in Albury, and I'll move here? We can buy somewhere close to your work. The North Shore's lovely.'

She wondered how long this would go on, with Rob slipping and sliding around the conversation, and she pretending their life was a perfectly normal one.

'You'd hate living here,' he said. 'Your friends are in Albury. It's where the girls grew up. And I need an escape to the country on weekends after my busy week and you provide that so well for me.' He smiled his charming smile.

Flattery. Way too late. How could I have ever been seduced by that?

'I don't think I'd hate it here. I've had a great day today.' She took a slow sip of her bubbly. 'There's so much more to do in Sydney, don't you think? So many interesting people.'

'Sarah, it's not going to happen. I'm not winding back my work here, and you living in Sydney during the week wouldn't work. Sometimes my days don't finish until after midnight. You'd get lonely.'

The last refuge of the scoundrel. Make it sound like you're only thinking of my needs.

'Now, I need to order. I have to get back to the hospital for a late check of my patients.' He said it with the finality of an exasperated parent talking to a whinging child.

Sarah began to spread butter on her bread roll. 'You won't be staying with me tonight then?'

'That would mean driving back to the hospital after dinner, then back here again late, only to have to return to the hospital in the morning. I told you, it was inconvenient of you to come without notice. So no, I won't be staying here tonight.'

'Good. That's what I told the clerk on the front desk.'

'What?' Rob was examining the menu in the dim light of the restaurant, giving her half an ear as usual.

'When he offered me a room swipe for you. I said you wouldn't be staying. I told him you'd probably spend the evening at Madeleine Stevenson's'.

That got his attention. A flicker of disquiet rippled across his face but he shut it down in an instant.

'What on earth are you talking about?'

'You must know who Madeleine Stevenson is. Isn't she the one you see when you're in Sydney?'

Sarah could see panic rising in Rob's eyes, before he lowered his head, rubbed his forehead with both hands and frowned. He sighed before finally looking at her.

'It's not what it seems, Sarah.' He took a gulp of wine. 'Madeleine's not my girlfriend, if that's what you're implying. I've been trying to work out a way to tell you about her and I'm sorry I haven't talked to you yet. The truth is, many years ago, I donated to an IVF Clinic in Sydney, to help infertile couples. It was before you and I had talked about sperm donation and decided we wouldn't go there. Madeleine, it turns out, is the product of my one and only gift. And she managed to track me down a few weeks ago wanting contact. She was curious about me. I can't tell you what a shock it was, because when I donated, we were promised details would never be released.'

Sarah continued to look directly at Rob, but he shifted his eyes.

'Is that the truth? That you only met her recently?'

177

Rob nodded with fervour.

'I promise you. I admit I've visited her once, to get to know her a bit.'

'What does she do? Where does she work?'

Rob shrugged. 'She's, she's a … a physiotherapist, I think. Works somewhere in the city. I don't know a lot. It's been such a surprise. I'm disappointed you'd accuse me of having an affair. I wouldn't jeopardise our marriage, what we have in Albury.' He leaned across the table and rested his hand gently on hers. 'It needn't affect our future.' In that moment, Sarah lost the last atom of respect she had for him.

She withdrew her hand. 'But if that's the case, why do you live in a Balmain apartment when you're in Sydney? Why is your name on the letterbox there, next to Penny Stevenson's? And how could you have celebrated Madeleine's graduation five years ago if you only met her recently? And don't forget Matt Brown and Ben Wilson and Nathan Pickering. Oh, and Scott Jacobs too. What about them? You know, the sons you're in contact with but never bothered mentioning to me. Or did they all magically appear in the last few weeks too?'

He shifted in his seat, mute. At least he had the decency—or was it only common sense?—to realise that in the face of her detailed knowledge, a denial would be pointless. She had the upper hand at last, and not only in their conversation.

'So, you can see why our marriage isn't working for me anymore. What a sham. For years you've been trashing the relationship we had, and for that, I hate you.' She gathered her room pass and reading glasses from the table, ready to leave. 'I've seen Richard, my family's lawyer, so you'd better get a solicitor sorted out soon. They can arrange the settlement. And don't bother coming home to Albury tomorrow—I'll be calling the locksmith as soon as I'm back. The removalists will pack up all your stuff and deliver it to your Albury rooms. Or would you prefer it goes to Balmain? Apartment 24, isn't it?'

She grasped the half-filled bottle of champagne to take with her to the suite. There was a whiff of flowers and berries as she lifted it. The waiter had been right. It was indeed a celebration.

Chapter 26

Libby ranged through the contents of her now dated wardrobe—her clothes were so two years ago. Most days, she was as confident in choosing the perfect outfit as she was in applying her cosmetics, but today she was shilly-shallying, laying every shirt, dress and pair of trousers in her wardrobe on the bed.

Relax, she berated herself. *This is just an informal business meeting to set up the website.*

But presentation was so important, and today she wanted her self-confidence to come to the fore.

She stepped into her favourite wrap dress and checked the mirror. Yes, an oldie but a goodie; the peacock blue suited her colouring well, and the style showed off her figure without screaming 'all dressed up'. She slipped on a pair of pumps and then changed her mind for ballet flats. She was tall enough; there was no point in towering over Kate.

This wedding planning venture could put her back on the path to security. Her nervous flutter had everything to do with that and nothing to do with Martin.

When she arrived at Kate's house, his white Audi was already parked in the driveway. Libby hurried up to the front door, gave a quick knock and went in without waiting for an answer.

'It's me,' she called, as she walked towards the kitchen-cum-family room where Kate and Martin were set up at the large table.

Kate's golden retriever came bounding up in her usual frenzy of welcome.

'Hi Molly! How's my favourite girl?' She bent to give the dog a tickle under its velvet chin. 'You can smell the treat I brought, can't you?'

Kate was pouring Martin a glass of wine across the table, and looked up with a welcoming smile. 'And a treat for Libby, too?' she asked, hovering the wine bottle over an empty glass.

'Yes, please. I need a drink. I barely slept last night. Can't wait to get our website up and running. And thank you so much, Martin.'

She joined them at the table and lifted her glass. He was wearing light tan chinos with a checked shirt, his cuffs rolled up ready for work—all efficiency, but still relaxed.

'We couldn't do it without you,' Libby added.

Martin had refused to take any more money for their extra tuition. He'd said it was all part of the service. Libby knew, from a recent flyer in her letterbox, that creating professional websites cost *'from only $395'*. It made Martin's offer seem almost too generous.

'Before you praise me too much, you should know that I've set up all of one business website before,' he said, 'for my daughter-in-law.'

'They call that SODOTO at TAFE,' Libby said. 'See One, Do One, Teach One. A few weeks ago, Kate and I wouldn't have dreamed of doing something like this, so you're still way ahead of us.'

Martin smiled at her. 'Tell me a bit more about your business. I need a clear idea of what you're after.'

Kate took up the reins. 'We're organising every detail of a wedding, so we'd love the page to reflect that we're a friendly *team* who can take the worry out of a wedding day. I've looked at a few other wedding planner websites and I know the ones I like best. We want our personality to show through,' she said. 'And our service will be a bit different to others, because we're offering Libby's make-up skills as well. Not every client will use her, of course. Some brides have their own beautician.'

'And we'd like a great photo gallery,' added Libby. 'Some sites I checked were too wordy. Photos make you sit up and take notice. Neelam's been a terrific help in showing us how to choose flattering angles and lighting—we've got a great selection now.'

She took a USB flash drive from her bag and passed it over to Martin who plugged it into his laptop. Several icons flashed onto the screen when he opened it, some of them relating to administration at TAFE. As Libby pointed out the photography icon, Martin leaned in and his arm brushed against hers very lightly as he clicked it open. It was the briefest moment, but she went on feeling the touch on her skin even as he looked at the screen.

He scrolled through the images, taking his time to look at each one of them, while Libby held her breath. Amy and Michaela were younger than she was, and although they didn't look like professional models—Michaela had squinched a bit *too* much, and Amy could still do with highlights in her hair—their images fitted with her message: anyone can look vibrant and beautiful with the right help.

Then Kate had decided that the mothers of the brides might like Libby to work her magic on them too, if they knew what she could do for them. So they'd added photos of Kate and Libby themselves after makeovers, as well as some of Kate's neighbours who'd found the whole experience a hoot. The pictures of Kate and Libby glowed; they had a depth about them that charmed even Libby. She knew before she'd started the process she could transform them both, but even she wasn't prepared for the mature beauty that emerged in the final shots.

Martin looked at them for a long time, his eyes narrowing as he scrutinised each picture. 'These are very good,' he said.

Libby blushed at his praise. Martin was switched on when it came to the internet, so his opinion was worth something. But she mustn't get carried away, he was probably only thinking about them as headshots to go on the website.

'I can see now what you're offering.' He looked up at Kate. 'You said you wanted online payment?'

'Yes, with a credit card or PayPal,' Kate said, walking around to the computer.

'Not sure that's necessary. Customers can pay directly into your business account.'

'Whatever you recommend. We're in your hands.'

'Totally,' Libby agreed.

Kate turned to her. 'Did I mention that Neil's joining us for lunch?' She gestured to the end of the table where four places had been set. 'We can discuss the ins and outs of setting up the financial side of the business now it's expanding. That's his forte. He began with a two-person legal firm—Neil and his secretary—and now he's the principal with a whole bunch of staff, so he knows what he's doing.'

*

183

'Excellent timing.'

Kate was at the oven as she welcomed her husband with a kiss. He greeted Libby with a hug and gave Martin a slap on the back.

'Good to see you again, mate. You almost managed to keep up with the peloton on Saturday morning! Beer?'

'Give me a few more months and I'll be ready for a spot in the Tour de France.'

'You two know each other?' Libby asked.

Martin took the beer he was offered. 'Neil's been introducing me to the bike tracks of Albury. And every hill for miles around. Seems to know the steepest ones, unfortunately.'

'That's called initiation! Can't have the newest member of our cycling fraternity beating all the old hands.' Neil turned to Kate. 'Need any help?' he asked as she carried a golden-crusted pie from the oven to the table and placed it by a large bowl of mixed salad.

'All organised. You sit down and relax. It's your brains we're after today, not your brawn.'

She poured him a glass of wine, before cutting the pie into portions for everyone and gesturing for them to help themselves.

'You're new to Albury too, Martin?' Libby served a slice and passed him the plate. 'How long have you been here?'

'A few months. These lovely people,' he indicated Kate and Neil, 'have been helping me settle in and meet a few locals. I'm retired so it's not easy making friends in a new town, even though my son and daughter-in-law are doing their best. The cycling group's great fun, but I doubt I'll ever reach their standards.'

'You better not! They'll never forgive me if the newcomer starts out-performing us. At least not for the first few years,' Neil said.

'I hardly knew anyone when I arrived a few months ago, either,' Libby said.

'So you've made a tree change?' Martin passed her the salad. 'How's it going?'

'Working at TAFE has helped me link up with a few people, but Kate's been my saviour. Without her, I would never have joined our computer group and got to meet so many great people.'

Martin lifted his glass and smiled at her. 'In that case, I think we should propose a toast to our new besties, don't you?'

Libby raised her glass as her eyes met his.

'Couldn't agree more,' she said.

Chapter 27

Andrea tried Sarah's number yet again. No doubt this would be another message left on her home phone that was ignored. She'd first reached out the day after their troubled conversation over the phone, though she was unsure when Sarah was returning to Albury.

'Sarah,' she'd said into the silence of the message bank, 'I can't tell you how sorry I am.' When there was no return call, she moved on the next day to: 'You've every right to be angry. I made a terrible mistake. I let you down.' And as time passed, she began to beg: 'Please, Sarah, please talk to me again, even if you yell and scream.'

Of course, ladylike Sarah had never yelled and screamed at anyone, as far as Andrea knew, but bitter recriminations would be better than this. The gulf between them was vast and unnerving.

'Hello, are you there, Sarah?' she said now. 'Please pick up.'

But there was nothing.

She sent another text message to Sarah's mobile, although she'd already left countless texts. Almost like some forlorn suitor in an unrequited love tryst: *Please call. Any time. I'm so sorry. I miss you.*

Nothing.

When she heard the ping of her iPhone a few hours later she scooped it off the kitchen bench to look at the message, but it was from Telstra, reminding her to pay her bill.

All right, she'd try another tack. She logged into the website of an Albury florist and trawled through the colourful posies online, all with given names like 'Sabrina', 'Colette' and 'Molly with Chocs'. There was even a 'Sarah'—one of the more expensive bouquets, a mass of delicate pink roses. Soft, feminine and refined, the site promised. Brilliant—pink roses were one of Sarah's favourites. Andrea sent them off and waited a few days.

No response.

She'd expected Sarah's grace would ensure some kind of contact, even if only a deckle-edged thankyou card. But the empty silence indicated the flowers had failed their mission.

Or perhaps Sarah hadn't received them. What if the roses had been delivered but left to wilt in a box on the front step?

Very well, Andrea would drive up to Monument Hill to check.

When she arrived, Sarah's car was sitting in the carport, and Andrea's step lightened at the knowledge her friend must be home. She walked along the side of the house, as she usually did, past a glorious pink hydrangea bush. The drapes were open and she could hear the radio playing. She rapped on the window, hoping to be heard above the ABC announcer.

After a moment she went back to the front door and rang the doorbell.

Nothing.

She felt a physical pain, as though something vital inside her had twisted. Sarah had to be home. Her house was perched way up on the hill, much too steep for her to be out and about without wheels. She was choosing not to respond.

There was such a harsh finality about this tactic. It screamed: 'You're dead to me.'

Andrea returned to her car and drove off, shattered. She needed to regroup, think it through, and try something else. Maybe it was time to take a step back.

When she was home in her kitchen she brewed a chamomile tea so she wouldn't be awake all night, and took it out onto the front verandah. How could Sarah not understand her dilemma when she'd learned of Rob's visits to the IVF lab? Sinking into one of the comfortable cane chairs with the warm sun on her legs, she imagined she was giving advice to a client in similar circumstances. Work had thrown her a few doozies over the years. She had a vivid memory of the woman who admitted that when her husband couldn't get her pregnant she'd found a man who could, but now that the child was needing a kidney transplant, the woman was terrified her husband might discover the truth. That had taken all Andrea's tact and experience to handle. But this was different: it was so close to home.

What would she recommend?

Don't push it, wait a while, try again when Sarah's reached some sort of equilibrium. There'd be so much for her to work through at the moment that repairing this particular relationship was probably low on her agenda.

The truth was, as Andrea had come to realise over the past two years, when you lived alone your friends were more important to you than you were to them. Why not leave it a few weeks until Sarah came up for air and offer support then? She might have had time to think it over and understand why Andrea had never spoken about Rob's activities. Even longstanding, close friends didn't bluster into each other's marriages telling confidential tales with no background knowledge.

True, she'd known Sarah even before Rob came on the scene, and in those days they had told each other everything, but the nature of friendship changes after marriage. What if Rob and Sarah had discussed his potential donations all those years ago and decided it was something they wanted to do for childless couples? What sort of a sneak and a dobber would she have looked then?

She took a sip of her tea, scalding her tongue a little. She'd keep busy until Sarah made contact again, maybe volunteer an extra day at MAMA.

And there was the IN-group, although that might become a problem. If Sarah wasn't willing to forgive, she'd be unlikely to return, especially as she hadn't wanted to change from book club to the IT sessions in the first place. It was only because of that wretched vote that they even had an IN-group. Damn, she should *never* have switched camps—it must have seemed like a betrayal.

Maybe she should be the one to quit instead, a kind of atonement so that Sarah wouldn't be forced to choose.

She pushed the idea out of her mind for now. Sarah wasn't around and there was another IN-group meeting tomorrow. It would be good to catch up with the others and be with friends again.

Chapter 28

Why does the phone always ring when you're in the shower?

Libby wrapped a towel around her dripping figure and grabbed her mobile from the kitchen bench. One advantage of living in a shoebox was that you never missed a call. And at least with the outdated Nokia, there was no FaceTime to be caught almost naked on screen.

'Libby, hi, my name's Chelsea. We haven't met, but I run Soul Hair. It's the hairdressing salon in Brick Lane.'

Libby knew of it. The first thing she'd done on arriving in Albury was to ask around for a good hairdresser. The name Soul Hair had come up time and again, with everyone raving about the salon. When she found full time employment, she'd be their customer for sure.

'Oh yes, I've heard great things about you.'

'Thanks! I'm ringing because I saw your website offering bridal make-up, and I adored the photos.'

Libby was astounded—the site had only been live for a few days. But before she could ask any questions, Chelsea continued.

'We do a lot of hairstyling for brides, usually on a Saturday of course, so we have a beautician who comes in that day, but often she's inundated with work. I wondered, if you're not too busy, would you be available as a back-up sometimes?'

Libby suppressed a laugh. Too busy? She had all of one booking—through Kate—and not for six weeks!

'A back-up? Yes, yes, I'd love to. That'd be terrific.' Libby was dripping over the floor and beginning to shiver. 'Sorry, you've caught me at a bad time, but I'm thrilled you called me. Can I drop into your salon to discuss it? I'm free on Tuesdays and Fridays at the moment, whenever suits.'

'I've a better idea,' Chelsea said. 'I'm having a barbeque at home on Saturday. I heard you're new in town. Why don't you join us? About twelve thirty. Very informal, a few people from work.'

She gave Libby the address several kilometres out of town, said how much she was looking forward to meeting her and then hung up before Libby could ask any more questions.

What a strange call. Maybe Kate knew Chelsea and had mentioned they were setting up a business. And there was no denying that their new venture was a good fit with a hairdressing salon.

*

On Saturday, a polite period after twelve thirty, Libby pulled up outside Chelsea's house on the south side of Table Top, a rural area north of the city. The old homestead was on a large, flat block in an area predating what real estate agents would now call 'lifestyle alternatives'. The front garden was well established with spreading plane trees and pencil pines along the circular drive. A central lawn, bordered by box hedging,

191

housed masses of brightly coloured plants in terracotta pots and variegated bushes in garden beds.

A young woman, perhaps mid to late twenties, came hurrying towards her from the house, her footsteps crunching on the gravel driveway. It had to be Chelsea; she was so on-trend with the latest hairstyle—shaved very close on one side with long, blonde hair that swept across her forehead. It suited her pixie face. Libby held out her hand in greeting, but Chelsea gave her a bear hug instead.

'I feel I know you already!' she said. 'Come and meet my husband, Phil.'

She was swept into a group of Chelsea's friends and introduced to her husband, who also sported a fashionably choppy hairstyle. He grinned and shook her hand warmly. He looked vaguely familiar, but before Libby could ask if they'd met before, Amy from TAFE gave a shout out and came over.

'Hey Libby, great to see you.' She struck up a model's pose, tilting her head coquettishly, fingers pointing to her professionally made-up face. Not only that, Amy now had blonde highlights.

'You like? I had it done this morning. Has your pupil exceeded expectations?'

'She sure has,' Libby said, giving her a hug. 'You look fantastic. And your hair is fabulous.' Suddenly Chelsea's phone call inviting her to be a back-up beautician at her salon made some sense. Amy must've mentioned it to her.

'You wouldn't believe the compliments I've been getting since you taught me these skills. I love it! Though I'm beginning to wonder if I've looked like a dog all these years. When I saw my photo on your website I decided to get Chelsea to do something with my hair.' She took a sip of her white wine and looked around. 'Are you here on your own? I never knew you and Chelsea were friends. Do you go to her salon too?'

'No, I wish I did. I don't know her at all. She rang me out of the blue, offering work with some of her brides on Saturdays. When I saw you here, I assumed you must've told her about me,' she said.

'No, but it's a great idea.' Amy's smile was enthusiastic. 'You'll be perfect for it.'

Chelsea came by with a bunch of wildflowers somebody had brought, looking for a vase.

'Oh good, you know Amy too. What would you like to drink? Martin was over by the drinks table, last I saw of him, if you want to head over.' She popped the flowers in a pale green jug. 'That's if he hasn't commandeered the barbeque by now. What is it with men and tongs?'

'Martin?' Libby swivelled to look for the drinks table. There was a big ice bucket of chilled tinnies and white wine, and glass bowls of red punch, but her mind was trying to compute how the one Martin she knew in Albury might appear at Chelsea's barbeque. This would be too ridiculous a coincidence.

'Yes, Martin. Phil's dad. He doesn't know many other people yet, so it'd be great if you could go and rescue him.'

Libby could almost hear the cogs moving in her brain before clicking into position. Chelsea was Martin's daughter-in-law! At last it all made sense.

Chapter 29

As predicted, Martin was in control of the barbeque under a spreading walnut tree, holding a beer in one hand and tongs in the other as he joked with a younger man in a striped T-shirt.

Martin turned and smiled as Libby approached.

'Oh good. You made it,' he said. 'I hoped you'd come.'

She lowered her head a little, trusting he wouldn't notice her face glow. His young mate wandered off for another beer. Great.

'Seems like I have you to thank for my latest job offer, on top of all the help you gave us with the website. The extra work from Chelsea will be a godsend.'

'It's all her idea.' He flipped several large chops—well charred—and tossed a heap of onion rings around.

Libby felt ravenous all of a sudden. Blame that waft of fried onions.

'Chelsea's an unstoppable force when she gets a bee in her bonnet,' said Martin. 'Best to let her run with it.'

'You must have loved her joining the family then. She's so positive,' Libby said. 'And I've met Phil. Now I know why he looked familiar. Do you have other family?'

'Another son. Andrew works in New Zealand, but we're hoping he'll come back to Oz in the next year or two. Might even settle down one of these days. My wife would have loved that.'

'Losing her must have been hard. Was she sick for long?'

There was a momentary hesitation. Martin moved a chop aside with more attention that it needed. 'No. It was a sudden death. Christine drowned. An accident.'

Libby took in a sharp breath and blinked. Her fingers fluttered to her mouth.

'Oh Martin, I'm so sorry. I had no idea.' *What an idiot I am, blundering in like that.* 'How awful. I can't begin to imagine ...'

No, she couldn't imagine what it would be like to lose, with such horrible finality, the person who'd shared your life. It explained a lot—Martin's aura of aloneness, even vulnerability, that she'd picked up on. She'd known he was widowed, but not because of something quite so tragic. Was he having sleepless nights, dreading each morning, wading through life with leaden feet, through ground that seemed thick with sludge and wondering what was the point of it all? That's what her life had been like after Gerald disappeared without warning. And his absence wasn't as unexpected or as brutal as Christine's must have been. Or as final.

'It must be tough, finding the strength to get through every day,' she said softly. 'Everything you've come to depend on isn't there anymore. Life's rhythm changes overnight.'

Martin looked at her directly then. 'That's so true. I was at a loss for months. That's why Chelsea and Phil suggested I come and live here for a while. And like I said, when Chelsea gets an idea into her head, it's easiest to give in to her.'

'Being welcomed into someone's life is a bonus when you're on your own, isn't it?' she said. 'Kate's been my saviour. I'm glad you took Chelsea's advice.'

Martin took a sip of his beer. 'So am I. It's working out better than I imagined. Love the countryside, too.' He gave an easy laugh. 'Though perhaps not the steep hills. But I haven't offered you a drink, and that's supposed to be my job today.'

'A cook AND a bartender. Throw IT maestro into the mix and is there anything you can't do?'

''Fraid so. A red jumper got into my wash load yesterday, so I might turn up to our sessions in pink shirts now.'

A chocolate and white border collie scampered towards them, making a beeline for the barbeque. He sat on his haunches, looked at Martin with big brown eyes and licked his lips.

'Not a chance, Jake,' Martin said.

Libby squatted and extended her hand towards Jake who licked it gently before turning pleading eyes in her direction.

'He's gorgeous. I'm sure Chelsea wouldn't mind if you gave him a small treat.'

'Forget dog whisperers, I had you picked long ago as a dog-spoiler. Don't think I haven't seen you slipping treats to Kate's dog. If I let you and Chelsea have your way with Jake he'd end up looking like a butter ball.'

'He's yours, is he?' Libby asked, rubbing behind the dog's furry ears. 'Lucky you. First thing I'll do when I move into a larger place is get a dog.'

'You're welcome to come walking with us tomorrow,' Martin said. 'I'm planning to do the Sculpture Walk again. I discovered it the other day—one of Albury's hidden gems.'

'Sounds interesting. Or should I ask the right questions first? Is it sculpted out of a sheer rock face that calls for special climbing gear?'

'Not at all. It's a very flat walk ...' He paused for a second. 'Well, at least the first few sculptures are on level ground.'

'Aha, then the sheer cliff starts.'

'What's this about sheer cliffs?' The man in stripes had returned and was standing at Libby's shoulder, proffering Martin another beer.

'Thanks, mate. Libby thinks I'm withholding crucial information.' He looked at her with a playful smile.

Perhaps she was being too careful. Her hesitation wasn't only about the difficulty of the walk, but because she'd rushed into things with Gerald. Maybe this was different, though. Martin wasn't looking for a partner; it was clear he was still grieving for Christine. There couldn't be any harm in accepting the offer of a stroll, walking the dog—that's all it was. He hadn't asked her out on a date. He was looking for a walking companion.

*

The sun was so high in the sky that they stood in small pools of their own shadow as they looked at one of the sculptures on the Yindyamarra walking trail. Martin was right about this track being an unknown treasure. The contemporary works of art by local Wiradjuri people were nestled in the bushland between a wide lagoon and the Murray River, and already they looked as if they'd belonged there for all time. Libby gazed at the Reconciliation Shield, an elongated piece that featured an abstract human figure whose separate halves were a deep earthy-brown on one side and white on the other.

'That's wonderful. It says so much, without a word,' she said.

Martin walked close to the shield and examined it. 'Interesting to know how the artist managed to score those circle patterns on the surface. She's done each one individually, I'd say.'

'And in such a fantastic spot. The water so still, all the birds calling out nearby.'

'"Yindyamarra" means to go carefully and respectfully,' Martin read from a plaque. 'Let's hope Jake takes that on board.'

Almost as if on cue the dog stopped near a log and gave a brief, gruff bark.

'That's his "alert" signal,' Martin said. 'Maybe a snake … What is it, fella?'

There was a rustle and then a blue-tongued lizard appeared for a moment before plunging into the grass. Jake let off a riot of barks and growls, pulling on his lead before giving up hope.

A little further along the track, a cyclist in hectic blue lycra whizzed by and raised one hand from the handlebar, but apart from him, there was nobody to be seen. It could have been miles from town, miles from TAFE and all Libby's usual worries. Jake continued to lead the way forward in a sprightly jog-trot.

A huge fish trap sculpture made of wire stood close to the river, its filigree shadow extending its beauty.

'Nifty design,' Martin said as they walked up to it. 'The currents would help take the fish right to the opening of the trap.'

'These sculptures are so clever. Look at this one!'

They'd reached another sculpture, a large empty picture frame that could be viewed from either side. From where they stood, the scene within the frame looked like a landscape painting, a foreground of rocks, with a grassy hill sweeping up towards spindly gums. The image might have been a work from the Heidelberg school, yet here it was in the bush, a living, natural picture.

'I'll take your photo in the frame,' Libby suggested. 'Kate and Neil will love to see this.'

Using his iPhone, she snapped a picture of him, the bush as the backdrop.

'The sun's in the right spot for a shot of you from the other side,' Martin said. 'And with a different background in the frame.'

He took the mobile back and Libby glanced over her shoulder at her backdrop, the placid river in its valley, and the road that led back home.

Martin came in closer for his snap, then took another and another one again. He drew close to the frame and lowered the camera as he gently moved his head and touched her lips with his.

Ah, she thought as she kissed him back, delighted that she'd been wrong, that she hadn't understood him. *So this is a date after all.*

Chapter 30

When Andrea pulled into Kate's driveway right on time the following Tuesday, only Libby's little Corolla and Martin's Audi were parked on the street. She stopped in the drive behind the cat's eyes of Kate's BMW. It looked as if the IN-group would be a quiet affair tonight.

As soon as Kate opened the door she seemed to sense something was wrong. 'Where's Sarah?' she asked. 'I haven't heard from her. Is she okay?'

Kate's questions didn't surprise Andrea. If anyone had picked up on the hand grenade that had been launched into their cosy group via Rob's screensaver it would be Kate, always so acutely attuned to the moods of others.

Andrea gave what she hoped was a relaxed shrug and handed over her jacket. 'Sarah's having a holiday in Sydney,' she said, and left it at that.

It was unlikely to allay Kate's concern but now wasn't the time or the place for the truth, and Andrea wasn't going to discuss Sarah's torment publicly. In a town the size of Albury, the rumour mill would be on overdrive and news would ricochet around the place soon enough.

Poor Sarah. It was so unfair. There'd be plenty of people who'd be gloating, not because Sarah had ever done anything mean or hurtful to them—she had *enormous* community spirit, and had raised more money at one MAMA ball than had been raised in the previous three years. But in the eyes of many, she was too beautiful, too successful, too privileged. That was all it took for some people to exult at such a tall poppy wilting.

When Andrea walked into Kate's family room, Martin and Libby gave a simultaneous little cheer.

'Ah, here she is,' Martin said. 'We were starting to worry that you wouldn't show either. I wondered if I'd scared you all away.'

Andrea laughed, warmed by their welcome. 'Denise mentioned she'd be away in Sydney for Stan's operation. She's being magnificent—he's lucky to have such a tower of support.'

'Yes, and she might be away a wee bit longer than she planned,' Kate added as she passed around a board of pâté and cheeses. 'By the way, those biscuits are gluten-free. Stan's had complications—nothing serious—so she's tied up in Sydney, poor thing. She asked us to take *meticulous* notes.'

Being beholden to Stan's illness might seem like a nuisance, but in the scheme of things, it wasn't. Andrea remembered having to drive Brian to his therapy sessions at inconvenient times, and those irritations seemed so trifling now. Denise probably didn't know how lucky she was to have someone in her life who needed her.

'Denise'd hate missing out on a lesson,' Libby said. She rummaged in her bag and produced a biro, testing it first on her notepad. 'I'm happy to send a record,' she added.

'Are we still waiting on Neelam?' Andrea asked.

'I doubt it,' Libby said, glancing at Martin. 'I think she might have some issues at home.'

Martin gave a little nod as if he were privy to whatever was keeping Neelam away.

So, he and Libby seemed to be in touch, Andrea thought, even appeared to share gossip. Perhaps they'd become friends; for all she knew they were already an item. It made sense. They were both new to town and likely to be looking for adventures, and they seemed as if they would grab life with both hands.

By the time Martin had finished showing them about Pinterest, the usual dull ache in Andrea's neck and shoulders had eased a little. She had to work out a way for Sarah and her to sort out their problems. It would be too sad if either of them felt obliged to leave. No, she wouldn't give up the IN-group. She'd done more than enter these women's homes—she'd begun to enter their lives.

*

As she drove home, Andrea realised what a godsend Ken's regular emails from Queenstown were. Not quite the same as a longstanding friendship, with its relaxed give and take, but great anyway. It was fresh and exciting, and stopped the internal monologue that was running an endless loop of self-blame in her brain.

My box of tricks is empty, she'd told him in her last message, having filled him in on Sarah's outrage and her futile attempts to make amends. *There was no luck with flowers, even though I sent her absolute favourites.*

She pulled up outside her house. The air was cold as she closed the car door and dragged open her heavy iron gates.

They were a barrier to slipping in and out whenever the fancy took her. Perhaps she should think about getting automatic doors, if they weren't way out of her price range—it would make life so much easier.

When she went inside she checked her email inbox right away. Because of the time difference in New Zealand she could never predict when Ken's emails would arrive, but tonight there was contact. The sight of his name beside the blue dot was as if the lights had been turned on.

Well done, you, he wrote back. *Sounds like you've gone the extra mile finding her favourite flowers. Have I ever mentioned that I bought flowers for my wife after an argument years ago? Didn't realise then that a bunch of wilting carnations picked up at a 24/7 convenience store on the way home would be about as welcome as dog poop on her shoes. But I'm a fast learner.*

Ha-ha. Many a man has fallen into that trap, Andrea messaged back. *Pity we didn't learn useful tips at school like how to make an apology and what flowers will bring forgiveness. I can't say my algebra classes did me much good.*

His response was immediate. *Hey, steady on there, lass. Not sure planes would stay in the air without algebra.*

Lass. She liked his use of the word—it was familiar and endearing. What she wouldn't give to be able to visit him, to speak face-to-face. How long had it been since anyone outside the family had even given her a hug?

The thought pulled her up with a shock. No embraces, no touching, no kisses for such a long time. Not since Brian's death and funeral, when people had been terrific and brought casseroles and flowers and comfort, but had then returned to their own worlds after a few weeks and support had petered out. It was understandable, she wasn't blaming them—to be honest, she'd never have given someone a big hug, for the sake of it, months after their bereavement. But it felt like one more missing moment in her life.

Maybe the fact that she was thinking about it so much meant she was ready to move to the next stage with Ken, take their relationship up a few notches. Maybe she could try to Skype him, but when she looked up his address in Skype contacts there was no match. Then she remembered. Ken had told her about his poor internet connection—he lived in a valley outside Queenstown, so he couldn't get Skype.

Perhaps she could be daring and fly over to visit him for a few days? But it would be a longish trip. By the time she got to Sydney and then took a connecting flight, it would take the better part of a day—and certainly most of her own inner resources. Her hands and shoulders would likely play up on such a long trip, and with the added stress of this business with Sarah her energy stores felt empty. Organising flights and accommodation, packing and lugging suitcases around—the thought alone was like a steamroller had flattened her.

And she must remember the etiquette of online friendships. A Google search—what would she do without Google?—had emphasised that the woman should not be the one to do the travelling. That was the man's role. A shocking regression from the liberated seventies when she and Sarah insisted on paying for themselves on a date and making their own choices, thank you very much. But awful to look needy or desperate now. Best obey Mr Google and wait a while.

She typed a cheery sign-off to Ken and went to bed thinking about how to meet up.

* * *

Denise hadn't expected for one minute that the planned three days at her sister Kay's small home, post-surgery, would turn into weeks of drama. Already she and Stan had been in Sydney for nearly three weeks, and it looked as if they'd be there a few more. Stan's recovery had been derailed by complications after the operation—infections, bleeding, you name it—and they spent their days visiting various specialist nurses trying to get things sorted. Apart from two postoperative visits, they hadn't seen the surgeon again. Perhaps the fact that he'd blasted the tumour cells meant his job was done, or perhaps he was uncomfortable with complications.

Today she was trying to find a park in one of those oversized shopping plazas with cavernous multi-storey car parks.

'Steady, careful,' Stan warned her, as she finally backed into a space up on the fourth floor. At least they were in the right place. Yesterday they'd set out for an appointment in Matraville only to realise halfway there they should have been heading for Marrickville. Denise knew the general layout of Melbourne from childhood trips to stay with her grandfather, but Sydney was a bit of a mystery.

She looked around and made a mental note of Bay F6. A few weeks before this Sydney trip, Martin had shown the IN-group members with iPhones how to download an app called Find My Phone in case theirs was ever lost, but what she should've asked him for was a Find My Car app. That's if such a thing existed, but she couldn't be the only person who had trouble remembering where she'd left her vehicle. Every car park in Sydney seemed to have level upon level where each one looked *identical* to the other, and stretched out for what seemed like acres of grey cement. How could she possibly remember where she'd parked?

Today was yet another visit to the community nurses at a clinic in some obscure place, for a follow-up session about a temporary bladder catheter that Stan *himself* had had to learn to change.

'You want me to put it *where*?' she'd overheard him saying to the continence nurse at his first visit. But today he seemed more at home with the nurse specialist, almost jovial in fact, chiacking with her as he followed her into her room, and using a friendly tone he didn't bother to use with Denise, who, after all, was only an ex-wife and therefore privy to all his complaints and his moaning *ad nauseam*.

'Why did I try this new-fangled treatment?' he demanded of Denise when he realised he'd have to manage the catheter himself. He was beside himself with that one, more so because he was living at Kay's home. And compared to what he was used to in Albury, this was one tiny house.

'My plumbing's never going to work again. Never,' he would mutter to Denise in an aside if Kay was out of earshot.

And then the clincher: 'I should never have let you talk me into this.'

Denise sank back and picked up a women's magazine, grateful for the respite. She was weary, as if her very bone marrow were being leeched from her. How good it would be to get back home to Albury and see her IN-group friends. They'd be streets ahead of her by now.

It wouldn't have been a problem if they'd stayed with the book club meetings. Missing one or two discussions about the latest novel was neither here nor there, but losing out on so many of Martin's sessions was a huge loss.

There was that Instagram tutorial she'd been looking forward to, and some other thing—what was it called again? Pinsit? Pintress? That could be a real goer for her netsuke collection. What other pearls was she missing? Probably Sarah had organised them into filming a full-length documentary on 'Understanding Social Media' by now.

'Thanks for everything, you've been wonderful,' Denise heard Stan say as he left the room with the nurse. He was ushered over to the receptionist after an appointment that had taken only a few minutes for the nurse to be wonderful in.

'Bloody hell! Medicare is supposed to be free,' he said to Denise once the nurse specialist was out of earshot. He handed the receptionist his credit card.

'Never mind, we'll be getting home soon. It'll be all right,' Denise reassured him as they entered the lift, although he had a point. The bills were mounting up faster than she'd expected. How were they going to find so much money for all these extra costs?

Chapter 31

After another three weeks with no Sarah, no Denise, and no Neelam, who was now away on holiday in India, the IN-group meetings had become rather subdued affairs.

It was then Andrea made up her mind. She and Ken were chatting—admittedly via email—every day, and getting on so well that it was time to bite the bullet, especially after his most recent message. It ended with the words, 'Wouldn't it be lovely to meet?'

She felt excited and young again, like when the nicest boy in her class had asked her out. And he'd turned out to be a real keeper.

Checking out the local Airbnbs, she found plenty of appealing houses offering affordable accommodation within walking distance of her home. Why not suggest he come over for a week? See if they got on together in real life as well as they did online.

Would you like to come to Albury for a short holiday? she typed. *There are places to stay close to where I live, and I could show you around the area. Lots of aviation history. You'd love it!*

A great believer in sleeping on an idea before acting, she left it in her Drafts folder. If she sent it then and there, she might have been horrified a couple of days later and wished she never had.

If only there were someone to talk it over with, but she would *not* be ringing Nicole. More giggles, and suggestions she look for a furry friend to pamper, would be no help at all. She'd have to take this plunge all on her own.

A rather formal note from Sarah acknowledged the flowers, but her movements remained a mystery. Andrea called in to her home again, but now the gates were locked. The front fence wasn't high, and as she stood there peeking over it she could see that the drapes were drawn across the windows and the garage was bolted. Sarah had disappeared.

Andrea's skin prickled with anxiety as she turned away. Maybe she could telephone Rob's rooms, and ask … what, exactly? She didn't want to speak with *him*; she'd never felt close friends with Rob, and his staff would never breathe a word to her of Sarah's whereabouts. Loyal to their boss to a fault.

She returned to the car and drove down the hill towards the centre of town. It was there she had a lucky encounter, when she dropped into Vital Ingredient on her way home. While she idled at the biscuit selection, trying to decide between Parmesan crisps and red pepper crackers, she found out what she wanted to know. Thank goodness for chatty Barbara Spencer—or at least that was her first reaction. According to Sarah, Barbara—who was married to one of the younger partners in Rob's clinic—involved herself closely in the practice. *Too closely,* Sarah had confided.

Andrea knew Barbara would leap at the chance to talk with someone who knew both parties to this salacious piece of gossip. If Andrea approached this with care, and made it seem like she knew more than she did, then Barb was likely to let slip information on Sarah's whereabouts. She wouldn't be able to help herself.

Barb gave her a little wave and hurried over. The large sunglasses on her head were like satellite dishes awaiting a signal.

'Hello,' Andrea said. 'Haven't seen you in ages, Barb. You're looking great.'

'I don't feel great!' she said, her silver earrings jangling as she shook her head. 'Haven't had time to see Chelsea at the salon for weeks. Too busy at Tom's rooms.'

'Yes, I guessed they'd be in turmoil,' Andrea said, though she had no idea how far the ripples of Sarah's marriage breakup had extended to Rob's Albury rooms. She had a hunch that all the exquisite details of Sarah and Rob's problems were bouncing off the walls of the city's medical establishments at this very moment.

She felt a sudden stab of pain, probably the guilt of standing in public ready to discuss her friend's shattered life with this woman who wasn't a friend of either of them. But how could she find out where Sarah was and whether she was going to remain in Albury?

'Turmoil! Tell me about it!' Barb said with an eager smile. 'Two great truckloads of Rob's belongings were delivered to his rooms, for goodness' sake! Even though Rob is only there a day or two a week. Tom was tearing his hair out—suitcases and boxes dumped in our waiting room one weekend. Even Rob's old hockey stick. I've been on overtime arranging storage for it all, believe it or not.'

Andrea hid a grin at the image of dumbstruck patients fumbling around in the waiting room on a Monday morning, trying to find somewhere to sit among all Rob's parapher-nalia. *Go Sarah! That's the way to tell him it's over.*

'I guess Rob might move to Sydney full-time now,' she said matter-of-factly.

'Oh, I doubt it,' replied Barb, beaming. She had the information that Andrea wanted and it gave her a sense of importance. 'Sarah'll get over it when she gets back from overseas. London—or was it New York? Wherever she's gone. You watch this space. She'll make amends with Rob once she realises what she's giving up. He's a *specialist,* after all. And anyway, what's she going to do on her own? A woman in her sixties is well past her prime. She'll never find anyone else, certainly no one as good as Rob. No, he's been a naughty boy and he got well and truly caught this time, but it'll all blow over. It's a silly overreaction.'

How galling of Barb to insult her best friend! Her comments were monstrous and unfair, and standing there with her gossiping among the nibbles and teapots and pastry brushes made Andrea feel intrusive and grubby by association.

This was more than a slap in the face to Sarah, it was deeply insulting to every woman of her age. Andrea's cheeks were almost stinging.

'You're so wrong, Barb,' she said. 'It's about self-respect and Sarah has that in abundance.'

She'd assumed society had moved on, matured, but now the message was still 'You're nothing without a man'.

Naughty boy indeed. Like so many powerful men, Rob surrounded himself with people who adored him, who believed he could do no wrong. Andrea had long ago concluded that Rob didn't have friends, he had disciples. It seemed Barb was one of those disciples. That's how the Robs of the world got away with anything.

No wonder, with her ambivalent view of Sarah's husband, that Andrea had never quite felt part of Rob's inner circle.

But she knew Sarah. There was no doubt that the marriage was over. Packing up your husband's belongings and dumping them at his rooms was a pretty powerful statement. She wondered if Rob would have a tin ear towards Sarah's pain and the finality of her decision as Barb seemed to have.

What if Sarah decided to stay in London? Or New York?

Andrea saw her friend retreating, like a ship towards the horizon, slipping over the edge, out of sight and out of her life. She had a searing sense of loss, a pain under her ribs, reminiscent of how she was when she'd lost Brian.

She paid for the biscuits and left, relieved to escape Barb. As soon as she returned home she plonked herself in front of the computer and opened her draft invitation to Ken.

She took a deep breath and re-read the message. Her pain began to lift and she was dizzy with a mix of anger and determination. She'd never been so ready to take the next step in her life. She'd dive head first into the future, to show the world that a woman in her sixties was far from past her prime.

She pressed 'send' and sat back, excited for the first time—in, oh so many years—about the path ahead.

Chapter 32

Kay seemed unusually cheery on Denise and Stan's last morning in Sydney when they loaded up the car—or rather Denise and Kay stacked the bags in the boot, because heavy lifting was still a no-no for Stan.

'Goodbye, Den, I'll phone you over the weekend,' Kay said with a bigger smile than she'd had in weeks. Although, in all honesty, she hadn't given any indication they were unwelcome, or that her haven had turned into a claustrophobic rabbit warren for the period. That's if you discounted a few sighs when Stan was being extra petulant.

It would be a long trip home, and for Denise the allure of getting back to her comfort zone was intoxicating. She couldn't wait to drop Stan off at his home and scuttle back to her own for much needed breathing space. Surely she could be less attentive now than a real-deal wife would have to be?

*

The morning after their return, Denise stood at the entrance to Stan's house, carrying the groceries she'd picked up for him at IGA. So much for all her resolutions. He couldn't help with the bags when she brought them in two at a time and began to stack the various items in the fridge: the fish fingers and frozen pizza and the large bottles of Zero he'd requested. Seriously, he should eat more fresh fruit and veggies—he was eating like a teenager whose parents were away.

'And look at this,' Stan said. He glared at his most recent medical bill. It was way above any rebate, and had come on top of several other costs for exclusive 'not on the Pharmaceutical Benefits Scheme, I'm afraid' medications and catheters.

'Are those things lined with gold?' he went on. 'Having that operation's like buying a top-of-the-range Mercedes. You can rustle up the cash for the initial outlay, but pity help you if you need spare parts or repairs and service. I hope I don't have to borrow extra.'

He was more fretful than Denise had seen him in a long time.

'I've had to borrow on my credit card and the interest rates are a joke. How am I going to pay all this back?'

'Why don't you put the kettle on, Stan?' She was *not* going to make the tea as well. 'We need to get back to normal. Time to check what's happening on eBay.'

'You're not wrong there.'

As he clattered around his neat kitchen, opening cupboards and finding tea bags and mugs, Denise took out her iPad and logged onto her eBay page. The fate of the 'Netsuke for Sale' project had dropped out of their minds completely during his illness. Thank goodness they'd set a long timeframe for the auctions.

'Whoa! This'll cheer you up. Have a look!' She stared at the page, trying to make sense of it.

'Every single netsuke has been snapped up. Looks like they've all turned a nifty profit.' She checked more closely before adding, 'The perspex box and stands have all gone, too. Again ... a tidy profit. Why didn't I know it was this easy? I would've retired from teaching years ago!'

Stan was opening the Tim Tams she'd brought. He gave a low whistle and actually smiled. 'You beauty! I wasn't sure your plan'd work, Den. For the life of me, though, I still don't get why people would pay more for something they could've bought themselves with a bit of searching.'

'They haven't the time to spend hours trawling through websites—sometimes it's easier to outsource. And we've made the netsuke look so enticing, people will want to own one.' She took a sip of her tea and pulled a face. Why did Stan never remember she had it with sugar?

'I mean, when we were kids, our parents would've died laughing if we'd told them that one day people would pay more for bottled water than for petrol. Even though "unbottled" water's safe to drink and available on tap. Literally. It's all in the marketing.'

Stan looked thoughtful. 'Maybe that big loan's not going to be such a problem. At this rate, we'll have it paid off in a few months. Good decision to have that surgery.'

Denise stared at him in astonishment, wondering if he was pulling her leg. Where was all the worry about money she'd been listening to for weeks? It was at that moment she remembered why she rather liked being single and living on her own.

Now that Stan had recovered, and was free of the disease, he could blot out the whole dark experience in the space of ten minutes. Like magic. Suddenly, the fretful, complaining Impossible Stan was gone, replaced by the light-hearted, encouraging Good Stan. Thank heavens. She couldn't have put up with Impossible Stan for too much longer.

'We made more than a hundred per cent profit on a couple of them,' she said after doing a few quick calculations on the sales. 'To think that dolling them up would have such an effect. Maybe I've got more artistic skills than I give myself credit for.'

'I'd better get to and make more of the fancy boxes, then.'

'I wouldn't mind looking at lots more auction houses now, find a bigger pool of netsuke to dive into. Ones that won't take a big chunk out of our profit.' Denise rubbed her hands together. 'Time to branch out, dive into the unknown. Find ones that appeal to collectors. And I still have my heart set on finding a hare with amber eyes. For me.'

'The ultimate prize, eh? If you ever do, I'll build you a whole cabinet to showcase it.' And with that promise, Stan picked up his mug of tea and headed out to his workshop.

A handcrafted cabinet for a treasured netsuke? As far as Denise was concerned, that sounded mighty close to a thankyou.

*

Once she'd packaged and despatched the sold netsuke to their new owners, Denise plunged into the task of finding more to trade.

She needed to do research at reputable auctioneer websites, like Christies with their eye-watering array of options. Should she go with mythological creatures—perhaps an elaborate dragon, or a gryphon with its bird-like head and lion's body? Or stay with the ever-popular Japanese zodiac animals, like coiled snakes and rats with evil eyes.

The sweet-faced tiger protecting its cub was bound to appeal to buyers. Kabuki actors who did their elaborate dances in flamboyant costumes beckoned her, but on reflection, she'd better give Japanese literary heroes a wide berth. What did she know about the topic? Japanese language and literature didn't exactly have a starring role on the student syllabus in Australia after the Second World War when Denise was growing up.

While she was browsing, an email landed in her Gmail inbox. In the blurb she'd written for her netsuke auction, she'd mentioned reading *The Hare with Amber Eyes*. How exciting—someone was responding, and as she read, she thrilled to the buzz of finding a kindred soul.

Hi, the woman wrote, *my name's Nancy Tanner and I live in Wisconsin. Like you, I simply adored* The Hare with Amber Eyes *and now I want to buy a netsuke for myself. I missed out on buying the adorable mice you sold a few weeks ago—I'm not so clever on computers, and was outbid.*

Join the club. Up until a few months ago, Denise wouldn't even have been confident to place one bid online, let alone understand the intricacies—and thrills—of making a successful bid seconds before an auction closed. Such an adrenaline hit.

The reason I'm contacting you, Nancy's email continued, *is to ask if you will have any more coming up for auction? I want an animal with the perspex box and stand. Thank you for your response.'*

Hi Nancy, she responded. *Nice to 'meet' you. Isn't it amazing that two people on opposite sides of the world can read the exact same book and both love it to bits? In answer to your question, yes, I'll be getting more netsuke for sale, and they'll have the stands and boxes. Do you prefer any particular animal?*

It didn't take long for Nancy to reply.

A hare with amber eyes! she wrote, before adding ... *only joking! I could never afford that, but I love animals. I see squirrels on my front lawn eating acorns or walnuts they've stolen from my tree. Oh, my, they're so cute. My maximum price is about $120, so I know I can't get ivory. I'm retired and a carer for my mother who's in her nineties and a shut-in.*

Leave it with me, Denise replied. *I'll let you know when I've sourced one.*

She turned back to the web immediately, looking for the ideal netsuke for the poor soul. She knew exactly what Nancy was going through as a carer and decided she deserved a gorgeous ornament to lift her spirits, something special.

Ivory rabbits, a monkey crouched over a bowl, even a bulbous toad all presented on the web, but finding a squirrel in the right price range proved impossible. There was, though, a playful puppy that would bring a smile to anyone, and at a reasonable price. It would certainly be easy for her to resell and Nancy was ecstatic when she saw it after Denise had uploaded it, showcased in all its glory.

This should be affordable, Denise told her. She'd paid sixty-five dollars for it, and could expect to on-sell it for around ninety to a hundred dollars. But she was wrong—the revamped little treasure flew out the door for $150! Nancy was almost inconsolable.

Don't worry, Denise typed, *I'll find another gorgeous one that you might have more luck with.*

But exactly the same thing happened as Nancy was outbid on a pair of foxes that she'd wanted.

You know my taste so well, Nancy wrote. *Could you sell it to me privately?*

No, sorry, Denise answered. *I don't have the payment facilities for it.*

What if I wired money to you first, before you send me the netsuke?

Are you sure? Denise asked. *That could be considered a risk for you.*

Not at all. You've got a 100% rating on your eBay site and everyone is glowing in their comments about you.

Denise basked in Nancy's compliment. She found a beautiful bone rabbit with a mischievous expression that her new friend loved at first sight. When payment was forwarded to her account immediately, Denise despatched the little mounted treasure the following day, hoping Nancy would love it as much as she did.

'I'm getting good at this,' she told Stan, when she dropped in to see how he was going. He was getting stronger every day. 'Bypassing the middleman and making a better profit is the way to go. It works brilliantly. We'll raise your money for the treatment in no time. And then some!'

Yes, she was boasting, but why not? Denise was buoyant. It was hard to believe how good her life had become. From joining a sedate book group to mastering eBay sales—who'd have guessed?

Chapter 33

For once, Libby didn't dread fronting up to the ATM for a withdrawal. In fact, as she waited in the bank's lobby for her wad of cash, she felt positively exultant.

She took the banknotes from the machine and counted them. Two hundred crisp, untarnished dollars. She hadn't withdrawn so much in one go in ages, and it was all thanks to her new friends: Kate most of all, but also Martin and Chelsea. Their belief in her was an incredible boost. Her make-up business was soaring, and the credit card that had lain untouched for so long was being given a workout now too.

She slipped her wallet back into her handbag and walked out onto Dean Street. Moving from Melbourne to start afresh had been a brilliant step.

But not everything was perfect. A new worry was starting to nag. What would Martin think about what had happened in Melbourne? She'd been so naive—or, if she were honest with herself, stupid. This problem with her ongoing debt all went back to Gerald. Charming, lying Gerald. How much should she tell Martin? Was it better to get secrets off your chest early in a relationship, or wait until there was a solid foundation?

'Good morning. Or is it afternoon already?' Libby turned at the familiar voice. Andrea was exiting the bank building right behind her. 'What a gorgeous jacket,' Andrea added. 'That looks like a Beechworth find?'

Libby smiled. 'Yes, I discovered the alpaca shop there. They've got some lovely things.'

'They always do. That soft crimson suits you. You look happy.'

'I am. Life's good!'

'Then let's celebrate. Lord knows I need something to perk me up. Lunch? Or are you rushing back to work? My shout.'

'Plenty of time. Friday's the "calm before the storm" day.'

'Ah, yes … your wedding business,' Andrea said. 'My daughter's friend was married in that rustic wedding Kate organised. You know, the one in the converted barn out at Howlong? Everyone was raving about it.'

'It's all Kate's doing,' said Libby. 'She has the most amazing ideas, more than anyone I've ever met. But the best bit is that she can transform her "out-there" schemes into reality.'

'Like changing staid old book club into the IN-group,' Andrea said, shading her eyes. 'I admire that skill. I don't have the chutzpah to take things to the next level.' She gestured ahead as they walked in the autumn sunshine. 'So … what about Black Zebra Cafe?'

'Ooh, yes please. I've heard lots of positive things.'

They were a little ahead of the rush hour and the only others there were a youngish man tapping on a computer with a ginger beer in front of him, and two women who looked like a mother and daughter on their weekly outing.

The older woman was a bit deaf, and fretting loudly about concert tickets for the following day.

'Andrea, good to see you,' said the waitress. 'Your usual spot near the window?'

'Thanks, but we might tuck ourselves away,' Andrea replied, pointing to a table in the far corner.

On the wall was the specials menu chalked in curling handwriting. Andrea didn't even bother to glance at the long list of house-made pastas and sauces, Libby noticed. She must know them by heart.

'I'll order some coffees,' Andrea said as she turned towards the hissing espresso machine.

Libby picked up the menu. Andrea had chosen such an out-of-the-way nook that it seemed they were about to have a private conversation. Good. Not only was she itching to know what had happened to Sarah, but she was worried that the IN-group was losing momentum. So many of them had been away over the past few weeks. It'd be awful not to have a reason to see the others, especially Andrea. She had such a careful approach to problems and a calm manner that gave you confidence.

Come to think of it, Andrea would be the ideal person to ask for advice about Martin. It was good timing, running into her like this, an opportunity for a one-on-one conversation.

She followed Andrea to the counter and ordered the pumpkin ravioli with sage butter and wilted greens that she'd heard Michaela rave about at work.

'I'm a bit worried about the group ...' Libby began after they'd returned to their seats.

Andrea's response was immediate. 'So am I!'

'Is Sarah really in Sydney for a holiday? I got a sense something bad happened when she brought her husband's mobile to the meeting. Do you remember? You hear awful stories about women discovering on their husband's phone that he's leading a double life … or gay or something.'

'You're not far off the mark,' Andrea said. 'You might have heard rumours.'

'No, nothing.' Libby didn't know enough locals to be a part of the grapevine.

'Well, her marriage is over,' Andrea continued in a voice so low that even Libby could barely hear, let alone any eavesdroppers. 'But she's not in Sydney now. She's overseas. London or New York, I'm not sure.' She gave a soft sigh. 'She's not communicating with me and I'm not at all sure that she'll return to the group. And it's all my fault.'

'Your fault? How?'

'I'd known for years that Rob—that's her husband—might not be quite the man Sarah believed, that he was keeping a secret from her, but I kept it to myself. Big mistake, as it turns out.'

Libby sat back in her chair. 'Gosh, don't beat up on yourself. A friend warned me about Gerald—that's my ex—before we married, but do you think I listened to her? I put it down to jealousy. Back then, I was in *lurve*. Gerald was so charming and so good at covering his tracks. Maybe Sarah's husband's the same.'

'All of that and more,' Andrea said. 'And you're right. I had no evidence, only suspicions. But now Sarah's paying the price and at a time in life when it's going to be hard to start again.'

'This is sounding too familiar,' Libby said. 'The end result of my failure to listen is that I've now been tainted with the brush of Gerald's criminal behaviour and left paying off debts. My lawyer called it an STD. That didn't help my self-esteem.'

'Sexually Transmitted Debt? Yes, I know about that, saw it a bit in my work. Women left holding the baby, and massive debts as well, because they're legally responsible for their *partner*'s borrowings.'

What a relief. Someone who understood, someone who wouldn't judge her. Libby felt as if she'd been locked in a claustrophobic cell and the door had been opened a teeny bit. She could sense her bottled-up shame begin to lift, and now she wanted to talk about what had happened.

'I can't tell you how awful it was,' she continued. 'I was the personal assistant to the CEO at a big engineering company, and Gerald was their senior finance officer. He was the one who got me the job. I was thrilled he was being so supportive, and that he thought it would be fun to work together. I realised later it was nothing like that. It was so he could track the movements of the CEO through me.'

Goodness. Was she gabbling? It didn't seem to matter. Andrea was giving all her attention, not even taking her eyes off Libby when the waitress arrived with their pastas.

'I'd only recently joined the firm—we were newlyweds. When I found an anomaly in the work accounts I drew it to Gerald's attention because it was his area. It seemed the right thing to do … not having any idea, never thinking for a *moment …*'

'… that he was to blame,' Andrea said. 'How did he react?'

Libby swallowed, her gaze far off in the corner of the cafe. 'He said he'd look into it, and later he said an internal investigation was underway but told me to keep it confidential.'

'And did you?'

Libby gave a bitter little laugh. 'That's what helped him. It was only afterwards, during the horrendous court case, that it dawned on me that I'd tipped him off, allowed him to cover his tracks early. If I'd suspected for one moment, or if I'd reported it to someone higher up the chain, my life wouldn't have come crashing down.

'When the company discovered over five-hundred thousand dollars was missing—and it only came to light by accident—forensic accountants and detectives came into our workplace and to the house in Prahran, seizing computers and papers and bank statements. It was dreadful. They went through our personal finances with the proverbial toothcomb.'

'How terrible,' Andrea said, pouring Libby some water.

'It was a massive theft ... What a nightmare.' Libby's eyes filled at the memory, but she blinked them away when Andrea leaned in to give her arm a sympathetic squeeze.

'And the worst of it was ... people didn't believe me. I truly had no idea what he was up to. I was *so* stupid.'

'No, you were trusting,' Andrea said, her untouched pasta in front of her.

'Yes, completely trusting. I guess I hadn't known him long enough before we married. I'll never make that mistake again, never trust blindly. You know, you hear comments like "she was happy to spend the money" but Gerald was squirrelling it offshore in a tax haven,' Libby said in another rush. 'I didn't see any of it, I swear. We were both on great salaries. We *were* living well, it's true—weekends away on the Barrier Reef, all that kind of thing, but it was off the money we earned.

'Gerald, it turned out, had "form". He'd used other names at earlier firms—Carter, Atkins, I'd never heard any of them. He got bail, but that was a big mistake. He scarpered off overseas with his ill-gotten gains and hasn't been sighted since.'

'Oh, poor you! I had no idea you'd been through so much.' Andrea looked genuinely distressed. 'But we all make mistakes—even the magistrate was fooled by him, it seems.'

'That hadn't occurred to me.' Libby felt her spirits lifting, and the tightness in her chest start to ease. Andrea was such a good listener. 'That was the end of my great job. And Gerald had taken out loans without me realising what he'd done—guess what dumb brunette didn't look at what she'd signed or even remember doing it?—so I've been paying off that debt ever since. Even selling the house and car left a hundred-thousand dollar shortfall.' She gave a wry smile.

'Did you think about declaring bankruptcy so you wouldn't be in debt for years?'

'Yeah ... for about thirty seconds. But that felt shameful too and I needed some sort of ... redemption, if that doesn't sound too silly? Mainly for my self-esteem, but also to set an example for my son. This time, with Gerald, I wasn't left holding the baby. That happened with boyfriend number one when I was nineteen. Paying the debt is something I need to do for Marcus. I don't want him thinking that it's okay to run away from problems like his father did—and Gerald. I can't stand people who take no responsibility.'

'Except it wasn't your responsibility.'

'But apparently, I'd signed the loan papers—though I've racked my brains over that one and I don't remember doing it—but I must have. Interpol still have warrants out for Gerald, as far as I know. With Kate and my new business going so well, though, I can see the bank debt being cleared much sooner. That's why you caught me looking so happy.'

'Well, good for you. Your son's lucky, having you for a mother. What does he do?' Andrea finally picked up her fork, and began to eat. Her pasta must be getting cold by now.

'Pretty much everything—computers, engineering, project management. He moved to Western Australia during the mining boom and struck gold for a few years. We always had to be careful with money—a single mum, you know how it is—so he's sensible with finances and he's bought a house. Now he's married to lovely Georgie with a six-month-old boy, and works for a building firm in Perth.' She couldn't resist. She reached for her wallet and flipped it open, showing her adorable, sleeping grand-bub. 'His name's Orson—it means bear. I sent him a gorgeous teddy and made a T-shirt for it with Awesome Orson printed on it.'

'It's a shame you're so far apart,' Andrea said.

'Mm, Martin's lent me an old computer so we can Skype, and it's fabulous being able to see them, even if I can't pick up Orson and give him a cuddle. I do miss Marcus, but I don't want to become an interfering mother-in-law.'

Andrea laughed. 'You'd be anything but! Now tell me about you and Martin. I sense good things are happening there too.'

'Is it that obvious?'

'Only if you know what to look for. Let me order another coffee first. Latte again?'

The cafe was buzzy now, crowded with lunchtime diners, so it took a few minutes for Andrea to return. Libby sat back in her seat and drank in the atmosphere, the friendly intimacy of the space, the glorious burst of roasted coffee beans. Looking around, she noticed the shelves loaded with jams and chutneys, specialty tins of exotic teas and quality spices. It was as if opening up to Andrea had made her more receptive, able to enjoy her surroundings again. This was what she'd missed and what she was loving now, that sense of belonging to a vibrant community.

'So, where were we?' Andrea seemed to feign vagueness as she rejoined Libby, before smiling. 'Oh yes, you and Martin.'

Libby ducked her head. 'It's true. I like him more and more every day. But … I could do with some advice, if that's okay.

I'm scared to plunge in too fast, after all that's happened. Trust is so important. Martin *seems* trustworthy, nothing like the men I've always been attracted to. He's so steady. I lean towards the bad boys, the slightly dangerous ones.'

'How's that worked out for you so far?' Andrea asked.

Libby giggled. 'Ooh, you're good!' It was like having your very own Dr Phil at the table. 'And you're right. My love life started with a complete tosser—although he did give me a gorgeous son—followed by other exciting flings, mostly ending in a complete train wreck. Are you saying that something different mightn't be bad idea?'

'I think you've got a keeper in Martin. And speaking from experience, keepers are winners.'

'There's something else—I haven't told him about my past, or the debt that I've got. It's not fair to get involved with that hanging over me. Should I tell him straightaway, or should I see how we develop? He might be understanding, but he might be horrified too, and want nothing more to do with me.'

Andrea paused before saying in a quiet voice, 'What makes you think that Martin doesn't know some of it already?'

'How would he …?' Libby asked, puzzled. She thought for a moment then groaned. 'Of course! He's a computer guru, an ex-army investigator. He'd have to know. Even I've done the odd stickybeak Google search on people now and again!'

'So that means it probably hasn't changed his opinion of you. I'd be astounded if he rejected you once you explain. My guess is that he's waiting until you're comfortable enough to tell him. A sign of a mature man, I'd say.'

'You are so wasted in retirement!' Libby said. 'Here you are paying for lunch—by the way, the pasta was as good as its reputation—and you're tossing in pearls of wisdom as well.

But that's enough about me. You must be missing Sarah. Is that why you said you needed something to perk you up?'

Andrea hesitated a second, and pulled her shawl closer around her shoulders. 'Sarah's absence has created a big hole in my life. Amazing how big. When a relationship ends people are sympathetic and rally around. But nobody notices if a friendship breaks down. It's like it's invisible.'

'Perhaps this is a hiccup,' Libby said, unsure how to cheer her up. She'd never had a friendship that had mattered as much as this one seemed to matter to Andrea. Her happiness was always dependent on her relationship.

'I don't think Sarah will ever forgive me. She was so angry. But on the plus side, I have met a very nice chap online.'

'On the *internet*?' Libby couldn't help betraying her shock. Andrea of all people finding romance that way was the last thing she was expecting. 'Is that … safe?' she asked, pulling back.

'It's fine, I ran it past Martin,' Andrea said. 'He showed me how to check a person's identity, so I know this man's the real deal. His name's Ken Ashton and he lives in New Zealand. He's coming over for a visit soon.'

'How exciting,' Libby said. If Martin was advising Andrea, it should be fine. 'We're hoping Neelam will return to the IN-group when she's back from India,' she said by way of changing the topic. 'Kate and I overheard a family argument when we called in a few weeks ago. Remember her husband Vinod? He sounded annoyed with Neelam for "neglecting him for this cooking foolishness". Kate had been tweeting high and low about Neelam's vlog, gaining her some followers, but that might have caused problems.'

'If anyone can come up with a creative solution, it'll be Kate,' said Andrea as she stood and took out her purse. 'What a find she's been!'

'For me most of all—a real life-saver.' Libby stood and pushed her chair back. 'My shout next time.'

She went over to the deli section and picked up two jars of lavender honey. She felt so much better, and it was only after she'd paid for the honey and pressed a jar on Andrea and they'd said their goodbyes outside that it occurred to her that while she'd told Andrea about her time with Gerald, and about Kate, and their awkward experience with Neelam, she still had no idea what Sarah had seen on her Galaxy phone or what Rob's secret was.

Chapter 34

Sarah had long promised herself this treat. To stand 'Upon Westminster Bridge' as the light of a yawning sun rose over the city, and see for herself what had inspired Wordsworth to pen the words that had thrilled her all those years ago.

Earth has not anything to show more fair:
Dull would he be of soul who could pass by
A sight so touching in its majesty:
This City now doth, like a garment wear
The beauty of the morning; silent, bare ...

It was a spine-tingling moment, and to be able to share it with Anna was precious.

Sarah and Rob had lived in the UK in the early eighties when he was doing the obligatory Australian rite-of-passage after graduation, working long hours as a surgical registrar in Sheffield. She was teaching English Literature at an exclusive Public School, so they'd managed no more than a handful of trips down to London. An early morning walk across Westminster Bridge had beckoned her on each visit, but its pull had always been beyond her reach.

After they returned home to Australia, Rob had never been keen to visit the UK again, probably because it wasn't a hub for cosmetic surgery. There were few tax-deductible junkets there on smart ways to remove fat from one part of the body and deposit it in another. On the few occasions Sarah had accompanied him overseas, it had been to Los Angeles or Las Vegas or Miami. None made for a memorable experience, especially for someone like Sarah whose formative years and spiritual home leaned much more towards Mother England. Rob would be away all day, immersed in talks and meetings, or 'networking' late at sessions that seemed to involve a lot of whiskey and wine.

She shuddered at the memories, for the bleakness of those holidays, and most of all for her submission to *his* needs during her married life. How could she have lacked a backbone for so long? Perhaps that was why Anna had deliberately chosen to live in London, knowing he'd be unlikely to visit.

She turned to her elder daughter and smiled. 'So, what do you think? Worth getting up at the crack of dawn?'

'For sure.' Anna's gaze wandered over the splendour of the architecture around her, magical in the light of the emerging sun. 'I should have trusted you.' She slid her arm around her mother's waist and snuggled in, like she used to as a little girl. 'This must be such a shock, but you know you've made the right decision, don't you? You deserve to be happy.'

'Did you think I was unhappy, when you were growing up?'

There was a pause before Anna spoke again. 'No, not unhappy,' she said. 'But as we got older, Lucy and I realised how selfish Dad could be, and that he didn't see how he was treating you. We always hoped you'd leave him. Though the circumstances beggar belief. Even we didn't think he'd treat you so ... dismissively. But the good news is, we'll be *much* more likely to come back to Albury to visit now.'

Sarah was pierced by these words. How sad that her daughters hadn't wanted to return home, all because she'd closed her eyes to the obvious cause of their self-imposed exile.

She leaned against the green wrought-iron railing of Westminster Bridge and looked down, calmed by the waters of the Thames as its ripples rose and fell in an almost hypnotic rhythm below her. The traffic was beginning to pick up, and the city would soon lose the gentle sheen of early morning and turn into a busy, noisy metropolis again.

'So what's it like, putting yourself first for a change?' Anna said. 'Liberating?'

Sarah laughed, throwing her head back like a carefree twenty-year-old.

'Oh darling, you have no idea! The freedom is intoxicating. I can go wherever I want, whenever I want. Yorkshire this afternoon to check out Bronte territory and Stratford-upon-Avon next week. And seeing I forced you to get up so early this morning, I'm taking you out for breakfast. Hungry?'

'You know me—always starving! A big English brekkie would go down a treat.'

They found a small cafe a short walk from the bridge, offering a 'grand' cooked breakfast and acclaimed 'world-class' coffee, though when Sarah took her first sip she was dubious about who'd voted for it. Coffee was something Australia did so well.

As Anna studied the menu closely, Sarah's gaze lingered on her firstborn. The high, almost noble, forehead, the glossy black hair that fell to her shoulders from its central parting, the grey-green eyes she knew so well. Nothing like that Madeleine. Superficial similarities only.

She'd worried how to tell the girls—they were still the 'girls' in her eyes—what had been going on. It wouldn't be fair to turn them into her confidantes. She'd told Anna about Rob's other family, about the woman who had a passing resemblance to her, and about his numerous male offspring too, but to her surprise, Anna had shrugged, as though anything her father did was of little concern to her.

'I don't want our separation making you think you and Lucy have to sever ties with Rob. Your father loves you both in his own way,' she said. She didn't want to turn the girls against their father any more than they'd already turned, to become one of those monster wives who spent their life excoriating their ex-partner. It was up to them to make their own decision about him.

'He has a funny way of showing it,' Anna put down the menu and ordered from the waiter. 'I think, if you analyse it, Dad loves himself more than anyone. I mean, how narcissistic is it to want to endlessly replicate yourself? It would be hilarious if it weren't so tragic. He would've done better to concentrate on the children who lived with him, even if they weren't the perfect specimens he'd hoped for. Like Brian did. Lucy and I used to wish Dad could be that kind of father.'

'Brian? Andrea's Brian?' Sarah was stunned.

'Remember the time we stayed with them for months when you and Dad were in the States on his sabbatical? Nicole and I were in Year 10, I think, and Lucy and Jason Year 8. We had a ball. Brian was such fun. He never lectured, he would talk about anything we wanted to discuss, and he was a good listener. And Brian and Andrea actually did stuff with us.'

'What sort of ... *stuff*?'

Anna's eyes lit up as her full English breakfast arrived. The whiff of bacon had preceded it. She ground sea salt and fresh black pepper over the fried eggs and took a few mouthfuls of sausage before speaking again.

'Yum! Oh yes, Andrea and Brian. Well, they used to take us to all our netball and tennis matches on the weekends—Dad didn't do that *ever*—and they'd stay to watch and cheer us to the end. Then we'd have a barbeque lunch in the park and kick a footy or throw a frisbee for Smithy, their crazy kelpie.

'Can you imagine Dad ever organising a spontaneous picnic and rolling around on the grass in public? It was heaps more fun than that multi-hatted Sydney restaurant he made a song and dance about taking us to once in a blue moon. You must remember the one—where he once got into an endless discussion with the sommelier about French wines. I can hear him now: "The acidity and clarity of the Sauvignon blanc produced in the Upper Loire Valley is an interesting comparison to Chenin blanc harvested from the Middle Loire Valley."' Anna mimicked her father's pompous wine-tasting voice to a tee.

Sarah recalled one day vividly. The girls had become bored and restless during the meal, irritating Rob no end. 'They don't appreciate anything I do for them,' he'd grumbled to her later. 'Why do I bother?'

'And thanks to Brian, I can do all sorts of small repairs too,' Anna added. 'Nicole and I loved helping him in his workshop. Jason's ADHD didn't make life easy for them, but they were so patient with him, and still had plenty of time for us.'

'Who said Jason had ADHD?' Sarah was almost breathless with the shock of all the information she was hearing. *Why hadn't she learned any of this before?*

'Well, think about it. He was such a bundle of uncontrollable energy. Mind you, as bright as a button—that made it harder for them in some ways. What was your diagnosis, then?'

'I don't think I had a ... *diagnosis*.' Sarah felt a pang of regret that she'd never stopped to consider why Jason had been so challenging. 'I wonder what he's doing in Thailand these days?'

'He's running a diving and adventure business in Koh Samui called *Don't Thai Me Down, Sport*. It's fantastic. Nicole gave me his address so I did a quick detour there on hols in Nepal recently. He's got a new partner to expand into more activities.'

She continued chatting about her adventurous holiday, but Sarah was only half listening, lost in memories of the girls' long-gone childhoods and a time when life seemed uncomplicated.

'So you and Nicole keep in close contact then?' she said.

'All the time. Facebook.'

Sarah almost shuddered at the name of that accursed site.

'She and Tim and the kids are coming to the UK via Thailand for a holiday in a few months,' Anna went on, 'so we'll be catching up. But I guess Andrea fills you in on all that news. She must miss Brian. They were so good together. How is she these days?'

Sarah hesitated. Should she tell Anna about their falling-out, about her inability to forgive her best friend? But she didn't want Anna to judge her. She mightn't understand why she couldn't bring herself to answer Andrea's emails and phone messages.

'I haven't seen her for ... well, for a few weeks,' was all she said.

'How come? You see each other all the time. Is she in Canberra with the grandkids?'

Sarah fiddled with her napkin. 'No. We've had a ... a parting of the ways. It turns out she knew years ago that Dad might have had other children—*lots* of other children—and she didn't tell me.'

'Whoa! She *knew*?' Anna raised her eyebrows and laid down her cutlery. 'Are you sure? Why wouldn't she have told you?'

'Okay, Sherlock, she didn't exactly *know*, but she *suspected*. She worked at the Royal Charlotte at the same time Dad was doing his secondment there. She came across information when she was counselling infertile patients that made her suspicious.'

'So, it was through her *work*. That makes it confidential medical information then.' Anna was tucking into her mushrooms again with the intensity of someone who'd not had a cooked breakfast in ages. 'If that's the case, she couldn't have told you even if she'd wanted to.'

Sarah smiled at her forthright daughter. Life was so much easier when you were young and free of responsibility. Decisions could be black and white then, the myriad shades of grey that came to confuse life's palette didn't appear until later. How could someone as inexperienced as Anna understand the humiliation of discovering your best friend knew something so intimate about your life that you didn't know yourself?

'Maybe she couldn't have told me,' she said. She hesitated for a moment, contemplating the possibility. 'I guess … maybe …'

Chapter 35

'I've had another email from Nancy,' Denise said. She was leaning over her dining room table, arranging the latest acquisitions. Stan was delivering perspex boxes at a rapid rate, almost faster than she could paint the small mahogany plinths.

'Who's Nancy?' he asked.

Denise stood upright and leaned backwards, stretching her lower back with a slight frown. She glanced at him to see if he was joking, but his expression was bland.

'Only our best customer!' she said. 'You know, my email friend in the US, the one who's always wanting animal netsuke. She's bought several already for goodness' sake!' How could Stan not know who Nancy was?

'Oh, that one. The last of the big-time spenders?' He plonked a box full of his latest mini constructions onto the table, not noticing that it scattered several of her plinths.

'Well, true, she hasn't spent lot of money on them ... so far,' Denise said, stooping to rescue two on the floor before Stan stood on them. Apart from one sale worth a hundred and eighty dollars, Nancy only ever paid in the double-digit range.

Stan shrugged. 'Higher priced sales would be better. Find wealthier customers prepared to pay in the hundreds, rather than the tens. We'd clear the debt much faster if our trinkets could get a better price.'

Trinkets? Stan didn't get netsuke collectors. Soon he'd be calling them *baubles* or perhaps *trifles* to be even more insulting.

'Anyway, what I'm trying to tell you is that Nancy has come into some money. Her mother died—she was very old—so Nancy's asked me to find her the squirrel netsuke she's wanted for ages. A *top-of-the-range* squirrel netsuke.' Denise grinned. 'She says she'll spend thousands if she falls in love with it.'

Stan gave a low whistle. 'You're kidding me! That's brilliant, but seriously? Someone'd pay *thousands* for one of these little knick-knacks?'

'For the last time, they're not *knick-knacks,* Stan. They have provenance and history. They're works of art! You'd never say that if someone paid that sort of money for a painting.'

'Wanna bet?' Stan chuckled.

* * *

Andrea's calm dissipated as she read Ken's latest message. He wasn't coming for a visit after all. At least, not in the short term.

She propped her chin on her hands, staring blankly at the screen, the disappointment as visceral as when a promised childhood picnic was rained out. She'd already begun making plans for his trip over—a visit to the scene of a daring aeroplane rescue back in the thirties that gave Albury a place in aviation history; a canoe trip down the Murray River with one of her more intrepid friends; a drive to view the 'waterfall' pounding through the weir gates after heavy autumn rains. All things she hoped he'd enjoy.

She daydreamed about him all the time now, wondering what he was doing, how he'd react to a certain news item that took her fancy, musing as to whether he was a beef or lamb sort of man. She couldn't imagine him being vegetarian. Chatting online every day was wonderful, but she couldn't find out the quirky little habits that contributed to a whole person without spending time with him.

The distress would be even worse for Ken, being told he had a heart problem. Andrea knew how bad it was for a pilot to fail a medical. Instant license suspension and no guarantee it would be reinstated until the health problem was resolved. A friend of Brian's had had his flying permit revoked, never to be returned, the moment they discovered his dodgy heart valve needed replacing. She understood the need for the utmost safety, but if flying was your livelihood, it was a brutal system. Poor Ken must be shell-shocked. He said it had come out of the blue.

To make matters worse, he wrote, *my damned insurance company won't pay income protection for the first eight weeks I'm off work. They want to know exactly what's wrong with my heart and how long it will be before I can fly again. As if I know! It means the business is short a pilot now—and, if I do say so myself, it's the pilot who brings in the money—so I can't leave. And wouldn't you know, the insurance on my fleet is due, too. Cash flow problems are the scourge of the self-employed. Don't ever think of setting up a business, Andi, unless you win the lottery!*

Andrea glowed as she read that. He'd switched from calling her *lass* to *Andi* and she liked the new nickname.

But who'd need to set up a business if they won the lottery, eh? he continued. *The worst part is postponing my trip to Albury. I'm so sorry about it. I've returned the money you sent me for the internal flights. You didn't have to do that.*

It was the least I could do, Andrea typed back, *seeing you were prepared to take time off work to come and visit. Get better soon and look after yourself—and the business.*

She'd found the money returned to her account that morning so she added, *And if you need a loan while you're waiting for the insurance company to pay, please let me know. I could help.*

You're too generous, he replied. *I'll see how things go. Don't want to strain the friendship. You're a very special woman.*

A very special woman. Andrea felt a surge of ... what? Anticipation? Excitement? She hadn't felt appreciated for such a long time. Could she be falling in love? Possibly. Maybe scientists would declare it was nothing more than a rush of dopamine to her brain, but whatever it was, her life was changing for the better. She could see a future now and it was thrilling. She had comfortable savings, a buffer against emergencies, so if Ken did need a loan, it was in her account, ready and waiting for him. Insuring aeroplanes would be costly, but she could always borrow against the house. And when Ken's income protection came through, he would send her the money back. She and Brian had never considered their money to be 'yours' or 'mine'. It was always 'ours'. How good it would be to have that sort of relationship with Ken.

It was satisfying to be able to help someone again, to have a new purpose in life. She felt like a hurdle had been jumped, one that had been blocking her view of the future for too long now.

*

Ken *did* need a loan, though he raised the topic again with great reluctance. He was still waiting on income protection payments, stuck in the eight-week no man's land, with little income and needing money urgently to insure his planes.

I hate asking for this, but the business could go under. And my team will grind to a halt if I can't raise the extra $50,000 to insure the planes. I promise I'm good for the money. True to his word, he included a copy of his policy to prove his worth.

Andrea logged into her bank's website to transfer $50,000 across to Ken's account. But her bank was having none of it. Five thousand dollars a day was her limit, it scolded her, unless she got 'permission' to increase her daily limit, a process that was going to take time and paperwork. She felt like she was back at school. It was her money after all!

She sent the five thousand to Ken's account with an apologetic email to him explaining why it would take ten days to transfer the entire amount.

By the time she'd transferred twenty-five thousand dollars in instalments, she had an idea. Why not spread these fledgling wings of hers and fly, but this time literally? Make the trip to New Zealand and delight Ken by turning up in person, cheque in hand, for the last twenty-five thousand dollars.

She'd been more energetic lately. Her hands weren't stiff, she was walking much more freely. She felt like a bird released after years of incarceration, wanting to stretch her wings and soar. What love could do for a woman.

It would be so daring to fly off on a whim. She normally needed to plan her spontaneity. But it wasn't like New Zealand was so far away—Sydney to Queenstown was a mere three hours' flight, same as the drive to visit Nicole in

Canberra, except she wouldn't have to be the driver. She could manage the short flight, and she'd only need hand luggage. Nothing was stopping her taking the plunge.

The IN-group meetings were in hiatus, Sarah was still missing in action overseas—apart from the brief thankyou note, Andrea hadn't heard from her, only knew what Barb had told her—and there was no other pressing business to keep her in Albury.

No business whatsoever, she realised, apart from the dreaded job of making inroads into Brian's shed full of stuff that she had no idea how to sell. If she left Albury this Thursday and returned the following Monday, she wouldn't even miss her shift at the gallery.

According to the address on its website, Ken Ashton Aviation Services was located near the Queenstown airport, a logical place to site a flying business. She could get a cab straight there after passing through customs.

Andrea wasn't sure if Ken would be at work the day she arrived. He might be in the middle of investigations and treatment for his heart, or be too snowed under with paperwork at home to take time out for her, but she was willing to play it by ear. She wanted her visit to be a surprise, no pressure on him, more a meet and greet session.

With the ease of a seasoned travel agent, she navigated the internet, and after arranging her flights, booked four nights' accommodation at a small self-catering apartment near Lake Wakatipu.

Chapter 36

Andrea had an uneventful flight to New Zealand, punctuated only by the steward's air safety demonstration and the arrival of a spongy Spanish omelette. The plane banked on approach to Queenstown, descending into the most picturesque airfield she could ever have imagined.

What an entrance! It was so glorious it could have been one of the Seven Wonders of the World. Nestled in a valley of lush green fields beside a mass of turquoise blue that must be Lake Wakatipu, it was surrounded by majestic, snow-dripped mountains. Andrea was instantly smitten. Imagine living somewhere so beautiful. No wonder Ken had his 'flightseeing' business here.

She passed through customs in no time—older women weren't considered a threat, she guessed—and was able to hail a small, cute-as-a-button green cab once she walked outside.

'I need a lift into town, please,' she said, giving the address of her accommodation, 'but could you stop at Ken Ashton Aviation on the way there? It's at ...' She glanced down at the website address. 'Sir Henry Wigley Drive, it's called. I'll only be calling in there for a sec.' The driver nodded and in less than two minutes, he pulled up in front of a building with a sign outside announcing 'Heli tours'.

'No, it's not helicopters,' she said. 'It's light aircraft. Sightseeing tours. Ken Ashton.'

'I'll take you over to Air Fjordland then,' he said. 'They'll know where it is.'

Another short trip and Andrea found herself in front of Milford Sound Scenic Flights.

'This sounds more like my friend's business,' she told the cabbie before ducking inside. She had to wait a few minutes while the man behind the counter finished his telephone conversation. 'I'm looking for Ken Ashton Aviation. Can you tell me where it is?' she asked. 'I was told Sir Henry Wigley Way.'

He leaned forward. 'Drive, you mean, Sir Henry Wigley Drive, not Way. But I don't know Ashton's. We do most of the scenic flights on this side of the South Island, so if it's a booking you're after, you're in the right spot.'

Andrea had a fleeting sense of being in a dream, caught in a strange place with people who couldn't understand the language she was using. This man must be mistaken.

'Ken Ashton Aviation,' she repeated. 'He runs scenic flights out of Queenstown airport.'

'Not from here, he doesn't.' It was said with a firm shake of the head. 'I've worked at this place for over twenty years and he's never flown out of this airport. But there is a smaller airfield north of here. You could try there.'

'How far is it?' Andrea asked. She could ask the cabbie to take her now.

'Forty minutes or so.'

Andrea gripped her overnight bag. That plan wasn't going to work. She'd have to hire a car herself to get there. Best to check into her accommodation, call Ken and sort out the confusion.

*

'I'm after a local telephone directory,' Andrea said.

The hotel clerk was a tanned, sporty-looking girl with a smiley-face badge on her T-shirt that read *Ngaire.* Andrea handed her the completed registration form.

'I'm chasing up details of a charter flight company but I might have the wrong address.'

She was itching to settle into her digs and arrange a meeting with Ken. What a surprise for him!

'First visit?' Ngaire said with a welcoming smile.

'It is, but I'm only here for a few days. I'm hoping it won't be my last trip. From what I've seen so far, Queenstown is stunning!'

'Gorgeous, isn't it? You'll love your room—it overlooks the lake. But I'm not sure I can help you with a telephone book. Everyone uses their smartphones these days. And there's free wi-fi in your room. Let me look, though. I might have a hard copy of a directory … somewhere …' She squatted beneath the counter, scrambling about, hidden from view.

'Ah, here it is …' She stood up and handed it to Andrea. 'And I can give you pamphlets for all the charter companies, if you like. What are you after? A helicopter trip over Milford Sound? A day trip across to Doubtful Sound? Even bungee jumping, if that takes your fancy.'

'Bungee jumping? At my age?' Jump off a bridge with a big rubber band attached to her feet? Andrea was simultaneously horrified and pleased. She must look younger than she was.

'Never say never. We had a visitor last month who did a jump for her eightieth birthday.' That put Andrea back in her place. 'Said it had always been on her Bucket List.'

'My Bucket List is a Thimble List,' Andrea said. 'Coming to Queenstown on a whim has it spilling over. I'd be terrified the jump might go horribly wrong.' She could think of nothing worse than all of Albury saying, 'Ah, Andrea Thompson. Wasn't she that woman who died doing what she loathed?'

She opened the phone book at the 'A's, but finding no entry for him under either Ashton or Aviation, tried under 'K'. No luck with that either.

'I'll look it up for you online,' Ngaire said. 'What name was it?'

Andrea couldn't help noticing that despite Ngaire's fingers flying over the keyboard with the confidence of a Millennial, she needed help with the spelling of both 'Ashton' and 'Aviation'. What would Denise think?

'Sorry, there's no Ken Ashton in Queenstown. In fact ...' She inspected the screen more closely, 'there's no Ken Ashton coming up in all of New Zealand. There's a Keith Ashton? Is that any help? Maybe your chap's moved away or retired.'

Andrea recalled the website for Ken Ashton Aviation she'd visited when checking the authenticity of Ken's photo. Why was that not coming up? Maybe it had been taken down since his illness; maybe flights had been suspended. Poor Ken.

'Not to worry. Thanks so much for your help. I'll settle into my room and sleep on it. I can decide tomorrow if I'll go ... bungee jumping.'

Ngaire nodded, and Andrea realised then that the girl was serious. She truly believed Andrea might give it a try.

She took the lift to her room and opened the door with her security card. Ngaire was right. Inside the open plan room, decorated with striking geometric designs, a floor-to-ceiling view of the most beautiful lake she'd ever seen greeted her. A deep, crystalline blue, flanked by soaring mountains. It was so glorious, and the view so romantic, her heart squeezed in anticipation.

She drew a chair close to the window, kicked off her shoes, and pulled out her iPhone. As mysteries go, this was one out of the box. Here she was, holidaying alone—a first for her—in a city she didn't know, looking for a man she'd never met, who seemed to have disappeared. Where was Ken's business? More to the point, where was Ken?

She put down the iPhone. She'd heard so many stories of outrageous charges for overseas roaming that she was loath to use it as a way to track Ken down. Better try with her iPad and the free wi-fi. And there, like clockwork, was a message from him, dated that very morning.

Hey, Andi, How are things with you? she read. *I'm so grateful for the money you sent. But it's only $25,000 and we'd agreed on $50,000. Hope there are no problems at your end. I need it rather urgently.*

She smiled with suppressed excitement. Little did he know that she was no more than a few kilometres away with a cheque for him in her handbag.

The weather in Queenstown has taken a turn for the worse and grounded all our planes, his message continued. *And MetService tells us with these wild winds there'll be no flying light aircraft for at least a week. I'll need that extra $25,000 ASAP. It's urgent, I'm afraid.*

The message went on in flattering terms about her generosity, about how soon he'd be able to repay her, and ended with gentle murmurings about their future once all these troubles were over and they could meet at last.

Andrea stopped reading. She gazed beyond her iPad at the view through the window of a cloudless afternoon in Queenstown, of a perfect duck-egg blue sky, and of the winter sunlight shimmering on the still waters of Lake Wakatipu.

Nausea overwhelmed her. She made it to the bathroom in time to see her very ordinary airline meal reappear.

Chapter 37

Denise had found the ultimate squirrel netsuke. It was intricately carved from a creamy, faultless piece of bone and Nancy was ecstatic, thrilled that Denise knew her taste so perfectly.

I love it to pieces already, she wrote after seeing it displayed as the work of art it was. *I'll transfer the money so you can send it ASAP.*

Excited to forward it to her friend—after almost daily internet chatting and numerous sales, Nancy rated as a friend now—Denise put it in the post the next morning. She'd sent Nancy several parcels before without waiting for payment to arrive in her account, and there'd *never* been a problem.

But now, three days later, desperation overwhelmed her as she looked at her bank balance. This couldn't be right. Where was the ten grand she was owed? Fear ate into her solid core of confidence, leaving her hollow. Please, please, the money had to appear.

She'd experienced the same inevitable sense of doom only twice before in her life. One occasion was during that awful school excursion to the weir when two of the pupils had pinched a rowboat and disappeared for a while.

The other was when she was nineteen and had borrowed her father's car, a gleaming new satin silver Holden Premier, for a quick trip into town. She'd ended up in a ditch, unhurt, but the same couldn't be said for the car.

Now the panic was rising to a crescendo again. Logging into her bank account for the tenth time in thirty minutes wasn't going to make ten thousand dollars—for a work of art *she'd already despatched*—appear miraculously in her account, but it was all she could do. Each viewing made her heart pump harder. Could there be a delay because it involved so much money this time?

Two days later, and still no sign of the payment, she sent a frantic email.

Nancy, the money hasn't arrived and I posted your squirrel package days ago. What's happened?

A reply arrived the following day, but it wasn't what she was expecting.

Dear friends, it read. *Our dear Aunt Nancy is in hospital after suffering a stroke. The stress of her beloved mother's death recently has played its part and the doctors can't say how well she will recover, so we ask for your thoughts and prayers at this very sad time. Stacey (Nancy's niece)*

Denise stared in horror. Poor Nancy. But what a terrible time for this to happen. It would surely delay the money being forwarded. Denise's heartburn became a little worse.

She wouldn't tell Stan that there'd be a wait for the payment. It was nothing more than a nuisance. Sure, she'd spent all the money they'd earned so far, plus extra she'd borrowed on her credit card for this latest acquisition, but this was a minor set-back and she could wait.

She sent an email back to Stacey, saying how sorry she was to hear the news and how she hoped for Nancy's full recovery, but received no update. She waited a few days before sending another email to enquire about Nancy's health, but rather than hearing from Stacey, the return message did nothing more than increase her fears.

ERROR CODE. MAIL SERVER UNABLE TO DELIVER. CHECK RECIPIENT'S ADDRESS.

Denise tried emailing several more times, checked and rechecked the address but every subsequent message bounced. Something terrible must have happened. She couldn't contact Nancy or her niece online and she didn't have a telephone number or a home address.

Was there any way she could retrieve the parcel? Or be reimbursed for its value? It was the most expensive netsuke she'd ever bought. But where would she start?

No one on any website could help, because she'd ditched PayPal ages ago to have private transactions with Nancy and it had been working brilliantly. But private sales weren't covered by any seller's insurance.

Martin had warned them about exactly those risks during his sessions on using eBay, but she'd convinced herself that it was different if your customer became a friend and was always reliable. Now though, if the money never came through, and it was looking pretty ominous, there'd be no hope of recovering her cash.

Nancy lived fifteen-thousand kilometres away. Almost as far as she could get, without being in outer space. End of story. It was also the end of the expensive netsuke, the end of all that money she'd outlaid and, worst of all, maybe the end of Stan's friendship if he found out. She dreaded the prospect of telling him. Somehow, some way, she'd have to recoup the money, and quickly.

Andrea would be the one person she could trust, and someone who might even suggest a way out of this morass.

She wouldn't be judgemental, either. But Andrea had left for a holiday on Thursday and wasn't due back for a few days. She might appreciate being picked up at the airport on her return, though. It would be possible to ask her for advice then.

Denise had always believed that the fewer people who knew her business, the better, but drastic times required drastic measures. She had to find out what had happened to Nancy's emails. Asking Martin could work, but Denise would need to be frugal with the truth and hope he wouldn't tell the others. They'd think she was a complete fool for ditching PayPal and parting with her treasures before receiving payment.

'Martin?' Denise tried to keep her telephone voice light, untroubled. 'Could I ask for some advice? My emails to an eBay customer aren't getting through and I wondered if you could check out why. I'm a bit worried about payment.'

'Happy to.' Martin's confident, reassuring tone soothed her nerves but only until his next words. 'But don't worry. That's the beauty of eBay and PayPal. Any losses should be covered.'

'Sure, I understand that completely.' Boy, did she under-stand that—now! 'But this customer has bought several items off me already, and she's always been an excellent payer. I'm a bit puzzled as to why the emails are bouncing now.'

'No problem at all,' Martin said. 'What's her email address? I'll check it out straight away.'

Promising to get back soon, he hung up quickly and for once Denise was relieved that phone conversations with men usually cut to the chase with minimal small talk. None of the chatty, rambling interactions she had with Kay or her Melbourne friends on the telephone. She'd managed to avoid too much embarrassment.

*

'I've got the information you're after, Denise.' It was Martin on the phone again, a mere twenty-four hours later.

His tone didn't inspire confidence. Denise went cold but managed to suppress any note of anxiety about her missing money. 'That was quick,' she said.

'It's not too hard if you know what you're looking for and have the right tools. It isn't good news, though. I tracked the email account to Wisconsin, but it was closed recently.' He paused for a moment.

'And I'm sorry to tell you, but it's because your friend has passed away.'

'No.' Denise was genuinely shocked. 'Poor Nancy. That's awful news. She's only a year older than I am.'

'I wish it were better news,' Martin said.

'I do, too, but thanks so much for your investigation,' Denise managed to say, though her voice sounded raspy. 'Remind me to recommend you if any of my friends need internet mysteries solved.'

There was a distinct note of sympathy as he said cheerio and hung up.

Denise sat for several minutes after Martin's phone call. So Nancy was gone and with her, any chance of receiving payment. And because she'd ditched PayPal, all for the sake of a few more dollars, there was a snowflake's chance in hell of getting the netsuke back. She'd have to recoup the loss. Confident of her ability to buy and sell online, surely she could bring in more money that way.

But what else could she trade? Without an ounce of fashion sense, trying her hand in the world of clothing or footwear was out of the question. She didn't know much about the latest trends in homewares and designer pieces either. And she'd reached the peak of her horticulture skills a few years earlier when she'd managed to keep an African violet alive for—oh, what was it—almost six weeks?

The sad truth was, at this stage of life, she had no discernible skills to market and no other ways to make easy money.

It was then she remembered the offer for a 'virtual' fifty dollars she'd received from some company with a name like FunBet or SafeBet when she was gambling months ago. Would it still be valid? What harm would there be in giving it a whirl now? Imagine if she had the same luck as that Mr Queensland they'd been promoting, who'd won a fortune on his first spin. What if she could recoup even half the money she'd lost? It wasn't like it was her money she'd be risking, after all.

She trawled through her old emails until she found it. No expiry date on the offer. Fantastic. After all, it wasn't her fifty dollars, it was SafeBet's fifty dollars. No risk at all there.

Three hours later, Denise was still playing roulette. The world and her financial troubles had receded into the background and she was more relaxed than she'd been for weeks. In the zone, like a surfer in a perfect barrel, confident that a jackpot was a mere spin away.

She was oblivious to the fact that her fifty-dollar 'gift' was in credit no more. It had well and truly switched to the dark side.

Chapter 38

Home had never looked so good. First from the air, when the plane dipped over the city and again, as Andrea glimpsed Albury's Monument shining with reflected morning sunlight like a welcoming beacon. As she headed towards the arrival gate, she saw Denise waving though the glass windows, her welcoming face like a warm embrace. Carrying her hand luggage with its Air New Zealand tag still attached, Andrea hugged her gratefully as soon as she passed into the arrivals area.

'What a lovely surprise. Being met when you fly back home is one of life's most comforting moments,' she said. 'Like being brought a cup of tea in bed.'

'Well, you're easy to make happy,' Denise teased. 'And even though you've only been out of the country for a few days, can I say I've missed you a lot? I'm not joking.'

They navigated their way through the car park in minutes and turned onto the main road for the short trip into Albury.

'So how was your holiday? Did you have time to see everything you wanted?'

'It was ... it was ...'

Andrea tried but failed to keep the waver out of her voice. How do you put into words the sheer awfulness of visiting a country, expecting love and finding nothing? Of being cheated out of a future you could almost touch? Of being lied to, robbed, and betrayed by someone you'd never even met? How could she have been so stupid? She tried to hold back her tears, but it was pointless.

'It's been awful,' she managed to say before putting her head in her hands and letting out the shuddering sobs she'd been holding back for days.

'Hey, it's okay. You're home now. You're safe!' Denise took her hand off the steering wheel and touched Andrea's arm. 'It was brave of you to travel on your own. A solo holiday isn't for everyone. I know you must be missing Sarah, but I'd have come with you, if you'd wanted. Anytime.'

Andrea lowered her head. 'That's kind of you, but I don't deserve sympathy. I'm a foolish, foolish woman.'

'Can I say that you don't have a monopoly on that?' Denise said. 'Let's get you home, though. I've bought some milk and a fresh Boston bun. I, too, have a sad story to tell, and the phrase *foolish, foolish woman* fits me as well. We can sit down and compete to see who's been the bigger chump, okay?'

Andrea gave a hiccup-y laugh, reaching for her handkerchief and wiping her nose. 'Oh, it'll be me. I'd have jumped up and down and waved my arms screaming *WARNING! WARNING!* if a client had told me she intended to do what I've just done.'

Though the day was unusually sunny for early winter, her house seemed unwelcoming when she opened the front door to let them both inside. She went around opening the curtains and pulling up the blinds.

Denise proved to be a good listener, but it wasn't an altogether comfortable session for Andrea. She was so used to being the one to dispense wisdom that admitting she'd been duped was hard. And confessing she'd sent money to a man she'd only spoken to over a computer sounded, in the light of a new day, like insanity.

'You know what's so embarrassing?' she confessed. 'I've heard about women being scammed and losing their home or their life's savings. I've always been so smug! But to think I'm one of them.'

'Well, you didn't lose the whole fifty thousand. Not that I'm saying twenty-five thousand dollars and having your heart broken isn't an awful loss, but your house is safe isn't it?'

Andrea's shoulders dropped. 'No, not at all. The money I sent over was a big part of my nest egg. I'm going to have trouble keeping up with the rates. It didn't cross my mind that the loan wouldn't be repaid.'

'Will you have to sell?'

'It looks like I'll be forced to. But preparing the house and packing up will be hideous. I've been wrestling with how to offload all Brian's collectibles. That shed's a nightmare.'

'Selling his stuff is where I could help. Trading online. I'd enjoy doing that for you.'

'You've been so kind to me, but I don't deserve it,' Andrea said. 'I wasn't at all friendly towards you when Book Club started. And I'm so sorry.'

Denise gave a slight shake of her head. 'Nothing to apologise for. I can be full on at times. Probably a bit intimidating.'

'No, it wasn't just that. You won't remember, but you did meet Brian and me years ago. You were the new head at East Albury Primary and we had a meeting to discuss our son, Jason. He was in Year 6 that year ... He was playing up a bit.'

'Jason Thompson?' Denise seemed to be turning his name over in her head. 'Wasn't he the lad who pinched a fisherman's boat during a school picnic at the Hume Weir and rowed out into the middle? Nearly gave me a heart attack! If my memory serves me, I suspended him.'

'Yes, that was Jason. You told us he was heading nowhere fast and would end up in jail if he kept on that path.'

Denise almost visibly flinched. 'No wonder you didn't like me. What a tactless thing to say. Yes, I remember now. It was my first year and I was way out of my depth. Some of the school community got the full brunt of my inexperience and I'm sorry you and Brian were among them. If it's any consolation, my communication skills did improve over the years. And I remember your husband now; he handled Jason so well. I'd be honoured to sell his collectibles. But before you trust me, I have my own confession to make ...'

* * *

Denise related her news about the lost netsuke and her fear of telling Stan what she'd done, a prickly rash climbing up her neck as she admitted that she'd dismissed Martin's advice by moving away from PayPal.

'I'd never take that risk again,' she said, as she helped herself to another slice of tea cake and spread it liberally with butter. 'I do love a good Boston bun, don't you? But getting back to our problems ... I'm not sure who's won the chump competition. We need to ask ourselves: Is losing twenty-five thousand dollars and maybe having to sell your house equal to losing nearly ten grand and worrying your ex might drop you *a second time* if he finds out? Perhaps we should call it a draw.'

'And there's nothing either of us can do,' Andrea added, sipping the last of her tea.

'That's not entirely true. Well, for you at least. I asked Martin to look into my overseas contact—though I didn't tell him the full story so, please, cone of silence—and he was able to find out where the emails had originated and why they were bouncing. But seeing your guy hasn't twigged yet that you know he's a con man, he hasn't given up the game. Maybe Martin could get the police or Interpol involved. At the very least, it might stop the bastard doing it to someone else.'

'Do you think Martin's that good?' Andrea rose from the table, looking hopeful, and began to clear up.

'Oh yes, sure of it. It only took him a day to find the details I was after.' She handed her empty cup and saucer to Andrea. 'Give him a call, you've nothing to lose. Meanwhile, I'll work out some way to make up my loss.' She stopped short of saying losses. For some reason, admitting to Andrea that she'd gambled away even more on a night of computer roulette was a step too far.

* * *

As the Boeing 777 reached its cruising altitude for the Atlantic crossing, Sarah sipped on a glass of champagne in business class, marvelling again that leaving London after lunch for the eight-hour crossing to New York would have her there in plenty of time for dinner. Incredible.

She pulled out a copy of *So Much for That*. With a stay in the United States ahead of her, catching up on Lionel Shriver's social satire of the crippling cost of their health system could be an interesting read. She'd finished a few lightweight 'chick lit' novels on the lengthy trip over, but after her invigorating four weeks in the UK with Anna, she was ready to tackle something with more gravitas on this leg.

But the fictional world of Shep Knacker and his terminally ill wife Glynis, on their downhill trajectory, failed to draw her in. Real life was intruding as Anna's words about Andrea and Brian disrupted her concentration. *She must miss Brian. They were so good together.* Anna and Lucy would never say that about Rob and her, would never slip the words 'Mum and Dad were so *good* together' into any eulogy they might give.

She wondered if she'd done enough to help Andrea during Brian's illness. Possibly not, but then, they were a very private couple—they didn't seem to need help, even though she'd offered meals and visits and transport. At least in Australia illness didn't bankrupt people like the US health system could. She'd discussed it with Rob, but offering financial support would have seemed patronising and unnecessary.

It must have been a draining and emotional time for them. Watching the weight peel off Brian and knowing he was in pain had taken its toll on Andrea, whose own weight loss and rheumatoid diagnosis was proof of that.

There might be some truth in what Anna had said about Andrea wanting to tell her about Rob's secret. What would she, Sarah, have done if the roles were reversed? But that wouldn't have happened. Brian would never have made such a monumental decision to father children without telling his wife, nor have skulked off to another town to lead a secret life. At least Andrea knew she was loved and valued all through her marriage, always on safe ground.

Not like herself, now teetering on the fault lines of a life gone haywire. And anyway, there *must* have been some way Andrea could have forewarned her without breaching confidences, if she'd bothered to try. Instead, because Sarah had been left in ignorance, years of her life had been wasted since the girls left home.

She tried to push away all thoughts of Albury. It seemed such a long time since she and Andrea had spoken, but Andrea was probably having a marvellous time learning new tricks with the IN-group and not missing her at all. She could think about mending bridges when she got home. Right now, there was New York and time with Lucy to look forward to.

Chapter 39

Andrea sat in front of her computer, ready to open her email. Her skin prickled.

Would there be a message from 'Ken'—whoever he was—or had he somehow found out she'd visited Queenstown and discovered that the whole 'Ken Ashton Aviation' show was a phantom? Did he even live in New Zealand?

He might be hooked up to a computer in Nigeria, or Russia, or anywhere on earth for that matter. Though how he could know so much about aeroplanes—and cryptic crosswords—if he were an everyday, run-of-the-mill internet love-rat was a bit of a puzzle. Somehow, she'd managed to snare herself a high-quality specialist scammer prepared to do his homework, to create false websites and take photographs of men who might authentically look like a 'Ken Ashton' from New Zealand. But how she despised him for pretending to care about her and for allowing herself to betray Brian by thinking she loved him back.

There were a few routine messages waiting in her inbox—a reminder about the next IN-group meeting, and a message from Woolies Rewards—but it was the most recent email that made her tighten her grip on the mouse. Yes, from Him. Not Ken anymore. Him. He'd contacted her again. The Phantom.

She glanced over her shoulder into the darkened room behind her where, despite the bright sunshine outside, she hadn't bothered to open the curtains, suddenly uncomfortable, a target, as though she was being spied on. When she turned back to the computer, she caught sight of the eye of its camera and took in a sharp breath. What if He'd been watching her all this time? He might know her even better than Woolies did.

Remembering Mark Zuckerberg's strategy, she leaped out of her seat and raced to the laundry with an unusual burst of energy, looking for the small toolbox Brian used to keep under the sink. She heard its familiar rattle as she dragged it out, then scrabbled through the screwdrivers and spanners, searching for something to keep this stalker at bay. Gaffer tape, insulation tape, it didn't matter, as long as it blocked the view through that all-seeing camera eye.

She managed to control her unsteady hands long enough to tear off a short strip of brown packing tape and returned to her study, creeping up on her computer from behind. Leaning over, she slapped a cover on the camera's lens with the sticky block-out tape. Only now could she breathe easier and open his message.

Not sure if my emails are getting through to you, Andi, but I'm in dire straits, he wrote.

Now it read like a self-pitying wail, not the worries of a businessman. How could she have ever read it in any other way?

The weather in Queenstown is still bad, planes grounded for another few days, and the twenty-five grand you sent, marvellous though it was, is only going to tide me over for a short while, so I need the extra twenty-five thousand you promised as soon as you can send it. You've been so kind, so caring. I don't know what I'd have done without you. I realised as soon as we linked up that I'd found a soulmate.

Andrea wrapped her arms across her chest, gripping her upper arms for security, fingers pressing into her flesh, close to bruising the skin. It was all she could do to stop gagging. What a load of tripe. And to think she'd fallen for it. The gall of the man, using honeyed words like that to swindle money from her. Who was this shyster? Was it even a man? It could be a woman, some loser who spent her day by the computer in fleecy-lined trakkie daks, who knew what another woman wanted to hear to make her feel loved again, to make her worth something. Andrea could almost taste the bile in her mouth.

She shook her head as if to remove something foreign, exorcise a demon. Another woman must have taken over her mind for a few weeks. This wasn't the real her.

It dawned on her then, though, that her scammer might have been a little too clever for his—or her—own good. Andrea had fallen so heavily for the image of Queenstown with the glamorous business that had been created for her she'd stepped way out of character in making that lightning dash across the Tasman.

In a funny way, what had seemed like an ill-fated journey was, in fact, what had saved her. It had prevented her from transferring a small fortune to this charlatan without any face-to-face meeting to confirm his existence. Imagine if she'd insisted the bank follow her instructions and she'd lost the lot.

Maybe she should send the manager a thankyou note for preventing her accessing her own money in the one outsized transaction. Bet that didn't happen to them very often.

Remembering Denise's advice to keep this 'Ken' person in the dark until she'd had a chance to speak with Martin, Andrea logged off her email account. There was no need to respond to 'Ken' yet. Let the Phantom sweat a little.

*

Martin was not at all judgemental when she rang the following morning. How embarrassing to have to admit to him that she'd been scammed after all his warnings about security. Her cheeks warmed as she spoke. Yet even knowing all the clever tricks, given to her by a professional security expert, she'd sent a wad of money *to a complete stranger in another country.*

'I'll be in touch as soon as I find out anything, so if you could stall this "Ken Ashton" for a day or two, that'd help a lot,' Martin said, once Andrea had confessed every detail of her brain fade. 'As soon as these people know the authorities are onto them, they shut their operation down so it's very difficult to trace them.'

'Stalling shouldn't be a problem.' She frowned, thinking it over. 'I'll email him to say that I'm getting all the money together, but the bank's delaying things. I bet the promise of another pile of cash will keep him happy for a while longer.'

Andrea hung up. Poor Martin. After he'd given them all such clear instructions. He must be horrified at how idiotic she'd been. There's only so much a person can do to protect complete and utter fools from themselves.

But if there was even a slight chance of getting her money back—though admittedly, that was unlikely—she'd realised she had to come clean and tell him everything, including the saga of her ridiculous, wasteful trip. And even if the only benefit of telling Martin was that she could prevent this particular scoundrel from tricking another vulnerable woman, that would be worth something.

She went into the kitchen, turned on her electric pie-maker and removed a couple of sheets of ready-made pastry from the freezer to thaw. It was as though she'd been let out of a cage. Martin had investigations in hand and Denise would be calling in soon to help her sort through the stuff in the garage and see what items might sell on eBay. There was no doubt that she'd rushed into a new relationship without taking care to sort through and store the memories and good times of her life with Brian. Denise's offer had come at the perfect moment.

She took the chutney from the pantry and spooned it into a small dish. How lovely to have someone over to share lunch. Even Sarah, back in the days when they were always in each other's lives, had been too busy for that most weeks. She and Denise could eat in the dining room and catch a glimpse of the gorgeous pink camellias outside once she let in the light. Time to remove the cobwebs.

Who'd have imagined she'd form such a warm bond with *Mrs Robertson* of all people? You never did know.

Chapter 40

'This is brilliant stuff.' Denise brushed the dust off the sleeves of her old shirt as she and Andrea stood looking at the large pile of assorted aviation artefacts they'd dug out from the bowels of the garage.

They'd sorted through all the memorabilia and displayed the items in piles on the large rectangular stone table in the backyard. From *Biggles* books to aviation magazines meticulously indexed—beginning with the very first copy dating back to the sixties—through to badges, pins and model aeroplanes, it was a cornucopia of flying.

'You could set up an aviation museum,' Denise said.

Andrea flipped the idea away with a wave of her hand. 'No, thank you. It's time to leave all this behind. Until your offer of help, I couldn't imagine how to tackle it and I didn't realise quite how much it was holding me back. But you've given me an idea. I'll call the Temora air museum and see if they want any of it.'

'Over my dead body.' Denise looked aghast. She picked up a badge depicting a giant 'A' flanked by eagle's wings. 'At least, not before we've tried to sell every last item that'll possibly make you some money. Temora can pick over the bones after everyone else. I reckon you'll make a tidy sum out of all this and, besides, I need to reassure myself that I learned to do *something* well from our classes.'

She put down the badge then scrutinised the rest of the collection with the eye of an eBay expert. 'I'd recommend we start with the smaller items, like the pins and badges. Nice and easy to handle. They're tarnished now but they'll look like must-have rare collectibles when I've finished with them, I promise.'

After they'd cleaned, polished and buffed all the chosen items with a soapy detergent and soft cloth, Denise tipped her head in satisfaction.

'I'd suggest the badges and pins be attached to backdrops for photographing. It can be a bit fiddly, but I'll stick them on and you can take the shots. The dark background shows them to advantage.'

'You have a great reputation, don't you?' Andrea said as she scrolled through Denise's buyer ratings, reading the comments on screen.

Great eBay-er. Would recommend A++++.

A pleasure to deal with. Will definitely buy from this seller again.

Denise glanced at the last critique. 'Oh, that post was from Nancy. So sad that she won't ever be in touch again.'

'She was your netsuke soulmate, wasn't she?' Andrea said. 'She must have had quite a collection by the end. But do you think people will pay for Brian's stuff? They're not quite works of art like netsuke.'

'Watch and learn.'

Denise typed 'Original Airplane Pins' into the eBay search site on her iPad. Andrea gave a surprised gasp when neat rows of stickpins flashed onscreen, listing crazy prices for similar badges to the ones on the table.

'Oh, my goodness. And I expected to *pay* someone to take them away. Twenty or thirty dollars for one pin? Are you serious? To think I've kept them in old cake tins in the garage. And these are the least of our stuff ... the model aeroplanes might be worth even more.'

'I'm sure they will. I've been doing some research since we talked about it,' Denise said. 'I'm guessing they'll bring in a reasonable sum, and that small, solid silver DC-2 model you showed me the other day?—it must be worth thousands. But are you sure you want to sell it? It's so lovely.'

Andrea sighed, resting her chin on one hand as she gave a long look at the compact model, running her eyes over its smooth-edged wings and satin sheen. 'Isn't it a beautiful piece? It was Brian's favourite, too. It's such a wrench, but I've frittered away twenty-five thousand dollars that I have to recoup somehow.'

'Well, see how you go once I've listed all these. This is so exciting. There's a whole world of collectors out there waiting for your treasures.'

'And they'd still be waiting if it weren't for you,' Andrea said. 'I'm indebted. Literally.'

*

Andrea's front doorbell rang its synthesised version of 'Für Elise' as she and Denise were in the study finalising the eBay postings for her pins, magazines and books. For a brief second the possibility that it might be Sarah quickened her step, but then she saw the silhouette of a man through the frosted glass. More likely a delivery. Would Sarah ever come home?

'Martin, hello!' she said, as she opened the door. 'This is a pleasant surprise. Have you discovered something? Do come in. Denise is here, helping me sell some items on eBay.'

Martin murmured a greeting before saying, 'Sorry, Andrea. I should have called. If it's not a good time ...'

'No, no, it's fine. Come in,' she repeated. 'Denise knows all about my crazy behaviour. She'll be as interested as I am in what you've discovered, and I'm sure you'll keep it confidential.' She made a move towards the kitchen. 'Cup of tea?'

'No. I can't stay, but I wanted to give you a heads-up that the news won't be helpful.'

Martin greeted Denise and took a seat at the table where she and Andrea were photographing the pins. He had a slight frown, one of concern rather than concentration.

'My investigations aren't complete, but there's no doubt that this 'Ken Ashton' doesn't exist, and his business website is a fake, created only days before you got his first email.'

'A con man? I've been duped by a professional!' She leaned back, folding her arms across her chest.

'So this scam artist set out to trap poor unwary women on a dating site?' Denise said. 'The bastard! These low-lifes think they can get away with anything.'

'Hmm.' Martin's gaze wandered over to the garden. 'It was a targeted post. Meant for someone with an interest in aviation. That's unusual.'

'My cryptic crossword clue on the profile page ... that was about aviation,' Andrea said. 'Could he have worked it out and decided to choose me especially?'

'That's looking possible.' Martin hesitated a moment, jiggling one foot. His usual calm, confident manner had disappeared. 'Do you know a "Dylan Woodforde" by any chance?'

Andrea rolled the name over in her mind, concentrating. 'My memory's not so sharp these days, but no, it doesn't ring any bells. Do you think that's his name? Does this mean you might know where he is?'

Martin hesitated again, avoiding Andrea's direct gaze. 'I'm not sure I'll be able to pin that down,' he said in a quiet voice. 'This one's good at covering his tracks.'

'But you know his name's Dylan Woodforde, isn't that a start?' Denise was leaning in, her eyes darting from Martin to Andrea as she began to quiz him. 'How'd you find that out? Does this Dylan have a police profile? Are there other complaints about him? Where does his website originate? You had no trouble finding Nancy's details.'

'Whoa, whoa, some trails are easier to follow than others,' Martin said, holding up his hand. 'One path led to his name, but then it came to a sudden dead end. Dylan Woodforde seems to have sprung into existence only in the last two years, so I'm not confident.'

'But this chap doesn't know that Andrea's suspicious. Surely that makes it easier?' Denise wasn't prepared to let this go.

Martin leaned his elbow on the table, his fingers tapping his mouth as he spoke to Andrea, still avoiding her gaze. 'I'll keep digging, but it may be best if you tell him that you've been advised not to send any more money and to finish it now.'

'What, before the investigations are over? Can't you contact Interpol or something if you know his name?' Denise's persistent questions were becoming embarrassing. She'd slipped into Principal mode interrogating a student or a staff member.

'Andrea could keep him on the hook a bit longer, tell him she's planning a trip to New Zealand to meet him,' she said. 'He doesn't have to know that she's already been.'

Martin looked directly at Andrea, at last. 'I wouldn't advise that. I think you've had enough stress already.'

'You think I should let it go?' Her tone was subdued, even to her own ears.

'Unfortunately, yes,' he said. 'I'll make more enquiries, but …' His voice trailed off.

'Your advice has always been spot on. I'll let him know tonight that he won't be getting any more money from me.'

*

Denise was hovering over her iPad as Andrea returned from seeing Martin out.

'Nope, there are too many Dylan Woodfordes listed on Google to be much help,' she said. 'Martin was a bit cagey, don't you think? I mean, he found out that Nancy's website had been closed in no time and that she'd passed away. To suggest you let it drop before he's thoroughly investigated it, and before this "Ken" has any idea you're onto him is odd. Something's fishy. Did you notice how he couldn't wait to get away?'

'Well … he wasn't himself. And I was a little surprised with his advice, that's true. But I put that down to him being embarrassed for me. I mean, I've been a complete idiot after everything he's taught us. I hope he doesn't blame himself. Or maybe he's worried that this scammer's dangerous. I'm sure Martin knows what he's doing …' She gave a feeble shrug. 'Look, the money's gone now. I'd rather we focus on our sales.'

'Hmm, I might do a little more digging into this Dylan Woodforde, if you don't mind. I have a hunch there's more to this than we think.'

'If you can out-investigate Martin, I'll be in awe of you,' Andrea said. 'But if you can sell all the items in my garage, then you'll be a legend.'

'What if I can do both?' Denise said with a grin.

Chapter 41

'I have to tell you something. Something you're not going to like.'

After agonising for days about how to admit her loss to Stan, Denise decided the best way to any man's forgiveness was the same as the way to his heart. So here he was at her table, sitting in front of a lamb roast with all the trimmings. He looked at home as he drizzled thick gravy over a plate piled high with meat and a mound of oven-roasted veggies.

'Uh oh. Is this a case of "there's no such thing as a free meal"?' he asked, his tone jovial. 'Okay, hit me with it while I'm enjoying your cooking again.' He licked a dob of gravy on his forefinger. 'Did I ever mention that Angie became a vegetarian? Wouldn't have so much as a slice of ham in the house.'

Denise spluttered on her first mouthful, and took a long gulp of water. Her netsuke loss paled into insignificance on the scale of what constituted bad news for Stan. Money could be recouped but, for Stan, there was no coming back from vegetarianism. So that was why his second marriage hadn't lasted.

'Really? No meat at all? I had no idea.' She'd been aware that Angie didn't like cooking, but this was thrilling information. 'Was this a moral stand or a health issue?'

'Both. It was like a crackpot religion.'

'Where was she on desserts?'

He shook his head, a picture of woe. 'Sugar was poison. God, I missed your pavlovas. Now, what did you need to tell me?'

Denise spooned out an extra crispy potato for him. 'Oh … nothing major, but you remember the American woman, Nancy, I've been dealing with? The one who inherited some money and was going to pay ten grand for the antique squirrel netsuke I found?'

Stan was following with interest.

'Unfortunately I didn't receive payment from her and now my emails are bouncing back—'

'Bloody hell. So she's done a runner,' he said. 'There are some people … if they swallowed a nail, they'd pass a corkscrew. Oh well, there'll be another buyer out there.'

'The problem is the netsuke's already been sent. We don't have it anymore.' Denise paused, and took another sip of water. This was so humiliating; she couldn't look him in the eye.

Stan remained intent on his meat as it disappeared off the plate, but Denise could tell he was listening.

'I sent it to Nancy *before* she'd sent her payment, but then she had a stroke and died.'

That slowed him down a little, but he still managed to scrape his plate clean before lowering his knife and fork. 'Seriously? That sounds a bit shonky. Do you think it's true? Maybe Smarty-Marty can chase it up. He's supposed to be a computer wiz.'

Denise gave a resigned shrug. 'He's tried. Nancy was genuine, but because I don't know her family's details, there's nothing he can do now.'

'So, we've done ten grand then?'

'Oh, no. Nowhere near that much,' Denise said quickly. 'That's what I planned to sell it for. I bought it for five.' She wasn't going to tell Stan about her foray into online gambling with SafeBet if she didn't need to. It was her own money she'd gambled there, not his. 'I'm so sorry, though. After all the effort you've been putting in. Our business was going gangbusters, so I guess I got carried away.'

She pushed back her chair, stood up and leaned over to clear the plates.

'Would you fancy some apple crumble? Not that I'm suggesting a dessert makes up for my stupidity,' she added.

Stan nodded, leaving Denise wondering what part of her statement he agreed with.

'I promise I'll make up the money that's been lost, even if I have to borrow from Kay, so don't you worry. It might take a bit longer than planned. But I'm prepared to work my butt off if I have to.'

Stan leaned against his chair, swinging back a little as he gave her backside a friendly slap.

'I've always liked your rump, so don't you go losing too much of it. Look, I won't pretend I'm thrilled about it, but anyone can make a mistake. I know I did twenty years ago. And I mightn't have recovered from the surgery without you supporting me all that time. We'll work something out.'

The muscles around Denise's neck and shoulders relaxed in an instant, as though invisible fingers were massaging them. She hadn't realised how tense she'd become over the prospect of telling him, and how important it was that he didn't hold it against her. And was he admitting to a mistake when he left her for Angie? That was about twenty years ago, come to think of it.

'You're right,' she said. 'Together we'll work something out.'

Stan stood and helped her clear some plates. 'Hey, you wouldn't have some ice cream to go with the crumble, would you?'

*

A light fog was enveloping the Croquet Club as Denise's yellow ball veered away from the hoop right in front of her and careened across the closely mown lawn to the far side of the court, ending up metres beyond the boundary line.

'Now why did that happen?' she said. 'Is there a magnet under the green hurtling balls astray? I followed the coach's advice to the letter, I'm sure.'

'You may have lifted your head before you struck it.' Andrea was leaning on her mallet, having watched Denise's ball skitter away as they practised shots after their lesson. 'But don't rely on my advice. I only have a few more weeks' experience under my belt. I still can't remember when it's my turn, or what colour ball I'm trying to knock out of the game. You need your wits about you. It's so strategic—and devious.'

'That's what makes it a lot of fun. *Sabotage while you exercise.* And not too hard on my ageing knees and hips either. I'd never have tried this if you hadn't twisted my arm, but it's quite manageable.'

'Think of it more as sport for the mind.'

'Easier for you, with your cryptic-crossword brain. Unfortunately,' Denise tapped her temple, 'these little grey cells have been in repose since I retired.'

'Ah, that reminds me, Monsieur Poirot. How's your investigation into my scammer going?'

Denise winced. 'Not great, but I'm still digging. I can't get rid of the nagging sense that Martin wasn't telling you the full story. It's not like I'm a student of body language or anything, but if any of my pupils ever looked off in the middle distance and covered their mouths when they were talking, I was pretty sure they were fibbing.'

'Why would Martin do that? He knew I was realistic about the chances of getting my money back.' She strolled over to her blue ball, lining it up with the hoop.

'Why does anyone hide the truth? To protect themselves and avoid getting into trouble. Or could it be to protect someone close? A family member maybe?' Denise pinched her lower lip between her thumb and forefinger for a second. 'Or to divert attention from the real villain, perhaps?'

Andrea raised her eyebrows. 'You've been watching too many *Midsomer Murders*. This is lovely Martin we're talking about, and we live in peaceful Albury, not some pocket of violent criminality in the English countryside.' She ran a perfect hoop and raised a fist in satisfaction.

'True. I'm over-thinking. But you're going to have to make up your mind. Am I Hercule Poirot or Chief Inspector Barnaby?'

They walked to the far corner of the court, Denise puffing a little as she bent to pick up her errant ball. Straightening to take her next shot, she assumed a passable Botswanan accent. 'But if you should even hint that my 'traditionally built' shape bears a closer resemblance to Mma Precious Ramotswe than Poirot or Barnaby, I will forthwith hang up my mallet and you will be forced to play alone.'

'No resemblance at all—yes, that's better, you didn't lift your head with that stroke—even though she's a very fine lady detective. I mean, *another* very fine lady detective. Speaking of mysteries, I ran into Kate yesterday, and she's itching to have a meeting on Tuesday at her place to tell us what she called "very good news". Expect an email.'

'Does that mean Sarah's back?' Denise asked, careful to keep her eye on the ball. She hit it with a satisfying *clunk* and it rolled slowly until it blocked Andrea's black one. '*That's better* ...'

'Not that I've heard.' Andrea assessed her position before swinging her mallet onto the ball. No need to admit that she'd be the last person Sarah would contact. 'It'll be Kate, Neelam, you and me. Libby and Martin are away for a few days together, but Kate said they already know her news.'

Denise interrupted her planned shot, lifting her head abruptly. 'Ooh, this sounds interesting.'

'I know. I tried to weasel it out of her, but she said I have to wait till Tuesday.'

'No, I mean the bit about Libby and Martin being away *together*. Have I missed something big?' She focussed again and swung at her ball.

Andrea gave a sly look. 'Let's say the slow burn of the past few months seems to have caught alight. But more than that I don't know. We may find out on Tuesday. Now, I'm about to attempt a clever jump shot to make that hoop, so with your excellent investigative eye, would you analyse it please and tell me afterwards why it failed?'

Chapter 42

If there was one thing the IN-group needed now, Andrea decided as she changed out of her slouching-around-the-house gear before their meeting that night, it was some uplifting news. Thanks goodness for Kate. Whatever she had to tell them sounded like it was better news than everything that had happened to date.

Switching to IN-group had turned into a recipe for disaster. She drove over to Kate's thinking over the past few months. Unbelievable that such smart women could get into so much trouble. It'd make a great soap opera, if only they weren't living it. No doubt she'd get over the fraudulent Ken soon enough, but whether she'd ever regain the confidence to re-enter the shark pool that was the dating scene was questionable.

At least Libby, after circling Martin for so long, looked like she'd caught a perfect wave and was swimming straight into a safe harbour. Finally, something was working.

*

Andrea was already sitting at Kate's dining table with Neelam, sipping her wine and cutting an oozy wedge of

Castello Blue, when Denise arrived for the meeting, bearing a sheaf of papers and huffing like a late steam train. She plonked herself down opposite Neelam.

'Sorry, everyone,' she said. 'Got distracted by my latest internet search and didn't notice the time. What you can find out online these days would amaze you.'

She looked rather pleased with herself, as if she were enjoying some special knowledge. Andrea had a throb of anticipation, although she didn't want to give it full rein. Perhaps Denise had gone on with her dogged detective work and uncovered something about the disappearing Ken.

Kate rose to pour Denise a glass of wine before topping up her own, then cleared her throat and remained standing.

'Welcome, all,' she said. Her smile was an embrace. 'As I mentioned in my email, Martin and Libby are away for a few days, so we can start without them. And yes, I'd have to agree with you, Denise, the internet's a wondrous thing—and why we're meeting tonight.'

The others clasped their wines and looked at her like chicks waiting for a mother bird's offering.

'We all know how wonderful Neelam's YouTube vlog on Indian cooking is,' Kate continued, 'but I can officially report that it's now gone viral.'

There was a momentary pause as her news sank in.

Denise's groan punctuated the silence. 'Surely not. You wouldn't credit it, the trouble we seem to get ourselves in. Martin was supposed to prevent things like this.' She ran her fingers through her hair, distracted and upset. 'Has it infected all our computers?'

It was Kate's turn to look taken aback. 'No, no, Denise, this is good news. Well, *great* news. I'd give a drum roll, if I knew how. When a posting on your computer goes viral—not *gets* a virus—it means it's having lots of views. It's become a popular site. Like a quarter-of-a-million-visits popular!' Her face was alight. 'Please raise your glasses for a toast to Neelam.'

Neelam's hands flew to her mouth. 'How could this be?' Her dark eyes widened with excitement. 'I am doing it only for my enjoyment and to help my son. How could this have happened?'

'Wow!' Andrea put down her glass, clapped her hands, then leaned over to give Neelam a hearty pat on the back. 'Fantastic. And so well deserved. You've inspired us all to cook Indian delicacies here in little ol' Albury, so it was only a matter of time before the rest of the world caught up.' She turned to Kate with raised eyebrows. 'Trust you to be the mastermind of this amazing success. Do tell.'

Kate laughed. 'It wasn't all me. I got into tweeting first, and then I began posting on Instagram. Well, it didn't take long to realise that if you catch the eye of a few influential tweeters and Instagrammers, and you have a killer product'—she gestured towards Neelam—'it goes ahead in leaps and bounds. So, one post liked by a hundred friends becomes four hundred in no time, then a thousand and so on.'

'It's basic maths,' Denise commented. 'A bit like compounding interest.'

Kate looked at her and chuckled. 'Me? Using maths? Anyway, when I read that *MasterChef* was so popular in India, I asked my daughter-in-law—she's a PR guru in Sydney—to get involved too, because her office has branches on the subcontinent and we both did some heavy-duty promotion.'

Neelam was looking as if she'd been pinned with a rosette. She gave Kate her complete attention. 'In India? It has gone viral in *India*?'

'Yes. An Indian television network has been in contact with my daughter-in-law and they want to interview you for one of their English-language morning shows.'

'Good heavens. Well done, Kate,' Denise said.

'This will make my Vinod so much more at ease. He is of the old-fashioned school, thinking an Indian wife's cooking should stay inside the home. But as young Raj and I tell him, he is living in an India in his mind from twenty-five years ago and has not understood that even his beloved country has moved way beyond that.'

'Then I have more news that might make him even happier. They're excited about how you fuse Indian and Australian food. With so many of their viewers having family or friends living in Australia, it fits their demographic. You'll be famous.'

Neelam's eyes shone. 'I did not know I have fused Australian cooking. I must have become more westernised than I realised. Oh yes, this will make Vinod most pleased. And Raj will think all his festivals have come at once. How wonderful it has been to join this group. Who would have believed we could be so successful, first with Kate and Libby and their popular wedding business, then Denise so very clever at buying the beautiful ivory, and now this.'

Andrea exchanged a furtive glance with Denise. They'd discussed earlier how they'd tell the group about their online disasters, but this didn't seem quite the right time. It might look like they were raining on Neelam's victory lap for one thing, and then shouldn't they wait until everyone was present? Although Martin, of course, knew all about what had happened, so that meant Libby probably did too.

'To further celebrate this momentous news,' Kate added, 'I've tried my hand at making some *kulfi*. Who's game to sample it?'

Winter it may have been, but Kate's bowl of smooth, rose-flavoured Indian ice cream was the most satisfying dessert Andrea'd had in ages, and judging by the sounds of scraping spoons and pleas for seconds, the others felt the same. After they'd finished, Denise began riffling through the papers she'd brought with her and cleared her throat.

'Look, it may not be the best time to bring this up, but ...' She hesitated as she looked down at the table, then at Andrea, before stroking her chin. She took a deep breath.

Not too many worries about raining on a parade, Andrea thought.

'Andrea and I have had nasty experiences on the net.' She cut off Kate's small shriek of concern with a wave of her hand. 'We won't go into the full story now, but we've both lost money—among other precious things. My beautiful squirrel netsuke, plus its payment, has gone forever. Anyway, we asked Martin to investigate, and though he could trace my problem in no time, he was ... I'd have to say, a bit less than forthcoming about Andrea's scammer, who claimed to be a chap in New Zealand.'

Denise was in full flight now. It might have been a school assembly.

'Martin gave us a name—a Dylan Woodforde—but seemed to suggest that this Dylan character hadn't even existed until a couple of years ago. Then he claimed that the trail had gone cold and he was doubtful he could find anything else, and pretty much clammed up. Now, we know how good he is at this sort of thing, so it was all a bit odd. He seemed to be ... I don't know, hiding something?'

'Surely you don't think Martin's involved?' Kate's blue eyes widened in shock.

Denise pulled back. 'No, I guess not. But the more I've been thinking about it, the more I wonder if he *does* know who this Dylan Woodforde is, but is protecting someone. And then this afternoon, doing some Google investigations of my own, I came across some information that has me a little worried.' She picked through the papers she'd brought, found the printout she was after and placed it face up on the table for everyone to see.

It was a photocopy of the front page of a Melbourne tabloid, dated over twelve months ago. And there, taking up the entire front page, was a photograph of Libby, looking harried and distraught as she walked up the steps to the Magistrate's Court, hand in hand with a man who had a guilty-as-all-get-out briefcase obscuring his face. The banner headline read: 'SHOW US THE MONEY!'

Andrea should be over shocks by now, after the hit of the Anna-but-not-Anna screenshot on Sarah's phone and the Queenstown bombshell that Ken was not Ken, yet her stomach flipped as she took in a sharp breath.

Poor Libby. How awful for her. So, this was what she'd been talking about that day they had lunch together. What a shocking experience she'd been through.

Andrea glanced at Kate, whose face flickered with disbelief for the briefest moment before she managed to suppress any further sign of surprise.

'You're not suggesting it's *Libby* who Martin's protecting, are you?' Kate asked.

'From the details,' Denise said, 'it sounds like Libby was a victim, snared by a crooked businessman. But one paper hinted that they both benefited from the theft ...' Her voice petered out at the look in Kate's eyes.

'This is ridiculous!' Two pink dots lit up Kate's cheeks. 'Next you'll say that the man in the photo with her is *Martin* in disguise.'

Andrea put on her reading specs and leaned forward with Neelam and Denise to examine the grainy shot, their shoulders almost touching. The man in the photo was impossible to identify, his briefcase ensured that, but she could see the solid build was not Martin's. Mortifying that she'd even considered looking. The three of them drew back, avoiding each other's eyes.

'And if you think that Libby has a heap of money stashed away somewhere, you're crazy. Have you ever seen where she lives? The car she drives?' Kate's whole face went red now, her voice raised. 'I knew about her problems, of course I did. We're in business together. I knew that's why she came here to start afresh. What I didn't realise was how humiliating it was ... all that publicity ... and this little exposé isn't helping one iota. She's the most honest person you'd ever meet—she has a strength of character I can only admire.'

Andrea twiddled the arm of her glasses. 'I agree. Libby was quite upfront with me too, about her run-in with the law and how she's trying to work her way through the debt her husband left her. She wasn't the criminal here—he was. They hadn't been married very long.'

She pointed in the direction of the newspaper report with its 'gotcha' photo and its strident headline. 'Typical sensationalist media. I promise you, she wasn't convicted and that's because she did nothing wrong, nothing at all. Except love the wrong man, and we've all been there.'

So easy to be seduced by Ken's words of flattery. This con man sounded the same, hurting a vulnerable woman.

'Libby's ex scarpered off overseas leaving her with a heap of debt. Meanwhile she lost her good job for no other reason than her husband's guilt.'

Kate whipped around. 'How unfair, being sacked for your husband's crimes.'

'Anyway, she was. And Libby wasn't in any position to fight it. So she moved to Albury to start again, work off her debt, and be in a town where people wouldn't judge her.' Andrea looked at Denise. 'Libby's not my scammer, I'd put my house on it.'

Denise had the grace to blush a little. 'It came as a shock, that's all I'm saying ...'

'You would be shocked,' said Neelam. 'Of course. That is to be understood, especially as you, too, have suffered an unexpected loss. I am very sorry to hear of it. But I, too, do not believe that Libby would be dishonest in any way, so we are all in agreement, isn't it?'

'We are.' Kate smiled at Neelam. 'And we're here to celebrate, not point fingers, so who'd like to finish off the last of the *kulfi*? No point putting a few spoonfuls back in the freezer. If Neil gets a taste of it, he'll want me to make it for him every week.'

Chapter 43

'So, tell me about your alpine holiday with Martin,' Kate said. 'Was it everything you hoped for?'

Libby took an invigorating breath as she and Kate paused on their morning walk up Nail Can Hill. A chilly haze was hanging low over the city, hiding the buildings, and the trees were shawled in fog. But from this elevated vantage point, they could have been on top of the world.

'Everything I hoped for,' said Libby. 'And more. Martin's wonderful. Considerate ... fun. I can't believe my luck, meeting him. Still trying to get my head around the fact that something so good could happen to me.'

They started walking again, turning onto a winding uphill track. The magpies were in full morning song.

'And why shouldn't it? The world's not full of men like your father or your ex, you know. There are good ones out there, and Martin's one of them.'

'I know, but ... There are times I think maybe I don't deserve to be this happy. Very negative, I guess. But I worry something's going to collapse, so until I'm on my feet again with a healthy bank balance, I'll be taking it slowly.'

'Speaking of finances …' Kate puffed as she quickened her stride, so Libby slowed a little. '… as I mentioned, we had a meeting last Tuesday night about Neelam's success with her vlog. It turns out that Andrea's been scammed, and because Martin couldn't trace who it was, Denise has been doing a bit of amateur sleuthing. Where she found out—'

'Hang on a sec. Andrea's been scammed? Not by the man she met online? The New Zealander?' Libby glanced at Kate. 'She mentioned someone at lunch a while back … We were at Black Zebra.'

'We didn't get the full details, but it sounds like that's the one. New Zealand *was* mentioned. Martin looked into it, but his trail went cold. So, then Denise took up the search herself.'

Libby's pulse quickened. Martin hadn't said anything about Andrea's problem or that he'd been asked to investigate. She was silent a moment as she led the way, picking out a path around a large fallen log. Fair enough, it was Andrea's business—but she and Martin were a couple now. They'd enjoyed four days of blissful togetherness, walking and talking in Victoria's beautiful High Country. And not one word about Andrea. Didn't he trust her enough to share at least some of the story with her?

'Anyway—' Kate stopped again and bent over, hands on knees as she tried to catch her breath, '—sorry, I'm not as young as you, and this isn't called Hernia Hill trail for nothing. So, for some reason Denise became suspicious that Martin wasn't telling them all that he'd found out. She went looking online and found news stories about your court case. She brought them to our meeting. She shouldn't have done that without talking to you … it was unfair. And I'm so sorry for what you had to go through in Melbourne. I knew you'd had a rough time with your ex, but nothing like that.'

Libby shook her head, her gaze on the scribbly gums. 'So, everybody knows now. I should have told you all the details, but—'

'No, you shouldn't. It wasn't our business and it must've been bad enough for you, going through all that, and starting afresh with nothing. The last thing you'd have wanted was to tell everyone you met all about it. The only reason I'm bringing it up is so that you know it's out there, and that we're behind you.'

Kate wrapped her arms around Libby and gave her a bear hug. 'Don't you go doubting yourself. I think you're marvellous and Martin does too. I've seen the way he looks at you.'

'I hope that's true,' Libby said, but her inner confidence was fading as she spoke.

Even Kate wasn't quite getting it, didn't seem to understand how important this information was. Martin hadn't shared any of this with her. He'd kept quiet about it all weekend. To think he was in secret communication with others in the IN-group, and she'd had no idea.

It must mean he didn't trust her, or didn't see her as so central to his life that he'd want to share what was going on.

She stared at the bush track ahead, trying to understand his silence. Perhaps Denise was right and Martin was hiding something, but whatever it was, it certainly wasn't about her.

＊

'Are you sure this is a good idea?' Libby asked. 'What makes you think this Ken character's emails will tell us anything that'll help Andrea?'

'I'm not doing it for Andrea,' Kate replied, checking her rear-view mirror as they drove into Andrea's tree-lined street. The remnants of old autumn leaves had now turned the ground into a litter of winter brown. 'Well, not only for her. I'm doing it because I think you've become suspicious of Martin and I'm worried you might self-sabotage your relationship. Neil and I have become great friends with Martin too, you know, outside of our friendship with you. We're sure he's not involved.'

'You've discussed it with Neil?' Libby looked across at Kate's serene profile. She wasn't sure how comfortable she was that she and Martin were the topic of conversation in Kate's household, but she placed a lot of trust in Neil's opinion. 'So, what does he think about Denise and Andrea's predicaments?'

'Exactly what I think,' Kate said, slowing down to a crawl. 'I can't believe Martin is behind their problems. Much as I love them both, you'll notice they got themselves into trouble by NOT following all of Martin's advice.'

Libby was silent for a moment. 'You have a point there.'

'I certainly do. And another thing, you never told me you were fired because of your husband's theft. That sounds so wrong.'

Libby shrugged. 'It's ancient history. Nothing I can do now.'

'Maybe not but it's still unfair ... Meanwhile, in other puzzling news, guess who I ran into at the supermarket? Sarah. She's back from the US, still jetlagged. I suggested we all get together at my place on Tuesday night, to get the IN-group going again, but she said she wasn't sure if she'd be rejoining. She declined in the nicest possible way, because that's Sarah, but I was a bit stunned. She was so *involved*.'

'She'd be a real loss ... but it fits with what Andrea said—that she might not rejoin. I hope it isn't the end of the IN-group.'

'Not if I have anything to do with it,' Kate said. 'When I asked her why, she mumbled something about having too much to do. I didn't believe that for a nanosecond. If anyone can multitask, it's Sarah. So, what have *you* heard? The grapevine tells me her marriage is over because her husband cheated, but why would that stop her returning to our friendly, harmless group?'

'Friendly, yes. Harmless? Not based on recent history. I don't know the details, but I think it's because of Andrea. She told me over lunch that Sarah couldn't forgive her for not telling her information she knew about Rob. What it was, I don't know … something linked to the cause of the marriage breakdown. I know Andrea's missing her terribly and somehow feels guilty.'

Kate parked the car and turned off the engine. 'That's awful. I'll give Sarah a call—invite her around on her own.' She tapped her chin, as if agreeing with herself, already planning some action. 'I'm sure they can reconcile … with a bit of help from a friend.'

*

Inside, they were soon settled in Andrea's warm study. Kate straightened the computer. 'Let's get started and search for pointers about your scammer in his emails. Something may have been missed.'

'Allow me, this is the same as my work computer.' Libby took control of the keyboard and opened all Ken's saved emails as Kate and Andrea read them over her shoulders.

'What are we looking for?' Andrea asked.

'This, for starters,' Kate said, pointing to one particular email and turning to Libby. '*Well done, you … Dog-poop on her shoes.* Can you hear Martin's voice in this email? At all? Have you ever heard him use these terms?'

Libby read and re-read the words on screen. 'No. Look, I don't suspect Martin of being the scammer. Not for one moment. It's just ... I don't know if he's ever mentioned it to you, but his son lives in New Zealand ... and he's a computer wiz.'

Kate took in her breath in a mock gasp. 'If that's your reason for suspecting Martin's involved somehow, maybe I should confess now that one of my sons is a computer geek too and he worked in Auckland a few years ago.'

'You know what I mean. It seems a bit of a coincidence ... We start learning about computers from Martin who has a son in New Zealand, and then Andrea gets scammed by someone in New Zealand.'

At this point, Andrea chimed in. 'But we don't know if my scammer is from there, he could be from anywhere. I've only spent a few days in Queenstown, but I could pretend to live there if I had to. I could even do a mean New Zealand accent, if push comes to shove.' To prove her point, she pronounced it as 'uff push comes to sh've'.

'Exactly,' Kate said, giving Libby's shoulder a friendly nudge.

Libby stopped her slow scrolling. She took in a sharp breath. Good heavens! 'Hey, this is a bit odd.'

Kate and Andrea leaned in.

'For the first month, all Ken's emails were addressed to your Gmail account through the RSVP site. Remember how we set up anonymous addresses for all our online shenanigans? But here,' she pointed to the screen, 'Ken suddenly switched to your private Bigpond address for a couple of posts. Did you give it to him?'

Andrea looked horrified. 'Goodness, no. I'd never be that reckless. I hate giving out my private email address at the best of times. I wouldn't take a risk like that in a fit.'

Libby raised her eyebrows a few millimetres.

'Sure,' Andrea added, 'I'd send wads of cash overseas to a total stranger who asked for money, but give out an email address? Never! Who knows where that might end ...?' She gave a self-deprecating chuckle. 'But you're right. This is odd. I always contacted Ken through RSVP, so his switch must have slipped under my radar. I guess I was getting excited about the new relationship and didn't notice. Do you think it's important?'

Kate leaned back in her chair, folded her arms and frowned. 'It makes it look more like the messages came from someone who knows you. That this wasn't a random scam, but you were ...' She seemed to be floundering for the best word.

'Please don't say *targeted*,' Andrea said. 'That's already crossed my mind. See ... I've put sticky tape over the computer camera ...'

'*Selected* might be a better word then. Or *chosen*. A bit of a coincidence, meeting someone online whose interests are so like yours. Don't you think?'

'No ... Yes ... Maybe a little. But when you have weird interests like aviation history and cryptic crosswords, the thrill of finding a match online overrides any suspicions. We nerds don't get a lot of excitement in our lives.'

'Someone who knows you? That's a bit creepy.' Libby shuddered. It had been so awful discovering Gerald had targeted her for his own dishonest purposes.

'I can't think of anyone who'd do this to me,' Andrea said, 'but maybe I should give Martin a call in the morning.'

She stood up and patted Libby's shoulder like a proud parent. 'Wonderful bit of detective work on your part, Libby. I'd never have picked that up. And Denise'll be green. Up till now she's been the ace sleuth around here.'

Libby stretched her legs under the desk. She should have been excited about her discovery, but her doubts about Martin were only growing. If she'd picked up this clue, it was unthinkable that Martin wouldn't have too. And if he knew that Andrea had been targeted, why was he keeping it a secret?

Chapter 44

As Libby tramped along Eastern Hill track past the lookout, she watched Martin flick Jake's favourite rubber ball across the trail. The dog ran in a manic blur to retrieve it before dropping it at his master's feet, ready for the next wild chase and capture.

At any other time, she would have loved this hike. It was part of a walking track, an epic trail that followed old explorers' routes. Standing there on the rugged terrain, the pair were treated to a vast three-sixty-degree panorama, extending from the snow-tipped mountains of the Victorian Alps up to the Hume Weir.

But today she was empty. Try as she might, Libby couldn't suppress the niggling conviction that Martin had more knowledge of Andrea's scam that, for some reason, he wasn't prepared to share.

'Has Andrea been in touch about her scammer?' she asked casually as he picked up Jake's ball again. He nodded, but said nothing. Why wasn't he telling her anything? Wasn't that what partners did, share their news or their worries? She'd told him about their email discovery in detail in the hope he'd respond with a snippet of his own information, but he was giving her nothing.

If she and Martin were to have a chance at being a couple, he had to be honest and upfront with her. This time she wasn't going to turn a blind, trusting eye to problems that arose.

'Because Andrea was quite worried about it, thinking the con man might be someone who knew her,' she persevered. 'Maybe stalking her. Were you able to tell her anything helpful about this scammer?'

'Not really,' was his short reply. He threw Jake's ball again, hard.

Libby looked at him with exasperation. Was he being deliberately obtuse? 'What does "not really" mean? Surely you either know something or you don't.'

'It's complicated, Libby.'

She wasn't sure if she heard a frustrated sigh escape his lips or if he was getting breathless from his activity, but she ploughed on.

'So, you do know more than you're letting on. Denise thought you did. Why can't you tell me? We're all worried about it. It seems a bit strange that as soon as we start taking your lessons and creating passwords and using social media, we get into all sorts of trouble, and poor Andrea gets scammed.'

Martin stopped in his tracks and turned to her. 'What are you saying? You think I had something to do with it?'

'No, that's not what I mean. But you obviously know who does. It seems you don't trust me enough to share the information. And if that's the case, then I'm not sure what I'm doing here. It isn't the sort of relationship I'd want to continue.' Surely he understood that, especially after she'd bared her soul to him about Gerald's disastrous betrayal and its repercussions.

'Don't be silly and melodramatic. I do trust you. It's information I can't divulge, that's all.'

Libby had a surge of fury. *Silly and melodramatic.* 'You mean you *won't* divulge it.' She managed to keep her voice even. 'So, it's "confidential"?'

Martin nodded, throwing the ball with even more force than before, causing Jake to become confused and miss its trajectory. The ball careened down the hill at speed and out of Jake's line of sight as he sped off in the wrong direction.

'So, it's okay for you to know but not for anyone else? I have to "trust" you and ask no questions, when you're clearly not prepared to share information with me.'

'You're blowing it out of all proportion,' Martin said.

'You're not in the army now, there's no need to mark the information "Top Secret". Tell me one thing then. Does it have anything to do with your son?'

'Phil? Why on earth would Phil be involved?'

'Not Phil.' She could hear the annoyance creep into her voice. 'Your other son. The one who lives in New Zealand. Andrew, isn't it?'

'What? You think *Andrew's* involved? Well, that's absolutely ridiculous.'

'I don't know what to think anymore. But I know we won't work if you don't confide in me and you dismiss my worries because you think I'm *silly and melodramatic.*' She stood clenching her fists, willing herself not to cry. Why couldn't he understand her need for trust?

'Look, you're upset, but you're not thinking straight. Accusing Andrew now—'

'Then put my mind at rest.' She placed her hands on her hips and glared at him. 'Give me something, anything, without betraying confidences. Is that too much to ask?'

'It is,' he said. 'Because it's not your business.' He glared at the dog, who was looking up, panting, his pink tongue hanging out. 'Damn you, Jake. Now I'll have to go and find the ball myself.'

'And whose fault is that?' Libby shot at him. 'Jake didn't throw it so bloody far. He doesn't know where it is. Seems like I'm not the only one who thinks you're being unreasonable.'

With a loud *harrumph*, Martin strode off down the hill after the missing ball, Jake loyally at his side.

Libby watched him go in dismay. So that was it. She was on her own. He wasn't prepared to talk, wasn't even going to throw her the tiniest scrap. She couldn't be with a man who didn't take her into his confidence, and it was obvious now that Martin wasn't prepared to trust her with any of his information. Maybe it was better she found this out sooner rather than later.

Blinking back tears, she turned and marched back to the stile they'd climbed not fifteen minutes earlier. She'd come directly from work and was relieved that her Corolla was sitting in the car park, aiding her escape. Because there was no way she was spending another moment out here with a man she couldn't trust and who didn't trust her.

* * *

It was time to act. If there was a vendetta against her, Andrea had to know who was behind it. She reached for the phone. Martin was the only one who might provide an answer.

This is all my fault, she thought, as she waited for him to respond. *Who'd have predicted that one tiny decision could ruin so many lives?*

If the vote had been different, Denise would never have risked all her savings. Sarah would be living the dream, exploring the canals of Europe with Rob as she'd always planned, instead of being—who knew where? And Libby's past would have remained a secret, instead of being exposed in such humiliating detail.

Andrea herself hadn't been spared either. If they'd stayed with book club, she'd still have her best friend and her self-esteem, and her home would be safe.

Stupid, stupid, stupid.

*

Martin was at Andrea's house a mere twenty minutes after she called him again.

'I'm still worried,' she said, placing a jumbo mug of coffee on the table in front of him, 'and I hate to keep on hassling you, but something new has turned up that's making me uneasy. Kate and Libby were here yesterday—Libby may have mentioned it to you—and we discovered that this "Ken Ashton" character used my home email address a few times. My *personal* one, not the Gmail one. I didn't ever give that to him. So, it sounds like he's somehow gained access to my computer, or … I don't know, maybe he knows me. It's spooking me out a bit. It seems someone's gone to the trouble of targeting me.'

Andrea searched Martin's face, holding his gaze, willing him not to reassure her that everything was fine when she knew that it wasn't.

'Did you discover anything else? You mentioned a … what was the name … Dylan Woodforde? I've searched my memory bank, but I can't recall ever hearing the name before.' She took a deep, calming breath, wanting her voice to sound as controlled as possible. 'If you know something, or even if you suspect it, I'd rather be told the truth. It's hard to defeat an unknown foe.' That comment must resonate with a former army man.

Martin remained motionless, his expression unreadable, his face still. This time, he didn't avert his gaze or shuffle in the seat like he had when he'd met with her and Denise.

'I don't know who Dylan Woodforde is,' he said with a slight shake of his head, 'other than having suspicions that the name was adopted by person or persons unknown about two years ago, for fraudulent purposes. But I do know where his emails come from.'

Andrea sat bolt upright. So, Denise had been right. He *had* known more than he let on, and here he was, about to tell her in that stilted police-investigator manner used on TV cop shows.

'As your surname's Thompson,' he continued, still with a sphinx-like demeanour, 'I'm assuming you know Jason Thompson, an expat Australian running an adventure business in Koh Samui?'

A vice grasped Andrea's chest as she inclined her head a few degrees. Was this what a heart attack felt like?

'He's my son. But he would never ...' She paused for a moment, chasing possibilities around her brain. 'He would never ...'

She was aware that Martin was sitting in front of her without a word as her thoughts floated, refusing to be corralled. She was viewing herself from the outside, like a spectator to her own life, even registering that Martin was behaving as she would have when telling a client bad news: pause a few moments for it to sink in, don't overload them with details, wait for them to speak. It was extraordinary that she could remain so analytical, so detached, as she watched Martin watching her.

'I know my son,' she said, her voice even and firm. 'He would never cheat me.'

'I wanted to spare you this. All I can tell you,' he said in a low voice, 'is after you notified "Ken" that you knew he wasn't who he claimed to be, Dylan Woodforde vanished. And that your emails came through a server registered to a business in Koh Samui. A business called *Don't Thai Me Down, Sport.*'

*

Andrea picked up the secateurs after Martin had left. She did her best thinking in the garden. As she ruthlessly pruned the roses, she knew that Jason would never scam her. True, Brian had had to bail him out several years ago when he was out of funds in Europe, but he'd matured so much since those days. If he were in trouble now, he'd come to her or, at the very least, Nicole, and ask one of them for help. Martin didn't know him.

She tossed the cuttings into the green bin and rammed them down. Jason wasn't a thief or a swindler. He'd made mistakes in the past, but stooping to this sort of criminality was not in his DNA.

Chapter 45

Sarah was on a mission. Since returning to Albury the day before, she'd already stocked the pantry, aired the house and watered the garden. Moving from room to room, she now wanted to erase every last trace of Rob from their home.

With his personal items long gone, the house had gained another spare room, created from his old study, but it was empty, awaiting its next phase. Small reminders of him were all around the house, though. She found a couple of CDs she hadn't sent off to his rooms. Music they'd both enjoyed listening to once upon a time. She never wanted to hear them again. A medical journal that she'd overlooked was sitting under a pile of books. She threw it in the kitchen bin together with the unwanted barbecue sauce in the pantry.

The house was going to be too big, too reminiscent of their married life, daily reminders that she'd been living a lie for so long. Once the lawyers had sorted out the details—and Richard had been busy with that in her absence—she could sell and move into a place that would be her own. She needed somewhere smaller, with less maintenance, that would allow her to travel on a whim. Where exactly that would be, she wasn't sure. Perhaps away from Albury if the rumours grew too loud. But Albury and Sydney were the only cities she knew, and even Sydney might not be big enough for her, with Rob's work there.

There was a huge hole where Andrea had been, but with this long estrangement, it wouldn't be easy to reconcile. After their tense telephone exchange, and being ignored for so long, Andrea might not be all that welcoming, either.

It was all very well to build protective barriers, Sarah thought, but if they stayed in place, she'd become a prisoner. While life without Rob was turning out to be liberating, Albury without Andrea's friendship might be too empty to contemplate.

*

Sarah pushed the passenger seat back to accommodate her long legs and stretched out, loving the space and the pure luxury of Kate's BMW.

'I'm so pleased you rang and asked me to come,' she said as they meandered along the back roads to Beechworth, past bushland and hills nourished by recent rains. 'I never believed I'd say this, but I've missed the Australian bush a lot. Especially the light ... the openness. Even our shrill bird calls. The cockatoos sound awful, and sure, the maggies are no nightingales ... but they're *ours*.' She opened the window a few centimetres and took a deep breath, savouring the scent of the eucalypts. 'London and New York are marvellous, but after a while they hem you in, and all you want to see is an uncluttered horizon, the odd lone eucalypt and blue, blue skies. We're so lucky living here. When I flew in last week, the land seemed sparkling and exhilarating and wonderfully *empty* from above.'

'What a relief to hear that you still call Australia home,' Kate said. 'I've been worried you mightn't return. I think we all have.'

'I was tempted to stay on, to be honest. Spending time visiting the places where great writers lived and worked was so inspiring. And there are tons more to see. But much as I loved my time with the girls, they have their own lives. The last thing they need is a mother hanging around with no purpose to her life. Anyway,' without thinking, she let out a deep sigh, 'I have so many things here I need to sort out.'

Kate muttered, 'I'm sure you do,' in a sympathetic voice that made Sarah wonder how much she knew about her changed circumstances.

'I'm glad you could make the time to come, then,' Kate continued. 'It's so helpful looking at potential wedding venues with an experienced set of eyes. Especially ones that appreciate design, like yours. And just back from the UK and the US. Did I mention you're looking terrific? Love that cashmere jacket.'

'That's something I *will* miss about New York. The fashion's amazing and so are their hair stylists.'

'I'd need more than a top-drawer hairdresser and a gorgeous, tailored jacket to help me out. A healthy dose of Botox and a surgeon's scalpel more like.' The moment after she spoke, Kate lifted one hand from the steering wheel and clapped it over her mouth. 'Oh, what a klutz I am. Tell me to shut up. I'm so sorry.'

'Don't worry. I'll have to get used to it. I take it you've heard that I've split from Rob?'

'Whispers around town, that's all.'

Sarah wondered how many of her IN-group companions knew the full extent of the havoc that one wretched Galaxy screensaver had wrought on her life.

She gave Kate a sideways look. 'What's Andrea said?' If Andrea had spoken to anyone, it might be Kate.

'Nothing much.' Stripes of light passed over her as they drove under the gum trees. 'She told us you'd gone overseas for a while to see your daughters, that's all. Someone who knows you—I can't remember who it was, probably a guest at one of my weddings—mentioned you'd left your husband … that he was unfaithful. Hard to keep things like that quiet in a small town. I do know Andrea's missing you. A lot. Especially since her blossoming romance turned to dust and left her with a mess to sort out.'

'Sorry. What did you say? Andrea met someone?'

Sarah wondered if Kate had meant to say Libby. She couldn't imagine Andrea going in search of a partner again, nor finding one in such a short time. Though as she'd discovered from Anna in London, there were parts of Andrea's life she'd known little about. Or worse, hadn't bothered to find out.

Maybe she was doing Andrea an injustice, thinking she wouldn't be open to a new life. Or had her own recent experience turned her into a distrustful, suspicious person? She winced. She'd spent the last few weeks soul-searching over her blind—some might call it wilful—ignorance about Rob's other life, and now it appeared she'd been oblivious to her best friend's needs as well. What sort of a person was she?

'An online romance,' Kate continued. 'She'd followed most of Martin's advice about setting up safeguards and checking identities, but the bit about never sending money to someone overseas escaped her.'

'Andrea's sent money to … what … to an international scammer? *Andrea?*'

Kate may as well have said that Andrea had lost fifty grand on a 200-to-1 outsider at the greyhound races.

'Oh, yes. She lost a heap. Denise has had a bad experience, too. She's out of pocket, but I doubt it would be to a catfish. She's being a bit cagey about her problem. But she's been single-minded lately, trying to find Andrea's con man. You can see why we've all missed you—and your common sense.'

She slowed down as they drove into the old goldmining town and gestured at the imposing, high-walled building on their left. It was a notable nineteenth-century construction, built from local rock, probably quarried on site.

'This old gaol's one of the places I want to look over with you,' she said. 'It's been bought by some consortium who are going to develop it. Those granite walls are stunning. They'll make great backdrops for my brides. But I missed breakfast. Fancy a quick bite and a coffee first?'

'Sure. I'm in your hands today. Anyway, it sounds like there's a lot of news I need to catch up on. At least reassure me your business is chugging along well.'

'Oh yes, we're almost too successful. Shame that nearly everyone wants to be married on a Saturday. It'd be so much easier for us if wedding celebrations were spread out over the week.'

Kate pulled into an angled car park at the front of a small cafe with a new sign promising gourmet treats and barista coffee.

'But Libby's had a big bust-up with Martin over ... who knows what? She won't tell me, but I sense it might be over nothing much. Now they've stopped seeing each other, so Libby's knee-deep in the doldrums. Are the doldrums something you can be knee-deep in? Anyway, she's distracted and vague and not herself at all. And Martin doesn't call in after riding with Neil, in case he runs into Libby. Neil says he's been quite morose too. Such a mess! Please return to the group. You're one of the few sensible people left. Seriously.'

Sarah had only to listen during their snack of toasted fruit bread and cappuccinos, her input unnecessary as Kate unpackaged the complicated stories of the other women. It was amazing they'd managed to get themselves tied up in so much trouble in the two months she'd been away.

As Andrea's saga emerged though, Sarah became uneasy. She spooned the froth on her coffee deep in meditation. Maybe if she'd not cut off her friend with such finality, been so unforgiving, she'd have known about Andrea's plans and she'd *never* have let her send money overseas.

Sarah tried to listen with half an ear to Kate's continuing chatter—something about Neelam's cookery blog—but she was acknowledging to herself that, even before her decision to cut ties with Andrea, she hadn't been there for her. Oh no, she'd devoted her life to Rob, vainglorious Rob, who hadn't appreciated her sacrifice.

And that focus had been at the expense of her girls and a loyal friend who'd needed her more than she realised. Maybe Andrea could have found some way to warn her about Rob's visits to the infertility clinic, to let her know about the risk to her marriage, but perhaps the time had come to let go of her own anger. Hanging onto all this bitterness would only make her small and mean, and it was hurting Andrea.

'At least one good thing's come out of all this,' Kate said as she stood and lifted her oversized shoulder bag from the floor, ready to go to their first inspection. 'Denise is helping Andrea sell Brian's things, and I hear they're playing croquet together every week. They're as thick as thieves.'

The blood pumped in Sarah's ears as they began walking back to the car.

'Oh, are they?' she said. 'That's … great.'

Thick as thieves? Andrea had positively disliked Denise Robertson at the start! Sarah slid into the passenger seat, snapped the seatbelt with a loud clack and folded her arms. This new chumminess was hard to believe. Croquet, of all things.

'So … you were mentioning the possibility of a meeting next Tuesday,' she said. 'I think I should be able to make it after all. There's no hurry with the jobs ahead of me, and it'll do me good to see everyone again.'

It sounded like Kate and the group wanted her back—no, *needed* her back. It was welcome news. Her new life might lay unmapped before her, but it seemed she had a vital role to play in the lives of the IN-group, and play it she would.

'Wonderful,' said Kate. 'And hearing about your trip has given me an idea. What would you think of taking literary tours around the UK in the northern summers? I think you were born to conduct luxury guided jaunts. Could you see yourself doing that?'

Sarah opened her eyes wide. 'I certainly could. Very much so. But—I have a liking for Alice Munro and Emily Dickinson's works too, not to mention Harper Lee, so it'd be remiss of me not to include North America. Especially while Lucy's there.' What an invigorating thought. Spending half the year in Albury and the other half closer to the girls, doing something she loved, hit the sweet spot. A bright future after all.

And Kate's suggestion to return to the IN-group was spot on. Attending the next meeting would be a way of seamlessly reuniting with her friends, and any momentary discomfort with Andrea would be diluted by the presence of all the others.

Chapter 46

Andrea and Denise arrived at Kate's house seconds apart on the following Tuesday evening. Their sales on eBay were chugging along and Denise's latest news on her successes remained upbeat.

'You've found your niche doing this, haven't you?' Andrea said as they strolled into the living room together.

She stopped her chatter on seeing Sarah sitting among the cushions on the couch. It was as if she'd never been missing in action from the IN-group, as if Andrea's nightmares that they'd never reconcile had not occurred. Excitement, trepidation, joy and diffidence competed for space in her mind, but there was no clear winner. She had no idea what to think.

Sarah was the first to make a move. She stood quickly, placed her wineglass on the side table, and walked over to Andrea before enveloping her in a warm embrace.

'I'm back,' she said in a soft tone.

Andrea clung to her tightly for a few seconds before releasing her hold, lest she embarrass either of them. After all, no one else knew what had gone on between them, or how harsh their estrangement had been. 'I'm so pleased,' she whispered back, although the word was much too tame. The hefty weight of grief, loss and guilt at having let her friend down all those years ago became feather-light in that instant.

As soon as Libby and Neelam arrived a few moments later, the room filled with voices as Sarah fielded a multitude of questions about her travels, her daughters, and the state of both the UK and the USA. Amazing how a brief visit was enough for the others to treat her as the instant expert on the two countries.

It was some time before they took up their favourite positions on Kate's couches.

'It's so good to have everyone together again at last,' Kate said, flitting around like a proud mother hen rounding up her flock and finding them treats—though in this case they were a laden cheese platter and glasses of wine.

'Not everyone,' Neelam said. 'Is Martin to join us tonight? Our group is not complete without him, I am thinking. It is he I must thank—as well as you, Kate—' she inclined her head towards their hostess, 'for bringing my little hobby of the Indian cooking to such an audience.'

'Thanks, Neelam, but I think you had the biggest part in your success. And I'm sorry Martin's not here tonight but, well, it's an evening to welcome Sarah back,' Kate said, 'rather than focus on social media training.'

Andrea caught her flicking a concerned glance in Libby's direction as she mentioned Martin's name, and wondered if there was a problem between the two lovebirds. Unlikely. They seemed so right together. She was concerning herself for nothing. Sarah was back and all was right with the world. She had a thrill of pleasure that was more than the wine. The return of her friend was enough for the time being.

* * *

'From what Kate's told me so far,' Sarah said, 'our social media skills seem to have gone a bit feral. More lessons might be needed.' She ran her fingers through her New York bob and took a sip of wine before sweeping her gaze around the group to include everyone.

'You've possibly heard rumours about me by now, so I'm glad to have a chance to tell you all, face to face, what's happened. I've split from my husband. For good. He's now moved out of our Albury home.' She managed a wry smile. 'I discovered he has a second life in Sydney and other adult children.'

There were several gasps from the others. Kate placed the tray and bottle on a side table and sat down to give Sarah her full attention. This was difficult. These were matters usually only spoken about in the absence of the people involved, matters to be gossiped over in low voices, but Sarah was determined to put her side of the story.

'All secrets exposed courtesy of the screensaver on the Galaxy phone. The one Martin got working for me,' she added. 'You may recall that meeting.' Kate and Libby gave a nod of recognition, but not so Denise and Neelam who looked as if this was news to them.

'What a terrible thing,' Neelam said. There was genuine sympathy in her voice.

'It is what it is,' Sarah continued. She took a slow sip of wine. 'At first, I wished I'd never discovered the truth, but you can't un-know something once it's out, so ... I've been re-evaluating my life. I realised was living in a bubble, and bubbles always burst, if you think about it.' She swallowed and went on with a little less certainty. 'I realise now that

Rob would have left me one day when it suited him, so better I had some control over it.'

'What will you do? You're not leaving, are you?' Libby sounded anxious. 'Please say you're staying in Albury.'

Sarah relaxed a little, touched by Libby's concern. 'I'm not leaving any time soon, that's for sure. I don't want to rush into a decision. Right now, it's lawyers at twenty paces, but I'm keeping the house. Rob's life will be in Sydney. He does most of his operating there anyway. I'll probably sell my share of his practice to the other partners. There's lots to sort out.'

* * *

A hush descended on the IN-group after Sarah's huge announcement, looks of shock and surprise replacing coherent comment. Possibly nobody had ever heard such a candid announcement before, and good on Sarah for telling it the way she had. There weren't too many who would have the chutzpah.

Andrea took a calming breath. At least Sarah, by telling her own story and seeing the women's genuine reaction, would realise Andrea wasn't responsible for any gossip wafting around town, nor have concerns that she'd disclosed any secrets to the group.

'Don't be too shocked, and please don't be sorry for me,' Sarah continued. She managed to sound upbeat. 'The past eight weeks of my life have been the best since, well, since forever—catching up with Anna and Lucy and doing all the things *I* want to do. No more walking on eggshells. Very liberating. The future looks quite rosy from here on. Thanks to Kate's suggestion, I'm thinking of organising a small group to go to the UK in a few months—a literary tour. If that works out, the road ahead is all positive.'

'When I am retired, that is something I would love to join,' Neelam said. Her face lit up at the thought. 'I am sure no one would do it better than you.'

A murmur of approval suggested the others weren't going to ask any more questions, and as Kate and Denise were starting to chat together, perhaps this was the moment for Andrea to tell them her own story, and make Sarah less like the odd one out.

'I'd like to fill you in on my latest news too,' Andrea said. Her quiet words stopped all other conversation and the living room was silent. The earnest faces of her friends were unnerving.

'As most of you know, I thought I'd found love online, but it turned out I was the victim of a scam.' She gave a weak laugh. 'When Libby very cleverly discovered that whoever was stringing me along knew my confidential details, I rang Martin again with this information. He's now filled me in on what he'd found out.'

'I knew it!' Denise couldn't hold back. 'I told you he was hiding something.'

If confirmation were needed that Andrea had to clear the air, it had been given in Denise's look of triumph. She wouldn't have stopped harassing Martin about it, second-guessing him all the time, and bailing him up again with more of her probing questions.

'At first, I made Martin promise to keep his investigations confidential, but on reflection, I think that was unfair to him, and to all of you. Scammers could target any of us, so you're entitled to know the full truth.'

It registered in the back of her mind that Libby had sat up slightly at her words about asking Martin to keep it confidential, but she needed to plough on and explain what was happening.

'Martin found out that a Dylan somebody was behind it, but the name rang no bells with me. Apparently, it was an identity created to be used as an alias.' She hesitated now, dreading what she was about to reveal to her friends.

'So, I pressed him *again* about what exactly he knew and he said ...' She stopped, swallowing as she tried to free up her vocal cords and formulate the right words. 'He told me that the emails had come from a computer registered to a business in Thailand.' Her voice dropped and she could barely stop it wavering. 'A business registered to my son, Jason.'

Her friends sat staring at her, hands flying over mouths, heads shaking in disbelief.

'No. Surely not.' Denise's eyes were round with shock as she placed a comforting hand on Andrea's and gave it a squeeze. 'He used to be a little mischief-maker, sure, but never unkind.'

Kate leaned forward, too. 'It sounds unbelievable. Is Martin certain about his facts?' she asked.

'I don't doubt his investigations,' Andrea said, grateful to both of them. Their support made her braver and she managed a smile. 'But I know Jason. I'm positive it's not his doing. He wouldn't cheat me. Ever.'

'I'm sure he wouldn't,' Kate said with her usual warmth. 'He's your son. You know him better than anyone.'

'The trouble is,' Sarah said in a low voice, 'we think we know a person well but then they betray us horribly.'

Andrea spun around to face her. 'If you're comparing Jason with Rob, then don't.' Her voice was like a knife. How dare Sarah. As welcome back as she was a moment ago, she didn't have the moral high ground here.

'No, no, I'm not saying that at all.' Sarah looked mortified. 'But sometimes we have to be prepared to accept the truth, awful though it might be. You have to admit Jason wasn't always the perfect child. Wasn't he suspected of selling marijuana back when he was a teenager?'

'What? *Selling* dope? He was not! Where did you hear that?' There was a pounding in her ears.

Sarah pulled back, flustered and embarrassed. 'I … I don't remember. I … it was a rumour I heard, that's all.' She seemed to be physically retreating into Kate's large cushions, shrinking with embarrassment.

'And you believed it?' Andrea shot back. 'You never mentioned it to me. Did you think it was okay for *you* to hear something important about my child that *I* didn't know? Why didn't you tell me about it?'

Sarah shook her head. 'Because it wasn't definite, it was something I heard once.' She bit her lip nervously. She was back-pedalling fast now, but Andrea gave her a laser stare, her cheeks warming with anger.

'I didn't *know*.' Sarah looked Andrea in the eye as she continued. 'It might have been untrue, spread by whoever was dealing the stuff. Jason might have been an easy target to blame.'

The others sat in strained silence as they watched the accusations play out. Libby opened her eyes wide at Kate, universal language for *this is so uncomfortable*.

'I see.' Andrea leaned back a little, her voice clipped and controlled. 'Because people would believe it of Jason, is that what you're saying? Impossible Jason, hyperactive Jason, of course he'd sell drugs. But tell me this—if the story *was* a mere rumour whirling around town, why did you think it was okay not to tell your good friend, the very friend whose child it involved? It's not like you'd heard it in a *confidential setting at your work*, where you were duty-bound not to divulge it. When did these double standards of yours come into effect?'

She could hear her own voice getting louder and edgier, but Sarah's false accusation had been too much to bear. 'Because I've always believed a decent person is able to keep quiet about information that's confidential. Whereas I'd have hoped sharing rumours with a friend who could address them and nip them in the bud would show genuine friendship. Silly me.'

Sarah's shoulders dropped. 'I'm so sorry …' she began.

Andrea stood abruptly, holding up her hand to quell Sarah's stammered words of apology. 'Too little, too late,' she said. She grabbed her handbag and turned to the others sitting in watchful silence.

'My apologies, especially to you, Kate. You're a wonderful hostess, but I need to go. Now.'

Grabbing her car keys out of her bag, she glared once more at Sarah and swept out of the room before even Kate could stop her.

Chapter 47

Libby was standing by the window of the converted office she shared with Kate, staring at the winter plumbago on the trellis outside: it was brown, shrivelled and close to moribund. She heard Kate's footsteps behind her and turned.

'A penny for your thoughts,' Kate said. 'Want to tell me what's going on between you and Martin?'

Libby's whole body sagged. 'How long have you got?'

'As long as you need.' Kate pulled out two chairs, placed them facing each other, and gestured for Libby to take one as she sat on the other. Her approach seemed almost formal. 'The doctor is in,' she said.

Molly, hearing them talking, came into the room, gave them a languid bow and slumped at Kate's feet.

Libby sank into her chair, relieved to take the weight off her heels at least. If only the emotional weight could be lifted as easily.

'I don't know ... I behaved like a petulant child, accused Martin of not trusting me. Then made it worse by suggesting his son—the one in New Zealand I've never even *met*—was Andrea's scammer, and Martin was covering for him. And I capped it off by telling him I didn't want to be with someone who didn't trust me. Can you believe it? I stormed off, leaving him on Eastern Hill when we were out walking.'

Kate waited until it was clear Libby had nothing more to tell.

'If that's the worst of it,' she said in a reassuring voice, 'go and talk to him about it. I'm assuming you regret what happened. What's made you change your mind?'

'It was something Andrea said last night. About a decent person being able to hold confidences. I think I might have let a decent man slip through my fingers.' She groaned, resting her elbows on the armrests as she put her face in her hands. 'Martin wouldn't tell me what was going on with Andrea's scammer, even though I piled on the guilt trip. I was sure he didn't trust me, that he was hiding stuff from me like Gerald did. I freaked out.'

Kate gave Molly's golden fur a rub. 'Understandable, given your experience,' she said. 'And now?'

'Well ... now it's obvious it was nothing of the sort.' Libby lifted her head. 'Andrea had asked him to keep the information private, so he was doing the right thing, while I was acting like a spoilt brat demanding my own way. And then I made a very quick judgement in the heat of anger—not the way to make good decisions.'

'That's it? A misunderstanding about where each of you was coming from?'

'Isn't that enough? I've blown it. He withdrew from me in an instant. I don't think I deserve happiness somehow.'

'What poppycock!' Kate's words burst out like cannon fire. She stopped stroking Molly and frowned. Libby looked at her with surprise. She'd not heard Kate use that tone before, or have the stern look a mother might adopt when she'd run out of patience. 'Very few things can't be fixed with goodwill on both sides. And before this tiff, I saw two people very happy to be together.

'Seriously, Libs, you weren't caught having a torrid affair with his best friend, and Martin wasn't photographed naked, drunk and disorderly on Monument Hill. You jumped to a silly conclusion that you now regret. So, fix it. You know what works best when you have a major disagreement with someone?'

Libby couldn't prevent a tiny smile. Kate was taking this counselling seriously.

'No. What?'

'If you're sorry, then say so. Tell him you made a mistake. But avoid those awful add-ons like, "I'm sorry if you're so sensitive that my words offended you". Saying sorry isn't that hard, you know. He'll either accept it or he won't, but at least he'll understand you know you got it wrong, and regret your behaviour.'

'You think it'll help?' It was as though a shaft of sunlight had spilled into the room and given it a lift.

'I'd wager my house on it.' Kate looked directly at Libby. 'I'll bet Martin's sitting at home wondering how to fix this. The poor chap doesn't quite know what he's done wrong, so he's got no idea how to approach it. Someone's got to make the first move. If not for yourself, then, please, do it for me. Martin's had nothing but his bike-riding to concentrate on and now he's beating Neil. And let me tell you, if Neil's not happy, I'm not happy.'

'That's the last thing I want,' Libby said. She sat up straight with renewed resolve and pulled out her phone. 'I might contact him now ... find out when I can see him. Time to eat humble pie.'

Are you home for visitors? she texted.

For your visits, always, Martin responded.

＊

'And if I'm ever so irrational in future,' Libby concluded, 'march me around to Kate's for a "tell it to her straight" session. She's a gem.'

She and Martin were sitting on his enclosed front verandah sipping a crisp pinot gris.

'Fights do happen, you know. Christine and I had our moments, too. My army ways drove her crazy sometimes. Back then, my job was in security, so I hadn't always shed the skin of secrecy by the time I got home. I need to learn how to open up more, now that I'm retired.'

'No, this was me being unreasonable.' She took another sip of wine. 'Andrea's business is her own business, not mine, and you were only doing what she asked.'

＊

Libby nuzzled Martin's shoulder as they snuggled together under the warm doona. At minus two degrees outside his bedroom window, and around six degrees inside, neither was keen to leave their cocoon, even to head to the kitchen to put on the kettle.

'What time are Kate and Neil expecting us?' she asked.

'Neil said around nine.' Martin pressed his lips briefly to her forehead before glancing at the clock on his bedside table. 'Seven thirty. Plenty of time. He sent a thumbs up when I texted him last night that we were having dinner, and I had no intention of joining him for a 6 am ride. Huge relief for me, too.' He chuckled. 'Don't get me wrong. I like cycling, but I can't continue at the pace I've set lately. Not sure my heart could take the strain. So please don't leave me again.' He turned to face her. 'I'm serious, though, about us breaking up. When I think of the future, I see you always by my side. These last few days have made me realise it even more.'

Libby traced the contours of his face with her fingertips and smiled. 'Me too. I just don't want to saddle you with this debt I have hanging over me. But I'm working my way through it, so fingers crossed it won't be a problem for too much longer.'

He stretched out and gave a contented sigh as he ruffled her hair then rolled over, pinning her gently to the bed. 'Whereas our only problem right now is whether we have enough time for ...'

'That would be a "yes",' Libby said, before wrapping her arms around his neck and drawing him closer still.

*

They could smell the mingled coffee and bacon as they entered Kate's kitchen, hand in hand. She greeted them with an excited hug.

'This is what I wanted to see,' she said. 'I told Neil if those two don't get back together, I'm throwing in the towel.'

She turned the sizzling bacon slices over and began to crack eggs into the pan. 'He shouldn't be long, he's taking a shower. His ride was a PB this morning, so he's in a very good mood. You might find yourself facing an uphill battle next time, Martin, and I mean that literally.'

The eggs spluttered and she turned down the heat.

'See what you've done to me, Lib?' Martin slid his arm around her waist and drew her towards him for a kiss. 'Set me on an impossible course.'

'Hey, get a room, you two.' Neil came up behind them, slapping Martin on the back as he simultaneously kissed Libby good morning. 'Good to see you both. And together.'

'Talking about getting a room—or, at least, a bigger room—reminds me,' Libby said. 'I'm on the shortlist for a full-time job at TAFE. Fingers crossed, but it's the one I'm doing already, so not having to train someone should appeal to the powers that be.'

'They'd be mad not to promote you,' Kate said. 'Well done.'

'Are we having chutney on these?' Neil had taken over buttering the bread rolls. 'And tomatoes? You know I like those sweet-bite tomatoes you get. Can you buy them in winter?' He sounded like a hungry six-year-old.

'You can have your egg and bacon roll with anything you like, sweetheart. And anybody who did a Personal Best today is allowed as many as they want. A couple of the chickens are laying again.' Kate loaded two trays and inclined her head to the back verandah. 'Let's eat there. The sun's out, and there's a heater.'

After breakfast, they finished off the contents of the coffee pot. Nearby, birds were competing for seeds around the birdbath. Neil turned to Libby. 'Hope you don't mind me asking,' he said, 'but Kate told me you lost your Melbourne job and were left with your husband's debts. Is that right?'

'Uh-huh. I'd co-signed a loan document so I was liable for that debt. Though to be honest, I usually checked what I was signing and I've no recollection of that particular one.'

'Where's your ex now?' Neil asked. 'Any chance of finding him and getting him to pay?'

Libby gave a dry laugh. 'Good luck with that. I've no idea where he is. I haven't worked out how to divorce him, so technically, he's not even my ex, though we've been separated over twelve months now.'

Kate gave Neil an eloquent glance. 'I could help you with that,' Neil said. 'Would you like me to set the ball in motion?'

Libby hesitated. She'd like nothing better than be rid of all trace of the man, but she didn't have the money to hire Neil at the moment. Maybe in a few months' time …

'It'll cost you nothing, Lib.' Neil had read her mind. 'An uncontested divorce is a piece of cake. I'll get some details and your authority to act and set things in motion. Shouldn't take long at all.'

Libby bowed her head in assent. The morning air was crystal clear, the sun was caressing her with its gentle warmth, and the spotted doves were having a ball in the birdbath. With Martin at her side, friends like Kate and Neil, and a promotion in the wings, life was getting better all the time.

Chapter 48

Andrea heard 'Für Elise' ring through the house. She opened the door a couple of centimetres, not in the mood to speak with unsolicited callers.

A massive bunch of flowers with a glorious scent hovered in front of her. Stargazer lilies, magnolia and roses in stunning crimson hues, encircled by eucalyptus leaves, smiled a greeting, but no face was visible. Judging by the floral apparition, the slender legs and the smart shoes poking below—probably those Manolo Blahnik's the magazines talked about—it had to be Sarah.

'I couldn't find a big enough bunch to match the apology I owe you.' Sarah's contrite voice floated over the top. 'And I'm afraid it's not called "The Andrea".' She lowered the massive display and sought out her friend's eyes. 'Totally understand if you're not wanting to speak to me. I'm so, so sorry. My comments about Jason were unforgiveable.'

Andrea stepped back and glared. 'Yes. They were,' she said.

She was damned if she was going to make this easy for Sarah. Weeks, she'd suffered, weeks of guilt and worry and endless thought-loops of how she might have handled things differently all those years ago. Beating up on herself, wondering how she could have found a way to tell Sarah her suspicions about Rob's activities without breaching confidentiality.

And now, *now,* it turned out that Sarah had known about Jason's youthful dalliance with marijuana and *hadn't told her.* It wasn't the point that she and Brian were aware of it and had diverted Jason to other pursuits like scuba diving and indoor rock-climbing. It was the hypocrisy, Sarah's double standards, that galled her the most. As if she, Andrea, was supposed to inform on Rob, but Sarah didn't have the same obligation regarding Jason—a mere *child.*

'And Anna spoke so fondly of Jason when I was in London,' Sarah continued, still embracing the huge bouquet, 'telling me how well he's doing ...'

Andrea opened the door a little further. Devious of Sarah to bring that up, knowing that if she came bearing news about Jason, Andrea would want to hear every last morsel of information. She couldn't possibly close the door in her face.

'I guess you'd better come in,' she said wearily, standing back. She doubted Sarah would ever understand how she knew—with every aching fibre of her being, as only a mother could—that Jason wasn't behind her scam.

After Andrea took the flowers, she led Sarah through the dark hallway and into the living room. 'These will look lovely in here.'

Sarah gave a small gasp. 'You've opened all the curtains,' she said. She looked around. 'It's so bright. And you've cleared out the papers. It looks great.'

'Denise has been a fantastic support, helping me sort through things,' Andrea said pointedly, before gesturing for Sarah to sit down on the upright Shaker chair. She wasn't going to offer a nice comfy armchair. Sarah still had some penance to do. 'Tea? Coffee?'

'An Earl Grey, thanks.'

Sarah parked herself on the edge of the seat with all the comfort of a raw trainee at an important job interview. *Good.*

'I'm glad she's stepped up,' Sarah continued. 'I know I haven't been much of a friend to you lately.' She dropped her shoulders, looking down at her feet. 'No, worse than that. I've been horrible. I've had my eyes opened to so many of my failings these last few weeks. Failings as a wife and as a mother, and, I'm afraid, as a friend too. And then I blundered in with more cruel and unnecessary comments towards you, of all people.'

Andrea paused to study Sarah. Having been so over-whelmed and excited to see her friend back at the IN-group meeting, then hurt by her tactless observations about Jason, she'd failed to notice the lost kilos, the drawn look, the dark circles under her eyes. Most people would still admire Sarah's slender appearance, notice the clever bob, the subtle highlights, but Andrea had no doubt she, too, had suffered weeks of sleepless nights.

'I'll put the kettle on,' she said in a more conciliatory tone as she headed for the kitchen. 'Then you can tell me all about Anna and Lucy.' *And any news of Jason.*

Sarah left her uncomfortable perch to follow Andrea out the room, passing boxes on the floor filled with tissue-paper-wrapped items.

'Are you moving?' Sarah sounded shy, polite.

'Yes, I have to sell. I've lost too much money. Anyway, the house is way too big for one person and the garden's getting unmanageable. I'm tossing around the idea of buying a small apartment in Canberra, closer to Nicole.'

'Canberra? But all your friends are here.' Sarah quickened her steps to keep up with Andrea. 'And you love your garden so much. Are you sure that's a good idea?'

'I have to do something. Denise is selling everything in Brian's shed, so that's one less worry,' Andrea continued. She gestured to the boxes of ornaments and crockery on the floor. 'These things are all going, too.' She was about to say how she couldn't have done it alone, but rubbing salt into the wounds would be shabby and mean, and Sarah looked miserable enough.

'So, tell me all about the girls,' Andrea continued, lifting the pitch of her voice a notch. 'Any photos?'

Sarah pulled up her usual stool at the kitchen snack bar, kicked off her shoes, and took out her new iPhone, locating the shots she'd taken and scrolling back to find the most flattering ones of her daughters. Ones that made them look like minor celebrities. There was Anna beaming beside the Serpentine with the Houses of Parliament in the distance, then Lucy standing and waving beside a horse-drawn carriage in Central Park, and laughing outside the elaborate Plaza Hotel.

Andrea softened at the sight of the images, remembering how Lucy had loved animals. 'They're looking fabulous. We did have great times together here, didn't we? Remember when she was tiny and you had her on a pony out at Jindera and she burst into tears the moment it stopped walking?'

'Fun days. And we'll have them again. Our four stay in touch too, so we did something right. They're scattered around the world—here, London, the States, Thailand, and they're still all good friends. Didn't think I'd ever say this, but Facebook does have its uses.'

Andrea poured the tea and passed the cup across to Sarah.

'You mentioned that Anna spoke about Jason. She was always like a little mother to him—quite protective when he was young. I heard she called in to Koh Samui on her holiday?'

'Yes, says his adventure business is pretty impressive. He's "living the dream", I think were her words. I guess you know he's taken on a new business partner?'

'He told me he's expanding. More adventures, I think.'

'Adventures is right. Anna scored a 'mate's rates' helicopter ride and a scenic flight when she was there.'

'Jason doesn't have a pilot's licence, as far as I know.' Andrea was puzzled. 'Scuba diving and water-based activities are his thing.'

'It's the new chap. That expat Kiwi with flying credentials. Showed Anna all the sights. Woody … somebody or other.'

Andrea froze on hearing the name, and everything began to slow down. Her hands couldn't control the teapot. Her tea spilled on the bench but she was too agitated to notice at first, or to register that the brown liquid was trickling over the edge of the bench and dripping onto Sarah's designer shoes.

'Woody …?' she said.

'I'm sure Anna called him Woody. I remember thinking it sounded like those doubles players from the nineties. The Woodies. You know—a typical knockabout nickname.'

Andrea stared at Sarah, her hands trembling as she mopped up the tea on the bench with her tea towel. 'Not Dylan Woodforde?'

'I don't think Anna ever mentioned his full name,' Sarah said. 'Who's Dylan Woodforde?'

Andrea dropped the tea towel and headed towards the study as fast as she could. The shock had given her a charge of energy. If it weren't for her arthritis she would have actually sprinted.

'Come on, Sas. We've got to Skype Nicole. *Now.* You may have cast a monumental ray of sunshine on my mystery. And if it solves it …' She waved her hands in the air with a victory jiggle.

As the *bom-be-dom, bom-be-dom* tone of the Skype connection sounded, Andrea riffed her fingertips on the desk. *Come on, Nicole. Pick up.* Finally, the blurry face of her daughter appeared, a close-up on the screen.

'Hi Mum. What's wrong? This is an odd time for you to call … Oh, Sarah, you're back home. Hi. Good to see you.'

'Sorry, darling, but I have to ask you something important,' Andrea interrupted. 'What's Dylan Woodforde up to?'

Nicole paused, staring at the screen. 'Who told you about *him*?' she said at last, her expressive face for once guarded.

'You mean, who told me that he's a scammer and a thief?'

Nicole's mouth opened, but nothing came out. *Damn, Skype must have frozen.*

'Can you hear me, Nic? I think we've lost the connection.'

'No, no. I'm here. How on earth do you know that? Jason didn't want me to tell you.'

'I know Dylan Woodforde better than you think. But I'd like details. What's going on? What exactly didn't Jason want me to know?'

Nicole scrunched her face and sighed. 'Well, if you know about him, I suppose there's no point keeping it a secret anymore. He joined Jason's business a few months ago—to expand into heli-flights and the like. But he recently disappeared, taking a chunk of Jason's money. And it turns out, his real name's not even Dylan Woodforde. We don't know who he is. But Jason thinks someone might've put the wind up him because he vanished overnight. Though that turned into a godsend, because Jase had had no idea what a low-life he was. Another few months and the business would've been run into the ground.' Nicole rubbed her temples. 'Jase is furious with himself for not checking him out thoroughly, but the bloke seemed the real deal: licensed to fly, experienced, charming.'

'Don't I know it,' Andrea muttered.

'Sorry, didn't catch that,' Nicole said. She leaned in closer.

Andrea shook her head. 'Nothing, darling. Go on.'

'Woody was running the flying side of things—his pilot's licence was the real deal even though the rest of him wasn't. And he claimed to be an expert in business management, creating websites and the like, so before long he'd taken over the paperwork and finances. The company was booming. You know how Jason hates being tied to a desk so he couldn't wait to hand it all over to someone who seemed to enjoy it. But the bastard's scarpered, leaving a pile of debt—unpaid bills stretching back for several months. He was pocketing all the takings for himself, while Jase assumed the bills were being paid. The local police are involved, but no one has any idea where he is, so it's unlikely he'll face charges. Probably left Thailand by now. The guy's a professional grifter. But how did you know? Jason didn't want you to find out, didn't want you to worry.'

'I'm afraid this Woody character tried to scam me too,' Andrea said, nudging Sarah's leg under the desk with her own as a silent warning. No point telling Nicole at this stage that Jason wasn't the only one who'd lost money. Her 'donation' must have come in handy for Dylan Woodforde's flight from Thailand. 'I might even be the reason it came to light. I let him know I was onto him.'

'My God. How did he try to scam you? Online? I guess he got your details from Jason's computer. It's great you woke up to him. I hope you didn't lose any—'

'How bad is Jason's loss?' Andrea interrupted smoothly. 'I'll help him out if he needs money to tide him over.'

'Oh no, Mum. You're not in a position to do that.'

Wasn't she? She'd been prepared to lend a stranger with a supposed bad heart fifty thousand dollars only a few weeks ago. As if she wouldn't work out a way to help her son.

'That's why Jase didn't want me to tell you,' Nicole continued. 'He said you've had enough on your plate these last couple of years and he's a big boy now. Tim and I offered him a loan, but he said his local reputation is good and he's worked out a deal with his creditors. He'll be fine. So how did this Woody get you involved?'

'Long story, darling,' Andrea said. 'I'll tell you when we have more time. Meanwhile, if you're talking to Jason tell him I understand how easy it is to be fooled by a shrewd con man who provides you with what you're after.'

'I guess you've come up against these sorts of stories through work.'

'Something like that,' Andrea said, before signing off. She turned to Sarah as they walked back to the kitchen. 'Mystery solved. Thank you. Thank you so much.'

'I can't tell you how pleased I am.'

'Me too.' Andrea raised her arms in triumph. 'And that's despite both Jason and me being cheated by a con-artist. Goes to show how all things are relative.' She lowered her hands. 'Oh no … oh my goodness!'

She bent down and picked up Sarah's wet shoes. Ugly dark tea stains had spread over the soft leather, leaving huge marks. The shoes were unwearable. 'I'm so sorry, I'll fix you up for them.'

Sarah gave a dismissive gesture. 'I wouldn't consider it.' She put her arms around Andrea's shoulders and hugged her. 'When it comes down to it, it's only stuff.'

Chapter 49

'You've made me *how much*?' Andrea stared at Denise, who'd dropped by unannounced late in the afternoon.

They were sitting in a sunny spot in the garden while they discussed her latest eBay coups. Near Andrea, a little flurry of bright blue fairy wrens dived and ducked around the emerging bottlebrush. She'd miss them when she left.

'Forty-five grand,' Denise repeated. She looked quite chuffed at Andrea's response to her news. 'And counting. There are still a few more items to sell, so there'll be more …'

'But it was less than a quarter of that the last time we spoke—and that, I might add, was already a fantastic sum for a shed full of bits and pieces. Are you sure? Forty-five grand?'

'Oh yes,' Denise said. 'I call it my 'Redemption from the Great Netsuke Debacle'. And not before time. A bidding war broke out on one of the antique model planes Brian had in his collection. My research suggested it was quite rare so I sent strategic emails to our keenest buyers. All you need is two bidders where neither can bear to lose. They pushed each other up to stratospheric levels. Watching them compete on eBay was like having a front row seat in the dying moments of a Grand Final where the teams are tied. The roar of the crowd was replaced by the rush of blood to my ears. I'd placed a twenty-grand reserve on it, but the buyers pushed it up to thirty-five! Sometimes you gotta love big egos, big wallets and testosterone.'

'I think I love clever friends the most, though,' Andrea said. This was an extraordinary turn of events. 'I'd never have dreamed of targeting buyers like that. You're amazing.'

'Keep talking,' Denise said. Her eyes shone with pride. 'It's thrilling at my age to discover there's something I'm not half bad at. I've made some spending money for Kay already so I'm selling more for her, and Debra at croquet asked me to offload her old table and chairs, too. I love doing it; there's a real future for me with this, I think.'

'And you've restored my nest egg, plus some. I won't have to sell my home,' Andrea said. She was beaming. All those ornaments, books and good linen she believed she'd have to abandon. Now she could pick and choose the ones to keep. 'I may still have some more work for you, though. Nicole's already given me the big thumbs-down to her grandmother's crystal fruit bowl set, and I don't need it. Honestly, the stuff you accumulate over a lifetime …'

'Happy to keep on selling. But I need to ask you about this.'

Denise rummaged in her carry bag and took out a tissue-paper-wrapped display box, containing the solid silver replica plane that had been Brian's most treasured keepsake. Polished to a lustrous sheen, it stood on its plinth under the perspex square, looking like it wouldn't be out of place in the Jewel House at the Tower of London.

'I was going to list this next, but bearing in mind the profit you've already made, you might want to keep it. A memento. Stan made the deluxe display box for it, and, well, we think it's too beautiful … too sentimental to let some stranger buy it. At least think about it first.'

The little knot in Andrea's chest loosened at that moment. She picked up the box and gently turned it around in her hands. Memories of the day she and Brian purchased it flooded back, of the old auction rooms they used to haunt, and of Brian's glee at picking up a rare item now and again that others had overlooked or under-appreciated. Such good times. She wrapped her arms around it, aware that her eyes were prickling with tears.

'I … I don't have to think about it,' she said. 'I'd even say it's going straight to the pool room, except it's much too good for that.' She pulled out a handkerchief and wiped her eyes. 'Another thing, though. Because I was going to send most of these unwanted goods to the recycling shop, I'd decided when you began selling that I'd give you twenty-five per cent—' She held up her hands on seeing Denise about to protest. 'And no correspondence will be entered into. So, you've made yourself over eleven grand. And counting. I hope that'll go some way to clearing your debt for Stan's surgery.'

Denise shook her head as they watched the tiny birds darting in and out of the undergrowth in their hunt for insects.

'Wow,' she said. 'Just wow!'

*

Andrea switched on her living room lamps after Denise had left. How wonderful not to have to pack up her home and sell after all. She glanced up at the high ceiling with its elegant Art Deco design. Sure, the house might be too big for her, but trading it in for a broom cupboard in the city, without any garden, would have been heart-wrenching. Now she had a healthy nest egg again, she could even upgrade the tired kitchen and get the electronic gates she'd thought about. A new skylight would flood the dark hallway with light, too.

The ring of her mobile interrupted her imaginary redecorations. Sarah's name flashed on the screen.

'I've had an idea I want to run past you,' she said when Andrea answered. 'I can't wait to discuss it. Are you home if I call in now?'

When Sarah was settled with a gin and tonic, Andrea looked at her expectantly.

'I couldn't bear to lose you to Canberra,' Sarah began, 'so I'm hoping you'll think over my plan—'

'But I don't have to sell anymore,' Andrea interrupted. 'Denise was just here. She got a massive price for one of Brian's old model planes. Financially, I'm better than ever.'

'Oh. Did she? Well, that's great.' Sarah leaned back, looking a little nonplussed.

'Sorry. I didn't mean to derail you,' Andrea said. 'This place is still too big for me, and I don't know how I'll manage in a few years' time, but at least there's no urgency any more. I belong in Albury, all my friends are here.'

Sarah clapped her hands. 'Brilliant. In that case, my idea might work after all. Your house is too big for you, mine's too big for me and has too much of Rob in it for comfort, but we both want to be based in Albury. We had such great times in that house in Glebe when we were at Uni, what would you think about us sharing again? We could renovate here to make it work for us.'

Andrea paused. 'That's not a crazy idea,' she said. 'In fact … it's close to inspired.'

They could have IN-group afternoon teas on the lawn by the rose bushes, enjoy drinks on the verandah before dinner and have the fun of each other's company every day. Even better than living in Queenstown.

'How could I refuse such an offer?' she said.

* * *

Denise had finished listing the remainder of Kay's unwanted goods on eBay and was about to start on Debra's furniture when Stan arrived unexpectedly. He was carrying a hacksaw and a large set of unidentifiable tools that normally lived in the mysterious darkness of his backyard shed.

'Now our debt's almost cleared, we could make a few more quid,' he said. 'I've dug out this old stuff I don't need anymore. Could you give me a hand selling it?'

'Not a problem.' Denise took the items from him and did a quick appraisal, identifying the saws and hammers among the jumble of goods. 'You'll have to tell me what some of them are called, though. It won't take me long to snap a few photos. At least we don't have to polish them, make perspex boxes and display them with an elegant backdrop!' Careful to follow Neelam's advice about lighting, she took several photos, humming a little as she framed the hacksaw with her camera.

'I haven't seen you this happy since you were teaching back in the day.'

'I think I like this more,' Denise said, as she rearranged the tools to take their photos at varying angles. 'The virtual world is so undemanding. No timekeeping, no meetings. Work when, and where, and if, you want to. While I'm doing this could you check Gumtree online and see what prices they're getting for this sort of stuff?'

Stan took over her iPad, keeping himself busy until Denise had finished her photos. She went over and stood behind him.

'*Trade Me?* What are you doing on a New Zealand site? Gumtree's better for us. Someone local's bound to want them.' She spotted a series of cars and vans on the screen. 'Wheels?' she said. 'You're a tinker, Stan Robertson. Unless you're actually building something, you never stay on task.'

'I'm on task, all right,' he said. Denise leaned over for a better look as Stan scrolled through the vehicles.

'You're not selling the Mondeo, are you?'

'More like thinking of buying, old girl. Look at this little beauty.' He pointed to a high-roofed campervan. It had its back door open, revealing a double mattress under a bright bedcover.

Very comfortable van, has never let us down, the ad promised. *Pick up only. Christchurch.* 'What do you say, Den? Shall we do it again?'

She recalled their trip to the South Island years ago as though it was yesterday. The clear blue waters around Picton, the ice-tipped mountains further south, the fun of never knowing what wondrous sight they'd discover the next day.

'We did have a marvellous time, back then,' she said.

'No reason why it couldn't be even better this time around,' he said.

Denise smiled at him. 'No reason at all,' she replied.

Chapter 50

'How's this for an intriguing message?' Libby held out her Nokia as she walked into the staff room for a morning coffee.

Amy and Michaela were about to head back to the front desk, but they rushed over to check her small screen, almost jostling each other to be the first to see the message.

CALL IN AFTER WORK FOR EXCITING NEWS Xxx K

'Ooh, what's that about?' Amy asked. 'I love a good mystery.'

'I've no idea. It's Kate. Sneaky of her to make me wait until after five.'

'Maybe a celebrity couple have booked a wedding, and the bride asked for you to do her make-up,' Michaela said. 'She probably saw your work on Kate's Instagram.'

'Or Kate knows Martin's bought *the ring*!' Amy's eyes lit up at her own suggestion.

She and Michaela were almost as invested in Libby's romance as she was herself. They asked every Monday morning, wanting to know the details of Martin's every move.

Libby laughed. 'Unlikely. It'll probably be much more mundane.' She slipped her phone into her pocket. 'But it is intriguing,' she added, wanting to support her friends' excitement. 'I'm surprised she didn't give me a hint. She's hopeless at keeping secrets.'

'In that case,' Michaela said, 'why don't you call her straight back and find out what it is? She won't be able to resist and it'll put us all out of suspense.'

'Or we could spend the day coming up with possible scenarios to fit the *exciting news* brief,' Libby said.

They looked at each other for two seconds before bursting into laughter. They wouldn't be able to get any work done after a tease like this.

'Okay, I'll call her.' Libby filled her cup with hot water from the urn. 'But I hope she hasn't put her phone on message bank. That'll stymie us.'

*

The front door was wide open when Libby arrived at Kate's after work. Her nose led her to the kitchen where Kate was at the oven, removing freshly baked cheese twists, all twirly and paprika-sprinkled.

'Do you have any idea what you've put us through today by switching off your phone?' Libby said, watching as Kate set the little snacks on the island bench. She stopped herself from swiping one from the tray.

'I had no idea people could have such vivid imaginations,' she continued. 'Tell me we're hosting a Royal Wedding or you've discovered that I'm the love child of a dying squillionaire who's desperate to make contact. Otherwise, I'll be facing a couple of very disappointed workmates in the morning.'

Kate clapped a hand over her mouth. 'Oops. Did I get everyone's hopes up? Sorry. I might have exaggerated a wee bit. I'm not sure what it's about myself, but I once read that the best message to receive is *"Ring me in the morning for exciting news"*, and I've been itching to use it ever since. All I know is that Neil told me he had information that would make you "extremely happy"—his words—and to ask you over at five and not to bother cooking dinner. We're going out. He should be here any minute.'

'No more clues?'

Kate shook her head. 'I tried to wheedle it out of him on the phone, but he wouldn't say any more. For some reason, he thinks I can't keep a secret, and even though I've been pestering him all day via text messages, he's ignored them.'

'Maybe it's about my divorce ...'

As they were speaking, Neil walked into the kitchen with his briefcase, carrying a lawyerly sheaf of papers—bound with legal red tape, no less, though Libby was surprised to see the ribbon was actually hot pink. His demeanour was much more animated than normal for a man coming home from work.

He swung the briefcase on the bench with an enthusiastic *thwack* and walked over to the bench where the cheesy twists were cooling. 'Something smells good.' He inhaled, then picked one up and took a bite.

'Hey!' Kate cried and flicked him lightly with a tea towel.

He took another bite. 'Bring out the good glasses, Kate. We have reasons to celebrate.'

He removed a chilled bottle of Moet & Chandon champagne from his case and began to unwrap the cork foil.

'You're serious about this, aren't you?' Libby said, as she set out three glasses along the bench. 'This is more exciting than Christmas morning.'

She parked herself on the bar stool and jiggled her foot as she waited for her glass to be filled, but Neil picked up the three glasses with one hand instead, gripped the bottle under his arm, grabbed his documents and ushered them both over to the table in the family room.

There, he untied the red tape and spread his papers with the panache worthy of a magician. He could have been David Copperfield revealing a fluttering dove from the depths of a top hat.

'First things first,' he said. 'Libby, you're now officially a free agent. Your divorce was the most straightforward one I've ever done—'

'Oh, my goodness, that's marvellous. I was dreading all sorts of complications.'

'There were none at all … so, if you'd care to affix your signature to the papers,'—he indicated a bright yellow stickie screaming SIGN HERE protruding from the side of the document—'congratulations will be in order.'

Libby grasped the pen, signed her name with a flourish, then held up her yet-to-be-filled glass and grinned at her friends. 'Fantastic news, Neil. And so speedy! Let's drink to that!'

'In a moment.' He glanced at her signature and smiled. 'There's more to discuss.'

As he cleared his throat, Libby tried not to let her disappointment show. Things were never as simple as you hoped.

'As your lawyer, I decided I'd look into your bank debt—the one you had no memory of signing up for. It's sometimes possible to negotiate reduced payments in cases like this. And I found something very interesting.'

He riffled through the papers in front of him, found a document with her bank's logo and placed it before Libby. 'Is this your signature?' He pointed to a large, looping signature: *Libby Morgan.*

She stared at the scrawl. 'No. It's my name, but unless I was blind drunk at the time, it's not my signature. I never curl my 'L's like that, and anyway, for formal documents, I always sign as Elizabeth.'

'Exactly. And it's not a match for the signature on the "consent to act on my behalf" form you gave me ... so ... to cut to the chase, it seems that it's fake.'

Libby was stunned into silence. Even Kate was struck dumb as they both stared at Neil.

'I ran it past a handwriting expert in Melbourne, who's prepared to testify that, on the balance of probabilities, they're not a match. In other words, it's likely to have been forged. Who did it, we may never know, but in view of your ex-husband's history, it wouldn't take a genius to guess, although bank executives have shown themselves to be less than ethical at times, too.

'I've been in discussions with your bank.' He tapped the logo on top of the document, 'and, surprise, surprise, (a) they refused to admit that it wasn't your signature even though they have the genuine one on record, and (b) the alleged witness to the signature can't be located. I told them in that case, we'd have to go to court to contest this alleged debt of yours—'

Libby pulled back quickly. Neil was speaking so fast with all his gobbledygook and lawyer-speak that she had trouble keeping up. But in the midst of his torrent of words one thing was clear in her mind—she never wanted to see the inside of a courtroom again.

Neil pressed on, ignoring her reaction. 'But after arguments and counter-arguments, they realised their position was about as strong as their public image, and we all know what people think of banks. So, we were able to reach an agreement. However, it's your choice, because there *are* choices.

'If you're prepared to sign a release confirming you won't pursue them for the money you've already paid, they'll accept that the debt is discharged and release you from any more payments. But if you accept these terms, they'll admit no liability for accepting a forged document.

'In the alternative, if you don't want to do that, we take them to court. And even though I think we've got an excellent case, it's not watertight, so there's no guarantee of the outcome. It could take years. Plus, if you lose, you'd be up for their costs as well as a continuing debt. But the final decision is yours.'

Libby blinked twice, as though she'd walked from a darkened room into bright sunlight and was too dazzled to see what was in front of her.

'Are you saying …?' She spread her hand flat against her chest. 'Does this mean?' Her voice trailed off.

She couldn't get her head around the news. Things like this didn't happen to her. She could make out Kate's huge grin—it was threatening to split her face in two—and was aware that Neil was beaming as well. Was he saying her debt could be waived so easily? That she had a real future, starting tonight?

The reality of it was so shocking, so thrilling, that she didn't even stop to consider Gerald's role in yet another fraud. Even he was in her past now, and she'd never have to think about him again. The road ahead was wide open and welcoming.

'Yes,' said Neil, 'I'm saying that with one more signature, you'll be free of this debt. But as I said, you may prefer to take the bank to court …'

Libby waggled her fingers, beckoning the pen. 'Come here, my precious …' She held it close to her heart as if it were a life buoy, read the document, then signed her name.

She heard the cork pop, was aware of Kate's crushing hug and excited congratulations, but it wasn't until she'd gulped a few mouthfuls of champagne and settled her cartwheeling stomach with a still-warm cheese twist that her mind became calm.

'I've booked a table for the four of us at The Farmer's Feast for seven thirty, to celebrate. It's my shout.' Neil said. 'I haven't told Martin the news yet—you should be the one to share it with him.'

'It's like I've won the lottery. Shouldn't tonight's dinner be on me?' Libby asked. 'But thank you, thank you for everything. I don't quite know how to process it all at the moment, but I'm so indebted to you ... to both of you.'

'No, no,' Kate said, with a wave of her hand. 'We were in a position to help a little, that's all. Now, why don't you call Martin? I'm dying to know what he says.'

'Or,' Libby said, 'I can go home and change, and we can both meet you at the restaurant at seven thirty.'

'Aren't you going to ring him now?' There was a plaintive note in Kate's voice.

Libby gave her lopsided grin. 'We can all tell him over dinner,' she promised.

But she needed to get in touch first. Pulling out her phone she sent off a text message:

MEET US AT THE FARMER'S FEAST 7.30 FOR *VERY EXCITING NEWS.*

Chapter 51

The following spring ...

Libby was smoothing the fabric of her graceful champagne-lace dress—it did show off her shapely legs rather well—as she stood beside Kate in their family room. When she'd first arrived in Albury, the move had been a mere step on an uphill path to recovery—a place to idle for a while, where she might be lucky enough to find work, make a few friends and tread a soft footprint while re-establishing her life. It was never meant to be permanent. Always in the back of her mind was a return to Melbourne and to the life she'd once lived.

And yet that wasn't how it had turned out. Here she was, ready for her wedding, facing a future that seemed so exciting it was almost scary.

'Do you think something's happened to Neil?' she asked Kate. *How much longer would he be? What if his car had broken down?*

She picked at imaginary fluff on her upper arm, brushing nothing away as she twisted around to check it out. 'I know Martin's the man for me, but my butterflies are working overtime.'

'Good. Then they'll wear themselves out faster. You do know they have a tragically short lifespan?'

Kate placed her hands softly on Libby's elbows and looked up at her. 'It's going to be perfect. Sure, Martin will be speechless when he sees you because, no exaggeration, a supermodel would be envious of how you look today, but he'll recover. So, there's nothing to worry about. It's all in hand.'

'What about Marcus and Georgie and—'

'Awesome Orson? Neil's already texted to say he's picked your family up from the hotel and delivered them safely to Chelsea's, where all is in readiness. My granddaughter's with them—she's a wonderful babysitter. Neil's on his way back here as we speak.'

Kate was ticking off all the jobs on her fingers. 'Marcus knows he's to greet you at the entrance and walk you down the aisle. Chelsea's done wonders with the garden. I see now why she was so adamant about the date. The roses are in bloom, the lawn is positively unAustralian it's so green, and that huge tree on the back lawn had a winter haircut, so now it's spread out like an umbrella to provide all-embracing shade.'

She dropped her hands and narrowed her eyes at Libby. 'And if further reassurance is needed, I know your wedding planner intimately, and she's left nothing to chance. Heard of clockwork precision? That's nothing compared to the seamless workings of *this* automaton.' She tapped her skull.

'Though I can't vouch for Raj and the choreographed Bollywood-style dance-athon he's planned for later in the evening. Neelam says he's so excited about being MC—his first big production. And might I add that whoever did your make-up could give master classes on the subject?'

'Is it okay?' Libby asked. 'Not too much?'

'Utterly beautiful.' Kate gave her a hug. 'I'm almost as proud as the day Louise got married. Though not quite as sad. At least you and Martin are staying in Albury. Now take a deep breath and Neil will be here before you know it.' She cocked her head slightly. 'In fact, that's him now … you won't even be fashionably late.'

As she said the words, Neil walked into the family room, jingling his keys. He was wearing a dark-blue tailored suit with an eye-catching tie, and Kate had pinned a small cream rose to his lapel. He put his arm around his wife and drew her in. With Kate in her lilac-blue silk dress, they made an attractive couple.

He gave an appreciative whistle when he saw Libby. 'Wow,' he said. 'There's a very lucky man out at Table Top who can't wait for you to arrive. If you're ready for the big day, your chariot awaits. Let's roll.'

With Kate on one arm and Libby on the other, Neil swept them out of the house and into his large BMW, all shiny and polished and glinting in the sunlight.

He tipped his head at the house opposite. 'Don't look now, but the neighbours are watching behind the curtains,' he said with a grin.

* * *

Andrea and Sarah arrived at Phil and Chelsea's Table Top home a comfortable forty minutes before the celebrant was due to commence the service, giving themselves time to unpack the car of its treasures—a selection of mouth-watering tortes Sarah had meticulously constructed and decorated.

In pride of place was the beautifully iced two-tiered wedding cake—Panama tortes with chocolate butter icing—that wouldn't have looked out of place in the front window of a European patisserie.

'Help me drop these into the kitchen first and then go and mingle,' Sarah said. 'I'll join you once I've arranged the dessert table. It'll only take a minute.'

'No problem.'

Andrea carried the wedding cake into the kitchen where the benchtops had been cleared in readiness for their offerings. She was in awe that such professional-looking desserts had sprung from her kitchen. No, correct that, it wasn't just her kitchen anymore.

But if Sarah believed that a mere 'minute' was all she'd need to display the dessert table fit for a wedding, Andrea would eat her hat. No mean feat, taking into account the ruched netting and silk flowers on the headpiece she'd had made.

She went into the living room where a lass in a neat waitress' outfit and white apron was waiting with a tray of drinks. She had a spray of freckles and her serious, attentive expression was touching.

'Would you like a sparkling wine?' she asked.

'Thank you.' With no one else in sight, Andrea continued the conversation. 'Are you a relative of the bride or the groom?'

'No, I'm Kristy, from Libby's TAFE. Studying hospitality. Thanks to her, Kate has us help at her weddings. I hit the jackpot this time. And Libby's so lovely … she's invited everyone in the course to join in for dancing and desserts later.' She flashed an excited smile. 'It's Bollywood-style, so the others will be in costume.'

'Then we're in for a treat,' Andrea said. 'Where will I wait until everyone arrives?'

Kristy ushered her on to the outdoor terrace, where Andrea paused to take in the scene. She'd been to all the Open Garden weekends in the area and had visited most of the impressive grounds around the Albury district, always on the lookout for new ideas, new plantings, new designs, but this particular garden had escaped her.

Several round tables, decorated with soft cream tablecloths, silver cutlery, and posies of colourful flowers, had been set up for about thirty guests with place names at each setting.

Beyond the terrace on the manicured lawn were several rows of beribboned chairs, bordering a central aisle leading to a rotunda with masses of pink-tipped Pierre de Ronsard roses in full bloom, trickling around its pillars. A well-established walnut tree was to one side, and the lush lawn spread out to the perimeter of the garden where masses of spring plantings, in varying stages of bloom, ringed the area.

By the time she finished her ramble in search of inspiration for her own patch, several others had arrived and the conversation was humming. Chelsea was flitting around, making sure everyone had a drink, and the wait staff were pressing yummy-looking Indian canapés on everyone. Neelam had excelled herself. Andrea checked out the seating arrangement at her table.

'Kate's split us up, I see,' she said as Sarah joined her. 'Where are you?'

'On Neil and Kate's table with Neelam and Vinod, and someone called Paul.' Sarah said, glancing down at the place names on Andrea's table. 'Oh, you're next to Stan. You're in for an entertaining evening.'

'I know. He's always a hoot.'

Sarah's phone pinged. 'Hang on a sec …' She glanced down at the message. 'It's Kate. They've left her place, ten minutes to countdown. Raj and I had better start marshalling the troops. Now who's that handsome young couple with the baby—and a teddy bear in an 'Awesome Orson' T-shirt?'

'It must be Marcus, Libby's son and his wife.' Andrea spun around to look for them. 'How adorable is Orson? I must go and introduce myself. Oh, I do love a wedding.'

* * *

As Denise watched Libby enter the garden, escorted by a young man who could have been a male model, she wondered if she should try to lose weight again.

But why bother? She'd never look anything like Libby, and besides, she'd glimpsed the forthcoming wedding feast while she was delivering her pavlova rolls to the kitchen—she'd made enough to satisfy the young ones who were coming later for the entertainment. Judging by the wafts of spices and the array of dishes she'd spied Neelam explaining to the wait staff, plus the dessert table—oh my goodness, Sarah had outdone even Sarah this time—it wasn't the day to think of dieting.

There was a hush as the music began and everyone—even Stan—craned to see Libby, calm and smiling on the arm of that young man who must be her son, as she began her slow walk down the herringbone-patterned pathway to the rotunda. It wasn't the 'Wedding March', in fact it wasn't a tune Denise recognised, but that was nothing new. Impossible to keep up with the latest pop stars, the Beyoncés and Rihannas and Adeles of the world, now she was retired.

Martin turned to watch his bride walking towards him. Denise liked that. Grooms who stood fidgeting, staring straight ahead with their backs to their intended, always made her think they were having last-minute regrets. Stan had turned to face her as she came down the aisle at their wedding, even given her a wink, much to her mother's disquiet. Winking in church in the seventies wasn't the done thing, but she hadn't cared.

She slipped her hand into Stan's for a moment and squeezed it.

'Brings back memories,' she whispered.

How good it was to be together again, even closer now since their debt-ridden phase was behind them and they were making money with more eBay sales—enough profit to pay for their upcoming New Zealand holiday.

Stan squeezed her hand back, turned to face her, and gave that same wink. Denise managed to stop herself laughing out loud. Incorrigible, that's what he was.

It was a short ceremony performed by a celebrant whose tone was warm and inclusive. Martin read a poem that, like the music, wasn't anything Denise recognised:

'"Love adorns itself:

It seeks to prove inward joy

By outward beauty.

Love does not claim possession

But gives freedom."'

How men had changed. Imagine any of them reading a poem in her day! But Martin seemed as relaxed and sincere reading these words as if he were dressed in khaki and giving orders to his men.

Libby's son, as well as Phil and another young man—most likely Martin's other son—spoke about love and marriage, and then Martin was kissing his bride and everyone was clapping.

As the couple drifted slowly back to the terrace, hand in hand, smiling and greeting the guests on their way, everyone cheered and the young men threw something in the air around Martin and Libby, who dodged and laughed. It wasn't confetti, Denise knew, because that wasn't used anymore—too difficult to clean up—more like rice, but in assorted colours. Probably some eco-friendly product that Kate had discovered.

*

After more nibbles, drinks and photos, and when they were seated at their places on the terrace, Denise extended a hand to the young man on her left, the one who'd talked about love and marriage during the ceremony. He looked in his mid-twenties, and was wearing a casual lounge suit with a tie that he'd loosened already. She guessed it would be off pretty soon.

'I'm Denise,' she said, 'and this is my partner, Stan.' She gestured to her right.

'Andrew deGraff.' He returned her handshake and leaned across to shake Stan's hand. 'And this is a friend of mine, Suzette,' he added.

A pretty young blonde, in a strappy, barely there dress that Denise was sure couldn't be warm enough, acknowledged her briefly. Another bonus of being older, Denise realised, was if you wanted to pop on a mohair cardy later, no one would look askance.

'Aha, so you're Martin's other son,' she said. 'Libby mentioned you were coming. Lovely to meet you. And welcome to Albury, though I guess you've been before.'

'No, first visit. Phil and Chelsea keep asking me to come, but I'm in New Zealand so it's a bit of a hike. I'm transferring to Sydney in the next few months, so I might become a regular then.'

'New Zealand? Stan and I are heading over soon. Grey-nomading in a campervan around the South Island for a few weeks. Where are you?'

'Dunedin. It's on the South Island too, but not on the popular routes. Bit too cold for most tourists. And wet. And out of the way.'

'Hmm. So, you don't work for Dunedin tourism, then?'

When Andrew laughed, she could have been hearing Martin. 'No, I'm in IT,' he said. 'Apple doesn't fall far from the tree and all that, pardon the pun.'

Denise leaned past Stan to attract Andrea's attention to introduce her to Andrew, but she was absorbed in a conversation with Michaela, so Denise gave up. By the time she turned back, Andrew was chatting with Suzette.

Out the corner of her eye, she noticed dozens of native birds lining the pathway from the rotunda, all the way up to their tables. Colourful grass parrots, their bright green wings flashing in the sunlight showing glimpses of red, honeyeaters, a few spotted doves, even an eastern rosella were gorging on something on the ground. How on earth had Kate—or was it Chelsea—conjured them up to provide such a display?

She kept staring at the sight and at the 'confetti' they'd used. Oh, my goodness. It was birdseed. Gorgeous coloured birdseed. She'd seen everything now.

* * *

Paul was Head of Department at the local TAFE and Sarah listened to anecdotes of the joys and trials of his work with interest. He was an entertaining raconteur.

His wife had taught English Literature at one of the private schools in Albury before retiring, and he related some of the howlers she'd come across in her time. What a pity she hadn't been able to join in the celebrations. Sarah would have loved chatting about books with her. Grandmother's duties in Melbourne, apparently.

'She would have liked that poem Martin read,' Paul said. 'Very modern.'

'Not so very modern,' Neelam said, entering the conversation. 'It was written by Tagore, the Bard of Bengal.'

'Then you might know who's done the catering,' Paul said as he tucked into the sumptuous feast on the table—platters of food for sharing. 'This is the best Indian food I've ever tasted.'

Vinod joined the discussion, beaming. 'That would be my wife, Neelam Sharma, the very lady you are speaking to. Now very famous on the subcontinent for her Australian-Indian inventions.'

'You're a lucky man,' Paul said.

'I am aware how lucky I am,' Vinod replied. 'Now my wife is so very well-known in India, we are able to travel there to present her delicacies on a most regular basis. We are even thinking of moving back when our boys have finished their schooling, though that will not be for another year or more.'

'Oh no, that's not good news. We don't want to lose Neelam.' It was the first Sarah had heard of a possible move. 'What will the IN-group do without her?'

'The IN-group, as you name it, has been very good for our family. I must thank you for being such an excellent organiser.'

Sarah bit her tongue. No point mentioning that she'd been dead against switching from book club, and that moving to the IN-group hadn't worked out so well for her own family. But now that the divorce was behind her, she was in a good place at last, about to lead another Shakespeare tour and visit the girls again.

She leaned forward to speak with Neelam.

'Those wedding canapés we had with drinks were fantastic. What would I have to do to score the recipe, Neelam?'

'You are very flattering. Can you tell me the ones you liked the best? I will do a video for you. Was it the spice-crusted paneer *tikka*, the cheese *kachor* or the *hariyali* chicken kebabs?'

'All of the above,' Sarah said. 'Why don't you include everything on this table as well? An Australian-Indian Wedding Banquet.'

'Then the time has come for me to learn how cleverly you are able to decorate your cakes, isn't it?'

*

Sarah always enjoyed the speeches. Martin's self-deprecating sense of humour was a surprise.

'I spent weeks willing the gorgeous dark-haired woman in the class to ask me a few more questions so I could impress her,' he told the guests, 'but do you think she could get a word in edgewise?'

The other IN-group members roared with laughter. He was right. Once over their initial reticence and fear of technology, they had devoured his attention at every session.

'But if there's one thing this group of women taught me, it's the need for cyber security,' he told them in a mock-serious tone. 'Something I hadn't been aware of when dealing with Chinese spies in my previous work.'

More guffaws—this time from his cycling buddies.

Phil spoke next, saying how delighted he was that his dad had moved to live closer, and remembering his mother, Christine, saying that he knew she'd love Libby as much as they all did.

Libby rose to speak then. 'Thank you all so much for sharing the day with us, and to you, Phil and Chelsea, for welcoming me into your family like this. To Kate and my IN-group besties and my workmates, you have no idea how you've made the move to Albury such a great experience.'

She turned to her husband. 'Martin, you came into my life and completely changed it, and for that, you have my undying love.'

Chelsea jumped up, saying she wasn't scheduled to speak, but she couldn't resist.

'It's time for a confession,' she said. 'I wasn't really looking for a new make-up specialist when I rang Libby,' she admitted, 'but, gosh, Martin was never going to make a move if left to his own devices.'

Soon, the tables were moved aside for Raj to bring in his team of dancers dressed in traditional Indian costumes, and the party music began, beating out its rhythm in a toe-tapping routine.

The students arrived—heavens knew where they'd found their outfits, but they certainly looked the part in their gorgeous swirling silks—and they swallowed up Libby and Martin in their rush to congratulate them.

Sarah edged towards Kate, who was looking over the gathering as she swayed to the music.

'What a wonderful evening. You're brilliant at this.'

Kate smiled. 'Thanks. How are the new living arrangements working?'

'Terrific. Even better than when we were at university. Now I've sold up, Andrea and I are renovating her place. You'll have to come and see it when it's finished.'

'I will. I bet it'll be fabulous.'

* * *

Andrea and Denise stood side-by-side as, late into the night, the gathering waved goodbye to Libby and Martin.

'What a wedding,' said Andrea. 'I haven't had so much fun in years. Raj sure has a future as a producer. I bet the students have been practising their dance moves for ages. Maybe once we've mastered croquet, we could take up belly dancing.'

'I think,' Denise said, 'if you can imagine me in harem pants, you've had way too much to drink.'

Andrea giggled. 'Maybe. But it's been a great night. What do you think we should do now we've graduated from the IN-group?'

'I suppose we could return to book club, but with Sarah away on her literary tours, Neelam so often in India, and Libby and Kate flat chat with their weddings, it might be a lame affair. No offence.'

'None taken,' Andrea replied. 'A friend of mine in Melbourne's part of a group that meets regularly, but instead of a book club, they ginger it up by planning different activities each month. An exhibition one time, learning to make home brew the next. We'd have to find more people though, and off the top of my head, I can only think of one other person who might be interested.'

'What if we invite her, and *she* has to invite the next one, and so on and so forth? Presto, we'd eventually have a gathering of new people doing new things. A voyage of discovery.'

'You,' Andrea's words were only slightly slurred, 'are a mathematical genius.'

She put her arm around Denise's shoulder.

'Mrs Robertson, I think this is the beginning of a beautiful friendship.'

* * *

Acknowledgements

While it doesn't take a village to write a book, it does take a team. Our thanks go to our two very talented editors, Nicola O'Shea and Dianne Blacklock, for their outstanding fiction workshops and for their incisive editing which brought significant improvements to this book.

Thanks also to Christa Moffitt from Christabella Designs for the beautiful covers she provided us, making our choice for the final design so difficult, and to the talented Laura Pike for creating the perfect logo for *Resisters*.

Without Joel Naoum from Critical Mass we could never have navigated the world of publishing, let alone digital publishing. We extend our heartfelt thanks to him for all his support and for finding such an excellent proofreader in Ariane Durkin.

Juliet Rogers at the Australian Society of Authors has been a font of advice and wise counsel for several years and helped us so much on the path to publication and for that, we are extremely grateful.

To the friends who read our manuscript before publication—Laura Pike, Angela Ramsay, Jane Downing, Mary Fisher and Nazli Munir—our heartfelt thanks for your generous feedback and suggestions.

And to all our friends—you are our inspiration. Thankyou!

CPSIA information can be obtained
at www.ICGtesting.com
Printed in the USA
LVHW041531180419
614686LV00002B/348